Praise for
MIDNIGHT ANGELS

"This superior religious [illegible] ller from Carcaterra [illegible] of Florence. . . . T[illegible] ed premise will keep [illegible]

—[illegible] ly

"This blood-splat[illegible] page-turner of a thriller could be the hottest action you get all summer."

—*Maxim*

"A fast-paced thriller so good, there's a solid chance you'll devour it in one sitting."

—*Cosmopolitan*

"The Italian setting is so intimate and sensual, the characters seem to leap from the printed page. Fast paced and brilliantly written, this book rings so true it grips readers and holds them until the very last page." —*Tuscon Citizen*

"A highly charged story . . . Packed with thrilling chases, intriguing characters, and vivid descriptions of Florentine culture and landscapes, the novel keeps up a dizzying pace with its captivating storyline." —*Las Vegas Review Journal*

"A wonderful travel book about this glorious ancient city . . . a genuinely thrilling thriller."

—*Sullivan County Democrat*

"Love, death and greed are here wrapped up in the world of high art. . . . This man can write anything, anytime." —*Crimespree Magazine*

Also by Lorenzo Carcaterra

A Safe Place:
The True Story of a Father, a Son, a Murder

Sleepers
Apaches
Gangster
Street Boys
Paradise City
Chasers

Midnight Angels

A Novel

Lorenzo Carcaterra

BALLANTINE BOOKS • NEW YORK

Midnight Angels is a work of fiction. Names, characters, places, and incidents are the products of the author's imagination or are used fictitiously. Any resemblance to actual events, locales, or persons, living or dead, is entirely coincidental.

A 2011 Ballantine Books Mass Market Edition

Published in the United States by Ballantine Books, an imprint of The Random House Publishing Group, a division of Random House, Inc., New York.

BALLANTINE and colophon are registered trademarks of Random House, Inc.

Originally published in hardcover in the United States by Ballantine Books, an imprint of The Random House Publishing Group, a division of Random House, Inc., in 2010.

ISBN 978-0-345-48391-1

Cover design: Carlos Beltran
Cover photography: Alessandro Villa/Age Fotostock

Printed in the United States of America

www.ballantinebooks.com

9 8 7 6 5 4 3 2 1

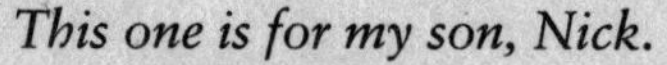

This one is for my son, Nick.

PREFACE

Summer 1989

FLORENCE, ITALY

THE ROOM HAD ABOUT IT THE MUSTY ODOR OF old clothes. The air was thick with dust, and dingy white drop cloths bunched along the walls. Each of the interlopers held a small penlight as they made their way toward a far corner, careful not to brush against the paintings stacked on the hardwood floor and the sculptures spread about the room. Rain nipped at the roof above as they ran their lights across the works of art around them. "Getting them out of here won't be easy," the woman said. "And that's assuming they're in here."

The man turned and looked at the woman. She was slim, with shoulder-length brown hair and chestnut eyes. "You're the confident member of this team," he said. "Don't panic on me now. Besides, they're in here and we *both* know it."

"Well, then I hope you packed a plan with these flashlights," she said, glancing around the shadowed room.

"Andrea, I *always* have a plan," he said.

"Of course you do," she said, not bothering to hide a smile. "I just hope it's an improvement over your last one. I don't think I'm up for another late night glider ride across open water."

"You have to admit it was romantic," he said. "No woman has seen Paris the way you have."

"Maybe so, Frank," Andrea said. "I would have much preferred a walk along the Seine and a quiet dinner at L'Ami Louis, but I suppose getting so close to the Michelangelo sketches was worth the risk."

"Next trip over," Frank said, touching a gloved hand to her face. "But now, let's see if what the old man told us is true. The Michelangelo designs should be somewhere near that wall, close to the fireplace."

"The old man spoke the truth." The voice was harsh and hidden, coming at them from the front of the room. "The sketches are here, and I can't begin to thank you enough for leading me to them."

Frank turned to Andrea and gestured for her to move toward a cluster of paintings to her left. They both had turned off their penlights and gripped .9 millimeter revolvers. They moved quiet as cats, their breathing slow and steady, marking the distance between themselves and the unseen voice.

"We've had a few good adventures these last years, haven't we?" the other person in the room said. "Together, I'd say we found at least ten percent of Michelangelo's lost treasures. But that masterpiece—the Midnight Angels—is still out there waiting to be grabbed. And that one I think I'll find on my own."

Frank turned and pointed his gun at the intruder. "You never found anything," he said. "You couldn't have. You didn't know where to look. What you did was follow. Without us to lead the way, you'd be lucky to find the airport."

"Maybe so, Professor," the man said, "but I'm the one who's come out of all this a rich man. You and your bride couldn't wait to deliver your discoveries to the first local museum to open its doors to you, ignoring the dozens of buyers waiting to pay millions for what you held in your hands."

"Only a thief would sell what isn't his," Andrea said,

crouched down behind a row of paintings, her grip on the gun still tight. "Those works never belonged to us."

The unseen man laughed. "If we had searched for lost gold instead of art, wouldn't we have kept it or sold it?" he asked, his voice full of disdain. "Sunken treasure as opposed to a buried bust? It's all of one piece and there for one purpose. To bring profit to whoever is so fortunate as to find it."

"Which leaves us where?" Frank asked, sensing now that they were not alone, that the man in the corner had others hidden about the room, all most likely armed. He knew from studying the floor plans there were only two escape routes. The closest was the large floor-to-ceiling window to his left, and that offered only an improbable three-story drop to gravel or a more manageable ten-foot leap to an adjoining rooftop. The front entry was the second and potentially more accessible option, but that came with its own difficulties, among them the numerous paintings and sculptures blocking the path. Not to mention the potential threat of unseen guns aimed their way.

"I'm sorry to say," the man said, "that our time together has come to an end."

Frank turned from the voice, looked at Andrea and pointed to the window behind them. "I'll cover and you go," he whispered.

She shook her head and clicked her weapon. "We head there together," she whispered back. "Spray the room as we run. Whoever gets to the window first cracks it."

Frank stayed silent for a moment and then gave his wife a knowing smile. "I don't even know why I bother," he said. "My ideas always get shot down."

"One of these days," Andrea said, returning the smile.

Standing back-to-back, they moved as one, firing rounds into all four corners of the room. Frank had read the situation correctly, and they were greeted by heavy return fire from all sides. Bullets chipped ancient sculpted busts and ripped through works of art that had survived for generations. Within seconds a room that for decades had been devoted to the cherished works of the masters became a fire zone.

Andrea was hit first, a bullet to the right shoulder that sent her spinning closer to her husband and dropped her to one knee. Frank pulled her up and wrapped his left arm around her waist. He put a fresh clip in the .9 millimeter and moved within inches of the window. "Hang on," he told her. "We're just about there."

A volley of bullets rained down on them, hitting stone, canvas, glass, and flesh, circling them in a cloud bank of gun smoke. "You know what bothers me the most about all this?" she shouted above the din, emptying the last of her rounds in the direction of the shooters.

"What?" Frank asked as he lifted the handle on the large window and swung it out and open, feeling the cool evening breeze of the Florence night rush in.

"I figured this to be the easy part," Andrea said.

Frank looked out the window, focusing on the red-tile roof less than a dozen feet to their left. "Not a simple jump," he said, "but not impossible. You'll make it. You're too good not to."

"So says you," she said, grunting as she began to move.

Frank sprayed the area around them with one final volley as Andrea climbed up on the ledge and timed her jump. "I'll see you on the other side," he told her.

"You better," she said.

He turned his head and watched as his wife made the leap, landing with a hard thud on the rooftop across from the open window, several red stone tiles falling harmlessly to the ground below and shattering. He reached for an edge of the open window and began to lift himself up onto the ledge, looking across at his wife, blood flowing freely out of a flesh wound in his right leg and several large gashes across his arms and neck. He was standing on the ledge, prepared to make his jump, when the bullet landed in the center of his back.

Andrea saw him jolt straight up and hid a scream with the fingers of both hands cupped hard against her mouth. Frank let the gun slip from his right hand, his knees losing feeling, his upper body now trembling and coated with sweat. He gazed across at his wife, gave her one final smile and lifted a hand up to caress his heart. He then fell backward into the room, landing with a dusty thud on the hardwood floor, his head ripping through a canvas resting on its side.

Andrea stepped back from the ledge, her hands still masking her mouth, and walked right into the arms of a muscular man in a thin leather jacket.

"He won't die alone, if that's your worry," said the familiar voice.

She lowered her hands from her mouth, her breath relaxed and her body calm and free of all pain and tension. She knew that given the countless risks she and her husband had taken through the years, a brutal ending should come with little in the way of surprise. It was, as Frank often told her, part of their job description. *As professors we lead tenured lives,* he once said to her. *As treasure hunters, we lead tenuous ones.*

"You'll grow old on this rooftop," she now told her captor, "if you're waiting for me to beg."

The man released his grip and spun her around. He stared into her eyes and held the look for several long seconds, a half-moon giving light to his gaunt face. "It could have been us," he said to her. "You and me. It *should* have been us. There was a moment . . . years back . . ."

"It takes two to make a moment," she said, her gaze locked down hard on his, "and you've always flown solo."

"No regrets, then," he said, stepping closer to her, pressuring her toward the edge of the rooftop.

"Only one," she said.

His eyes posed the question.

"That neither I nor my husband will be there to see who it is who finally brings you down."

"Be content with what you do know, then," he answered. "You both will have died knowing whose hand turned the wheel."

He removed one of his black leather gloves and gripped her neck with thin fingers, a large ring, marked with the head of a dark bird, catching the glare of a distant light. He glanced at her bullet wound, which had stained the ground around them in a circle of blood, saw the glint of fear in her eyes, and smiled. He lifted his right hand, the one holding the long knife, and plunged it deep into the center of her stomach. He held her in place and waited, watching as the life ebbed out of her body, a thin line of blood easing down her lower lip. Releasing the blade, he took two steps back, looked up at the open window across the way and nodded to two men standing there. "Come get her," he told them. "And bring the sketches with you."

"And the rest of the works?" one of the men asked.

"Burn them," he said, "along with the bodies."

He stepped over the fallen professor and stared out across the rooftops of Florence, hands folded behind him, knowing there now was no one left to prevent him from achieving his dream.

The secrets of the city would soon be his alone.

PART ONE

*"I saw the angel in the marble
and carved until I set him free."*
—MICHELANGELO BUONARROTI

CHAPTER I

Summer 2010

FLORENCE, ITALY

KATE AND MARCO MADE A SHARP LEFT ONTO Chiasso Altoviti, leaving the rushing waters of the Arno behind them, running at full speed across the cobblestones of the narrow street. Kate, her long brown hair held together by a blue butterfly clip, led the way as they dodged the occasional shopper, bumped against a parked Vespa, and successfully evaded an elderly woman hauling two plastic bags filled with fruits and vegetables.

"They are no longer chasing us, I think," Marco said, grinding to a fast stop. His English was accented, his light brown polo shirt marked with sweat as he rested his hands on the knees of a pair of Levi knockoffs. He was in his late twenties, thick dark hair flowing toward the nape of his neck, his strong features highlighted by rich olive eyes.

Kate slowed her pace and turned to gaze down the curved street. "Let's keep moving," she said, "just in case."

"Just in case what?" Marco asked.

Two men, dressed in track suits and sneakers, came tearing around the Borgo Apostoli. "In case you're wrong," she said as she grabbed his arm and sprinted down the street.

"I told you we shouldn't have done what we did,"

Marco said, as short of breath as he was filled with anger. "I told you we should have left things the way they were."

"No, you didn't," Kate said, not slowing down as she turned her head to check on the men. "You never told me any of that."

"And what good would it have done if I had?" he asked.

The men were closing in, moving through the early morning shoppers and tourists at a faster clip, more experienced in the art of pursuit than their targets were in the art of fleeing.

Kate and Marco made a full-charge run toward the Uffizi. "If we can make it in there, we might have a chance to lose them," she said, pointing toward the imposing gallery. "A guide who works there is a friend of mine. She'll find us a place to hide."

"Are you sure she's working today?" Marco asked.

"It's a guess," Kate said. "But right now, a guess is the best I can do."

"We should be in a café, drinking espresso, listening to Bob Dylan," Marco said. "Instead, we are running from two men who maybe want to kill us."

"I didn't know you liked Dylan," she said, turning onto Via de' Georgofili, closing in on the Uffizi. She wiped a strand of brown hair from her face, gave a quick glance at her pursuers and a nod of encouragement to Marco.

They both stopped when they saw the rope ladder hanging from an open double window three stories above them, a middle-aged man waving frantically for them to begin their climb. *"Fai presto,"* he shouted down. "Please, hurry. There is not much time. You have only seconds."

"How do we know to trust *him*?" Marco asked, reaching for the bottom rung of the rope, noticing the two men turning a corner and heading their way. "How do we know he's not with *them*?"

"We don't," Kate said, holding the rope for support and nodding for Marco to begin his climb.

In seconds he was halfway up the ladder with Kate right behind him, lifting the rungs as she moved forward, leaving the two men at street level staring at them in frustration. They banged against the thick red oak door that led into the building's entrance but were met by a series of dead bolts and unanswered buzzers. Marco looked up at the middle-aged man who was leaning outside his window ready to greet him with a smile and an open hand. *"Bravo, ragazzo,"* the man said as he helped ease Marco inside his apartment. "Now the signorina, no?"

"I'll help her in," Marco said, reaching down and offering both hands to Kate as she kicked clear of the ladder and stepped onto the window ledge and into the room.

"Now you must go quickly up to the roof," the man said. "In Florence, walking across the rooftops is the fastest way to get anywhere, better even than any bus or taxi."

"Why are you helping us?" Kate asked, looking into the man's eyes. He was short and overweight but carried it well, dressed in dark tailored slacks and starched white shirt, sleeves rolled up to the elbows.

"It looked to me as if someone should," the man said, his English as confident as his manner. "And I've never been one to stay out of other people's affairs. I take after my mother in that way, I suppose."

"The two following us might find you," Marco said, standing with his back to a large wooden hutch filled with old photos and memorabilia. "Not that I know them personally, but my guess is that they aren't the type who show much patience with anyone getting in their way."

"Make them *my* worry, then," the man said. "You concern yourself with getting up to the roof and finding your way to safety."

"What's your name?" Kate asked.

"Gian Lucca," he said with a slight bow of his head. "I was named after my grandfather, as most Italian boys seem to be."

Kate smiled at Gian Lucca, then leaned over and hugged him. "Thank you," she said. "What you're doing is very kind and very brave."

"And very foolish," Marco said. He caught the sideways glances of both Kate and Gian Lucca. "Not that I don't appreciate it," he said.

Gian Lucca turned away from Marco, looked across at Kate and let free a warm smile. "Please," he said, "I must get you to the roof. While I hate to agree with him, your young friend is correct. Those men will be here soon, and they will not be as happy to see me as you both were. Time is not a friend to us."

A few moments later Kate and Marco stood on the rooftop of the small building, the sun glistening off the Arno a short distance away, the grandeur of the Uffizi at their backs.

"The leaps from roof to roof are short and should not pose much risk," Gian Lucca said. "You need to reach the building closest to the Ponte Vecchio. The top door will be unlocked. Once you make your way out to the street, cross to the other side of the Arno and you will be safe, at least for now."

"What about you?"

"I need to prepare," Gian Lucca said. "I have guests arriving."

"You don't need to risk your life," Kate said, holding his right hand in hers. "We can stay and help."

"Better still," Marco said, "you can leave with us. Why get into a fight when it is so easy to avoid them? A lesson clearly not yet learned by my American friend."

"Your concern is appreciated," Gian Lucca said, smiling and patting his stomach. "But for me, jumping across rooftops is not the safest option."

"Will we see you again?" Kate asked.

"Only if you plan on being chased again," Gian Lucca said.

"Then I imagine we'll all be close friends," Marco said. "I've only known her ten days and already I've sweated through every shirt I own."

Gian Lucca heard footsteps coming up the stairwell, opened the thick black door of the roof and gazed down. "I must go and greet my guests," he said. He waved at Kate and Marco and walked back into the building, closing the door to the rooftop and locking it from the inside.

"How many rooftops have you jumped across in your life?" Marco asked Kate.

"Half a dozen or so," she said, "maybe more. I had a friend in high school who was very good at it, and I would go with her sometimes."

"I didn't have friends like that," he said. "Going skiing was probably the wildest activity we ever did."

"How good a skier are you?"

"One broken arm and one broken leg in three trips," he said. "What does that tell you?"

"It tells me I should jump first," Kate said.

And she did.

CHAPTER 2

CHICAGO, ILLINOIS

RICHARD DYLAN EDWARDS STOOD BEHIND THE large lectern and watched as the students piled into the small auditorium. He glanced down briefly at his notes and his class list and wondered how many of the eighty-three students attending his seminar on Michelangelo and his theory of art would actually apply anything they learned to their everyday lives. How many of them took up the study of art history because it fulfilled a hunger to connect with the masters of the past, as opposed to how many slid into it as a major, thinking it would come with an easy college degree attached? It was a question Professor Edwards often posed to himself, usually on the days he was preoccupied with matters that went beyond the walls of his classroom.

And today was one of those days.

At the age of forty-six, Edwards ranked as one of the world's foremost scholars of Michelangelo. He had devoted the bulk of his life to the study of a man who was born in impoverished anonymity and died eight decades later draped in both riches and respect. But it was not the works of the Divine One that weighed on Edwards's mind this early first semester morning, the weather outside still bearing the brunt of a brutal heat wave that showed no signs of surrender. It was the note folded inside the breast pocket of his denim shirt that consumed his full attention, the one that he had printed out of his e-mail box earlier that morning and read again and again. The note was from Kate Westcott, the young woman he had raised since the eve of her fourth birthday and who now found herself on a fellowship working in the city of Florence, devoting a year of her life to the study of his hero. It was a fellowship he had embraced with the pride of a parent, but now filled him with a sense of dread.

"Excuse me, sir?"

Edwards looked up to see a young man standing in front of him, his rail-thin body leaning ever so slightly against the edge of the lectern, his long blond hair masking half of a face that seemed to be always on the verge of a smile.

"Good morning, Stephen," he said. "And what major crisis do we need to put our heads together and overcome today? Or would you like me to guess?"

"I could give you a few hints," his student said, stifling a chuckle.

"I'll ask for a lifeline if I need one," Edwards said. "But for now, I'm going to throw my weight behind my gut instincts and take lost or missing essays for eight hundred."

"It's finished, sir, that I promise you. I may not know where I left it, but I know for sure it's completed."

"Were you drunk or sober when you worked on it?" Edwards asked.

"Sober," Stephen said. "But I guess I went at it pretty heavy once I was done."

"Do you remember any of it?"

"I remember *all* of it," Stephen said. "It was pretty much all I worked on for four full days, sir."

"Then it's not missing and you won't walk out of here with an incomplete."

"I don't understand, sir," Stephen said. "I can't hand in the essay today because I don't have it with me."

"But you *do* have it with you," Edwards said. "You just don't have it written down."

Stephen's blue eyes widened and he shook his head several times. "I don't think I could do what I think it is you're asking me to do, sir," he said. "In fact, I could swear to it."

"What you mean is that you couldn't do it this very moment. Which is perfectly understandable and not something I would even consider asking of you."

"Thank you, sir," Stephen said, the red flush gone from his face. "You had me there for a second, I admit. Thought for sure you were going to ask me to recite my essay out loud as soon as class started."

"That would be a tactic more in keeping with the Philosophy Department," Edwards said, walking from his side of the lectern and standing now next to Stephen, dwarfing the student in both height and build. "*But* I do expect you to recite it to me as well as to the class before our time is up. I'll leave it to you to signal me when you're ready."

"Professor, please," Stephen pleaded. "I don't think I'll be able to remember everything I wrote."

"You won't need to," Professor Edwards said. "Just remember enough of it to convince me you were telling the truth, that somewhere on this campus or in this state there is a finished essay on Michelangelo with your name on it. I will accept the fact that papers can be lost or stolen. I will never accept being made to look like a fool. Have I made myself clear?"

"Very clear, sir," Stephen said.

The boy turned slowly away, stopping in the middle row of the auditorium, and sat down, dejected.

Edwards walked over to a large bay window that looked toward the north, the upper part of his right shoulder braced against a wall, the warm sun reflecting off the dirt-speckled glass. He stared out at the tree-lined walkways, students lounging on the lawn or sitting on benches, iPods latched to their ears, textbooks open and spread across bended knees. Professor Edwards loved the serenity of campus life, a safe bubble from the risks of the world that lay beyond the brick-lined campus entrance. Here, life could be dissected and discussed without fear of reprisals, and answers to even the most complex questions could be found—at least within the context of a spirited discussion. An environment dedicated to breaking down the lessons of the past and applying them to the problems of the present. As an academic, he found solace in this tranquil setting. And if that were the whole of his life, then Richard Dylan Edwards would indeed be a man who had found peace on this earth.

BUT THE ACADEMIC WORLD did not command the youthful professor's full attention. Edwards's true calling, which more often than not put him in danger's scope, was chasing down lost and stolen works of art and returning them to their rightful owners. His academic work offered cover for those clandestine endeavors, affording him the luxury of traveling for months at a time and allowing him to seek what many considered forever lost.

He came to his calling well-equipped to handle its challenges. Naturally athletic, he worked his body hard to stay in shape. He was skilled in the use of a variety of weapons, from modern to medieval, and had spent decades studying martial arts. Even so, he didn't embark on his adventures alone, but was instead one of a number of scholars, academics, art restorers, historians, and treasure hunters belonging to a dedicated and secretive group. The Vittoria Society had been named in honor of Signora Vittoria Colonna, daughter of the grand constable of the Kingdom of Naples and the only woman known to have captured Michelangelo's heart. The artist had been sixty-one in 1536, when he met the beautiful Vittoria, by then the widow of a marquis who had fallen in battle, and Michelangelo would spend the remainder of his days in her grip. He wrote her numerous sonnets, drew dozens of pictures capturing her in various stages of repose, and spent as much time in her company as his work would allow. And when Vittoria died, on February 25, 1547, at the Convent of San Silvestro in Rome, Michelangelo mourned her loss more than that of any other who crossed his path.

They were art hunters.

In the past five years alone, half a dozen members of the Vittoria Society, spread across the globe, had discovered three paintings by Caravaggio in the basement of a soon-to-be demolished Paris hotel; found a soiled folio believed to have been written by William Shakespeare in a rusty freezer in the foyer of an abandoned farmhouse in the Scottish highlands; bought a complete manuscript thought to be written by Sir Walter Scott at an illegal auction held long after closing hours in a fashionable London row house; and were scouring Hong Kong seeking a sword used in battle by Genghis Khan. Each of their discoveries had been delivered with discretion to its rightful owner as determined by the leaders of the Society.

Edwards had been brought into this secret world by Frank and Andrea Westcott.

They were academic legends, a studious and brilliant couple long considered the most renowned Michelangelo scholars in the world. They were also among the six founding members of the Vittoria Society and by far the most active and adventurous of the group.

Edwards had been a shy twelve-year-old, living in an Indianapolis orphanage, when he first met them, standing in the hallway of that prison-gray dormitory he had learned to call home. He did not question why they wanted to see him, and had not the slightest clue as to their identities. Still, he knew from that moment that he belonged in their company.

The Westcotts taught him their methods and were as demanding in their work and study as they were effusive in their affections. "We're not out to change the world," Frank once told him, outside the Sir John Soane's Museum in London a week before Edwards would begin his college studies. "We're just looking to bring balance to it. No one should ever gaze at a work of art for what it's worth financially. You seek it out and allow it to tell you all it can about who you are as a person. Watch a man's eyes the first time he looks up at the statue of David and you'll know all there is to know about him in a matter of seconds. If you can't be moved by a great work, if all you can do is break it down to its financial value, then what more is there to say about you?"

THE PROFESSOR WATCHED a young woman walk across the well-kept lawn of the quad outside his second-floor classroom and his mind immediately conjured the image of Kate. She had been barely four years old when her parents died. He was in his mid-twenties then, unprepared for a family. But he owed his life and calling to Kate's parents. In turn he had devoted years to the raising of their daughter.

He taught her as he himself had been taught.

Her parents had left him financially well-positioned to

place Kate in the best educational environment he could find. But he realized early on that he would have to do more than simply enroll the quiet and studious child in a variety of classes to consider his job complete. He needed to provide her with a stable home and someone she could turn to and confide in during troubled days. And it had been important to him that her life not evolve into a series of mental and physical chores. He wanted her to cherish the moments they spent together and to pursue her studies and her physical regimen with a passion that matched that of her parents.

Edwards stepped back from the glare of the outside sun, turned and looked down the row of desks at Stephen. "Five more minutes," he said, "and then we'll get started."

He walked back toward his lectern. He reached down for his brown leather briefcase and skimmed through its contents until he found the folded piece of paper he sought. He pulled it out, leaned against a corner wall and held the paper against his right leg. It was a letter he had written Kate earlier that morning, one that was still missing the ending he required and she had grown to expect—the clues to a riddle.

It was a game they had been playing now for nearly two decades. It grew out of Kate's fondness for the TV show that featured her favorite childhood comic book hero, Batman. She was particularly taken by one of the villains he faced on a regular basis, the Riddler, and would devour any story where the two did battle. More often than not, the Riddler would attempt to snare his opponent through a series of "Riddle Me This" hints, many of which stumped Batman long enough for his nemesis to get away. Edwards noted how much Kate enjoyed that part of the story line, and soon enough a game of hints and clues built around most any subject they discussed became a signature part of their routine.

He recalled the last time the two had played the game, four months earlier as they walked through the airport terminal, two hours before her flight to Rome was to depart. "Remember," she said, "you promised you would visit as often as you could."

"And I will," he said. "But remember this trip is your time now. You've read all the books, you've taken all the classes, you're even teaching a few yourself. And you've excelled at all of it. But there's still one piece missing. One very important and crucial piece."

"What?" she asked.

Edwards looked over at her, realizing that behind the confident façade of the well-trained young woman still resided the frightened little girl whose parents had died years before she could get to know them, that he, and their shared devotion to the study of Michelangelo, was her only link to them. "Riddle me this," he said to her.

"Oh, no," Kate said, not bothering to hide the pleasure the game gave her, "not now. Not with something like this. I'll *never* guess the answer. You know how terrible I am at this game."

"I see some progress," he said.

"Richard, we've been playing this since I was in preschool, am I right?" she asked.

"Yes."

"And how many times have I guessed the correct answer?"

"That doesn't mean you're not good at it," he said.

He loved her as much as a father would a daughter, but because of their closeness in age, their relationship was much like that of an older brother and younger sister.

"How many times?" she repeated.

"Not once," he said with a shrug. "But I have a lot of faith in your abilities. I always have and I always will."

Kate stared at him for a quiet moment and gently placed her hand on top of his. "I never thanked you for everything you've done for me," she said. "You're the only family I've ever known."

"And you're the only family I've ever needed," he said, squeezing her hand. "Now, are you ready? And you don't have to give me an answer now. Think about it on the flight over and during your first few weeks in Florence. I'll include a new clue in each letter I write, and I don't want you to get frustrated. This will be your most difficult one yet, but I think you'll get it eventually."

"Is there a prize at the end?" Kate asked with a wide smile.

"A grand prize," Edwards said. "A prize for the ages."

STEPHEN WALKED UP the narrow aisle toward the professor. Edwards slid the folded paper into the side pocket of his jacket and gestured toward the lectern. "Has it all come flowing back to you?" he asked his student, watching him step in front of the lectern, his fingers gripping the side panels.

"Not exactly, sir," Stephen said.

"You might surprise yourself," Edwards said. He stood in the center of the classroom, hands in his pockets, and faced the student. "We always retain more than we think. The key is not to panic, but to allow the answer to come to the surface. Are you ready to begin, then?"

"I never seem to be quite ready, sir," Stephen said.

"Few of us are," Edwards said. "Despite that, we still

find it in ourselves to move forward. Sometimes, that's even more important."

"Yes, sir," Stephen said.

"Then let's both move forward together," Edwards said, taking two steps closer to the student. "Now riddle me this."

CHAPTER 3

KATE AND MARCO WALKED ON THE STONE STEPS of the narrow sidewalk, the Arno running hard to their right, leather shops and dress boutiques lining the street to their left, racing traffic the only buffer. The day was leaning toward dusk and a gentle mist hung on the air. Lights from the Ponte Vecchio and the apartment buildings and businesses lining both sides of the river cast the city in a soft glow.

"You have been so lucky, Marco," Kate said.

"In what way?"

"You've spent your life in this city," she said. "I can't imagine a more beautiful place in the world."

"It's even more beautiful when there aren't men with guns chasing you down every street," he said.

Kate glanced over at him, observing his dark hair flopping against the collar of his denim shirt, his round, handsome face doing little to hide the concern visible in his almond eyes. "I'm sorry I got you mixed up in this," she said. "It wasn't intentional, believe me."

Marco shrugged his thin shoulders and shook his head slightly. "It's not as if you forced me to go with you," he said.

"Yes I did," she said.

"What I meant is that you didn't drag me with you at the point of a gun," he said. "I went because I wanted to go. Not that you have a gun. I mean you don't, right?"

Kate stopped, leaned against the gray stone wall and

stared down at the Arno below. "The river is so much like this city," she said, "don't you think? So dark and majestic, beautiful and powerful, and yet filled with so many secrets."

"And don't forget to add dangerous," he said. "Not too long ago, the Arno almost brought Florence to ruin."

"The flood?"

Marco nodded. "You can still see the watermarks in some of the buildings and the museums," he said. "In some parts it reached the streetlamps. Can you imagine? The water came in strong. My father was my age when it happened, and a day never passed that he didn't think about the damage that had been done. My mother never spoke about it—the memories were too disturbing to her—but Papa told me a few stories before he died, and all of them had sad endings. There was a point during that flood, maybe just a few hours, when many people here, including my family, felt the entire city would be washed away. Disappear as if it had never existed."

"A lot like what Hurricane Katrina did to New Orleans," Kate said.

"Yes," Marco said, "except in one respect. No one here would dare to turn his back on Florence. No one would allow it to float away, not the government and most especially not the people of this city. Those might have been our darkest days and nights, but the lights stayed on."

"Do you think you'll ever want to live anywhere else?" she asked.

"America is the only place that interests me," Marco said. "If what I have heard and read is true, then so much is possible there. I never believed, as many did here, that the streets of American cities were filled with gold, but I do believe you have more opportunities to achieve your goals as an American than I do as an Italian. Here, ambition is not enough."

"America is bigger," Kate said. "With a larger appetite. And yet I feel more at home here than I ever did there. I feel like America is where I live and where I study and where I work. Here is where I belong. It's as if my history is here on these streets, down these alleys, in the museums and in the churches. And I've only been here a few weeks."

"I blame Michelangelo for that," Marco said with a smile. "He has turned you into a Florentine. And how could he not? You've spent so much time reading about him, studying his works. Already you know him in ways most scholars don't. I hear it in the way you speak about him in class. And if you know Michelangelo, then you know Florence."

"He's real to me, that's all," Kate said. "I never think of him as an historical figure, but as a man who lived life doing what he loved. All the books talk about how accomplished he was, how revered, but you never get a sense of him as a man living a day-to-day life. I guess those missing parts are what I've always looked for."

"Your parents wrote about those missing parts," Marco said. "I suppose that's one of the reasons their book has always been popular with art history students. You don't need a dozen *espressi* just to get through the assigned chapters."

Kate kept her eyes on the dark brown waters of the Arno and remained silent, her hands hanging over the edge of the wall, fingers interlocked as if in prayer.

Marco leaned his back against the brick wall and stared out at the passing traffic. "I hope you don't mind me mentioning your parents," he said. "I didn't know them, of course, but I do know their work. They had a big influence on me."

"I really didn't know them, either," Kate said, her

voice muted. "I was so young when they died that the work they left behind has been my only way to connect to them, same as you."

"Which then brings us back to Michelangelo," Marco said.

"And since the people chasing us seem to have gone on their break, now might be a good time to pay him a visit," she said.

"I'll go only because I know it will bring a smile to your face," he said. "I have my bike parked on the other side of the bridge and we could be at Santa Croce in ten minutes."

"If you don't mind, I'd rather walk," Kate said. "Such a pretty night."

"Every time I offer you a ride on my bicycle, you turn it down," Marco said. "I don't mind, really. I'm just curious why you hate it so."

"What's there to hate?" she asked, moving away from the wall and walking back down the street, Marco by her side. "Other than that there isn't a place for me to sit, the tires could use a little air, the chains squeak like a church bell, and there's so much rust on it you have to guess the color of the bike."

"Now you sound like an American," Marco said.

"What does that mean?"

"To an American, if something is old—and I mean months, not years—it gets tossed aside," Marco said. "I've read where cars are traded in every two years, televisions in your homes are thrown out as soon as a bigger screen is available, clothes given away by the season. Here, if something belongs to us or, more importantly, is given to us, then we do all we can to keep it forever. It becomes a part of who we are."

"Do you think Michelangelo would have gone with you for a ride on your bike?" Kate asked, nudging him with her shoulder.

"He would have more likely ignored it," Marco said. "He was, you know, indifferent to anything he himself did not design or construct. His eye would always be on *the next thing*. If it already existed and he had no part in making it, it bored him."

"With an attitude like that," she said with a smile, "he could have passed for an American."

They walked past the Ponte Vecchio, the jewelry stores on both sides of the street still doing a brisk business as the workday neared an end, and onto Via Girolami toward Santa Croce and the final resting place of Michelangelo.

CHAPTER 4

THE BALD MAN WITH THE FOUR-INCH SCAR RUNning down the right side of his face opened an aluminum-lined briefcase and took two steps back. He looked over his shoulder at the man behind him and smiled. "On time and as promised," he said.

"It's what you were paid to do," the thin man said, brushing past him to gaze down at the contents of the briefcase. "Little reason to gloat."

"It was riskier than either of us anticipated," the bald man said.

"That might be due to the fact that the police were tipped off within minutes of the lift," his client said. "And that tip came from the people you brought in to help with the operation. That end of the job was not well handled."

The bald man pulled out a crumpled white handkerchief and wiped at his neck and forehead. He was breathing through an open mouth, and his long-sleeve blue T-shirt was marred by circles of sweat. He had been an art thief and a forger going on fifteen years, mostly small-time lifts amounting to nothing more than a few thousand euros, the majority involving apartment break-ins of old-line Florentine families known to have paintings and sculptures that could easily be moved out of the city and country. "We were gone by the time they arrived," he said, his voice still steady, his upper lip twitching slightly. "And we left nothing behind that could be traced back to us."

The thin man turned away from the briefcase and glared at the thief. "There is no 'us,' " he said. "And as long as we conduct business together, I suggest you remember that."

"Listen, I didn't mean to imply we were partners," the bald man said. "Hell, I don't even know your name, which makes it impossible for me to tell anyone anything. I just meant I was doing this job for you."

"Roberto Mangini," the thin man said, leaning against the side of the wooden table on which the briefcase rested. "Is that your real name or the one you want me to believe is real?"

"The first name is real," the bald man said, "and that still puts you one up on me."

"How much would you say the art in the briefcase is worth?" the thin man asked.

"Depending on the buyer and how eager you are to move it, I'd say two hundred, maybe even 300,000 euros," Roberto said. "Minus any cuts that have to be paid out along the way."

They were standing in the center of the large kitchen of a shuttered restaurant on a small side street near the Pitti Palace. An overhead bulb shrouded by a thin shade swung above them. It was past midnight now, and the occasional footsteps of a late diner or a couple heading home after an evening walk could be heard.

"And how much of your time would that amount buy me?" the thin man asked.

"Depends on the job you want done," Roberto said. "If it's another break-in that turned out to be as easy as this one, then it would hold me for a week, maybe a few days more. Something more complicated always gets to be more expensive. But until I know what you have in mind, I can't say."

"Then I'll answer for you," the thin man said. "I give you this painting, allow you to sell it to the highest bidder and pocket all the proceeds. I'll even pay any commissions or cuts that are required along the way. Fair enough so far?"

Roberto nodded. "I like what I hear," he said.

"You can bank that money, invest it wisely or gamble it away all in one night," the thin man said. "It's of no concern to me. But in return for taking it, you will work for me on one other assignment."

"For how long?"

"It could be a day," the thin man said with a shrug, "or it might last as long as a year. The only point that matters to me is that you agree to do it."

"And if I choose to walk away instead?" Roberto asked. "Where will that leave us?"

The thin man stepped closer to Roberto, brown eyes still as stones, his angular face a blank slate, a hint of menace buried beneath. "How much do you know about me?"

"I know enough," Roberto said.

The thin man smiled. "I learned long ago that is an answer given by people who don't really know anything at all."

THE THIN MAN had been born in 1965 in a nondescript suburb of Detroit, in the middle of a late January blizzard. His father worked on the line in a string of auto factories, his hard-drinking ways always keeping him on the cusp of unemployment. His mother held down a part-time job at a diner a half mile from the three-bedroom house she had inherited from an uncle. The boy was their only child, and he was raised in a house that was free of books and empty of warmth. He attended the local public school and did well enough in English and art classes to catch the eye of a teacher who saw promise in a boy whose shabby clothes and silent demeanor hid an insatiable curiosity and sturdy intellect.

The teacher convinced his indifferent parents to allow their son to take a series of advanced courses at a nearby private school. Those classes propelled the boy to achieve academic credentials strong enough to earn him scholarships to both an elite prep school and Michigan State. He had escaped.

By all accounts, the boy—named David by his parents but called an assortment of cruel nicknames by his fellow students because of his reticence and his studious habits—was a quick study. He felt a personal connection to the works of the masters, specifically those who thrived during the Renaissance, and devoted his time to researching them. The hard work paid off, earning him a number of fellowships overseas, where he attacked his lessons with an even greater passion.

David's commitment to the study of art was extreme, and he allowed himself little time for many of the other activities enjoyed by students his age. He attended few parties, belonged to no one social group, and the few attempts he made at dating led to little more than awkward silences and quick endings. But David believed that the love of his work would help him overcome anything.

It was during those years that his name was brought to the attention of Andrea Westcott.

By the early 1980s, Andrea Westcott was working to expand the membership of the Vittoria Society. She especially sought talented students from the art history community, to reach out to them months before they entered the cloistered environment of academic life.

"We need to reach our recruits while they're still pure," she told her husband Frank one evening, over a meal at Sostanza, their favorite Florentine steak house.

"Get hold of them before some of those professors strip them of their sense of adventure."

"I am *nothing* if not adventurous," Frank said. "I mean, if you were paying attention, you must have noticed I was the one who ordered the wild berries."

"How Indiana Jones of you," she said.

"What can I say?" Frank said. "I live for the thrill."

"Do you think what we're doing is worth the trouble?" she asked. "Worth the risk?"

Frank glanced at her, reached for her hand and held it gently. "Yes," he said.

"It seems impossible sometimes," she said. "Especially knowing we could both live to be a hundred and still not even come close to finding it all. I mean, with Michelangelo alone, at least a third of his work is still missing."

"I don't think either one of us has to worry about living to a hundred," Frank said. "And, frankly, I'm not sure I would want to, even if I had the option."

"I think you'd be a very sexy old man," she said. "And it would be great fun to see you spend three hours every morning trying to find your slippers."

Frank laughed and waited as a young waiter in a crisp white shirt rested a plate of biscotti in front of them. "I wouldn't worry about it," he said. "It's the right thing, what we're doing. Our success can't be judged on the number of artistic works we find. Our success is simply in making the attempt."

DAVID WAS AMONG the first of Andrea Westcott's student recruits.

He first met her at a lunch she arranged at a small restaurant two miles from his college campus. He would never forget that initial encounter: Enthralled by her knowledge of the art world, enraptured by her beauty, he had pledged his allegiance to the goals of the Vittoria

Society by the time the waiter rolled the dessert cart toward their table. They kept in touch from that day forward, either by mail or in person. It was during those heady months, with the arrival of each new letter or the start of a fresh conversation over warm cups of coffee, that David fell in love for the first and only time.

One semester after he landed his first teaching position at a small college in the Pacific Northwest, he was on a plane bound for the Scottish Highlands, sitting in a first-class seat directly behind Frank and Andrea, about to begin his maiden mission for the Society, a trackdown of a stolen Modigliani painting.

David had learned about artists in schools, in books and walking the halls of many museums. But he learned about art from Andrea. She taught him to look beyond the books and venture past the lectures to see the work for what it was. Over time, though, what she saw and what he saw veered in opposite directions. Andrea loved a work for its combination of raw skill and inherent beauty, while David loved it for its financial worth. But that should not have come as a surprise. Andrea never had a need or a hunger for money, whereas David craved wealth and found himself at a loss whenever the Society donated a retrieved work when it could have been pocketing millions. But it went even further. David had pledged his love to Andrea, and learned quickly and painfully that such devotion would never be returned.

He broke free of the Vittoria Society in the spring of 1983 and spent the next two years traveling through Europe, taking the initial steps toward laying down the foundation for a new network. He wanted to emerge with a group that would rival the Society in intellectual power, financial backing, and museum and gallery connections, but whose purpose was radically different. His end goal was the accumulation of wealth, and there would be no boundaries to his cohorts' methods of operation, including the recruitment of professional assassins and experienced mercenaries.

David had absorbed a great deal of knowledge in his time with the Society, but no lesson had greater impact on him than the need to operate in secrecy. He felt it crucial that his group function in darkness, utilizing code names and third-person intermediaries, with no one knowing the true identities of their accomplices. Both the money and the art would be funneled down back channels, cleaned and washed by hired hands with no apparent connection, and then processed through a series of secured banks in Europe and the Middle East. He would travel alone and undercover, emerge long enough to lock in the transaction or locate the missing art, then fade back into the mist. He would require an identity cloaked in mystery and tinged with danger, but one that would still give him an identifiable signature in both the artistic and criminal communities.

By the summer of 1985 the pieces of the elaborate puzzle were in place. The Immortals opened their doors to the business of dealing in illicit art. And in that year, David, the quiet boy from a Detroit suburb who grew up to be an art history prodigy, ceased to exist.

He was now and would for the rest of his years be known as the Raven.

ROBERTO KEPT HIS EYES on the rows of cash in the briefcase, took a deep breath and nodded. "What do you need me to do?" he asked.

The Raven smiled, slid his hands into his pants pockets and walked toward the door leading out the rear of the shuttered restaurant. "For the time being, don't leave the city," he said, without turning to face the thief. "You will, at some point soon, be contacted by one of my associates. Follow his instructions from that moment on."

"I wouldn't worry," Roberto said. "I always hold up my end of the deal."

The Raven turned back. "I never worry about people like you," he said. "If you fail me or you betray me, someone will replace you that very day."

He turned, flipped the latch on an old wooden door, swung it open and stepped out into the darkness of the Florentine night.

CHAPTER 5

KATE WESTCOTT WOULD ALWAYS REMEMBER the moment.

She sat in a corner of a crowded gym, her T-shirt drenched, her brown hair clinging to her face, fresh from an hour-long treadmill workout. She held a thin envelope in her hands and stared at the stenciled Italian writing on the front. The letter had arrived in her office mailbox two days before, and she had yet to muster the courage to open it. She had been fretting over its arrival for weeks, as nervous on this late afternoon as she was three months earlier, when she dropped off the thick FedEx package filled with all the information her Michelangelo Fellowship required. She felt her odds were favorable. She had the proper academic credentials. She had completed a wide variety of high-level internships, starting as far back as junior high school. She spoke three foreign languages, including Italian. She had glowing letters of recommendation from some of the most prominent scholars in the field. And she was now halfway through her second year as an adjunct art history professor at a northeastern liberal arts college, giving her the type of work experience that helped round out a high-tier academic résumé. Still, she knew there were only six Michelangelo scholar positions open each year, and 1,200 equally qualified candidates from the United States alone had submitted their applications.

"It's not going to open by itself," a man said.

Kate turned her head, crumpling the letter as she did, and looked up at Sandy Walker, a first-year English professor she had befriended and helped as he navigated the school's bureaucracy. Sandy was tall, rail thin, with a thick head of curly blond hair that always seemed windblown. He was a decent teacher, but lacked both the passion for his chosen profession and the ambition to go further in the field. At twenty-five, he was already a man set in his ways, counting down the hours to the final bell, when he would be free to pursue the leisure activities that seemed to occupy the bulk of his time.

"It would make it so much easier if it could," Kate said.

"C'mon," he said, "crack it open, read the good news and then we can go out and celebrate. We'll hit Alfie's for fresh clams and as many beers as they can pour. My treat."

"Why don't you go ahead," she said, "and maybe I'll meet up with you later, good news or bad."

"The fellowship's a slam dunk for you, Kate," Sandy said. "You earned it. But you also need to allow yourself to enjoy it. And I don't know if you can get it together enough to let that happen."

"And getting drunk in a clam bar would prove you wrong?"

"It would be a start," he said. "And you wouldn't be getting drunk alone. I'll be with you every step of the way. Scout's honor."

"I had something else in mind," Kate said.

"Care to share it?"

"I'd rather not," she said.

"I'm at a loss here, Kate," Sandy said. "I've tried my best to get close to you, but I'm starting to feel as if that's something you would prefer I not do. I'm just looking to be your friend, nothing more."

"I don't make friends easily," Kate said.

"So I've noticed," he said.

"Maybe I expect too much," she said.

"Or maybe you give too much of your time to the past," Sandy said, "and not enough to the present."

"I trust what I know," Kate said. "And I'm not alone in thinking that."

"I'm sure there is a guy out there somewhere who feels the same way," Sandy said. "I'm just not that guy."

"I'll have dinner with you Saturday," Kate said, standing and facing him. "But there's something I need to do first, and if you are really a friend you won't ask to know any more than what I've just told you. Agreed?"

"Do I have a choice?"

"No," Kate said.

"Then it's a date," Sandy said, managing a weak smile. "But drinks and dinner are on me and I won't take no for an answer."

"Want to bet?" Kate asked. She turned and walked out of the gym, her head down, the letter still clutched in her right hand.

KATE STOOD NEXT to Professor Edwards, the sand at their feet soft from the rush of the ocean waves. She held two fresh batches of flowers in her arms and stared out at the angry waters, roiling and slapping hard against the turf. It was the middle of the night in the middle of the week, and the Atlantic Ocean seemed to be in no mood for company. Professor Edwards lifted the collar of his sweater against the sharp chill and took in a deep breath of air tinged with the flavor of salt.

"How do you always remember the exact spot?" Kate asked him. "You could have been standing anywhere on this beach, it's changed so much over the years."

"How could I *not*?" Edwards said. "Disposing of your parent's ashes was the hardest thing I've ever done."

"I miss them so much," Kate said. "I envy you the time you were allowed to spend with them. You got to know them in ways I never could. You were probably more of a child to them than I was. I hope that doesn't sound harsh, because I don't mean it in that way."

"I know you don't," Edwards said. "But believe me, I never saw them happier than when they held you in their arms. They were lucky in so many ways. They were passionate about their work, each other, their child. It's a rare gift they were given, even if it was for too short a time."

"I've had a fantastic life so far, so I don't want anything I say to sound like it hasn't been," Kate said. "And much of that is due to you, to the things you taught me and the love you showed. I was too young back then to be aware of how much you were giving up to raise me. To know what a sacrifice it must have been. But I'm not too young to know that now."

Edwards stared out at the ocean, the spray of the waves coating his face and arms. "I didn't give up anything, Kate," he said in a low voice. "I've been the one to benefit from our years together. Never doubt that for a moment."

"It took me a week to open the letter, I was so nervous," she said. "Not just for all that it meant for me, but for you and for them as well."

"The notion of you *not* getting it never even entered my thinking," he said. "I even got you your plane ticket *before* the letter went out."

"What made you so sure?"

"Well, for one, I know how gifted you are," he said. "For another, I called the university and spoke to the fellowship director myself."

"You called?"

"Oh, I hate surprises," Edwards said with a shrug. "Which shouldn't come as a surprise to you. And if you by some fluke were not getting the fellowship, I wanted some time to help brace you for the disappointment."

"My understanding was that they weren't allowed to give out any information regarding the program," Kate said. "I thought they couldn't even discuss it outside of private chambers."

"They can't," Edwards said, "which is why I never asked about the fellowship."

"What did you talk about?"

"Apartments, mostly," he said. "Length of lease. That was very important, as far as I was concerned. I was just curious if, in his opinion, the director thought a one-year lease was a better way to go than a short-term one."

"Follow all the rules but do so in as flexible a way as possible," Kate said. "I'm pretty sure that's one right out of your playbook."

"It was one of theirs, really," Edwards said, his eyes still focused on the crashing waves. "If I abide by any rules, they are the ones your parents taught me. And the ones I've done my best to teach to you."

"I haven't been able to sleep much since I applied for the fellowship," she said. "I can only imagine how happy they would be right now if they were standing here with us."

"This time for you in Florence is a turning point, Kate," he said. "It will allow you to take your work to an entirely new level. I'm not just being complimentary when I brag to friends about your abilities. You're very talented. And now we'll see those talents put to their proper use."

"I was just hoping to barhop and take in the sights," Kate said, smiling. "And maybe even latch onto one of those cute Italian guys whose only goal will be to break my heart."

"Then we're both on the same page," Edwards said, quick to return the smile. "Just remember, cute Italian guys are often joined at the hip by stern Italian mothers who are not quick to warm to the notion of their sons being swept away by beautiful young women. Or any women, for that matter."

"Does your cliché about Italian mothers hold true when it comes to their daughters as well?" she asked.

"Just as much," Edwards said.

"So your affair didn't work out?"

"We didn't allow ourselves the chance to work it out," he said. "It was no one's fault, really. There are dozens of reasons why love affairs come skidding to a halt, and they all seem important as they happen. But as the years pass, you realize how foolish those reasons were."

"Have you kept in touch with her?"

"Not initially," he said. "It's a series of stages. First you want to be with her every single moment of every single day. Then, after the breakup, you decide a cooling off period would be best, and before you know it fifteen years have gone by. And then, one day, with no particular motive, you pick up a phone and there's a voice on the other end that still brings a smile to your face and, if you're at all lucky, a friendship begins to develop."

"Still, none of it could have been easy," Kate said. "I'm the same age you were when my parents died. But instead of being allowed to go off on your own adventures, you were burdened with a four-year-old. You deserved an entirely different life."

"I haven't missed out on one single thing," Edwards said. "And if I have regrets, it's for the times when my work forced me to be away from you and our home. You were alone a lot more than you should have been. It's one reason I made sure you were kept plenty busy, hoping that all those activities in some way would help ward off any bouts of loneliness."

"Do you miss not having a family of your own?"

"You are my family," Edwards said, "as were your parents, and that makes me one very lucky man. And now here we are, the four of us, together again."

Kate bent down, her knees resting on the wet sand, and laid the flowers atop a wave. She watched as the foamy water pulled back, dragging the bouquets in its wake. She stood, moved closer to the professor and rested her head on his shoulder. "I'd say the four of us make a pretty formidable family, don't you think?"

He put an arm around her and the two turned away from the waves and began a slow walk back. "You have no idea," he said.

CHAPTER 6

KATE AND MARCO WALKED ON THE SOUTH SIDE of Via Ghibellina heading for number 70, the address of Casa Buonarroti. The residence had originally been three houses which were bought by the sculptor in 1508 and used primarily as rental properties. Upon his death, Michelangelo willed the homes to his nephew, Leonardo, who in turn opened a gallery in the home in 1612 to serve as a memorial to his great-uncle.

"This is the *last* street we should be on," Marco said, speaking in hushed tones even though the street was nearly deserted. "And that is the *last* house we should be walking toward."

"We've been followed and chased for the last five days," Kate said. "I think we both know what they want. What neither of us knows is who they are. Aren't you the least bit curious?"

"Not at all," Marco said. "And if we give them what they want, then maybe we'll never need to know who they are."

"Is that why you told your friends what it was that we found?" she asked. It came out sounding like an accusation, which wasn't what Kate had intended, but which also didn't seem wrong to her.

"No," Marco said, stung by the tone of her words. "I would never betray you. It wasn't anything at all like what you're thinking."

"But you did betray me," she said. "I asked you not to

tell anyone. I made you promise not to tell anyone. And then, not even two days later, we're being chased through the streets like fugitives. I need to know who they are, and I can't find that out if I spend my time hiding. It would be a big help if I knew who it was you told and why."

They were standing now across the street from the wooden front doors leading into Casa Buonarroti.

"We still have an hour until they open," he said. "Maybe that will be enough time for me to explain."

"The truth shouldn't take that long," Kate said.

Marco took a deep breath and gazed up and down both sides of the quiet street. "This is one of the few times I wished I smoked."

"But you don't," she said, refusing to budge from her hard stance.

"I barely made it into the fellowship program," he said, "and I'm sure one big reason I was picked has to do with the fact I'm from Florence and the director wanted at least one student from the city included."

"You're as good, if not better, than anyone in that class," Kate said. "And I'm not saying that to make you feel better. It happens to be fact."

"I love the work," Marco said. "I always have. It's just that it comes easier to you and to some of the others. It has never been that way for me. And many of my friends are working at good jobs, and some have started families already. They look at me, at my age still going to school, studying the work of an artist dead for centuries whose name they're sick of hearing, and they think I'm just wasting my time."

"And what they think is important to you?"

"Yes," Marco said. "I don't have anyone back home who's proud of me. My father died when I was a boy. My mother remarried a few years later, and the last person her new husband wanted to see every night when he walked through the door was me. I moved out as soon as I had the chance and don't see her much, and when I do there's not a lot for us to talk about. I'm probably the only single man my age in Italy not living with his mother."

Kate leaned against a stone wall and stared across at Michelangelo's home, letting a calming silence pass between them. "How many of your friends did you tell?" she finally asked.

"There were five of us in a bar," Marco said, "two nights after you and I made our discovery. We went for a long walk and then stopped at an outdoor café for a few drinks."

"How did it come up in conversation?"

"It started the way it always does," Marco said, "and I fall for it every time. Everyone else at the table had both a full-time job and a fiancée. I've got neither. So, when it got to me, they asked about my schoolwork, but it was with that tone in their voices that I had heard so many times before."

"And so you blurted it out," Kate said, "despite your promise to me."

"I was proud of what we had done," he said, "what we had found. And I wanted them to know I wasn't just wasting my days buried inside a classroom, that I was doing work that mattered."

"Were they impressed?" she asked.

"Not as much as I thought they would be," Marco said, "but enough so that it got them to stop talking about weddings and engagements and listen to what I had to say, at least for a minute. I didn't tell them that much, nothing more than the basics."

"Which are?"

"That you and I had stumbled upon a lost work," Marco said. "I didn't tell them how we discovered it and what we did with it, just that we had found something that, up to now, was only rumored to have existed."

"Did you tell them what it was?" Kate asked.

Marco shook his head. "But they were smart enough to figure out it had something to do with Michelangelo. Anyway, they bought a round of drinks, toasted me, and we called it a night. And that was the end of it."

"Not for all of them," Kate said. "One of your friends had to mention it to someone, and that someone had to care enough about what we found to come looking for us."

"The people chasing us are dangerous," he said, "and none of my friends know anyone like that. *I* don't know anyone like that. I get nervous around kitchen knives. I wish none of this had ever happened."

"You didn't know what it would lead to," she said, letting her voice soften now. "There's no reason for either one of us to have known."

"I don't mean just talking about it in front of my friends," he said. "I mean all of it. Finding the work and . . ."

"Meeting me?"

"In a way, yes," Marco said. "Now, please, don't walk away. Give me a chance to explain what I'm trying to say."

"I'm not going anywhere," Kate said.

"I like you," Marco said. "From the day you first walked into class. What's not to like? You're beautiful, funny, kind, smart, and from what the other students tell me, even rich. It's a dream for someone like me to meet someone like you."

"There's a but coming," she said. "I can feel it."

"*But* there is a part of you that scares me," Marco said. "I can tell just in the way you react every time we're in danger. You don't seem bothered by it. My body goes numb when we're chased, but you're in total control. I've never been around anyone like that, and it frightens me. Does any of this make sense?"

"All of it," Kate said. "And I'm sorry I got you involved in this, but I'm not sorry I met you and I'm not sorry we became friends. And just because I don't look scared, it doesn't mean I'm *not* scared."

"Really?"

"Yes," Kate said. "I'd have to be insane not to be frightened by what's going on around us. And while I may be impulsive, I don't think it's fair to write me off as crazy."

"What do you think is going to happen?" Marco asked.

"Maybe I shouldn't tell you," she said. "It might be better if you didn't know what I'm thinking."

"You see what I mean?" he said, stepping into the street, his hands spread wide. "What you just said scared me even more than those men who have been chasing us."

"I won't ever lie to you, Marco," Kate said. "No matter how good it might make you feel."

He took a deep breath and stepped closer to Kate, inches away from her face. "And I won't leave you to fight this alone," he said. "No matter how scared I get."

"I don't know who is chasing us," she said. "But whoever it is, they want to get their hands on what we found. If they wanted to kill us, they would have done it by now. They need to capture us—me, really, not you."

"Why you?"

"They don't know for sure you were with me when I made the discovery," Kate said. "And they might think I didn't trust you enough to tell you where I hid it."

"They have no proof to think that way," Marco said.

"They have no proof *not* to think that way," Kate said. "And since you let it slip to your friends that something was found, but failed to tell them what it was and where it is, only gives them more reason to believe I hold the key."

"We can't just keep running from one end of the city to the next," he said. "Sooner or later, we'll be caught."

Kate looked at him and smiled. "You're right," she said. "I should have thought of it from the start. I was so excited that we actually found something, I probably wasn't thinking straight. But *that's* the answer."

"The answer to what?" Marco asked.

"We *let* them catch us," Kate said. "Then we'll know who we're up against."

"That's not a good idea at all," he said, a touch of panic seeping into his voice. "It's one of the worst ideas I've ever heard."

"You said it yourself," Kate said. "We can't just keep running."

"It sounds too dangerous," he said. "We only *think* we know what they're after. What if we're wrong? What if they're chasing us for reasons that have nothing to do with what we found in the corridor?"

"Like what?"

"How should I know?" Marco said. "Two weeks ago I was biking through the city looking for good buys on used art history books. My only worries had to do with maybe finding a part-time job so I would have some coffee money during the school year."

"I have coffee money," Kate said, stepping out into the street. "And there's a bar just around the corner. Should be open in a few minutes."

Marco thought about this for a moment. "Can I get a pastry to go with the coffee?"

"We both will," she said.

He nodded and moved from the front of the building to stand next to her. "Is what we're doing worth it?"

"The coffee's the best in the neighborhood, and their pastries are better than anything I've ever had," she said.

"Is it worth it?" he asked. "Is it worth risking our lives for a work that's been hidden for centuries?"

"For you, I would say no, it's not even close to being worth it," Kate said.

"And it's different for you?"

"Yes," she said, "and please don't ask me to explain why, because I haven't even come close to putting it all together. I just know this is not only what I need to do, it's what I *have* to do."

"Even if there's a chance it might get you killed?" Marco asked.

"Yes," she said, "even then."

She squeezed her arm under the fold of his and together they walked toward the coffee bar, the late afternoon shadows of Casa Buonarroti at their back.

CHAPTER 7

KATE HAD HEARD TALES OF MICHELANGELO since she was old enough to walk. Her parents would refer to him often, both in conversation and in the stories they read to her each night—a practice continued by Professor Edwards for years after their deaths. As she grew older and began to read about him herself, she set aside questions to ask Edwards over dinner, knowing he would offer in return a series of hints and clues designed to help her discover the answer. Over time, she began to think of Michelangelo as a talented but eccentric member of her extended family, the uncle who is always talked about but never seen. She marveled at his accomplishments, stared with awe at his works, laughed at his numerous outrageous acts and statements, and always sought to unearth new and interesting details of his life in each book or article she read.

But it was the story of the snowman that won her heart.

Kate was twelve when Edwards told her of the rare snowstorm that blanketed the city of Florence, starting on the morning of January 20, 1494, and ending twenty-four hours later. It was a warm and humid summer afternoon, and she and Professor Edwards walked slowly past the Great Lawn of New York's Central Park, munching on soft toasted pretzels bought from a Sabrette vendor.

Michelangelo had been seventeen on the day in question and still mourning the recent death of his benefactor, friend, and the man closest to his heart—Lorenzo the Magnificent. The snowstorm had brought Florence to a halt, thick mounds of white covering every street and rooftop. An emissary from the palace was dispatched to the home of Michelangelo's father on Via Bentaccordi, sent there by Piero de' Medici, newly designated as Lorenzo's successor. Michelangelo listened to the messenger's words and then tossed over his shoulders a thick purple cloak, a gift from Lorenzo, and trudged through the heavy snow to the Medici Palace.

Forty-five minutes later, he stood before Piero, barely a man himself at twenty, and was asked to go outside and build a statue of a man made of snow in the family's honor. A sad-eyed Michelangelo stared at Piero in silence for several moments before nodding his head and reluctantly accepting the assignment.

"Why would Piero ask him to do something so stupid?" Kate asked.

"It only sounds stupid if we look back on it," Edwards said. "But in those days, it was an accepted custom to have sculptors design statues in the snow. In much the same way, painters were asked to make banners for the numerous processions and tournaments that took place throughout the country."

"But why call Michelangelo to do the job?" she asked. "I mean, you don't need to be a genius to build a snowman."

"There were a number of reasons, and all of them left Michelangelo no choice but to accept the challenge," Edwards said. "First, he was the family sculptor, which pretty much meant it was his job to do as he was asked. Second, with Lorenzo's death, Michelangelo was forced to move out of the palace and back in with his father."

"And what was so wrong with that?" Kate asked. "Didn't he love his father?"

"I'm sure he did," Edwards said. "But all the same, it would play to Michelangelo's advantage that he live within the walls of the palace, which meant he would need to design a snowman that would please his new master, Piero."

"Did he?"

"What do you think?" Edwards asked, smiling down at the girl, her cheeks red from the warmth of the day, her eyes bright and brimming with curiosity.

He marveled at the ways in which her young mind was evolving. She was always questioning, never shy about voicing her opinions, and, rare for a child her age, was not only quick to respond to a good story but also eager to wrap her thoughts around the different meanings it might carry. Edwards did all he could to feed her intellectual hunger, from museum visits to trips to the local library, where Kate would devour everything from picture books to Nancy Drew novels. She loved stories and art, and he took great pains to nurture that part of her, understanding that by doing so he was also teaching her about her parents. Which is why Kate, above all else, loved to hear stories about Michelangelo. The man known throughout his life as the Divine One was the most direct connection between the young girl and the mother and father she would only know through memory.

"I think he went outside and did as Piero asked," Kate said.

"And then some," Edwards said. "He designed a statue so large and so magnificent that it brought out thousands of visitors from throughout the city, this despite the clogged streets and blocked trails. It also so pleased Piero that not only was Michelangelo invited back to live in the palace again, he was given an honored seat at the de' Medici dinner table."

"How long did the statue stay up?" she asked.

"Even the great Michelangelo was no match for a spring thaw," Edwards said. "His work soon melted and disappeared. It is one of the few works he completed of which there is no visual image."

Kate walked in silence for several moments, her pretzel long since eaten, her jelly bean sandals landing soft against the park pavement, the Great Lawn packed with sunbathers and children running while holding on tight to the strings of overhead kites. "So then how do we know?" she finally asked.

"That he made the statue?"

Kate nodded. "We don't even know if it really snowed," she said. "So how can we be so sure he made a statue out of snow?"

"Riddle me this, young lady," Edwards said.

Kate covered her face with the fingers of her right hand. "I am not good at this," she said.

"Not yet, you aren't," he said. "But you'll get it right eventually. Luck along with skill will dictate the time. But this is one you should be able to figure out."

"Only if you make it an easy one," she said.

"A defective chunk of marble," he began, not bothering to hide his smile. "A debt that must be paid. A job that must be finished. And time is not your friend. Now, what does all that give you?"

Kate thought for a second and then nodded. "The naked man," she said.

"Known in some circles as the David," Edwards said.

"So I got it right?"

"Not quite on the money," Edwards said, "but close enough."

"But what does the naked man have to do with the snowman?" she asked.

"They are two sides of the same coin," Edwards said. "Both were jobs that, for their own reasons, needed to be completed quickly. And both came along at a time when Michelangelo was in need of funds and, as was true for most of his life, well behind on his assigned work."

"What was he working on when he did the snowman?" Kate asked.

"The statue of Hercules," Edwards said.

"Have I ever seen that one?"

Edwards shook his head. "No," he said. "Neither have I, nor has anyone else since the eighteenth century. When the piece was finally finished, it was sold to a man named Alfonso Strozzi, and then, years later, Francis I, king of France, took possession. It was kept in the Fontainebleau gardens, and there it remained until very early in the eighteenth century."

"And then?"

"And then it vanished, much like the snowman—only in his case, the disappearance could be traced to natural causes."

"I bet it's really hard to steal a statue," Kate said.

"If it *was* stolen," Edwards said, moving toward a wooden bench, the young girl fast by his side.

"You said it vanished," she said. "Doesn't that mean someone stole it?"

Edwards sat down and looked at Kate standing across from him, the late afternoon sun reflecting off the endless row of city high-rises. "In most cases it would, yes," he said. "But I don't think that's what happened with the Hercules."

Kate glanced up at him, absorbing his words and attempting to grasp their intent, and then she nodded. "Michelangelo hid it," she said, an excited tone to her voice.

"If not him, then someone working on his behalf,"

Edwards said, leaning forward, hands folded, arms resting on his knees. "And it probably wasn't the only time. If what I believe can ever be proven, then at least forty percent of his works are hidden in various parts of Europe. I'm not alone in thinking that way. Your parents believed it as well, and they did considerably more research on the matter than I have."

"But why would he do that?" she asked. "Why go to all the trouble of doing the work if all he was going to do at the end was hide it?"

"There are a number of reasons," Edwards said, "and they all make a great deal of sense when examined closely."

"Like what?"

"Well, it could have been done at the behest of the Medici family. They were consumed with the notion of power and knew their grip on the city could not last forever. Hiding works of the greatest sculptor of the day would ensure that they would never lack for funds, no matter how precarious their situation might become."

"Do you think Michelangelo would agree to that?"

"I doubt he would have had much say in the matter," Edwards said. "Remember, he was essentially their employee for large portions of his life, and he was as loyal to them as he was to anyone. So, in this case, I don't think he would put up much of a fight, as long as he was paid in full for his work."

Kate sat on the bench and stared up at the cloudless sky, her legs stretched out, two squirrels rummaging on the grass nearby. "Would he hide some of his works for the same reason as the Medici family?"

"Most likely," Edwards said. "Especially during the times he was either feuding with them or, worse, hiding from them. He was arrested and held prisoner by the Medicis quite a few times for infractions that would be seen today as minor offenses. And if anyone knew the true worth of Michelangelo's work, it was the master himself."

"Have any of the works been found?"

"Now and then," Edwards said. "Your parents uncovered a lost work very early in their careers, a small piece of sculpture done by a very young Michelangelo. They gifted it to the city of Florence."

"Have you found any yet?"

He shook his head. "I've come close a few times," he said, "or at least I thought I had, but all my leads came up empty."

"Do you think I'll ever find any?" she asked.

"I don't *think* so, Kate," he said. "I *know* so. I *know* it with all my heart, and I've known it since you were first born."

"What makes you so sure?"

"Because you will be the best one of us," Edwards said. "You will be guided by me and by the notes left behind by your parents, but you will take it further than any of us ever dared. That's what I believe."

Kate stood and began to walk back toward the Great Lawn, her head down, hands by her sides, lost in a swirl of a young girl's thoughts.

CHAPTER 8

KATE AND MARCO STEPPED INTO THE ENTRY of the Vasari Corridor and came to a quick stop. They gazed down the sloping hall, portraits wrapped inside gilded frames hung on both sides of the cream-colored walls, small circular windows letting in shards of late afternoon light, the sheer majesty of the room overwhelming them both.

"It's like it was frozen in time," Kate said. "The way it looks now is the way it looked when it was first built."

"They've added a few hundred more portraits and painted it a half-dozen times," Marco said, "plus they put in security cameras. But if you take all that away, we are in the city of Florence as it was in 1564."

The Vasari Corridor was built by designer and author Giorgio Vasari in a five-month period, ostensibly to commemorate the wedding of Francesco de' Medici and Johanna of Austria. Its true mission, however, was to serve as a link between the Pitti Palace, where the Grand Duke lived, and the Uffizi offices, where he worked, allowing him the ability to rule the city under the protection of one roof. The stone-covered walkway is just under a kilometer long, an overhead passageway that begins on the west corridor of the gallery and then moves toward the Arno River, following the flow of the water to the Ponte Vecchio. There it crosses over the tops of the shops, cutting through the Church of Santa Felicita and over the houses and gardens of the Guicciardini family before coming to an end under the arches of the majestic Boboli Gardens.

"The Grand Duke must have been such an arrogant man," Marco said as the two began their slow walk up and down the steps of the corridor, accompanied by an elderly guard, who stayed a few feet behind them. "And a frightened one as well."

"Why do you say that?"

"The Ponte Vecchio used to be the local meat market at the time Vasari began his work," Marco said. "It was the Grand Duke who had it moved, replaced by the gold merchants who remain there today. You know why?"

"He couldn't stand the smell of the butchered meat," Kate said, "especially during the summer months."

"And that doesn't sound like the action of an arrogant man?" Marco asked.

"Maybe he was just a sensible one," she said, stopping to gaze at one of the seven hundred paintings which, along with five hundred artists' self-portraits, hung on each wall and ran the full length of the corridor.

The Vasari Corridor was designed and built as a place to observe the daily activities of the town without any fear of being seen. The small windows can barely be discerned from streets below. Today, an unarmed guard walks the full length of the corridor every hour on the hour, and a series of prison bars blocks access from one section to another. While security cameras are clearly visible throughout the corridor, there is no alarm system.

"You would think with all the valuable art hanging here, there would be a higher level of security," Kate said.

"Truth is, not many people even know it is here," Marco said, "and that may well be the best security system of all."

"It's still a target," she said. "What about that car bombing in 1993? The one that killed five people? It happened just down the street from this window."

"That was a tragedy," Marco said, "but it had nothing to do with the corridor, even though a few paintings were damaged and one or two ruined."

"Some of the articles I read attributed the attack to homegrown terrorists," Kate said. "They had to be looking to damage either the museum or the corridor."

"If you want to call the Mafia homegrown terrorists, then those articles are correct," Marco said. "The bomb was set off to show displeasure at police crackdowns on their activities. The car was parked where it was because it was near the center of town, no other reason."

"You never think of the Mafia having any business at all in a city like Florence," Kate said. "I don't really know why, but the two images don't seem to fit together."

"If you spend enough time in Italy," he said, "you will see the Mafia leave their fingerprints everywhere. They are our original sin and we may never be free of their grip."

They turned into the second part of the corridor, crossing above Via della Ninna, which links one end of the Uffizi with the Palazzo Vecchio, the seat of the Florentine government since the thirteenth century.

"The windows are so small," Kate said, peeking through one to gaze at the bustling street below. "But even so, you can see pretty much everything you need to see."

She and Marco walked down a short flight of wide steps and stood before two large windows, the only two of their kind in the entire corridor, both offering a wide view of the Arno and the apartment buildings lining both sides of the river.

"These were not part of the original design," the elderly guard explained. "And they should never have been built, if you ask me."

"Why were they?" Kate asked.

"In 1938, Hitler came to Florence and decided he wanted to give a speech from inside the corridor," Marco said. "Not even Mussolini could talk him out of it. There was no other choice but to build the windows and allow him access to the people below."

"That dark day was the first and last time the windows have been opened," the old guard said, a look of pride on his face. "In return for the gesture of the windows, the Nazis blew up all the bridges in Florence except for the one you see standing on this spot. The same one Hitler saw, the Ponte Vecchio."

Kate and Marco walked in silence for a few moments, their footsteps muted on the carpeted stairwells, the guard following slowly behind them.

"He walked the same path we're walking now," Kate said, her eyes fixed on the white stone steps and the rich ornate tapestry covering them. "Most likely alone, lost in thought, troubled or relieved over one job or another."

"Who?" Marco asked. "Hitler?"

"Michelangelo," Kate said. "He would have had a dozen different reasons to walk through here, regardless of the time of day, most of them business-related, no doubt. But some of those walks were for reasons having nothing to do with work."

"Like what?"

"He was a celebrity, or as close to one as they had in those days," Kate said, always keen to reduce Michelangelo to basic human terms. "It must have been difficult for him to walk the streets without attracting public attention and running the risk of being stopped and asked questions he might not have been in the mood to answer."

"Like Mick Jagger," Marco said, smiling.

"Well," she said, "it's not crazy to think of him in those terms. Like a Renaissance rock star."

"So, if Michelangelo is Jagger, does that mean da Vinci was one of the Beatles?" he asked.

"Anyone but Ringo, I suppose."

"This corridor was probably used for so many purposes," Marco said, gazing up at a Bernini painting. "You walk through the streets of the city and you don't even notice its existence. Visible to all, but seen by none. In its own way, it is the ultimate Renaissance invention."

"If you feel that way, then you must believe some of the rumors are true," Kate said.

"As I am sure that you believe *all* of them," Marco said.

"Not all," she said, "just most. I never thought the rulers of the day kept prisoners here or used this place to dispose of bodies. There were too many other hidden haunts in the city to serve that purpose. Besides, this corridor wasn't built for bloodshed. It's too elegant, too regal to be stained that way. The Medicis were a methodical bunch, each movement planned, each site designed for its own specific purpose."

"Correct," Marco said, standing across from her now, his back against a stonewashed white wall, arms folded casually across his chest. "The purpose of the Vasari Corridor was to allow the rich and powerful a way to cross from one end of the city to the other without any worry of being seen. I don't think there was anything more sinister to it than that."

"That was only one part of it," Kate said. "They had other plans for this corridor, and they shared those plans with only a handful of people."

"Look, I love Oliver Stone movies, too," Marco said. "And I'm the first to listen to any plausible conspiracy theory, but I never lose sight of the fact that they are nothing more than what they are—theories."

"This was more than just a showroom, and a lot more than a passageway," Kate said, scanning the walls. "This was a hiding place, a long corridor that was both secure and free of prying eyes. This was the perfect place."

"To hide what?"

She turned and faced Marco. "What mattered most to the Medicis," she said. "Their treasure. You know from all the reading we've both done that the family's one fear was to lose the fortune they had amassed, either by takeover from another ruler or a fall from power. They were no different than any other rich family, back then or even today. It just makes sense that they would look to make sure they were covered, in the event that hard times ever hit them."

"So you think they hid their money inside the corridor?"

"Maybe," Kate said. "Or maybe what they thought would be even more valuable to them than money."

"If it's not money, then it could only be works of art," Marco said.

"But not just any works," she said. "The Medicis needed to be absolutely certain that the art and sculpture they deemed worth hiding would be of great value not only in their lifetimes, but to subsequent generations. And as far as they were concerned, that work would belong to only one man."

"You want to believe that it was Michelangelo," Marco said. "Which might be true, assuming any part of your theory is true. But he wasn't the only master working within the Medici inner circle. Raphael was part of that universe, as was Leonardo and a handful of others. Why Michelangelo? Why not one of the others?"

"His relationship with Lorenzo de' Medici for one," Kate said. "There was a bond that existed between them and carried through to the other members of the family for decades. Think about it, Marco. Through all the feuds they had with him, even the times they had him jailed or sought him out for condemnation, they always returned to Michelangelo and his work. Because they knew, they believed what the world back then believed—that it was work that would last and only grow in value. Work that would be worth hiding, regardless of the price or the risk."

"And what makes you so convinced that work is in here?" he asked.

"If you stop and just think about it for a minute or two, it does start to make some sense."

"Florence is a city of secrets, Kate. And there are many places to keep those secrets."

Kate and Marco, along with the elderly guard, approached one of the corridor exits, a short distance from Buontalenti's Grotto. "Let's go out this way," Marco said, nodding his thanks to the guard.

"Why here?"

"Because Buontalenti is one of *my* heroes," Marco said. "He is to me what the great Michelangelo is to you."

"I didn't know you admired the grotto so much," Kate said.

"I don't," he said. "I mean, it's an amazing piece of work, but it doesn't even venture close to what was his greatest contribution. He left us all a gift that no one can ever forget. One that even a conspiracy devotee like yourself can enjoy."

"What?" she asked, stepping out of the corridor and into the sharp Florentine light.

"Buontalenti invented gelato," Marco said, with a schoolboy grin spread across his face. "Now you tell me, what greater gift is there?"

CHAPTER 9

EDWARDS SAT IN A SOFT LEATHER CHAIR, HIS fingers wrapped around a cup of coffee, flames from the crackling fire to his right offering the only light and warmth to the sparsely furnished room. He gazed up at the well-dressed man standing with his back to the fire, hands thrust inside the pockets of what looked to be a hand-tailored suit.

"I wouldn't be too concerned," he told the man. "She just needs some time. If we allow her that, then we won't need to fear any disappointments."

The man—tall, wiry, thick strands of white hair resting against the tip of a starched white collar, cobalt blue eyes shielded by the smoke—turned his head slightly and gazed at Edwards. He was in his midsixties but looked at least a decade younger, an athletic body beneath an academic's face.

"*They* will know where she is," he said, his voice crisp, "if they don't already. And they'll know what she has gone there to find, before she even figures it out."

"That's always been the danger," Edwards said, resting the coffee mug on a three-legged wooden side table. "That's always been the fear."

"I still think it would have been the wiser course to tell her all she needed to know prior to her trip," the man said. "I said so at the time."

"That's because you don't know her as I do," Edwards said. "She's prepared for whatever dangers come her way. And let's not forget, we didn't put her out there alone. We have eyes on her, as many as she'll need."

"I've never doubted her abilities," the man said. "But I know those of her enemies as well. I don't need to give you any lessons as to the lengths the Immortals will go."

"I'm aware of the risks," Edwards said. "As will she be when the time is right. But for now, all our worries might be for naught. She may not find anything and may simply spend her time in Florence furthering her studies."

"Do you really believe that will be the case?" the man asked.

"No," Edwards said after a slight hesitation. "Her mother and father were brilliant at locating lost or stolen treasures."

"And as great as they both were, you have surpassed them," the man said, his thin lips parting slightly, coming close to breaking a smile. "The Vittoria Society has grown in power and prestige under your leadership."

"Perhaps," Edwards said, acknowledging the compliment with a small nod. "But we are no match for her. We each depended on a vast network of informants and allies. Local Art Squads. Insurance agents. And then there were times when we simply took advantage of mistakes made by our competitors."

"And she'll need to do all that as well," the man said.

"True," Edwards said. "But she brings with her that extra dimension we all lacked. A kind of internal radar every treasure hunter wishes he possessed."

The man smirked. "How can you be so certain?"

"It's been there from the time she was a child," Edwards said, doing little to hide the rush of pride he felt, his face more animated now, his gestures becoming more dramatic. "We would spend hours poring over her parents' volumes of notes. With only a few hints, she would arrive at sound conclusions." He smiled. "She favored conversations that focused on Michelangelo."

"Why do you suppose that is?" the man asked.

"He is as real to her as I am," Edwards said. "She has never seen him as a famous man from one of her textbooks. To her, he remains very much alive and very human. He is also the thread through which she can reach out to her parents. She has read so much about him, spent so many years studying his works and his methods. She has studied her parents' accounts of his documents, absorbed their opinions, and formulated a few of her own."

"Her own?" the man asked.

"Neither her parents nor I ever bothered to look beyond the artist to seek out the man," Edwards said. "It seemed to us much easier to let the work speak for itself. Kate simply allowed the man to lead her through and to the work."

"And this will lead her to a discovery that others have been incapable of finding for decades?" the man asked.

"I have little choice but to believe it," Edwards said. "And as a member of the Society, you would be wise to at least profess to the same."

The man looked away from Edwards and managed a slow nod. "What do you need me to do?"

"Be ready," Edwards said. "It is now up to Kate to decide our next move. Assuming that she won't walk away with empty hands, we must be well positioned to help."

"And you'll stay here?" the man asked.

Professor Edwards stood and stared down at the ebbing fire. "When the time is right," he said, "I'll be in Florence. The Raven and I have waited too long to complete our business."

CHAPTER 10

BUCA MARIO SITS IN THE CENTER OF PIAZZA Ottaviani in one of the quietest streets in all of Florence. The restaurant has been there, in the cellars of Palazzo Niccolini, since the early months of 1886, serving local cuisine at local prices to students, tourists, and longtime residents alike. The owners, a handsome husband and wife duo straight out of an early Marcello Mastroianni and Sophia Loren comedy, are always the first to greet any visitors to their sanctum of fine wine and excellent food. They are never without a warm smile, a big embrace, and a desire to end your evening on a happy note.

It was one of three such restaurants Marco had introduced Kate to soon after her arrival in Florence, understanding that, above all else, a young woman far from home would need a few very special places she would be able to call her own. And Buca Mario quickly became such a place for Kate.

She loved the fact that it seemed buried under the palazzo, a three-stone-step drop to the door that led into a large restaurant bustling with waiters in white jackets and patrons in casual wear, the smells of the homemade pastas and sauces and fresh grilled meats warming the air and helping to kick the appetite into full gear. Kate frequented the restaurant often, usually choosing a corner table less than a dozen feet from the front register. She was treated as a regular by both the owners and the staff, and had grown to trust the tastes of her favorite waiter, Louisa, often allowing her to select her meal.

"You can't be serious about any of this?" Marco demanded. He sat across from Kate, leaning forward, a thick slab of Tuscan bread hanging from the fingers of his right hand. "You do realize we would be arrested if we were caught? And you might even risk getting deported? You might want to think about all of that before you decide to move forward."

"You can stay out of it if you want," Kate said, undeterred by his outrage. "This is something I need to do. And whether it's alone or with you, I'm going to go ahead with it."

Marco quietly lifted his glass of red wine and took a long, slow drink. He glanced down at his bowl of rigatoni and grilled sausage mixed with a fresh tomato and basil sauce and shook his head. "What makes you so sure there's something in there?"

"It's a gut feeling, not something I can explain," she said. "But the only way for me to be certain that there *isn't* anything there is to look inside for myself."

"There is no one *allowed* in there," Marco said, lowering his voice as a middle-aged American couple sat down at the table to their left. "I'm sure they put a rule like that in place for a reason."

"If there is something hidden," Kate said, glancing over at the woman to her right, "that's where it would be."

"It's a small space," Marco said, "with limited access and right by the entrance to the Uffizi in full view of two security cameras. It's blocked off by a barrier and a yellow strip of tape. If we step anywhere near it, we are certain to be spotted."

"It's the one section of the Vasari Corridor that has never been open to the public," Kate said, "not now and not in the days of the Medicis. I checked the original designs of the corridor, both the ones we have in school and whatever I could find on the Internet. It's a little less than a quarter mile long and curves along the Uffizi and ends up at the north end of the Ponte Vecchio. It's one of the few places left in the city that hasn't been touched by the modern world. That alone is reason to walk through it, no matter the risks involved."

Marco rested his fork against his plate and leaned in closer to Kate. Buca Mario was now filled with customers, and a small squad of waiters, young and old, zoomed past them, platters of pasta and appetizers and baskets jammed with bread held aloft as they curved their way around chairs and trays stacked high with empty plates. Diners at many of the tables were loud and boisterous, while others kept their words soft and warm, content to eat their food and drink their wine in relative peace. "Let's say that by some miracle you actually do find something," he said to Kate. "What happens then? Will the discovery alone be enough? Or will you need to take it a step further?"

"Depends on what I find," she said.

"What is it you really want, Kate?" Marco asked. "What I mean is, why did you really come to Florence?"

"I don't have any sinister motives, Marco," she said. "I'm here to study, same as you."

"There's more than a good chance you already know all there is to know about Michelangelo," he said. "And what little you may not know, you won't learn from either the lectures at school or the books we are assigned to read. So there must be another part to your agenda. But I will understand if you don't want to share it with me. We've only known each other for a short while, and there's quite a bit you don't know about me, either. But if you want me to take a big risk and join you in an attempt to sneak into the sealed area of the Vasari Corridor, then I do need to know a bit more than I do right now."

Kate sat back and looked around the crowded restaurant. She understood all the reasons for Marco's confusion and his trepidation about venturing deeper into the corridor. She would feel much the same way if she were in his position. But more than that, she wished she could give him a satisfactory answer, one that would help relieve his doubts. The problem was, she didn't have an answer, or at least one that would make any sense. She was working on instinct now.

"I guess just being curious isn't enough?" she asked.

"I'm afraid not," Marco said. "Not when it involves something this important."

"You're right," Kate said, leaning back as a young waiter cleared the empty plates from their table. "It's too much of a risk for you to take. If we get caught in there, it could cause you all sorts of troubles. Might even get you thrown out of the program, and I wouldn't want to see that happen, especially after all the hard work that went into your getting accepted."

"But that will happen to you as well," he said. "And I *know* the program means as much to you as it does to me."

"So I better make sure I don't get caught," she said.

"But why do it at all?" Marco asked. "Is going in there really worth it?"

"Yes," Kate said, "it is."

Marco stared at the table, his fingers toying with the small white sugar bowl resting in the center. He was drawn to Kate and had been from the start of the program, recalling how easily she'd managed to navigate her way through that first day, when it all seemed like nothing more than an avalanche of rules and forms, intermingled with class instructions too complicated to write down, let alone remember. She had a comforting way about her, appearing to be as much at ease with herself as she was in the company of strangers. Kate didn't shy away from being the center of attention, but did so in a way that managed to ingratiate her to others. Yet beneath the warmth and charm she exhibited, Marco sensed a longing to both explore and exploit the boundaries of uncharted terrains, and he was as drawn to those elements of her personality as he was frightened by them.

"You scare me at times," he said, his voice barely a whisper.

"I don't mean to."

"I know," he said. "And it's as much me as it is you. I can't explain it, really. Maybe it's more envy I feel than fear. You shrug off any risks that might be in your way and are content to let your heart chart your course. In that sense, it makes you so much more Italian than me."

"I always factor in the risks of anything I do," Kate said. "It would be foolish not to. But sometimes the bigger risk is *not* taking the chance."

"Would you think less of me if I didn't try to sneak into the corridor with you?" Marco asked.

"Of course not," Kate said.

"But you wouldn't mind if I did come along?" he asked.

"It's always better to have company," she said.

"This could turn out to be one of those decisions I'll always regret," Marco said.

"Or it might be one that could change your life forever," Kate said. "Or it could end up being nothing more than an adventure for us both. But the potential for it to be any of those possibilities makes the attempt worth the gamble."

"When do you plan to do this?" he asked.

"Saturday at noon, thirty minutes before lunch."

"Why then?"

"That's when it will be at its most crowded," she said, "especially the area closest to the sealed-off corridor. The few guards stationed at the front of the Uffizi will have their hands full following the various tour groups coming in and going out of the halls. There's more than a good chance we can get in without being noticed."

"And what about getting out?" Marco asked.

"We'll stay inside until the crowds begin to return after lunch," Kate said. "We'll come out the Palazzo Vecchio side and blend in with one of the groups heading either in or out of the halls."

"You knew I would be coming with you before you sat down," Marco said, a smile spreading across his face.

Kate returned the smile.

"What makes you so certain there aren't any security cameras in the sealed-off area of the corridor?" he asked.

Kate lost the smile and wrinkled her brow, leaned in closer to Marco and lowered her voice. "Don't get mad, okay?" she said.

"That means you *don't* know if there are cameras in there or not," he said. "*Dio mio,* Kate. I will never live long enough to understand someone like you."

"There's no reason to have any security cameras in that part of the corridor," she said. "It's been sealed off since Michelangelo was *alive*. There are people who have lived their entire *lives* in this city who don't even know it's there. It's safely hidden in plain sight. As far as any of the guards are concerned, that section of the corridor might as well be invisible."

"If that's true—and I don't doubt you," Marco said, "then in all likelihood it has not been as well maintained as the rest of the corridor. It could have been used as storage space by the maintenance crews."

"There's only one way for us to know for sure," Kate

said, "and that's to make our way in there and see for ourselves."

A middle-aged woman in a light blue summer dress, draped around a body that was still shapely enough to draw stares, stood at their table, a box of biscotti cradled in her arms. "These are for you," she said, placing the box on Kate's end of the table, "to enjoy late at night, while you study."

"*Grazie,* signora," Kate said, glancing up at the woman's warm eyes and the dark hair that ran long down the sides of an unlined face and along the nape of her neck.

"*Per niente,*" the woman said with a wave and a smile, bustling off to a corner table to make small talk with an elderly couple.

"It's going to be hard for me to one day have to leave this city," Kate said. "I already feel as if I could live the rest of my life here."

"Most Americans do," Marco said. "And some Florentines, too, I would imagine."

"But not you," she said. "Why is that, Marco?"

"I love the Italian way of life," he said. "The strength of family, the ability to nurture our souls as much as we do our wallets, is the way we should all view our lives. There would be far fewer wars if we did, that's for certain."

"But you see negatives to this life as well," Kate said.

"Yes," he said. "They are not negatives to all of us, but to me they seem limiting."

"How?"

"Well, for example, in America it is assumed that anyone can achieve anything that he or she sets out to do," Marco said. "You're pretty much told that from cradle to grave. And in your hearts, whether it's true or misguided, you embrace the idea, no matter how rich or poor you may be. That's not the case in my country."

"You don't think you can make any of your dreams come true?" Kate asked. "What would stop you?"

"Of course I believe I can achieve what I set out to do," he said. "But like many Italians my age, I approach my dreams with a more realistic eye. Maybe we here in Italy learn early on not to set our sights too high. We are taught a simpler way to dream. And for many that's more than enough."

"But not for you," she said.

Marco nodded. "In so many ways," he said, "I'm so much more of an American than you are, maybe because I have seen a lot more television. Or perhaps it's just something that's rubbed off on me, living in a city that has so many American visitors. I seem to want more than what my other Italian friends want, and I'm not talking just about money. I want many of the things that are treated as nothing more than second nature to successful Americans and, for whatever reasons, are seen as beyond the norm for the majority of Italians. I'm not even sure I can point to any one specific example that would help explain what I mean. I just know the differences are there and are very real to many of us."

"You want to live in America some day?" Kate asked.

"I dream like an American," he said. "It would be nice to try to live like one."

"It does sound like we should just trade places," she said. "We might both end up a lot happier."

"You do seem comfortable here," Marco said. "From your very first day, you fit right in."

"Professor Edwards—the man who raised me after my parents died—always said I wasn't of my generation," Kate said, "that I was one of those kids who preferred the past to the future. And if there is one thing you can never escape from in Florence, it is the past."

"Which helps explain your fascination with all things Michelangelo," Marco said.

"In part," she said.

"And which also paints a clearer picture of why you are so determined to get into that sealed-off end of the corridor," he said.

"Yes," Kate said, "and it's a comfort to know I won't be alone. I'll have a friend by my side."

"A frightened friend, to be sure," Marco said, "but a friend to you all the same. And one who even pays for lunch."

"I don't recall agreeing to that," she said, a gentle tone of mock anger in her voice. "I thought we'd go Dutch."

"Actually, here in Italy we say, 'a la Romana,' " Marco said.

"Okay, then," Kate said. "A la Romana sounds like a plan."

"And a good plan it would be," he said, signaling a passing waiter, "*if* we were in Rome. But, we are in Florence, and today I insist on paying."

"You're going to make a fine American, Marco," Kate said. "I have no doubts at all about that."

CHAPTER II

THE RAVEN WALKED WITH A STEADY STEP INTO the duomo, head down and hands clasped behind his back. He was flanked by two men, both at least ten years younger and several inches taller, each dressed in a manner far too casual to suit their style-conscious companion. The Raven turned right to face the majestic altar at the center of the Duomo, the light from the frescoed windows surrounding it as if by drawn swords, thick shards of midmorning sunlight bouncing off the marble and chiseled stone.

"There was history made here, my friends," the Raven said, speaking in a low but strong voice, indifferent to the packs of tourists and guides who flowed past. "It was here that the scheme to kill young Giuliano de' Medici was carried out. At that very spot," he added, pointing, "Giuliano was murdered by Francesco Pazzi, at the time the banker to the Pope. It was the twenty-first day of April, 1478. The church was twice as crowded as it is today."

"The murder was done in front of witnesses?" the muscular man to the Raven's left asked. His neatly shaven head served as a waxed mirror to the candles burning bright around them. "Then, I doubt the killer got very far."

The Raven turned away from the altar and gazed at the man, his head tilted slightly. "Escape was not part of his plan," he explained. "He *wanted* the Medicis to know, wanted *everyone* to know, that it was he who had the courage to plunge a dagger twenty-one times into the body of one of the most powerful men in the world. There are some acts that are worth the price of a life. The earlier you learn this lesson, Piero, the better you will be able to serve our cause."

"I don't see how my death would serve the cause," Piero said.

"I do," the Raven said. "But that's a conversation for another day. For now, I need you to tell me all you have learned about the city's most curious student."

"She's done nothing out of the ordinary so far," the chubby man to his left said. "Ordinary for a young woman of her financial means, at least."

"I'm curious to find out, Gennaro, if you and I share the same definition of ordinary," the Raven said.

"She took care of the basics from the start," Gennaro said. "She found an apartment, a large one-bedroom on the second floor of a well-maintained home right around the corner from Casa Buonarroti, with the living room window looking down on a quiet street. She signed up for her classes on time and bought her books secondhand from the university shop. She maintains a disciplined daily routine, starting her day just about sunup with either a run through the streets or a row down the Arno. She walks to school, stopping at a café for a quick coffee and a bottle of water she keeps in her backpack. She has grown friendly with many of the merchants in her neighborhood and, occasionally, initiates a brief chat. She's quite a bit different from most of the other foreign students, not only in her line of study but throughout the school."

"In what way?" the Raven asked.

"She was at home here from the start," Piero said, jumping into the conversation. "She didn't need time to adjust or change her ways. It helps that her Italian is fluent. Plus, she's been here a number of times before, so the city is not alien to her. She eats her meals out every day—a panino or salad for lunch, which she normally finishes either sitting near the ugly Neptune or in the piazza in Santa Croce. She has her big meal in the evening and has become a familiar face in three restaurants. She buys and reads two newspapers a day—the *International Herald Tribune* and *USA Today*—and is rarely without a book in hand. She likes to window-shop and buys her notebooks in a place not far from the Excelsior Hotel."

"What about friends?" the Raven asked.

"There's a young man," Gennaro said, "a fellow student, Marco Scudarti. They seemed to hit it off from the start of classes and spend quite a bit of time together. If she's ever with company, it includes him."

"What do you know about him?"

"He's got a clean record and no prior links to either the girl or anyone from her family," Piero said. "His father died when he was barely out of diapers, and his mother remarried a few years later, but the boy spends as few hours at home as possible. I'm not sure why, but I'm guessing he and the stepfather are not close."

"How is he set financially?" the Raven asked.

"He's not rich, not by any means," Gennaro said. "He has an account at one of the local banks and draws small amounts of cash from there every two weeks. It seems to be some sort of small trust fund set up for him years ago, perhaps by his father, maybe even a relative also long since dead. Either way, it's enough to keep him in food and clothing and books while he completes the program."

"Are he and the young lady involved romantically?" the Raven asked.

"They're only friends," Gennaro said, "as far as I can tell. They make the rounds at the museums together, not a day passes when they don't go into at least one, sometimes for hours at a time."

"Can you get to him?"

"His family history comes up clean as far as any criminal links," Piero said. "There have been a few legal issues that have cropped up in the past, but nothing that goes any further than a landlord and tenant dispute. If we went to him with the right offer, he might listen."

The Raven turned from Gennaro and Piero and walked slowly toward an exit door at the rear of the Duomo, his head down, his hands resting casually inside the pockets of his expertly tailored gray slacks. Gennaro and Piero waited a few seconds, then followed.

"Do you have them both under watch?" he asked.

"Yes," Gennaro said. "Neither one makes a move without our knowledge, whether they go out for a gelato or to the library. We have people on their every step."

"Except for that one day," Piero said. "A few hours. They went into a section of the Uffizi we weren't allowed to go."

"It's not a problem," Gennaro said, rushing to defuse what he hoped would not evolve into an explosive situation. "They were the only two allowed in, a private tour arranged for them by the school. Other than the guards assigned to go in and out with them, they were alone. There was no one in there for the lady to contact anyone and nothing in there for her to take."

The Raven turned and looked at the two men, his eyes as still as stone. "Has either one of you been inside the Vasari Corridor?" he asked.

Both men shook their heads.

"Then neither one of you *knows* who else might be in there and what there would be in the corridor for her to take," the Raven said.

"Yes," Gennaro mumbled.

"When did this visit occur?"

"Three days ago," Piero said. "They went in the front end and walked out the back, same as anyone who is fortunate enough to be granted a tour through the corridor. The only other person with them was an elderly guard who escorted them to the exit."

"Have they gone anywhere near the Uffizi or the Palazzo Vecchio since?" the Raven asked.

"No," Piero said. "They've spent the bulk of their time since then doing research work in the library and then having dinner. Their night usually ends with a gelato and a slow walk back to her apartment."

"And the boy, does he ever go up to her apartment?"

"Never," Gennaro said. "He says his good-byes at the door. Maybe he's shy or just not interested in girls, or perhaps he's just waiting for the right moment. But he has befriended her without any hint of romance."

"Which makes him a lure by which we draw her in," the Raven said. "She will make a move, and he will be the one, willingly or not, to show us the way."

"A move toward what?" Piero asked. "It might help us do our job if we had some idea what she is supposed to be looking for."

"I could share my thoughts with you," the Raven said, "but that would be a waste of my time and yours. The short answer is I have no idea what she's looking for. But I don't believe for one second that her time here is simply in the interest of academic pursuits. She's a treasure hunter. It's in her blood."

"Are we the only eyes on her?" Piero asked.

"For the time being," the Raven said. "It should remain that way until a discovery is made. If that occurs, word will spread quickly, and there will be more than eyes on her."

"What happens then?" Piero asked.

"One of us will die," the Raven said in a matter-of-fact tone. "And our destinies will be fulfilled."

He cast a quick gaze up at the altar, then nodded to the two men standing at his side and turned, walking with soundless steps out of the crowded Duomo.

CHAPTER 12

KATE STOOD IN THE CENTER OF THE MAIN room of the Farmaceutica di Santa Maria Novella, the oldest herbalist pharmacy of its kind in the world. The former monastery was the medicinal hub of Renaissance Florence as the Dominican monks worked their magic within the flowered walls of their herb gardens, seeking to cure the ills of rich and poor alike. They had teas to settle an angry stomach; dietary supplements from devil's claw to a carbon and fennel mix, guaranteed to relax spasms and cure muscle aches; fruit concoctions packed with minerals and vitamins that promised to fortify a weak and tired body; and essential oils used to massage and refresh aging skin. Among the customers greeted as regulars by the attending monks were Dante, da Vinci, Raphael, and Michelangelo.

"He suffered from constipation, you know," Kate said. "Complained about it constantly and to anyone who would listen. He probably talked about that more than he did about any of his works."

"How would you even know something like that?" Marco asked.

"It's in a number of books and articles written about him," she said, scanning a row of bath powders and perfumes. "And it makes sense that it would be a problem for him or anyone living in Florence during that same period, since their diets were so restricted. Remember, it wasn't until explorers returned from America that

Italians saw things like tomatoes, oranges, and grapefruits."

"Then it was a Renaissance period not just for the masters but for the monks who ran this place as well," Marco said.

"Do locals still shop here, or is it now mostly a destination for tourists?" Kate asked. She glanced across the marble-tiled room at a girl in a basketball jersey and short pants posing indifferently next to an elegantly dressed older woman with a bemused look on her face.

"We all shop here still, when we can afford it," Marco said, "but we have learned to adjust our clocks to when the tourist traffic is light, which is often toward the end of the day. My mother likes to come here to gather her spices for cooking and organic olive oil for salads, and I must confess to a special fondness for the store-made hazelnut spread they sell. It's the best in the world."

"Let's get some, then," she said.

"And it would be an unpardonable crime to leave without buying a jar of their hand cream," a male voice behind her interjected. "Young and delicate skin deserves it."

Kate turned toward the voice and saw an impeccably dressed man in his midforties, his thick brown hair combed away from his eyes and forehead. He had a half-smile on his face and a harsh gaze that sent a shiver down her back. She had never seen the man before, but felt his presence was not a sight she should welcome.

"Ivory soap works for me," she said.

"An indulgence is always worth the extra cost," the man said, holding the half-smile, cobalt blue eyes peering through her. "It's a theory I've embraced for many years."

"Not all indulgences come with a price tag," Kate said. "Some have no cost at all."

"Point taken," the man said, bowing his head slightly.

"Would you allow me then to offer the hand cream to you as a gift?"

Kate took a quick glance around the main room of the pharmacy, the lines to the two registers long and winding, the crowds around them thinning. The man stood slightly off to her left, across from Marco, who stood resting his back to the counter, silent and wary. "No," she said, her voice firm, her face flushed red with an anger that sprang quickly from suspicion. "I don't care much for surprises—or gifts given to me by strangers."

"You're a student here, am I correct?" the man asked. "Your gentleman friend as well, I would imagine."

"What we are is our business," Kate said.

"You have a quick temper," the man said, his widening smile only making him look more sinister. "Very much along the same lines as your mother."

The mention of her mother froze Kate. She was not used to hearing anyone speak about her, let alone a stranger whose very presence she found unnerving. She held her breath and tried to stay in control of her emotions, but was overwhelmed by a feeling of sadness mixed uneasily with anger. A cold sweat formed at her neck and she fought back an urge to cry.

"Who are you?" she asked, her voice low but forceful, her teeth clenched.

"To describe myself as an old family friend would do an injustice to us both," the man said, his words spoken slowly and seriously. "I like to think of myself as much more than that. For a time, I had the honor to be both a student and a protégé of your parents. All that I know about art and its history, I learned from their works and their words. There isn't a day I don't recall them or their lessons."

"What do you do?"

"What I was always meant to do," the man said. "What I was taught to do. Suffice it to say you and I share a passion for art long regarded as either missing or stolen."

"I'm only a student," Kate said.

"For now," the man said. "But the taste for the quest is there, even if you have yet to act on it. There will come a time when you will take all you've learned and put it to use. When that time comes, please remember that I can be of great help to you."

"I have all the help I need," she said, giving a quick glance toward Marco. "But thank you anyway."

The man turned and nodded at Marco. "I'm sure your young friend means well," he said. "But I have my doubts as to whether he will be a match for your talents. No offense meant, of course."

"Don't worry," Marco said. "I agree with you."

"I know him," Kate said, "and I trust him. And that's all I need. But if I needed help beyond him, I wouldn't turn to you."

The man smiled and stepped closer toward her, the echoes of the shoppers' voices and footsteps bouncing off the pharmacy's thick walls, the air rich with the smells of sprays, soaps, and herbs. "Give some thought to our words here today," the man said. "Don't dismiss them easily. I ask it as a simple courtesy to someone who owes so much of who he is to your mother and father."

"I won't forget a single word," Kate said.

The man nodded, bowed slightly, and walked with mannered steps toward the front entrance of the pharmacy, Florentine sunlight creeping through the openings of the old monastery doors.

"Maybe I need to reconsider my career path," Marco said, "if your friend is any indication of the kind of people who populate the art history arena."

"He's not my friend," Kate said.

"He *did* seem to know a lot about you," Marco said, "and even more about your parents."

"I've never met him before today," she said. "But I'm sure we'll run into each other again."

"Do you think he's been following us?" Marco asked, not making any effort to hide his concern.

"I'm not sure," Kate said. "It could have been nothing more than coincidence. I mean, it's not like we have a tendency to visit out-of-the-way and difficult-to-find places and need to be tracked. There are two groups who are easy to spot in Florence—art students and tourists—and, in my case, I fit both profiles."

"I would have an easier time believing all that if he had approached you and just made general conversation," Marco said. "But you heard what he said, and I think you are pretty clear on what he meant."

"He caught me off guard," she said, "which was, no doubt, his intent. I'll be better prepared the next time we see each other."

"Prepared to do what?"

Kate put an arm under Marco's elbow and nudged him toward the lotions lining the left wall. "That's something I need to figure out," she said. "But for now, how about we check out that hand cream he was talking about? Let's see how accurate he was about that."

"I'm one big ball of nerves," he said. "I was never like this before. Not until I met you."

"German chamomile flower tea should do the trick," Kate said, guiding him across the tiled floor. "We'll pick up a box on our way out. It's the best thing this side of Fernet Branca for your stomach. Trust me."

"I hate tea," Marco said. "I'm Italian, remember?"

"Trust me," Kate repeated, her voice a bit firmer, her grip on his arm a little tighter. "It's all you need to do."

CHAPTER 13

PROFESSOR RICHARD DYLAN EDWARDS SAT BACK and stared across the empty baseball field, the sun warming his face and arms, a large bag of shelled peanuts between his feet. He was perched in the front row of a field box along the first base line in that quiet period after batting practice and before the start of the game, when a ballpark held the sanctity of an empty church.

As much as Edwards loved the game of baseball, he revered the major and minor league parks in which the game was played, putting them on the same pedestal he reserved for museums and art galleries. He had made it a personal goal to see at least one game in every ballpark of note in the country, and had so far completed only a third of his journey. He had sat through the madness of a Yankees–Red Sox contest played out in the heated confines of Fenway Park; seen the New York Mets take on the San Diego Padres in their home park of Shea Stadium, knowing it would be the last go-round for the crumbling arena; traveled to Los Angeles to watch the Dodgers swing away against the Cincinnati Reds in the massive ballpark of Chavez Ravine; and he spent a long weekend in St. Louis, managing to get in two games at Busch Stadium. But no park fed his baseball soul as heartily as the small bandbox of Wrigley Field, the home of the Chicago Cubs.

Edwards regarded Wrigley as the perfect American

ballpark, its confines allowing the fan to get close enough to shout at the players. The fans were knowledgeable and rabid, devoted despite the steady diet of disappointment. It was the combination of the beauty of the park and the indefatigable spirit of the diehards who gave comfort to Professor Edwards. He had spent many decades chasing works deemed forever lost by the art world, and so was at home with impossible quests. And much like his beloved Chicago Cubs, he had learned never to grow complacent but to embrace whatever victories came his way.

"This is our year, I can feel it," the man squeezing into the seat next to him said. "We have it all, hitting and pitching, and nothing can stop us."

"It shouldn't be called Opening Day," Edwards answered, smiling across at the man. "It should be named Optimistic Day. Would make a lot more sense. After today, it's a straight roll down the hill."

"Spoken like a true diehard, Richard," the man said, "which is one of many reasons I enjoy your company as much as I do."

"You surprise me, Andrew," Edwards said. "Here I thought it was because I always pay for the tickets."

Andrew MacNamera was one of six original members of the Vittoria Society, from that first meeting held in the back room of a small restaurant in a New York City suburb. Now in his late sixties and in the second year of a painful battle against the unrelenting demon of lung cancer, he was still as sharp and as focused on the group's goals as at the end of that first long night of food and drink, where he helped devise a plan intended to secure the future of lost artistic treasures. Though he was, on the surface at least, a soft-spoken academic, MacNamera provided the Vittoria Society with what over the years would prove to be one of its most crucial elements. He had established a worldwide network of informants and enforcers meant to help the group both achieve their goals and keep a step ahead of their adversaries.

The core of this group grew out of the connections MacNamera had made early in his academic career. While still an innocent and eager college student, he was heavily recruited by a variety of CIA officials and moved off the campus of Northwestern University and into a twelve-year stint as a Black Ops agent, running a number of clandestine and extremely dangerous missions across the European continent. This allowed him to build a connective network of loyalists, government officials, criminals, and Cold War agents he felt would be both sympathetic and helpful to the cause.

By the time he sat in his seat in the second row of a field-level box along the first base line at Wrigley Field, Andrew MacNamera had put in place his international operation of nearly five thousand sources, giving the Vittoria Society eyes in corners that were shaded and dangerous. The operation was funded by a well-stocked financial network of art collectors, dealers, academics, and historians who, across a twenty-year span, built a massive cash base to help support their various endeavors.

"Day baseball will soon be a remnant of the past," MacNamera said, scanning the ivy walls, watching the players leave the field after their pre-game drills. "Have you ever noticed it's always the things that give people the simplest pleasure—double features, drive-in movies, carnivals, amusement parks—that are the first to vanish whenever civilization gets the urge to go modern?"

"That shouldn't pose a problem for you or me," Edwards said, "since we live in the past. For men like us, nothing ever dies. It's just frozen in time."

MacNamera sat back and thrust his hands into the pockets of his worn Cubs jacket. He always dressed for the occasion, easily blending in regardless of the circumstances, making it a point never to be the one in any group who stood out. He was short, and now, due in part to the ravages of the disease coursing through him, somewhat frail, his once stout upper body reduced to a shell of bones and stretched skin, the booming voice of old replaced by a hoarse wheeze. But the eyes, so prominent in his gaunt face, told even the most casual observer that there was still quite a bit of fight left in the old man.

He glanced over at Edwards and rested a thin, withered hand, purple veins bulging over knuckles and fingers, on the professor's elbow as the game began, the crowd cheering the strike thrown on the first pitch. "Have you heard from Kate much since her arrival in Florence?" he asked as the cheers abated.

"Between the e-mails, letters, and cellphone calls, I'm surprised she has any time left for her studies," Edwards said, his eyes on the field, but his attention focused on MacNamera.

The older man's face crinkled, the edges of a smile forming around the corners of his mouth as he dug his hands deeper into the pockets of his warm-up jacket. "Did you know Wrigley was the first ballpark to use an organist?" he asked. "They tried it back in the summer of 1941, hoping to draw a younger crowd. Even back then, 'Bring Out the Youth' was the message of the day."

"I don't think you dragged yourself to the game to exercise your baseball trivia muscles, Andrew," Edwards said. "What is it you need to tell me?"

MacNamera turned from the field and stared at Edwards for several long seconds, then shifted his body closer. "They've made contact with Kate," he said. "Two days ago in the herbal pharmacy."

"She in danger?"

"Not at the moment," MacNamera said with the

slightest shake of his head. "They'll wait and give her the time she needs, see if she comes up with anything. If she does, then they'll make their move on both Kate and her discovery."

"Who approached her?"

"None other than the Raven himself," MacNamera said. "We shouldn't be surprised. He is probably as curious about Kate as he is about you. After all, had he stayed true to the cause, he would have been the director of the Society. And young Kate would have been groomed by him, not by you."

"How did she handle the meeting?" Edwards asked.

"She was fine, I'm told," MacNamera said. "My guess is she was initially caught off guard, but she seems fine."

"What are we doing about it?"

"To start with, I've doubled the eyes on Kate," MacNamera said. "I've also put two men on that friend of hers. But I don't need to tell you, our people are not out there alone."

Edwards leaned back, ignoring the home crowd cheering a Carlos Zambrano strikeout. "I wonder at times if the right thing to do would have been to keep her away from the ugly end of our business," he said. "Just let her live her life."

"She is what she is, Richard. And do not deceive yourself into thinking you had any say in the decision," MacNamera said.

Edwards took off his Cubs cap, ran a hand slowly through his thick, wavy hair and shook his head. "The Immortals," he muttered, his voice dripping with disdain. "He was always a pretentious twit."

"He fancies himself a warrior, and so named his group accordingly," MacNamera said with a slight smile. "The Immortals, after all, did defeat the Spartans.

Granted, the odds were more than slightly in their favor, but a win is a win."

"Let's assume Kate does indeed find something of value during her time in Florence," Edwards said, returning to the dilemma at hand. "How can we make sure we learn about it before the Raven does?"

"Not an easy task," MacNamera said. "Much will depend on what she finds and where she finds it. And also, what she decides to do with that discovery."

"My guess is she would contact me right off the bat," Edwards said. "In that case, we can hold a slight advantage, perhaps buy ourselves a few hours."

"Working on the assumption that she does contact you first," MacNamera said, "we then need her to be savvy enough not to use a landline or a traceable cell. We will also have to hope that her friend Marco can be trusted to remain silent."

"How does he check out?"

"No links whatsoever to the Raven or anyone remotely associated with him or his group," the older man said. "He is all that he appears to be—a student behind on his bills and his assignments who has developed a rather large crush on our Kate."

"Does she feel the same way about him?"

"I've never been able to judge which way a woman's heart leans," MacNamera said. "But my guess is that her feeling is simply friendly. At least for now."

"If Kate's going to find anything at all, she's going to need some time," Edwards said, "and we have to make sure she gets that."

"Which means bringing trouble down the Raven's path," MacNamera said. "That can be arranged."

"Then throw as many diversions at him as you can," Edwards said. "And let's not depend just on the strength of the Society. I'm sure the Rome Art Squad has him under their lens for one heist or another. Let's see if we can be of any help in that regard. He's also had a price on his head for several years now, with few venturing to make even an attempt. Why do you suppose that is?"

"He hires any potential assassins who might rise to the bait and pays them handsomely to work by his side," MacNamera said, "leaving the inexperienced and the desperate as potential prey. He also commands a certain level of fear and of invincibility in both the art world and the criminal underground. There are many who think we are the only ones who can battle him on equal footing, and we haven't been able to touch him for more than two decades."

"Do you ever think I've taken it too far in that regard?" Edwards asked.

"What choice did you have?"

"I often wonder if Frank and Andrea would have turned the Society into such a lethal force," he said. "In truth, how different are we from the Immortals other than in the methods we choose to dispense the lost art? Blood on both sides has been spilled in equal amounts."

"Perhaps it may one day revert to what Frank and Andrea originally had in mind," MacNamera said. "If Kate so desires."

Edwards turned to the game and briefly allowed himself the luxury of getting back into its rhythms, a respite from the talk of danger and deceit. He glanced at the scoreboard and then turned back to MacNamera. "The Society will defeat the Raven and ultimately bring his run to an end," he said. "I have never doubted that fact."

MacNamera nodded. "That and a well-played game is more than enough to bring a smile to a dying man's face," he said. "In the interim, I'll cause as much havoc as I can to the Raven and his illustrious Immortals, allowing Kate to pursue either her studies or our next adventure."

"I always take you for granted, Andrew," Edwards said. "I never mean to do it, it's just that you have been there for me for such a long time that it's easy to take your talents as a given. But I would be lost without your help and friendship."

"I fear you will be without both sooner than either of us would like," MacNamera said, avoiding eye contact. "It's spreading faster than the doctors anticipated. I doubt I will be of much use to you past this summer."

"Where do you stand on the question of miracles?" Edwards asked.

"I draw the line at dreams," MacNamera said. "And I have had the good fortune to have lived to see one of those dreams—the Vittoria Society—take root. Such a rare gift is worth more than any miracle I can imagine. However, if a miracle gets thrown on me, I won't fight it off."

"I think there's time for you to realize one more dream," Edwards said, "if you're up to it."

"It would take more than sickness to prevent it," MacNamera said.

The old warrior then stood, patted Edwards on the shoulder, bowed his head and turned, walking up the stone steps, heading out of the ballpark, prepared to engage in one final battle.

CHAPTER 14

Antonio Rumore stared out at the crowds filing along the stalls of the Mercato Centrale, the central market of Florence, the dueling odors of fresh meats, fish, poultry, and cheese thick in the air. He took a lazy gaze up toward the second floor, where the fruits and vegetables were stored and sold, giggles of children echoing off the partially open walls and filtering down to the street. It was ten minutes after nine on a Saturday, the early morning mist slowly giving way to a warm sun and rising temperatures.

Rumore reached into the front pocket of his tailored white shirt and pulled out a filtered British cigarette. He held it in his right hand and rested his head against the shuttered door of a long-abandoned Laundromat, keeping his dark eyes on the activity in the marketplace across the plaza. Then he glanced to his left, watching the older man slowly make his way to his side, two small paper cups filled with espresso in his hands, beads of sweat forming across his forehead.

"I have a sweet roll in my pocket," the man said, handing Rumore one of the cups. "We can split it, if you like."

"I'm good with just the coffee," Rumore said, holding the cup close to his lips and blowing.

"Did I miss anything exciting?" the man asked, finding a shaded spot next to Rumore and reaching for a sugar-dusted bun wrapped in a swath of napkins in the right-hand pocket of his crumpled tan jacket.

"I think they're running low on artichokes," Rumore said. "Other than that, it's business as usual."

"And what of our friend?" the man asked. "Did he hold true to his usual form?"

"Creatures of habit always do, Stefano," Rumore said. "He made his first stop at the butcher's stall, where he was handed two full plastic bags. He handed the bags off to a tall, bald man standing to his left, and then the two of them moved on toward the fish counter."

"God, how I do love police work," Stefano said, stuffing the last bite of the bun into a corner of his mouth. "You tell me. Where else could we find this level of excitement—and on a Saturday morning, no less?"

"He hasn't been coming to Florence these past few weeks because there's a shortage of fresh meat and fish in Rome," Rumore said. "He's caught wind of something and it must smell of a big score, otherwise there would be no need for him to get this directly involved this early in the process."

"I've been checking the stats every morning, as always," Stefano said. "What's out there isn't worth the squad's time, let alone the Raven's."

"It may not have surfaced on anyone's radar just yet. But the big hauls seldom pop up until those final hours before they're ready to hit the market. And it may not even be a discovery he's after. He might be here for a heist."

"The Florence police have been put on alert," Stefano said. "As have all the museum security forces. If he or anyone in his crew makes a move, we'll be sure to hear about it."

"It would be of great value if we heard about it *before* it happens," Rumore said.

"That was one incident, and if there was someone we

could point a finger at and blame, then I would have fired him myself," Stefano said. "It was a mistake on our part and a good luck landing on the side of the criminals. It happens sometimes."

"Never to me," Rumore said, his eyes focused on the activity in the marketplace.

"Then it's time you got over it," Stefano said. "I'm not talking to you like a partner here. I'm speaking as a friend."

"I will get over it," Rumore said. "As soon as I see the Raven in handcuffs or in a coffin."

ANTONIO RUMORE WAS a police captain assigned to one of the most prestigious units in the world—the Rome Art Squad. Since its formation in 1969, the squad had been responsible for the retrieval of more than 1.2 million stolen or missing works of art, 300,000 of them captured outside Italian borders. The Art Squad consisted of 186 detectives working out of eleven cities, its members expert in fields as diverse as art history, antiterror tactics, martial arts, and languages, with contacts—both legal and otherwise—deep inside the varied worlds of antiquities, money laundering, and drug trafficking.

On paper, Rumore would have been deemed an odd choice for the Art Squad.

He was the only son of a devoutly religious Neapolitan hotel manager, a hardworking and lonely widower whose wife had been yet another in a long line of innocent victims of Camorra street battles. They lived in an apartment along a section of the city known as Lungomare, a working-class district overlooking the bustling harbor and vistas of the Bay of Naples. Rumore had been a frail and sickly boy, often forced to miss as much as a full semester of classes due to a variety of ailments, from a bout with double pneumonia to a rheumatic fever scare to a leg broken in three places. The boy didn't spend time complaining, content to pass his days and nights alone in a world of his own making—spent in his corner bedroom reading thick volumes of art history and biographies of the great and the infamous. His father had wedged his bed against the small window that opened out onto the harbor, the rich sounds of Neapolitan love ballads filtering up from the open-air restaurant that filled the first floor of his thirteenth century apartment building.

He seldom saw his father, who often worked double shifts in order to save enough money to give his son more than a month-to-month existence. It was a quiet life that offered little in the way of promise and less in the form of opportunity. Then it got worse.

Three weeks before his twelfth birthday, Antonio Rumore lost his hearing.

No one from among the small squadron of doctors his father was able to round up could offer an explanation, some even concluding their examination with a simple shrug and a shake of the head. While Rumore's father and his few friends were distraught over the boy's plight, Antonio accepted his submergence into a silent world, longing only for the sounds of the love songs he so cherished. And in time he made an effort to turn his unexpected disability to his advantage. When out with his father, he would carefully study the way passersby walked, moved, and gestured, gauging their looks, the cut of their clothes, how they interacted with those around them. He would then compile a mental dossier on these passing strangers, a preteen body language expert at work on the streets of Naples.

He lived in silence for a full two years.

Then, one rainy Sunday morning as he stared into his bathroom mirror, adjusting a blue tie under the collar of a starched white shirt, as he readied for a pre-Mass breakfast, Antonio heard the refrain of a car horn repeatedly bleating beneath his bedroom window. He rolled up his tie, walked out of the bathroom and pulled a cassette down from the second shelf of a small bookcase, opened the case and slid the cassette into its slot on the portable player he kept next to his bed. The boy then sat on the chair by his desk, listening to the sorrowful lyrics of his favorite song, "Parle me di Amore, Mariu," fill the room. He lowered his head, his hands resting on his knees, thin lines of tears streaming down the front of his smooth, handsome face.

RUMORE HAD JUST COMPLETED his two years of mandatory military service, choosing to spend his time as a navy sailor, his adventures taking him to the coast of Africa and into the hotbed of the Middle East, and was enjoying a brief break from the mundane chores that constituted so much of a life at sea. He was twenty-three, just over six feet tall, with a lithe, muscular frame; a long-distance sprinter in a country that prided itself on leisurely evening strolls. He found comfort in the silences that running around an empty track or deep inside a tree-lined trail provided, allowing him the ability to clear his head and focus on the goals he had set for himself.

Rumore wanted to be a carabinieri, the governmental arm of the Italian police force and the most respected law enforcement officials in the country. It was a childhood dream that did not dissipate as he grew into manhood. He would often walk by the local carabinieri station located less than three blocks from his apartment building and watch the men head toward their squad cars to begin their afternoon shifts—dark uniforms pressed, white shirts starched, black ties firmly in place, shoes polished and hats low and firm.

It was all he wanted out of life—to be one of them. A

member of the best the country had to offer. And he sought to take it even one step further—not only to be accepted into their ranks, but to then be offered a position in the elite Rome Art Squad.

He submitted his application six months prior to the end of his military service, and still had yet to hear a word, either by mail or phone. He realized that the odds would not be in his favor. He was a southern Italian in a department dominated by men from the North. He was not a graduate of a university whose name would be enough to impress. He had majored in Art History, not exactly a degree that would make the higher-ups in the department seek out his application. Nor was he born to a family either prominent enough to have connections within the ranks or with a legacy of law enforcement. Yet Rumore vowed he would fulfill what he believed to be his destiny. And it was that belief, that wholehearted desire to be a member of the carabinieri, that led him one late summer afternoon to walk into a small, nearly empty restaurant just off the Via Venuto and approach the table of General Carlo Albertini, chief of the Rome Art Squad.

Rumore had devoured all there was to read about the general's exploits, following his career from the early years, which were highlighted by a series of top-tier drug busts, to his later notoriety in working undercover and rising through the ranks of the most notorious art theft ring in Europe, where he helped orchestrate their eventual takedown on the piers of the Rome waterfront. That success led to the formation of the Art Squad, which he had nurtured and directed until it stood as the pinnacle of excellence in its field and made him the most famous carabinieri in the world.

Rumore stood directly across from Albertini, the general calmly spooning sugar into a large cup filled with a foamy cappuccino. He was a small man, thin and wiry.

His thick gray hair was razor cut, and a small moustache, mixed with specks of gray and black, helped highlight a set of dark, penetrating eyes. He rested his spoon on the white linen spread and looked up at the young man before him.

"It was kind of you to wait until I finished my meal before you approached," the general said. "I usually don't receive such a courtesy when I'm being followed."

"I wasn't following you, sir," Rumore said. "I was simply trying to find the proper moment to come speak to you."

"Knowing when to make your move may be a luxury to some," the general said, sitting back and staring up at the nervous young man, "but to a policeman, it is a necessity. In some cases, it is a skill that may take years to sharpen."

"I'm not a policeman," Rumore said, a bit defensively.

"Not yet," the general said, "and perhaps never. But from what I've been able to observe, it won't be for any lack of desire."

"From the way I saw the situation, sir, I had nothing to lose," Rumore said. "Making my case to you is my best chance, my only chance, to join the carabinieri."

"How long ago did you submit your application?"

"Going on seven months, sir," Rumore said. "It's either still sitting in someone's in-basket or it hasn't even been opened yet."

"You're from Naples, am I correct?" the general asked.

Rumore nodded.

"From what both you and I know of that lovely city, it could also still be waiting to leave your local post office."

"There is always that possibility, sir," Rumore said

with a smile. "Which is why I mailed out two applications."

A middle-aged waiter approached Rumore, a small tray with two large cappuccinos resting in the center cupped in the middle of his right hand, a cloth napkin folded across the crook of his arm. The general calmly watched as the waiter rested one cup between the setting on the other end of the small table and the second in front of him. He then waved for Rumore to sit.

"I took the liberty to order you a coffee," he said, "which also gave me a perfect excuse to ignore my doctor's advice and enjoy a second cup."

Rumore pulled back a wooden chair and sat, resting his hands around the warm coffee and staring across at the general. "When did you first notice me?" he asked.

"The real question you need to ask is at what point did I realize you were not a threat to me," the general said. "Both sides—police as well as criminal—always get noticed, but the motive of the man following you is never easy to ascertain."

"And what was it that gave me away?" Rumore asked.

"Your body language does not yet have the feel of danger," the general said, "which either means you are an eager and impatient young applicant or a very bad and poorly paid tracker. But you did cause me a few minutes of thought. A sliver of hope."

"A good guess then on my part would be that you have also figured out why it is I needed to come see you," Rumore said.

The general stirred his coffee and smiled. "There were at last count well over five hundred applications resting in a large pile on my desk," he said, "winnowed down from close to twelve hundred. All of the applicants are worthy young men and women such as yourself, each one qualified, each equipped with the proper academic backgrounds. From that rather large pool, I will need to select two and assign them to my Art Squad. It would seem, on the surface at least, to be a daunting task, and in many respects it is. But in fact, it always comes down to nothing more complex than a simple gut reaction. I've been doing it this way for quite a number of years now, and I have yet to appoint someone to the squad who would be considered a mistake."

"The squad has never had anyone in its ranks from Naples," Rumore said. "Is that from a lack of applicants or does your gut deem all Neapolitans unacceptable?"

"Using bias as an argument may earn you a few points on a debating team," the general said, "but it won't help you secure a place in my squad."

"What would, then?"

"An answer as to why you should be chosen over any of the other applicants," the general said. "And save the details about how high your grade average is and how you get teary-eyed at the sight of Michelangelo's David."

"Most of your applicants would be worthy additions to your squad," Rumore said. "There is no denying that. We all come into the process with the skills and sensibilities needed to master the job—we all speak multiple languages, know our way around museums and galleries, are tops in our grade level in weapons and tactics, have our own independent network of street connections, and boast a working knowledge of the high-end criminal world. None of us would have bothered to apply if we didn't have those attributes."

"But you possess one other component that all the others lack," the general said. "I'm more than anxious to hear what it is."

"I can disappear into the criminal world," Rumore said. "Infiltrate their ranks, be accepted as one of them, welcomed into their group, and over time be included in their plans."

"Undercover," the general said, clearly intrigued.

"You've never had one in the Art Squad," Rumore said.

"I've never had need for one," the general said. "Our solve rate is the highest of any such unit in the world. We work all our cases much like a homicide investigation, piecing together clues, linking one to the other, until all the pieces are in place, a suspect is in custody, and a valued piece of art is returned."

"And it's been an effective process up till now," Rumore said. "I didn't come here asking you to change it, just update it."

"And if I decide such a change is called for, why would I choose you?" the general asked.

"I don't think you would have wasted even a portion of such a lovely day if you didn't already know the answer to that question," Rumore said, gently easing back his chair and standing across from the general. "It's been a pleasure to meet you and it would be an honor to work for you. I pray that whomever you finally select, it will be the correct decision."

Rumore bowed slightly and turned to leave, heading toward an array of angry drivers and congested traffic. The general sat back, crossed one leg over another and stared at the young man moving gracefully through the now crowded streets. "We share that same prayer," he said in a voice no one could hear.

TWO DAYS BEFORE the Florence stakeout, Rumore sat at his desk looking over an array of mug shots. It was early and quiet, the squad room empty, the phones silent. He held up one photo and brought it up closer to his desk light, staring at it for several seconds before resting it by his elbow. He wrote the name of the man in the photo on the top line of a yellow legal pad, then reached across his desk and grabbed a file folder containing the most recent prison release dates. On the second sheet, he found what he was looking for and transferred the information to the legal pad, writing it under the name of the man in the mug shot.

He sat back in his chair and looked out at the tree-lined street below, the chaos of a morning in Rome still several hours away. He glanced at his watch and was about to ease up from his chair and head for the Borghese Gardens and a quiet run when the phone rang.

Rumore picked it up on the second ring, noted the time and listened for a voice. "You're the only person I know sleeps less than I do," the man on the other end said. He was an American and a friend. He sounded old and tired.

"I think it's the coffee," Rumore said.

"Have you had your run yet?" the man asked.

"You didn't call at an early hour for me and a late one for you to check on my workout schedule," Rumore said.

There was a pause, and he heard the rumblings of a cough before the old man spoke. "Are you getting any hits on Florence?"

"Nothing out of the ordinary," Rumore said.

"Can you spare the time for a trip up?" the old man asked.

"If it would be worth my time," Rumore said.

"I wouldn't have called if I didn't think it would," the old man said.

"I have many old friends in Florence," Rumore said. "As do you. Is there anyone in particular you want me to see?"

"Yes," the old man said, "someone we both know all too well. But I doubt either of us would consider him a friend."

"An old enemy," Rumore said. "That's even better."

"Not just any old enemy, Captain," the old man said, and then hung up.

Rumore rested the phone back on the receiver, stood and walked out of the empty office of the Rome Art Squad.

CHAPTER 15

KATE AND MARCO STOOD WITH THEIR BACKS against a cold and jagged stone wall, their university T-shirts coated with sweat. They were fifteen feet inside the blocked off area of the Vasari Corridor, shrouded in dust and darkness, their white Puma sneakers stained red from the mounds of clay that coated the path.

"Are you certain no one saw us come in?" Marco asked.

"I think they would have chased us," Kate said, her words lacking their usual conviction. "They weren't looking for it, so there was no reason for them to expect it."

"That doesn't help explain why I'm still trembling like a child with a fever," Marco said. "I have never been as frightened in my life as I am at this very moment, and I'm not ashamed to admit it."

"Neither am I," Kate said, moving away from the wall. "Maybe we should start looking around. Help get our minds off what's outside and focus on what's in here."

"There's nothing in here, Kate," he said. "I've been trying to tell you that ever since you came up with this idea. There's nothing but dust, discarded portraits of mediocre noblemen, and a ceiling that looks like it will cave in at any moment."

"And let's not forget about the rats," she said. "There

must be a few hundred of them living inside these cracks."

"I *had* forgotten them," Marco said, "until now."

Kate moved slowly and with careful steps deeper into the corridor. She was surprised to see that this portion of the corridor was nearly as well-maintained as the main piece—the walls were painted with a fresh coat of white, and older, less recognizable portraits lined both sides, giving the enclosed space the look and feel of the adjoining sections. The ceiling did have thick round patches of water damage, and there were a number of areas that were in visible need of upkeep, but otherwise there was little to separate this section from the central hall. Unlike the main corridor, the sealed-off portion was designed to be hidden from view, and the historical rumor had always been that it was built in a manner to allow the Medici family to hide their most secret and valuable possessions.

Kate stepped over a large crack in the floor's foundation and ran a hand against one side of a wall. There were a number of thick white stones jutting out, edges sharp enough to draw blood, and when she rested her fingers across the top ridges of one of them, she felt it come loose.

"These bricks and stones could all come free with just a tug," she said, running her hands up and down the wall.

"They've been here forever," Marco said, taking a quick glance behind him. "Add in the humidity and moisture and I'm surprised they're still even holding up the wall."

"Or maybe they were designed to be moved without a struggle," Kate said, shaking one piece of stone free and clutching it in her hand. "This is still fresh, can't be more than two, maybe three years old."

"Which tells you what?" he asked. "Maybe the work

crews repaired it. They seem to be working on the ceiling and parts of the floor. No one's ever in here, so they can fix what needs to be taken care of at their leisure."

Kate took a step back and gazed up at the wall, her eyes tracking every nook, every corner of stone and brick, tracing it as if it were a map. Marco stood off to her side, watching closely.

"Let's take it down," she said after a long moment. "All of it."

"Why?"

She gave him a smile. "Just a hunch," she said.

"You understand, it may be one thing to sneak in here," Marco said. "That's trouble enough if we're caught. But to do damage to a national landmark, I can't even imagine what will happen to us if we're found out."

"It's worth the risk," Kate said.

"And if your hunch is wrong," he said, "will you promise me this will be the end of it?"

"Scouts' honor," she said. "I'll be the most law-abiding resident in Florence."

"They might hear us," Marco said. "The noise could echo through the other side of the wall."

"I don't think so," Kate said. "The bricks and stones have been layered in gently, just dirt and some spackle at the edges to hold them in place. They will come out with a slight tug. We don't need to pound at them to set them loose."

"How much of it do you want to take down?"

"We need to see what is behind the wall," she said. "When we can do that, we should stop."

"I just pray we don't find ourselves staring at the inside of the gift shop," Marco said.

IT TOOK THEM forty-five minutes to clear away enough of the wall to be able to look into the darkness beyond a circular opening. Kate peered into the hole, brushing aside dust and cobwebs, her face hit with a blast of cold air, her nose recoiling from a thick and acrid odor. She could hear rats squeal and scurry clear of the light infiltrating their once private lair and see the outlines of a small wheelbarrow and two shovels resting against one of the side walls.

"Give me a boost," she said to Marco as she lifted her right foot onto the side of a sharp edge of stone.

Marco bent to one knee and cupped his hands under the sole of her left shoe to lift her. Within seconds Kate was scooting over the side of the broken wall, her skin scraping the chunks of stone and mortar. She soon stood in the middle of a room that was much larger than it appeared from the outside, its solid walls made of a substance from another century, thick and coated with a pinkish hue due more to the passage of time than choice of color.

She walked the corners of the room, gazing through the mist, cool wisps of moisture flowing across her ankles, absorbing all that she could see, a wide smile stretched across her face. She turned a tight corner and came to a dead stop, looking down at a thing of raw beauty, mere inches from the edges of her feet, close enough for her to touch, feel, embrace. She dropped to her knees, closed her eyes for a brief second. She thought of her mother, father, and the professor, and knew how thrilled they would have been to have witnessed this sight. This was their moment, and she wished more than anything they could be by her side to share in its discovery.

She had stepped into another time.

She could feel her heart beating wildly, the coolness of the room mixing sharply with the icy sweat running down her neck and back. She had never known such a feeling of pure joy and exhilaration. She turned toward the opening of the wall at her back and saw Marco peering in.

"Come in," she said to him in a surprisingly calm voice. "You'll want to see this."

She waited while Marco struggled to make his way over the wall, grunting and groaning as he maneuvered across sharp rocks and mounds of dust and debris. He landed hard on one knee, stood, glanced quickly around the room and then walked over to her. She was pointing toward a darkened corner, the walls around it chiseled and hollowed out, three stone sculptures resting in the open alcove. He wiped the soot from the edges of his mouth and moved closer to the sculptures—three Angels, each about four feet tall and weighing less than a hundred pounds. They were perfectly proportioned, chiseled by the hands of a master, free of any of the dust or dirt that littered the rest of the room. "They can't be real," Marco whispered. "The Midnight Angels are not even *supposed* to be real. All the books I read claimed they were just another part of his legend, nothing more than myth."

"The books were wrong," Kate said.

Marco leaned down and placed a gentle hand over one of the Angels, his fingers stroking the perfectly chiseled shoulders and muscular arms, the angular face, the determined eyes, the proportioned wings.

"How did you know?" he said in a whisper. "How did you know they existed and that they would be somewhere in here?"

"The books follow history," Kate said, her eyes focused on the three angels. "It's how most people are taught. I followed the artist."

"Are there only three Angels?"

"I think so," she said. "One of the unproven rumors

was that Michelangelo planned and sculpted the seven archangels in secrecy, trusting no one other than maybe one or two of his closest assistants. They were meant to be a gift, a surprise, a gesture of love and admiration to someone he claimed had ahold of his heart."

"Do you know who?"

"A woman named Vittoria Colonna," Kate said. "The only woman Michelangelo ever claimed to love."

"That's another part of the myth of Michelangelo," Marco said. "All indications are he was either gay or asexual."

"More unproven rumors," Kate said. "Michelangelo lived his life shrouded in them. It was how he preferred it. The less people knew about him, the greater his legend grew."

"So what do we do now?"

"You mean with the Angels?" she asked.

Marco nodded. "We should let someone know we found them. The museum, our school, somebody needs to know they're here."

"Somebody already knows," Kate said.

"Who would that be?"

"Whoever hid them here," she said, "and kept them hidden for God only knows how many years."

"You do this all the time," Marco said, his voice cracking. "Just when I'm starting to relax around you, gears switch and you start talking in a way that scares the hell out of me."

"Just look at the Angels," she told him. "In a place mired in dust and soot, they are free of both. They're kept in the coolest corner of a sealed-off room, free of any prying eyes. But they can be checked on easily and often, judging by how little time it took for us to spread open the wall. They are in here for a reason. I just haven't figured out what that is."

"To sell them, maybe?" Marco asked. "The Midnight

Angels would be worth millions on the open market and millions more on the black."

Kate shook her head. "I don't think so," she said. "That could have been done anytime they wanted. It's not like people were out there looking for the Angels to be put up for sale. No one even knew they existed."

"*You* did," he said. "There could have been others."

"I was working off a little girl's dream," she said. "Art thieves and hunters require more than a dream to put them to the chase."

"So, if they weren't kept in here to eventually be sold, then why bother hiding them?" Marco asked. "They'd be much safer inside any one of our museums."

"To protect them, maybe," Kate said. "You can steal from a museum. It happens all the time. But in here, wedged behind a wall, in a sealed-off part of a corridor with few visitors, they would seem extremely safe."

"Not that safe," he said. "We found them, didn't we?"

"Right now, we're asking questions we don't have the answers to," Kate said. "And until we get to the people who have those answers, we need to do what we can to make sure the Angels stay as safe as they were when we found them."

"Easy enough," Marco said. "We just reseal the wall and find our way back out of here."

"That'll work for now," she said, "until I can think of a safer place to store them. In the meantime, we need to find out who it is who knew the Angels were in here, and who else is out there looking for them."

"What makes you so sure someone else is?"

"When it comes to lost or hidden art, there's always someone else," Kate said.

"You sound as if you already know who it is," Marco said.

Kate shook her head. "I only know who he might be. But I need to be one hundred percent certain."

"How are you going to do that?"

She looked across the room at Marco. "By calling in the cavalry," she said.

CHAPTER 16

CLARE JOHNSON STOOD ON THE FIFTH FLOOR terrace of her two-room Excelsior Hotel suite, gazing down at the heavy brown tug of the Arno River as it rumbled through the heart of the city. It was early morning, a good twenty minutes before sunup and church bells would waken the citizens of Florence to a new day, and she was already on her third cup of espresso, her inner clock still tuned to New York hours and revved to run at that city's wild pace. She was dressed in a Karl Lagerfeld tailored jacket and skirt, the outfit highlighting the shapes and angles of her workout-buffed body.

Clare was thirty-three years old, had a B.A. in Art History, an MBA from Harvard, and had been one of McBain International Securities' top investigators four years running. She was McBain's principal art retriever, the one agent most often chosen to chase down stolen works covered under the company's golden seven- to-ten figure policies. She approached her work with a passion not often seen in the pristine world of high-end art, preferring to operate in the heat of the action. She worked best on the road, where she was fed daily doses of information by a vast network of sources, working under the theory that it was also best to think like a thief in order to capture one.

Clare Johnson was born on the run, growing up in cities large and small, in both towns that were nondescript and places that would be on any traveler's map if only money were no object. She was thrust into this whirlwind environment out of necessity, the daughter of James Johnson, who everyone called "Cat" and who was one of the most infamous art thieves of his time. Cat Johnson was a unique figure in the criminal underworld, a man with a gift for the grab and an ability to plan a heist in any gallery or museum in the world with the care and studious dedication a combat general would bring to an upcoming battle. The fact that he was a black man born in a Bacon County, Georgia, one-room shack made his exploits all the more remarkable and gave added weight to his legend.

Cat had learned about crime on the dusty streets of a grubby childhood, while his taste for art was honed through the many books he borrowed from a public library less than a half mile from the interstate he would later use to escape his surroundings and embark on his criminal adventures. He devoured the books, staring at each magnificent portrait or sculpted work until his eyes stung, his mind absorbing all that he had read and learned. He grew up savvy enough to know he would never have the means to purchase even the most modestly priced works he admired, but shrewd enough to understand that a young man with a fast mind and the skill set of a top-tier thief had all he needed to at least try to reach for what had been drawn or chiseled by the masters. All someone in his position needed was a little bit of seed money and a whole lot of luck, and from the way he liked to look at the world and the problems they presented, he felt life owed him both these as payback for dealing him a poor set of cards from the start.

"You want to get lower than Bacon County, you need to dig yourself a ten-foot hole and jump in head first," he once told a friend. "It's not saying the world owes me a living for throwing me out in the dust to spend my days on the scratch for money and the sniff for food. But it does owe me some luck, and I intend to cash in on that."

He started small-time but didn't play on that turf for long. His string of well-planned and even better executed break-ins caught the attention of the criminal assembly line, and by the time the young thief had made his way to Chicago, his name was front and center on the mind of Arthuro Mastopiedi, the underboss to Anthony Accardo and owner of one of the finest art collections in the United States. Mastopiedi had made it a point always to get the up-and-comers to sign on with his crew, and he went all out to recruit Cat Johnson. They met for the first time in a downtown Chicago barbershop with blackened windows and large ceiling fans slicing away at the heat and the flies. It took less than twenty minutes for the two ambitious men to reach an agreeable arrangement, and out of that initial meeting a thirty-year friendship bloomed.

Cat Johnson specialized in home museum invasions and he always worked alone. He never did more than five jobs in any given year, devoting an average of three hours of research for every three seconds he spent inside a targeted home. He would move the lifted works that same night, transferring them to waiting vans in an area known only to Mastopiedi, who would then take control and navigate the hot art through the various alleys of the black market. In return for his work, Cat received an up-front fee of $25,000 plus a six percent commission on the final sales total of the stolen goods. In his entire career he never earned less than $200,000 on any one job, working under what he felt was a foolproof system. "I know I could have taken down bigger paydays," he once told his daughter, in the last months of his life, when the cancer had spread from his lungs to the rest of his body. "But there's a price for that kind of hunger and greed, and I wasn't willing to pay. Besides, I was all about the score. The money was a bonus, and not going to prison and being sent away from you? Well, what the hell kind of a price can you lay on something that sweet?"

He never hid how he earned his income from either his wife or his only child. They lived a simple life and pulled up stakes often, using Cat's cover as a Mutual of Omaha insurance salesman as the reasons for the frequent transfers. The family moved not out of any concern that the authorities were closing in on them, but rather as yet another part of Cat Johnson's approach to the criminal way of life—never get too close to people or places. There can be no room for friendship outside of business, or for nostalgia not tied into a theft. It was a cold way to live, but to Cat, keeping his personal circle tight was the best route to a prison-free existence.

He did, however, allow himself one personal luxury—he doted on his daughter Clare. She was his one steady companion in life. While he never strayed from his marriage to Cynthia, the union was one built on loyalty rather than love. But to Cat, his Clare was as lovely as any painting he had ever seen and as smart as any artist whose life story he had set to memory, and he did his all to fuel her education as he prepared her to lead an honest life in what he viewed as a corrupt world.

"Don't ever believe it when someone tries to tell you there's only two kinds of people in this world," he said to her when she was twelve, as the two toured the halls of a home museum in Houston, Cat making mental notes on each piece of work they passed. "There are all kinds of people in this world, and if you are going to do much more than survive, you will need to read each of them as if he were an open book laying flat across your lap."

"Is that what you do?" Clare asked.

"Every day, in every way," Cat said.

"How?"

"The same way you can read that picture hanging there," he said, pointing out what he knew to be an early drawing by Pablo Picasso. "You learn all you can about the painter, how old he was at the time he started and then finished the work, where he lived, who he lived with, what he did for money and what he did when he wasn't at work. You store all that and then look at the work. I mean *really* look at the work, as if it were alive and you could see it move, take it past the paint and come away with what the artist was looking to tell you. You take it far enough, it will feel as if you painted the work yourself. The same lessons apply to people, and trust me on this, little one, people are much easier to read than any painting that's hanging in any of the museums we've been in."

"Will that help me be like you?" Clare asked.

"That shouldn't even be in your thinking," Cat said. "You will be better than me, you and me together, we'll both see to that. One thief in the family is more than enough. There are higher steps out there for you to climb."

"Like what?"

"There will be plenty of time to work all that out," Cat said, resting one thin arm across her small frame. "You'll find it when you come to it. But for now, let's keep our focus on the lessons that sit before us waiting to be absorbed. The career call—in my experience, anyway—is one of those things that floats down and just lands on you, sometimes coming at you from out of nowhere or from a place you never even gave a second's thought. But you will for certain recognize it when it does. And you will be as good at whatever that career ends up being as I am at being a thief. And if I stick around long enough and teach you as much as you need to know, then you might—just might—end up being even better."

Cat Johnson did his job, and through the combination of the best schools stolen money could buy and the lessons he was able to impart, he lived long enough to see his daughter become the premier insurance investigator in her field. Specializing in art retrieval, she had an eye-popping sixty-five percent success rate in a field where forty percent success was considered the gold standard. She knew how to run down leads, gathering information from both cops and art dealers while giving up very little of what she had already learned about the case. In so many ways, Clare was very much her father's daughter—she preferred to work her cases alone, and her bosses gave her full rein in that area once they caught a glimpse of the end results. She trusted no one, and while friendly and at ease on the few occasions she was off the trail and in the home office, she shunned the habit of socializing with any of her coworkers. She did, however, make it her business to learn their tastes and habits, strengths and weaknesses, likes and dislikes. She loved logging the long hours the work required, the travel to faraway cities she had only read about in academic books and novels, the private tours inside many of the world's museums, places her father had devoted so much of his time telling her about.

What she loved most of all was breaking down a theft, and it was in this arena that Cat's lessons proved most priceless. She would be called in on a case within twelve hours of a theft, more often than not in the form of a late-night phone call from her direct supervisor, Edward Langley. He was a frail man in his late sixties who helped start the firm with the now long-deceased Shamus McBain, and he was always direct in his conversations and sharp in his commands, never stopping for idle chatter or wasted words. "A Monet was lifted out of a home museum in San Francisco," would be his typical opening remark on the telephone, in lieu of a hello. "The start and finish details will be downloaded onto your BlackBerry. The job was professional—alarm codes jumbled, rear access to the home contaminated, exit most likely through the front of the house in the middle of a quiet day, so they knew going in it would be empty."

"How much do we stand to lose?" Clare might ask.

"We're on the line for twenty-five million," Langley would tell her, or some other sum. "Do whatever you need to do to make sure we don't have to pay it out."

There would be no good-byes, no good lucks, just a silent second and then a dial tone, signaling both an end to the conversation and the start of her new assignment.

Clare always kept a bag packed and ready in order to make maximum use of her time, and would usually travel to the hit site by private plane, a rented car waiting for her within a hundred feet of the runway. Once at the crime scene, she would touch base with the local police to pick up whatever loose shreds of information they were willing to share, and then secure permission to scour the area on her own. She brought to her work the skills of an insurance investigator and the instincts of a thief, and this lethal combination enabled her to climb swiftly up toward the top rungs of her profession.

Clare Johnson was, hands down, the most feared and respected insurance investigator in the business.

THE RAVEN STOOD several feet behind Clare, on her Excelsior balcony, his eyes slowly scanning the shape and contours of her body, a warm cup of coffee cradled in his hands. "What a beautiful sight," he said. "It's enough to make a man's heart skip several beats."

"Save the sweet," Clare said without bothering to

turn around. "I've heard better lines from street corner peddlers."

"I was referring to the river," the Raven said, managing a slight smile. "But now that you've brought it to my attention, you still look great."

"Lots of coffee and little of anything else," Clare said. "It keeps the heart pumping and the body trim."

The Raven stepped out onto the terrace, the sun warming his face, the hard pull of the river water reflected in his dark wraparound shades. "I don't suppose it would do me any good to ask what brings you to Florence?" he said, resting his coffee cup atop the black railing.

"I had some vacation time coming," Clare said, "and when those rare occasions occur, this is the best place to find me. But I suppose you already knew that before you talked the cleaning lady down the hall into letting you in here."

"*Bribed* the cleaning lady," the Raven said. "And yes, I was aware this is your favorite city and also that you are owed two weeks paid leave by your firm. Still, the doubts linger."

"And you?" Clare asked. "Craving a Sostanza steak? Or is there a new exhibit in town I should check out?"

"Neither," he said. "Though I must confess to having developed a fondness for the brusque manner of Sostanza's waiters."

"Well, now that we've covered that territory," Clare said, "why don't we cut to the quick? You tell me as much as you're willing to share, I'll do the same, and maybe we can both come out of this with some answers."

"I will do my best to be honest with you," the Raven said.

"We're not going to get very far if you start off our conversation with a lie," she said.

"We both know there are three professional heists in advanced stages of planning," the Raven said. "One is at the Uffizi. I'm still trying to weed out the location of the other two."

"A second is at a private home somewhere in the historic district," Clare said. "Top-tier team from France led by an old hand named Duvalier."

"He was once one of our best safe crackers, prior to falling into some bad luck," the Raven said. "It was during his rather long recuperative period that he developed a taste for the finest in Renaissance art."

"Neither of the two jobs will fetch anything worth your time," she said. "On top of which, you have more than enough members in your troupe to serve as scouts. Which means either the third job is the one that promises to net a notable score or there is something else brewing in this city that's caught your evil eye."

"And the same will be true for you as well," the Raven said. "You usually only enter into the frame after the dust has settled, yet here you are, on vacation, within walking distance of three major jobs about to go off. And your firm not represented in any of those thus far discussed. If I could lay a wager, I'd put it all on the bet that you have as much interest in these potential lifts as I do. Which is to say none."

"In this city, there's always more to appreciate than the potential for a heist," Clare said, leaning her elbows on the black railing, gazing down at a young couple embracing under a streetlight across the square. "We both make a move if we sniff something like that. We've done so most of our lives, so why stop now?"

"Then you know she is in town," the Raven said.

"I know she's here to continue her studies," Clare said, "and that might well be the long and the short of it. She may be here for the same reason hundreds of others come each year—academia is, after all, very much a key part of her world."

"If either one of us believed that, neither one of us would be here," the Raven said.

"Not even for those brusque waiters?" Clare said, turning her head slightly, sliding a smile in his direction.

"I don't need to travel to find a good restaurant," he said. "But I would go to the ends of the earth to lay my hands on a rare find. Especially one from the master."

"And why are we both so sure she will be the one to find it?"

"It's what they raised her to do."

"Maybe," Clare said. "Or maybe she's just come along at the right time and might luck into finding herself in the right place. Maybe we're all expecting her to follow in her parents' footsteps when all she is is just a regular girl."

"We're both too smart for that," the Raven said with a dismissive wave. "The key ingredients of our profession are preparation, patience, and timing. She's been in preparation since she was a child. The work she does, blended with what she's learned as the ward to the distinguished professor, taught her the value of patience. As for the time, it might not be now, but my instincts tell me there will be no better moment than the one we currently find ourselves in. And if I needed any further proof, well, your presence here supplies that."

"How many of your crew do you have on her tail?" Clare asked.

"Now, Clare, how would I measure up as a worthy nemesis if I gave a direct answer to such a question?" he said. "Suffice it to say I have more than I need to cover her every movement, regardless of how uneventful her forays have so far turned out to be."

"Then you know where she was yesterday?" Clare asked.

"Sneaking into the sealed-off section of the Vasari Corridor is a rite of passage for any art history student worthy of an advanced degree," the Raven said with a nod. "It is as true today as it was back when we were young enough to call such endeavors an adventure."

"That may be true," Clare said, "but then we went in with no other intent than to eat our lunch in an off-limits place. Neither of us went in expecting to find anything of value."

"She and her young friend entered empty-handed and came out the same way," the Raven said. "I would not be here chatting the day away if that were not the case."

"What about their clothes?" Clare asked. "Did your eyes on the ground mention their clothes?"

"If it was important, they would have," the Raven said, turning away from the river, his full attention now on Clare. "But I'm gathering you were told a slightly altered tale than the one I was given."

"Or perhaps what I was told was inaccurate," she said, walking into the elegantly furnished living room and pouring herself a fresh cup of coffee from the room service breakfast cart.

"If you heard different, then I need to hear it as well," the Raven said, the hint of a threat to his words.

"No doubt you do," Clare said, sipping her coffee, not bending to the implied pressure, "you just don't need to hear it from me. Not unless we come to an arrangement that benefits us both."

"We've done our share of business in the past," he said. "I always found it to be pleasant, if expensive."

"You get what you pay for," Clare said, "or so I've heard say, usually from people with not enough money to get what they want. Luckily, that's not the case with you."

"It never has been," the Raven said.

"It's different this time," she said. "You need to know

that from the start. This is more like an expedition. It could lead us to a whole lot of nothing. But if there is a payoff, it could be bigger than anything you and I have ever seen."

"And are we still looking at Katherine as our main source?" he asked.

"Our *only* source," Clare said.

The Raven folded his arms across his chest and nodded. "How much will it cost to have you once again by my side?"

"Fifteen percent of market worth on anything she finds," Clare said without hesitation. "*Black* market worth."

"And if she comes away from all of it with empty hands?" he asked. "Or if the discovery made is not of the magnitude we expect? What's the price for your time should either of those events occur?"

"I'll let you off easy," Clare said, reaching for the coffeepot and refilling her cup. "Five hundred for each day. Plus expenses, of course."

"I will agree to all of your terms on one condition," the Raven said. "It's a simple one, really, and one I require from most anyone I do business with, especially at an elevated level of anticipated profit."

"We've done business in the past," she said, somewhat taken aback by both the request and the change of tone in the Raven's voice. "I don't recall any conditions."

"This one's different," he said. "It requires a greater degree of trust on my part. Therefore, I need an additional incentive in place and won't move forward until I have such an assurance."

"Let's hear it, then," Clare said.

The Raven walked toward her, reached for the coffee cup and rested it back on the tray. He then cradled her face with his hands, holding her gently, their eyes locked, thin lips inches from her right ear. "If you betray me," he whispered, "I will slice you into small pieces and feed you to the creatures in the river below. You have my word."

He brought Clare even closer to his side and placed a cold kiss on her warm lips. "Now, tell me all you know," he said.

CHAPTER 17

SANTA CROCE IS ONE OF THE LARGEST AND most beautiful of all the Franciscan churches standing today. Work on the marble façade, begun in 1294, was finally completed in 1443, though the neo-Gothic campanile was not added until well into the nineteenth century. The monks who ran the church in those early years were both pious in spirit and astute, and their shrewdest moneymaking venture was, at its core, as simple as the lives they led: In exchange for a considerable financial contribution, which the monks used to support the church and themselves, they would guarantee any benefactor a final resting place within the very walls of the sacred hall. It was a bargain many of the Renaissance giants found difficult to resist, which helps explain why the tombs of Dante, Machiavelli, Rossini, Galileo, and the Divine One himself, Michelangelo, line both sides of the church.

Michelangelo had intended to be buried in Rome and for the sculpture of the Pieta to mark his tomb. But three years prior to his death he had a change of heart, and asked that his body be laid to rest in Florence. His tomb is a nondescript and uninspiring marble design. Initially, a number of Michelangelo's associates, led by Daniele da Volterra, suggested using the statue of Victory as the funeral monument. It seemed to be a consensus choice until Giorgio Vasari, Michelangelo's friend and advisor, stepped into the discussion. He successfully argued that since the Divine One had never fought in a war or even worn a uniform, a statue dedicated to battle would be a poor choice. He then set upon designing the tomb that rests there today, complete with a bust chiseled by Battista Lorenzi and surrounded by the three symbols of painting, sculpture, and architecture. The final work was, according to Professor Edwards, "not a work that would have earned Michelangelo's stamp of approval. But then again," he liked to say, "he had little say in the matter."

KATE AND MARCO stood about ten feet away from Michelangelo's tomb, staring up at the large marble work, tourists milling about them on all sides. Despite the cool air filling the spacious hall, Marco's shirt and face were tinged with sweat and his breath came heavy and in spurts.

"You worry too much," Kate said, doing her best to reassure her frightened friend. "No one saw us go in or come out. And if anyone had heard us either tearing down a part of the wall or putting it back together, don't you think he would have rushed into the corridor?"

"I suppose," Marco said.

"What we *do* need to worry about is how to get the Angels out of the corridor, and then, once we manage that, where we can put them where no one else will find them," she said. "The first part sounds just about impossible, and the second could be even harder."

"Why move them at all?" Marco asked. "They seem perfectly safe right where they are. If our goal is not to let anyone know we've found them, then I would think the best way to accomplish that is to leave them alone."

"It won't take them very long to figure out we were in the corridor," Kate said. "We hid our tracks pretty well and put the wall back together as best we could, but it's not exactly the way we found it, which means we need to move the Angels out of there before someone else does."

"I have no idea how to do something like that," Marco said. "I'm an art student, not a cat burglar."

Kate turned away from Michelangelo's tomb and looked at him. "I need to protect the Angels," she said. "I know you're frightened, and I am, too. But we're not alone in this, or at least we won't be for very long. There will be people along to help us soon, a couple of days away at the most."

"If that's true, why don't we just wait until they arrive?" he asked.

"I wish we could," she said, "but I don't think we have that kind of time."

Kate glanced over Marco's shoulder, toward the entrance to Santa Croce, and caught a glimpse of the two men standing in the shade of the thick, ornate door. They were both young, thin, and dressed in casual tourist attire, their appearance and mannerisms designed to avoid attention and detection; just two more curious onlookers among the hundreds walking the halls of the grand church. The occasional furtive glances in her direction from the taller of the two were enough to cause her concern, but it was the way they both walked—slow, choppy steps, made in a tight and semicircular pattern—that gave off an air of indifference that was rare inside the walls of Santa Croce. She turned away from the men and looked at Marco.

"What's wrong?" he asked, quick to catch the apprehension on her face.

"Let's walk toward the back of the church," she told him. "Don't turn around and don't act any differently than you were five minutes ago."

"Five minutes ago I was frightened," Marco said. "Now I'm terrified."

Kate turned and slid her right hand under his left arm.

They moved away from Michelangelo's tomb and eased past Dante's much larger and more ominous final resting place, not bothering to turn around.

"Are you being careful?" Marco asked. "Or do you know for certain that we are being followed?"

"I don't know," Kate said, quickening her pace, pushing him along with her. "It's probably just my imagination. I guess seeing the Angels kicked it into high gear."

"Who is it exactly you think we might be running from?" he asked.

"If I'm wrong, then we're trying to flee from two graduate students from England," she said.

"And if you're not?"

"Two men neither one of us would want to be caught alone with," Kate said.

They neared the hall leading into the gardens, slices of bright sunlight guiding them toward the opening, a cluster of children staring up at the iron-railed walkways that encircled the top tier of the church. Kate picked up the pace and navigated her way around the children, each wearing a bright yellow T-shirt, blue shorts, and designer clone sneakers.

"There won't be as many people in the gardens," she said.

"Is that a good thing?" Marco asked.

"It is if we want to know if we're being followed," she said, pushing them both toward the entrance into the silent gardens of Santa Croce.

"What will they want from us?" Marco asked.

Kate could tell both by the sound of his voice and his body language that she was exhausting him. She knew she was very close to losing him as a companion and a friend and that not even the thrill of the discovery of the Angels would be enough to convince him to stay by her side. It would not be the first time she would lose a friend to her exuberant curiosity and her obsession with lost or missing works of art. She had not yet mastered the delicate balance that was often needed between maintaining a valued friendship and the nurturing of a compulsion she clearly relished. If she were forced to choose between the two, she would always come down on the side that chased the study of art, a quest she felt nourished her link to her parents. She could let a friendship fade, but would hold onto her parents for as long as she could.

"They will want to know what we know," she finally told Marco, "and to see what we've seen."

"And if we refuse?" he asked. "What will they do then? And please don't joke. I would like a truthful answer. Not something silly like they might kill us."

She glanced to her left, watching an elderly woman reach over and light a votive candle to a statue of the Blessed Mother, mouthing the words to a prayer. Then she looked to her right and saw a small group of Japanese tourists, always quick to pose, cameras ever at the ready, smiling before the large marble tomb of yet another Renaissance legend, Rossini. Then she looked out toward the garden, the brick and mortar overhead shielded from the blazing sun by stones set centuries earlier, the quiet of one of Florence's most magical sights now only minutes away from having a day of peace brought to a brutal end.

CHAPTER 18

EDWARDS STOOD UNDER A CONCRETE ARCHWAY leading to the tarmac of the small runway, a heavy wind and rain pounding at his clothing, soaking through his jacket and coating his face. He had his back to the black private jet, fueled and prepped for takeoff, waiting for the heavy storm clouds to pass as they marked their journey slowly up the East Coast. It was late afternoon but the rain and the overcast sky had turned the day into midnight black. Edwards stared out at the rain landing with a steady beat on the parched pavement, gazing past the low rumbling jet engines toward the dark void of the horizon. He didn't turn when he heard heavy footsteps approach from his left, keeping his eyes steady and his body tension-free.

"Why the rush?" the approaching man asked in a voice hardened by too many years of heavy smoking. "Weather report says all this will blow away in under three hours, maybe less. It's always better to fly into a clear sky than an angry one."

"I don't mind the rain," Edwards said, still staring off into the distance. "As a matter of fact, I prefer it. I've always felt safer traveling in bad conditions. I'm not sure why."

"I made the necessary arrangements as soon as I got your call," the man said, stepping up alongside Edwards. "Everything you need will be there waiting once you get to New York. And I also booked a two-night stay at your regular hotel under your travel name."

Edwards glanced over and nodded. "I'll only need one night," he said. "Just long enough to pick up what I'll need in Florence and to meet with Banyon."

"Banyon?" the man said, not bothering to disguise his surprise at hearing the name. "I thought the Society had severed its ties with him, especially after the last escapade."

"We can never sever our ties with men like Banyon," Edwards said. "You should know that by now, Russell. Academically? Financially? We can compete on any level with any group out there. But our battles are not just fought in libraries and on field research. Sometimes we need to get our hands dirty."

"I never think of men like Banyon as being on our side," Russell said.

"He is not a card-carrying member, okay," Edwards said. "But if the price we pay him outweighs what the competition has on the table, he will be a most valuable asset. And he won't be the only one we'll call on for help. I have a feeling we'll need as many men like Banyon as we can afford."

"Are you concerned she has yet to make contact?" Russell asked.

"She's being careful," Edwards said. "I warned Kate that there would be eyes on her while she was in Florence, not all of them friendly. She has a secure cell line that she uses under normal circumstances, but she was also given a list of names of Society members who can help her reach me without anyone else knowing. But she would only venture in that direction if she found something worth everyone's attention, and the fact I haven't heard from her in two days tells me that's indeed what has happened."

"We could just pull her out of there," Russell said.

"Get her to safe ground, see if she did indeed find anything worth a second look and send a team in to retrieve it."

"I've thought of that," Edwards said.

"And you decided against it."

Edwards nodded. "Kate will one day be in charge of the Society," he said, "and part of her job will be to confront risks and dangers on a regular basis. I need to find out—we all need to find out—if she is up to such demands."

"We're in place to provide as much help as she might need," Russell said. "But we've been outflanked by the Raven before. He is much better chasing down people than he is recovering art. If she has found something of value, he will do anything to retrieve it."

Edwards glanced at the dark clouds and closed his eyes for several seconds. He had long dreaded the arrival of this moment, despite the many years he had devoted in preparation for it. He had made use of the large sums of money at his disposal through the foundation to provide Kate with the best academic training available. Fearing the extreme dangers she might one day confront, he had tried to further insulate her from harm through the study of martial arts, archery, and advanced courses in weapons and tactics. When time allowed, he would take the classes along with Kate, helping him keep his instincts sharp while also providing him with more time with the young woman he had come to think of as his little sister as much as his ward.

And he had introduced her to men like Russell Cody, a dedicated twenty-year member of the Society who was its respected and somewhat irreplaceable director of security. Russell had taken a long and violent path prior to his time with the group, hired out as a mercenary in a handful of wars that led to a three-year spin in CIA counterintelligence before coming to the attention of the

Society. He took to the group's cause from the start and had rid them of many an enemy, eagerly working alongside a small army of esteemed academics, curators, and art hunters. He taught the mysteries of his trade to all who were willing to listen and obey, and he, in turn, absorbed as much as he could about the vast and unknown world of missing and stolen art and antiquities. It was a perfect match, one that suited both sides of the equation. And while Russell was loyal and protective to all members of the Society, there was no one he cared more about and devoted more attention to than Kate.

Let me put it to you this way, he once told Edwards. *Someone does her harm or attempts to hurt her in any way, they will have to deal with me.*

"Kate can handle herself," Edwards said now, his voice firm. "We've all made sure of that."

"Still, I would feel a lot better if we reduced her risk factor," Russell said. "The Raven's hired hands won't be difficult for us to spot. There's no harm taking out a few of them and giving the kid a more open field."

"Hold steady for now," Edwards said. "If this works out the way I hope, it's going to be our one chance to take them *all* out. To be rid of the Raven and his Immortals once and for all."

"In that case, Professor," Russell said, putting out a hand and giving his friend the closest he could get to a smile, "you have yourself a safe flight and a productive meeting with Banyon. I'll be there when you get to Florence, and I hope our girl finds what she's after."

Edwards shook Russell's hand and then grabbed for the leather satchel by his feet. "I hope we all do," he said.

CHAPTER 19

KATE AND MARCO SPRINTED DOWN A NARROW street, the two men from the church fast on them. They made a sharp right at the corner, Kate scraping her right knee against the side of a stone wall at the turn, and ran up a street dotted with parked scooters and vendors selling designer knockoffs. Marco was slightly ahead of Kate, his legs burning from the steep incline, short of breath and stamina. Kate turned to check on the two men closing in on her and tripped over the broken edge of a cobblestone, sprawling, hands spread wide, to the ground.

The thin man with the tan came to a quick stop, leaned down, wrapped a hand around her right arm and lifted Kate to her feet. He caught the frightened look in her eyes and nodded. "Just relax," he said, barely winded from the exhausting run, "and you'll make it through okay."

The second man, his skin much paler and his body not nearly in the same condition, stopped next to them, hands resting on his knees, fighting to catch his breath. "Let the other one go," he gasped. "She's the only one we need."

Marco slowed when he saw Kate fall. He hesitated for a brief second and then turned and ran back down the hill in her direction.

"Marco, don't," Kate said to him, watching him

come toward her and her captors. "Keep running. They won't chase you."

He walked up to Kate and the two thin men. "Are you okay?" he asked her.

Kate nodded, her arm still held by the man with the tan.

"Well, now that we're all together again," the man said, "let's go somewhere quieter where we can talk this out."

Kate glanced at Marco. "Why did you come back?" she whispered.

"For you," he said.

KATE SAT ON a stone bench, her back to a cold brick wall, the tan man still keeping a tight grip around her right arm. Across the path, facing a manicured lawn dotted with large pine trees, Marco was held in place by the second man.

"It's very simple, little girl," the tan man said, his brown eyes stripped of life and emotion, not bothering to hide his British accent. "Tell me what you found, and where, and we will let you and your friend loose."

Kate took a deep breath and glanced down at her hands. There were plenty of reasons for her to be frightened: Both men seemed intent on getting the information they were sent to retrieve, and they didn't appear concerned as to how they went about it. She also knew that in spite of Marco's brave front, he would eventually answer any question posed to him if he believed the threat against either one of them was real. Yet despite all apparent danger, she was relatively composed, her initial wave of fear slowly subsiding. And for that, she knew she owed Professor Edwards a debt of gratitude.

But she also knew there had to be a more complex reason to explain her demeanor than the words of wisdom passed to her by Edwards. Her reaction to situations others might find potentially dangerous had always, from her youngest years, bordered on the serene. It seemed an almost automatic response on her part to keep her emotions under control regardless of place or situation, an intuitive knack for finding comfort where others would succumb to fear.

"And if I don't tell you anything," she said to the man clutching her arm, "what happens then? Are you going to kill us?"

The man stared at her a moment and then leaned closer, his breath heavy with the odor of peppermint. "The most horrible acts can be accomplished in broad daylight and in total silence," he said, arching his brown eyebrows.

"Maybe," Kate said, glaring back. "But you're not that kind of man. Neither is your friend over there. We both know that."

"You have a lot of nerve, college girl," the man said, his anger rising. "I should just snap your neck and be done with you."

"If that's what you want to do, there really isn't much I can do to stop you," she said. She knew she was now waist deep into unchartered waters. "But, if you kill me, you leave without *any* information, and that won't make the man who pays you too happy."

"We still have your friend," the man said, tossing out his last card. "He sees you go down, he will talk."

"I know," Kate said. "I would, too, if I were in his place. But does he know what I know? Can he point you toward whatever it is you think I found? There are many ways this can end up going wrong for you."

The man eased the grip on her arm and leaned forward. He had quickly given weight to her words. "Sounds like you've covered every possible angle," he said. "Not leaving me much room here. But I bet you have an answer worked out for me on that, too."

"You're the master criminal," Kate said. "You decide."

"Decisions like that are well above my pay grade," the thin man said.

The second man strolled over, Marco nervously in tow. "Are we anywhere yet?" he asked, not bothering to hide his annoyance.

"We seem to be at an impasse," the first man said. "She won't talk, and I don't want to kill her. So, Ed, unless you have a quick solution, I suggest you drag your ass back where it was and wait."

"I'd have no problem killing either one," Ed said. "Just give the nod."

"How much do either of you know about art?" Kate asked, giving Marco a reassuring glance. "I don't mean knowing a Monet from a Picasso. I mean having an idea of what a portrait or a piece of sculpture is worth, financially."

"Not a clue," Ed said. "And I speak for both me and Phillip here in that regard. I just know what tailing you and finding out what you know or what you don't is worth to our boss."

"What's your point?" Phillip asked Kate.

"It's just a thought," she said. "And much of it depends on how loyal you are to the man who sent you after us."

"We're loyal to the wallet," Phillip said.

"In that case," Kate said with a smile, "I'm your girl. The man who sent you after us pays well. That's a fact. But while you may not know much about art, you must know about the group that stands behind me. And if you know that, you'll know how much more they'll pay to keep me alive."

"What are you saying?" Marco asked. "Are you thinking of having them *help* us?"

"Does he come with the package?" Ed asked.

"Don't worry," Kate said. "You'll get used to him."

"I doubt that," Ed said.

"So what's your deal?" Phillip asked. "And what if it isn't as sweet as the one we already have?"

"You know the answer to that," Kate said, "or you wouldn't have taken it this far."

Phillip looked at Ed and waited until he saw the other man give a nod and pull his hand away from Marco. He then turned back to Kate. "Where to now?" he asked.

"Into the piazza," Kate said. "I need a gelato. I'm certain Marco does as well."

"There's no need to concern yourselves with me," Marco said. "I don't wish to be a bother."

"Shut up," Ed said.

"There better be a plan to go along with that gelato," Phillip said.

"Only one way to find out," Kate said.

She stood, reached for Marco and put an arm under his before starting a slow walk leading down the gravel path out of the gardens, the two thin men in tow, heads down, hands jammed inside the pockets of their tailored slacks.

"I pray you know what you're doing," Marco whispered.

"Me, too," Kate said.

CHAPTER 20

THE STOUT WOMAN STANDING BEHIND THE jewelry counter was fifty-six years old, with long strands of gray hair and a sunny face distinguished by a thin four-inch scar just above her right eye. She had been living in Florence since the morning of August 16, 1982, the day she wed a tailor named Mario Branchi, who owned a small shop next to the money exchange across from the Ponte Vecchio. The marriage lasted less than a year and produced no children and much unhappiness for each of them. She was looking for a sense of adventure she had sought since early childhood, while Mario was merely seeking a level of security that had been sorely lacking in his life. She had a passion for fine arts and quality design; he thought himself a modern man locked within the limits of a medieval city. So, Mario and his bride, Josephine Maria Collins, let common sense take hold of them and decided to bring an end to what they viewed as a failed union. And out of a marriage in ruins, a friendship, now in its third decade, grew and blossomed.

"We didn't allow it to turn ugly," the Chicago-born Josie once told an old friend. "Instead, we kept alive what it was we both liked about each other and let it flow from there. Sometimes—in fact more times than any of us care to admit—a good friendship is worth more than a good marriage. You can count on a good friend to risk all he has for you. I don't know if you can say the same about the person next to you in bed. At least I know I can't."

In the spring of 1988, with money she inherited from an aunt back home combined with a loan from Mario, Josie opened a high-end art supply shop two storefronts down from Harry's Bar on the banks of the Arno River. The shop, which featured leather-bound sketch pads, monogrammed stationery, and parchment in assorted hues, was named Vittoria's, after the Italian historical figure Josie most admired.

Signora Vittoria Colonna.

The shop was an instant success, catering to a stream of regular customers, primarily art students from the university, local painters, designers in need of quality supplies, and American tourists looking for that perfect gift. In the middle of her second year running the shop, Josie renovated a back room and turned it into a place where artists both young and old could sit and discuss their works or gossip about the failures or success of others. It didn't take long for word to spread through the streets of Florence that Vittoria's was the place to be for anyone with dried paint lodged under his fingernails. The shop became a meeting and greeting ground, friendships and feuds were begun, and love affairs—both casual and long-lasting—were born, with Josie holding court at the center of it all.

It was also the shop that served as the Florence headquarters for the Vittoria Society.

Josie had first heard about the group in passing during a late night session at a back table in her salon. She found the idea of an organization dedicated to the retrieval of lost and stolen artifacts in order to return them to their proper owners inspiring, and quietly went about learning as much as she could about the group. It took her two years before she made the leap from interested bystander to full-fledged member, working through a friend to arrange a meeting with a Society liaison who then put her in the same room with Professor Edwards.

Josie was taken with the professor's passion for both his teaching and the lofty goals of the Society; goals she felt were noble in the attempt and dangerous in the achievement. She was also intrigued by the dark-haired, doe-eyed girl who sat quietly by his side, waiting for her cup of hot cocoa to cool, listening intently to their discussion. It seemed clear to Josie, even during that first eventful meeting, that one day in the not distant future, the demands and burdens of the Society would rest squarely on the shoulders of young Kate Westcott.

In short order, Josie became another valued member of the Society.

Both her home and the shop were now a safe haven for members of all stripes who arrived in Florence to work on a wide range of assignments, all of which required discretion. Josie showed no qualms about venturing into dangerous terrain, and as her reputation grew, so too did the peril of her endeavors. She could be counted on to hide a painting worth millions on the open market, often placing the work in plain sight of customers, framed in glass, hanging in the center of her shop, palmed off as yet another inexpensive copy of a masterpiece. She counted among her circle of street friends an array of gifted forgers, men and women with the talent to coat over a great work with a similar one of their own without fear of damaging the original. She had a solid network of buyers and sellers on both the open and black markets. And she could depend on her platoon of café regulars to supply her with daily doses of street gossip and museum and gallery goings-on.

Josie thrived in such a challenging and active environment, finding fulfillment in the work she did by day and satisfaction in her adventurous second life.

So it did not surprise her when she saw Kate Westcott

and a young man enter her shop just as the sun was setting on yet another beautiful Florence day. She had not seen Kate since that first meeting with Professor Edwards, but recognized her as soon as she stepped into the store, the sharp angles of waning daylight blending with the impending shadows of evening. The magnetic eyes that had first caught her attention, the calm yet confident manner in which Kate walked, the ease with which she quickly embraced her surroundings, were all there, highlighted even more now that the child had been transformed into a woman.

"I was just about to pour myself a cup of espresso," Josie said in English, the rhythms of her Chicago accent still vibrant. "I could just as easily pour out two more. You can drink them as you browse. I should warn you, though, my coffee is served hot, strong, and bitter. If you're not up to it, just say the word."

"Sounds perfect," Kate said. "Thank you."

"Save your thanks for when I do something helpful," Josie said with a wave of her right hand. "The truth is, I could use the company. It's been too quiet in here the last two, three days. Not sure why exactly, but it happens sometimes. You would think after all the years working this place I would get used to the pace, but my mother always said I was Chicago-stubborn, and I suppose there's a lot more truth to that than I would care to admit."

Josie poured out three cups of espresso and handed one each to Kate and Marco. She left her cup on the side counter next to the stove and looked over at the two students. "Your hands are too clean, so I'm ruling out art supplies, and you can get much cheaper posters to hang on your walls from the merchants by Neptune's fountain. And not very many students can afford the type of sketchbooks I sell. That limits you to notebooks and pens, and as you can see for yourselves, I have a wide variety of those to offer, if that's what you need."

Kate took a long, slow sip of the hot coffee and gave Josie a warm smile. "A friend told me how good your coffee is, and he wasn't wrong," she told the older woman. "But he seldom is, at least not around me."

"If your friend told you about my coffee, then he must have told you about me," Josie said.

Kate nodded. "He speaks of you often," she said, "and always with fondness. He told me you are one of his most trusted friends, and that I should come see you if I'm ever in need."

Josie finished her coffee in two long gulps and rested the empty cup in the middle of a bronze sink. She reached into a cookie jar and pulled out a long brown-filtered cigarette and a thin blue butane lighter. "We all have our vices," she said, clutching the cigarette between her teeth and lighting it with a quick flick of the lighter. "Hope you don't mind."

"It's your smoke," Marco said, "but it goes into our lungs. I mean no disrespect, of course."

Josie tossed him a look that was part bemusement and part distaste. "Is he always this annoying or is he just nervous?" she asked, her eyes on Marco, her question directed at Kate.

"A little bit of both," Kate said. "But don't worry. Marco's easy to warm to."

Kate's kind words caught Marco off guard, and he felt his face warm.

"Is he involved with you or just tagging along to keep you company?" Josie asked.

"We're not dating, if that's what you're asking," Kate said.

"I wasn't," Josie answered with a shrug, taking a deep drag off her cigarette.

"I came to see you because I need help," Kate said.

"Fair enough," Josie said, dropping the remnants of her cigarette into the bottom of her coffee cup. "What is it you think I can do for you?"

Kate glanced at Marco and then back to Josie. "Professor Edwards told me you helped him out of a number of very delicate situations, and that you were one of his—"

Josie put a hand on Kate's right shoulder, her fingers gently squeezing the soft flesh under the thin white shirt. "What is it you want me to do, child?" she asked, her voice easing toward tender.

"Break the law," Kate said.

CHAPTER 21

IT HAD BEEN THREE FULL DAYS TO THE HOUR since the discovery of the Midnight Angels, and Kate was flat on her stomach, hands braced against a hardwood floor, her eyes adjusting to the flickering shadows that swept over the tiny room. She glanced to her left and gave Marco a reassuring look, doing her best to silently calm his visible fears. She rested the heels of her feet against the base of an old wooden desk and began to run her fingers along the whitewashed floor, looking for the loose planks Josie had assured her would be there.

Marco's right hand reached for hers and he held it tight, his fingers clutched around her wrist. "I will only ask this one final time," he whispered.

Kate turned toward him, rested her other hand on top of his and gave him a calming smile. "I already know the question, Marco," she said, her words spoken softly in the near darkness of the room.

"And?"

"And yes, I'm sure," Kate said. "As sure as I've ever been about anything in my life. We are doing the right thing and we're doing it for the right reasons."

Marco nodded. "I believe you," he said. "I have no idea why, but I'm starting to think you know exactly what you're doing."

She patted his hand and nodded, then slowly eased her hold. "Help me find the loose planks. Josie said they would be no more than fifteen feet from the front right leg of the desk."

Marco slithered a few inches forward and tapped at the floorboards at his side. "These first two I can pretty much lift out," he said. "I might need a small knife or something like a letter opener for some of the others."

Kate reached into a rear pocket of her jeans and eased out a thin black penknife. "This should be good enough to get it done," she said, slipping the edge of the blade against the side of one of the floorboards. "Once I lift it, you grab it and slide it free. We'll need to clear away at least ten, maybe twelve boards to give ourselves room."

"And what about the layer that rests between the boards and the ceiling below?" he asked. "What if it isn't as easy to break through as Josie suggested?"

"It's a good plan, Marco," Kate said, digging into a second floorboard. "Josie did her part. Now we just have to make sure we do ours."

"How much time do we have until the next guard shift?"

"Twenty minutes, if they're right on the clock," she said. "That should be good enough for us to get the floorboards lifted and pencil sketch where we plan to punch out the hole in the Sheetrock."

"Then we wait for ten minutes before we break through," Marco said. "I know you already knew that. I just wanted you to know I remembered it as well. I hate that you might think of me as a coward."

Kate paused and looked away from the floorboards. "I would never think that," she said. "In fact, it's just the opposite. You need to be very brave and very trusting to even attempt what we are about to do."

"And don't forget to include foolish in there as well," he said, managing a nervous smile. "It often goes hand in hand with bravery and trust. Love, too, I suppose. But only if you happen to be a romantic."

"And are you?" she asked.

"I like to think so," he said, struggling now to find the words. "I like to think we both are."

Marco wished he could tell her, let Kate know how he felt, what was in his heart, that he cared for her not just as a friend but as something more. Much more. But he had never had such feelings toward any woman before, none that were this strong, that drew him in this close. And until he knew for sure how she felt about him, he feared venturing any further than he already had.

"We've come this far," Kate said, "let's not get caught now."

Marco stared at her for several seconds and then nodded as he quietly rested the discarded floorboards up against a side of the thick, mahogany desk that dominated the small room. He could feel the thin lines of sweat running down the center of his back, cool to the touch, his fingers and palms clammy as they reached out and grabbed the loose slabs of wood. And he could taste the fear, coating his tongue thick as a fresh dab of paint, his mind racing with the doubts that had filled his head since he first embarked on his dangerous journey with Kate.

He had no way of knowing if the noise they were making, as slight as it was, could be heard in the silence that engulfed the small room just above the sealed-off portion of the Vasari Corridor, less than a dozen feet separating the two of them from the resting place of the Midnight Angels. He wondered what it would feel like to be caught, dragged away by the authorities, forced to explain to unknown faces the reasons why they were attempting to steal a treasure that had been left hidden for these many centuries.

Resting a final plank against the desk, Marco glanced out the small window above his head, a full moon filling the late night sky above Florence. He took a deep breath and realized he was, as of this moment, no longer an art student working toward a master's degree and a teaching position at a prestigious school.

He was now a thief.

THE YOUNG MAN and the older woman stood in the shadows of the Ponte Vecchio, the rough tide of the Arno River echoing through the empty streets.

"Is the van in place?" the woman asked.

"Yes, Josie," the young man said, "parked just a few meters away, outside the towing zone, as you requested. And at this hour, it should take the driver no more than five minutes to get to his destination, even at reduced speed."

"And was the inside of the van properly padded?" Josie asked. "It doesn't help anyone if the product gets damaged in transport."

"Safe enough for a newborn," the young man said. "Moving them out was never the problem. *Getting* them out is what most concerns me."

"They'll make it," Josie said, lighting a fresh brown cigarette, her face briefly glowing from the flame. "They've got the guts and the plan. All they need is a little luck."

"Why'd you let them go in alone?" the young man asked. "Or go in at all, for that matter? We could have found a more experienced team."

"It's their find, Peter," Josie said, blowing a thin line of smoke skyward. "It belongs to them. They're the ones who should bring it out. It's how I want it to go, and how Edwards wants it done as well. The fewer hands on this, the better it's going to be for all concerned. There's going to be more than enough to keep us occupied once word of the discovery leaks."

"You think they're the real deal?" Peter asked. "We've gone down this road a few times in the past, thinking we made a rare find, only to come away with nothing to show for our trouble."

"We've had some solid finds these past few years," Josie said, glancing down the dark and empty street. "That Caravaggio we found buried near the Duomo two years ago was nothing to brush aside."

"That's not the point I'm trying to make," he said.

"Then what is?"

"We have yet to find a piece of work that was only rumored to exist," Peter said. "Anything the Society has recovered up until now could be documented in some archive in the basement of a museum somewhere. This would be the first truly lost work we've ever come across. I find it sort of stunning that, if it is indeed the case, a university student managed to do what a worldwide network of academics and art experts never could."

"That's because she's not just any university student," Josie said. "That young lady up in that office is herself as rare a find as anything you, me, or any other member of the Society could ever hope to unearth. If anyone can bring in a lost work, she's the one."

"She's better than Professor Edwards?" Peter asked.

"She will be, soon enough. Even Edwards would admit to that."

Peter glanced at his watch, pressing a tiny button that lit up the small screen in a greenish hue. "With a bit of luck, they should have cleared the Sheetrock away by now. They should be standing in the room with the find. If they had done anything to alert the security details either inside or out, we would have heard it."

"They will still need to get the Angels up through the opening and into the office," Josie said. "Which means we need to depend on the boy as much as we do on Kate. And he's still the one element in this equation unknown to us all."

"I can still get someone in there if you need it," Peter said. "A member of my team lives a few streets from here, just above the Ferragamo store. He can be inside in a little more than fifteen minutes, probably less."

Josie mulled it over for a few seconds and then shook her head. "Let's stay with the plan. No cause to make any changes."

"At least not until we hear the alarm bells go off," Peter said.

He leaned over and kissed Josie gently on her left cheek, lifted the thin collar on his brown leather jacket and stepped out onto the cobblestone street of the Ponte Vecchio.

"If that happens," he said, "you won't need to guess where I'll be."

Josie let out a smile and gave Peter a quick wave. "In the middle of the smoke," she said.

KATE STOOD ALONGSIDE one of the three Midnight Angels, her fingers gently tracing its lines. Marco looked down from the small office above, a flashlight focused on Kate and the Angels.

"These were the ones Michelangelo believed would be his greatest achievement," she said, still whispering, her voice echoing off the cold stone walls. "The ones that would seal his legend."

"Most scholars don't even think they exist," Marco said. "They say the works are nothing more than a myth."

Kate looked up at him and smiled. "Well, we can both see how right they were on that," she said.

"Do you think we'll ever find out who has been hiding them all these years?" he asked. "And why?"

"We'll start to get an idea once they are discovered missing," she said. "You eliminate the people chasing these pieces solely for their value and those who simply want to possess. The ones who are left will be able to provide some answers."

"You better start lifting them up to me," Marco said. "We still have plenty of time before the next shift swings this way, but the sooner we are out of here, the better."

"Remember to grab each one under the wings and ease them up through the slot," Kate said. "They're lighter than they look, but also more delicate. Whoever served as their guardian went to a great deal of trouble to keep them in near perfect condition all these years. Let's not ruin all that in just one night."

"In that case, make sure you catch them if they slip out of my hands," Marco said.

Kate lifted the first Angel, wrapping her arms around its waist, her feet planted firmly on a stone ledge, allowing her better balance and stronger traction as she gently eased the twenty-five-pound statue up toward Marco's outstretched arms. He had his ankles braced around the base of the desk for support and waited until the Angel was up high enough for him to get a firm grip. "Don't let go until I tell you," he said. "And even then, stay close enough to grab it in case it does slip."

"Glide him up slowly," Kate instructed. "Don't get up to your knees until the head is through the opening."

Marco wrapped his arms around the Angel's wingspan and then froze.

Kate caught the movement of his eyes and his concerned frown. "What's wrong?" she asked.

"A light just circled the walls of the room," he said. "I think it came from the street below."

"It could be a guard working the perimeter of the building," Kate said, struggling to keep her grip on the Angel, her arms and wrists starting to ache from the weight.

"What if it's not?" Marco asked, his hands, holding the Angel's wings, now trembling.

"Then we're in serious trouble," Kate said, trying to maintain her confident demeanor, but fully aware of the implications they would face if caught.

She had been taught, by both Professor Edwards and a handful of his acolytes, that fear was one of the few human emotions that could be confronted and defeated. She never argued with their theory, it all sounded so plausible sitting inside the safety well of a classroom, surrounded by the benign rituals of academic life. But now, in the middle of a silent night, her arms wrapped around a sculpted Angel hidden for centuries from the public eye, standing behind a secret wall of a sealed-off corridor, the fear she once thought so easy to manipulate felt as real to her as the cold sweat that ran down her chest and back. She found breathing to be a chore and wished she could control the aggressive pounding against her chest. She knew she had to keep control of the situation, and for perhaps the first time in her adult life, wasn't sure how to accomplish such a feat.

Marco's tugging on the Angel brought her quickly back to the task at hand. "I'll get this first one up," he said, "and then I'll go and take a look around. I didn't hear any footsteps coming our way, so I think we're still okay. But we would both feel better if I knew that for sure. Will you be all right?"

Kate took a few deep breaths, her fingers and arms starting to tingle, and looked up at him. "Just don't leave me alone down here too long," she managed to say.

"I won't leave you, don't worry," Marco said. "What kind of a man would I be if I were to do such a thing?"

"A smart one," she said, watching as he eased the first of the three Angels through the opening and then disappeared from sight.

CHAPTER 22

EDWARDS STARED OUT THE WINDOW OF THE private Gulf stream jet as it made its way across the choppy waves of an aggressive Atlantic Ocean. He was a good three hours into the flight and sat at an oval desk filled with open notebooks and legal pads marked with an extensive series of notes and designs. He poured himself a fresh cup of coffee from a silver serving pot and drank it down in three long gulps. He was drinking far too much coffee lately and he could feel its effects, from the occasional series of heart palpitations to the nervous tension. He made a silent promise that once this particular mission was complete and he had managed to survive it, he would once again return to the strict health regimen he had followed for most of his adult years. But now was not the time to fret over set routines and rigid schedules. It was, instead, the most important and the most challenging moment the Vittoria Society had faced—a golden opportunity to bring to light a centuries-old work that had previously existed only in the rumor mills of academic circles, combined with the chance to finally eliminate a man whose name and status had haunted Edwards for decades. He and the Raven had danced around one another for far too long. The moment was near for one of them to emerge from the shadows of their secret worlds and lay claim to victory.

And for that to happen, he felt sure one of them needed to die.

Edwards rested his head against the thick brown leather and closed his eyes. He was too exhilarated to sleep, and instead allowed his mind to wander to Kate. His visions ran on an endless loop—the young girl tossing her first karate kick toward the ceiling of a dojo, visits to countless museums in too many cities to remember, the long talks and the longer walks, listening to her speak with passion about Michelangelo and hearing in her words the voice of her mother and the clear thinking of her father. And now he pictured her in Florence, about to unearth a work that had only been discussed in private clubs and university lecture halls or at five-course dinner tables, and he wondered if she was truly prepared to handle the task at hand. Had he trained her well enough? And if not, would his presence and the full strength of the Society be enough to counter the assault he expected to be launched by the forces of the Raven?

Edwards knew the risks were great and the challenge the toughest he would ever face. He understood the consequences of the actions he would soon undertake, and didn't dare estimate the number of people who might perish in the pursuit of three chiseled pieces of stone. And he had no doubt that Kate could easily be one of the casualties of the battle that loomed so close at hand. He would do all he could to prevent such a calamity, but he had been through enough such battles to know that once wedged into a fight, anything was possible and almost none of it for the good. He had sworn his love and devotion to Kate, but had given his allegiance to the Society.

He also wondered if such risks were worth it. Had he betrayed his core beliefs in order to bring the Society to the point where it rested on an equal footing with the Raven and his Immortals? Was a rare discovery worth the loss of a life, and not just any life, but potentially that of the one person he loved more than any other? He had taken the Society to heights no one ever imagined it would achieve, but at what cost? And how much different was he, really, than the man he so wanted to bring down, a man once considered a friend and now his most lethal enemy?

Ironically, it had been Kate's parents who always preached that there should be no one person bigger than the Society. Little could they have predicted that one day that very theory would threaten their only child.

"Don't mean to disturb you," a woman's soft voice said, shaking Edwards back to the moment. "Just wanted to check to see if there was anything else you needed me to do before landing."

"Please," he said, "take a seat and let's see if we've covered every base."

Edwards watched as the woman he estimated was only a few years older than Kate eased into a plush leather seat on the other side of the oval table. She was wearing a tight-fitting pantsuit over a toned upper body and shapely legs. Her long, thick brown hair partially hid one side of a thin face highlighted by sparkling blue eyes. She held a felt-tip pen in her right hand and rested a yellow legal pad on her lap.

"The pilot tells me we're making excellent time," she said in a voice that proudly revealed her Boston roots. "We should be landing about forty minutes earlier than planned."

"This hour of the night, doesn't surprise me," Edwards said. "You're Rita, right?"

She nodded and smiled. "Yes," she said. "Sorry, I should have reintroduced myself. It was such a rush back there during takeoff."

"No, it's me," Edwards said. "I've always been bad with names. If you haven't been dead at least three hundred years, don't expect me to remember anything at all about you."

"Your motorcycle will be waiting for you on the tarmac, as you requested," Rita said. "And your bags will be waiting for you at the hotel."

"You checked me in under another name?" he asked.

"Yes, Professor," Rita said. "And there is a new passport in your carry-on bag to match the name. You'll also find a white envelope in there with five thousand euros, all in fives, tens, and twenties. And a fully loaded nine millimeter along with two additional ammo packs."

"Has anyone been made aware of my arrival?" he asked.

"We've kept a tight lid on that," she said. "Those who know stateside are your most trusted aides, and no one in Italy has been informed. Since it's not an anticipated visit, I think we can keep it that way for as long as necessary."

"I'll settle for one day's head start," Edwards said, reaching over to pour a fresh cup of coffee. "That's the best I can hope for, regardless of all the precautions that have been taken."

"Will that leave you with enough time to finish what you plan to do?" Rita asked.

"Not really, no," Edwards said. "But I'm grateful for any advantage you were able to secure. The rest will be up to me."

"We could send out an alert to a few of our aides in Florence," she said. "A little help might buy you some more time."

"I'll find them if I run into any trouble I can't handle," he said. "Or, as is more often the case, they'll find me. But I think, initially, that I can be much more effective working in the shadows. The time for fireworks will arrive soon enough. No sense striking the match."

"Okay," Rita said, poised to stand and return to her station at the rear of the private jet. "I won't be far if you need anything."

Edwards reached out a hand and held Rita in her place. "How long have you been part of the Society?" he asked.

"It will be four years this October," she said, apparently thrown off by the question. "I was recruited a month or thereabouts after I finished college."

"Why do you think you were sought out?" Edwards asked.

"I'm not really sure, to be honest," Rita said. "I had an art history degree, but that's grown into an area of study second only to the always useless English major. And I was about to start work at a museum in Denver. Perhaps the combination of those two arenas caught somebody's attention. Or maybe the Society was just short of its quota that particular month and needed to fill a space."

Edwards sat back, nodded and smiled. "Who recruited you?" he asked.

"A friend of one of my professors," she said. "He told me his name was Charles Agee, but somehow I never quite believed that to be true. He told me a bit about the Society, its goals and past achievements, doing his best to make it sound as glamorous as possible without really saying much about the group at all."

"But clearly he was successful," Edwards said.

"I wasn't a difficult sell," Rita said. "Mr. Agee pointed out the many opportunities that would be available to me—tons of travel, the chance to pursue a master's degree with Society money, working with some of the most prominent names in the art world. Toss in a salary that was three times what I would have earned in Denver and I had my pen out and ready to sign."

"And were all those opportunities made available to you?" Edwards asked.

"More or less," she said. "I've traveled to places I would never have dreamed of being able to visit and have worked with terrific people and been allowed to learn as much from them as time would permit. I've also made a number of very close friends, people who will always be an important part of my life. So, in that sense, the payoff has been huge."

"And where is it that you feel the Society has failed you?"

"I never did get to work on that master's degree," Rita said. "I could never manage to get enough of a break in the travel schedule to squeeze in a normal class load. No one's fault, really. Just the way the job assignments happened to fall."

"So, then, there are no regrets?" he asked.

"Not to this point, no," she said.

"Does that mean you won't be taking that job with the French company that has been actively recruiting you?" Edwards asked.

The question caused her to redden and go on the defensive. "The public face of the Society is well-known and respected," she said. "So it's not unusual for employees of such a company to get job offers. I'm certain I haven't been the first member of the group to be approached by an outside firm."

"And what position were you offered?" he asked.

"It's a moot point," Rita said, comfortably regaining her composure, though still a bit unsure how the professor seemed to know so much about her off-hour activities. "I turned down the offer."

"Why?" Edwards asked. "It's a younger and, many would argue, much savvier group, with the potential for growth that we may not ever see. At least as far as the public image is concerned. They stand to offer you considerably more money and a great deal more challenges and responsibilities. And I would imagine you crave both."

"I'm happy with where I am and with what I have," Rita said.

Edwards sat back and stared out at the batch of clouds floating past him thick as throw pillows. "How much do you know?" he asked, not bothering to look her way.

"About what?" Rita asked, fully grasping the import of the question.

"About who we are and what we really do?" he asked, turning slowly to glance in her direction. "About that side of the Society the public *doesn't* see?"

She drew a long and slow breath, giving weight to her choice of words. "There are a lot of stories," she said, "but nothing that can be pointed to with any assurance. And I don't put much belief in what I hear, only in what I can prove, and so far I've found no proof."

"And how would you feel if those stories you heard about the group's other activities turned out to be true?" Edwards asked. "Would it bother you enough to leave the Society and jump at the first job offer?"

"No, not at all," Rita said. "The only thing it would do was make me wish I were a part of it. If the stories are indeed accurate—and I can only suppose there must be some level of truth to them—then not only would I be doing important work, but there would be a lot more excitement to my life."

"And we can always use a fresh dose of that," Edwards said. He turned away from her and slid a folder from under a pile of papers spread across the counter toward her. "Read this and study it. We have less than four hours until we land. That should give you plenty of time to familiarize yourself with all the details. I've already notified your field officer that you will be staying on in Florence, working as my assistant. Assuming, of course, that's agreeable to you."

"Yes, sir," Rita said, clutching the folder and beaming

a smile across to the professor. "It is totally agreeable to me."

"That's the answer I was expecting to hear," he said. "And you might finally get a taste of that excitement you've been craving all these years."

"May I ask, sir," Rita said, "why it is you decided on me?"

Edwards shook his head. "Your work and your abilities, including those we believe have yet to be tapped, caught the eye of many within the organization," he said. "Now it's time to see if we can put your talents to greater use."

Her upper body stiffened and she rested the folder on her lap. "Am I being promoted because of my father?" she asked.

Edwards stared back and shook his head. "You're being promoted *despite* your father," he said. "He has no bearing on the current situation."

"I didn't know until after I joined the Society that the two of you were close friends for many years," Rita said. "He never mentioned it to me, not once, not even after he found out I was recruited for the organization."

"Given the dual nature of the work we do, it is usually a good idea to keep certain matters as private as possible," Edwards said.

"Even from your own daughter?"

"Especially from family members," he said. "Such a disclosure can often lead down only one of two paths—betrayal or disappointment."

"Neither of those will ever sum up how I feel about him," Rita said. "The truth is, I'm very proud of my father and of the work he has done."

"I hope you never allow those feelings to change," Edwards said.

"I won't," she said, "no matter what happens."

"It sounds to me like we're set to go, then," he said.

"I'm assuming we'll be in Florence for a bit of time," Rita said.

"As long as it takes to complete the task," Edwards said. "Is that a problem?"

"I'm wearing the only clothes I have with me," she said with a sheepish smile.

"You'll have plenty of time to go shopping," Edwards said. "Buy what you need as you need it. When it comes to clothes, if it can't be found in Florence, well, then, it can't be found."

"I should get to work," Rita said, standing. "I'd like to be as ready as I can be before we touch down."

"Just one more piece of business before you head off," Edwards said. He leaned down and pulled up a leather duffel bag that had been resting against his left leg. He undid the straps, flipped it open, reached in and drew out a thick brown package. From where she stood, Rita could see her name neatly stenciled across the front. Edwards stood and handed her the package. "This now belongs to you," he told her.

"What is it?" she asked, taking the package, conscious of its heft.

"It's your father's gun," Edwards said.

CHAPTER 23

MARCO LEANED AWAY FROM THE WINDOW AND slowly crawled back to the open hole in the center of the room. "They're gone," he whispered down to Kate, "at least for the time being. So, if we're going to move these Angels out of here tonight, I suggest we start to do it now."

Kate peered up at him, her hands, arms, and face covered in white soot and dust, the two remaining Angels surrounding her in the misty darkness. "Is the van still in place?" she asked.

"I haven't checked on it in a while," Marco said. "But there would be no reason for the driver to have moved. He was nowhere near where the disturbance occurred."

"Let's get them up and out, then," she said, slowly regaining her confidence and composure that had briefly abandoned her during those long and agonizing moments while she waited for Marco to return. "If we do this right, we can be out of here with time to spare before the next shift makes its way in."

They worked together in silence, gently easing each Angel through the opening in the floor, careful not to scrape the sculptures against the floorboards. Once all the Angels were in place, neatly lined next to one another in the small office, Marco leaned down and helped Kate up through the hole. She peered into the darkness of what had for far too long been home to the Midnight Angels and slapped the soot off her hands and arms.

"Let's put the boards back in place," she said, "and then make our way to the van."

"How do you know the driver?" Marco asked, reaching for a wooden plank at his back.

"I don't know anything about him," she said. "Not even his name."

"You're kidding, right?"

Kate checked the time and peered out the small window down into the darkened street below. "I can't see the van from here," she said. "But he shouldn't be more than a quarter of a kilometer from the building."

"Or he could have driven off the second he heard the commotion out front," Marco said, as angry as he was nervous. "I can't believe you put all your trust in someone you don't even know."

"I trust the one who sent him to us," Kate said. "And we can discuss the merits of that once we're in the van, but for now, let's move the Angels out of here."

They carried them out one at a time—Kate holding the top half of the sculptures, Marco the bottom—using the rear staircase, careful to take each step, conscious of not brushing the marble up against the concrete walls. They eased their way down the narrow steps and came out through the wooden double doors at the back of the small office building situated just above the sealed-off portion of the Vasari Corridor. There, they stood under the soft glow of an overhead light, the streets around them quiet, evening shadows blanketing the city.

"Which way?" Marco asked.

Kate nudged her head forward. "Down the street behind you," she said. "The van should be parked next to a pastry shop and across from a leather goods store."

They walked the first Angel along the cobblestone steps, making sure their grips were firm and their footing solid, conscious of any sounds they heard. Neither one spoke, but each would occasionally cast a glance down at the Angel they carried, and even in the still of night and through shafts of light, they could see what a magnificent piece of work they held in their hands.

"It's perfect," Marco whispered. "I've never been this close to something this perfect."

"And now you're close to something even better," Kate said.

"What?" he asked, keeping his focus on the Angel and on taking each step with care.

"The van," Kate said.

She rested her end of the Angel on the ground with gentle movements, leaned over, grabbed the handle of the back door and swung it open. Inside, the van was equipped to transport nuclear waste—side and door panels and overhead space wrapped in cloth and covered in strips of bubble wrap, all resting under thick white sheets to place the Angels on, to protect them from any potential damage from the trip through the bumpy side streets. The overhead light inside the cabin was not on, and the driver didn't move from his post behind the wheel. He glanced in the rearview mirror and watched as the two students lifted the first of the three Angels into the van and then shut the doors. He leaned his head out the driver's side window and nodded to them, holding a thick white cloth in his left hand.

"Take this with you," he said. "And before you leave with the last Angel, wipe down any area in that office you may have touched, from doorknobs to furniture, anything that can leave behind a fingerprint."

Kate ran toward the driver, grabbed the cloth from his hand, then rushed back to Marco's side. "See," she said. "I told you he would be here waiting."

"I wasn't worried about whether he would be here," Marco said as they made their way back to get the second Angel. "I wondered whether we could trust him, and for the record, I still wonder."

"Wonder all you want," Kate said. "Just do it while we walk. We still have two more Angels to go."

They rushed back to the unlocked front door of the small office building and took the stairs up as quickly and as quietly as possible.

As they carried the second Angel around a corner of the stairwell, Marco scraped the base of the sculpture against a wall, sending a flurry of dust particles to the ground, his sweaty hands starting to lose their grip. "Do you need me to lay down my end?" Kate asked. "Wait for you to get a better grip?"

"No," Marco said. "I think I'm okay now."

"Don't think you're okay," she told him, the words coming out harsher than she'd intended. "Make sure."

Marco looked at her for several silent seconds, reaffirmed his grip on the statue, then nodded. "I'm sure," he said, taking a move down the next step.

Kate shook the hair away from her eyes and continued her march toward the waiting van.

MARCO CLOSED THE REAR door of the van, the three Midnight Angels safely tucked away inside. He brushed away some of the white dust covering his arms and shirt as he moved toward the side panel entrance. The street was as quiet as it was deserted, the evening mist embracing him.

"Did you clear away the prints?" the driver asked, not moving his head, his voice startling Marco as it echoed down the narrow confines.

"Yes," Kate said. "As much as we could."

"Get in then," the driver said, "and let's get out of here."

Marco reached for the door handle, to slide it open. The blow to the head, coming at him from out of the darkness, stunned him and sent him buckling to his knees. His vision blurred, his eyes tearing and twitching.

Kate turned to face the assailant, her right forearm catching a glancing shot off the pipe the man swung at her. He was thin and tall, decked out in black slacks, black zippered windbreaker, and black running shoes. With a wool cap jammed down on his forehead and the lack of light, his facial features remained hidden. He neither spoke nor even grunted.

Kate swung away from the van and brought the attacker closer toward her, standing now in the center of the street. He held the pipe above his head as if it were a large sword, his steady steps inching closer toward her. She lowered her head, avoided a hard swing of the pipe and landed a well-placed kick to the side of the man's rib cage. That stole some of his breath but quelled none of his determination.

She was the one who spied the driver, out of the van now, moving toward them like a ghost, gently stepping over Marco's prone and moaning body. She didn't see the long thin blade clutched in his right hand, not until it caught a glimmer of light and was well on its way toward the center of the attacker's back. The driver never touched the man, letting the blade do all his work, moving it steadily through bone and skin and nerve endings, until it slashed and burned past any artery that carried life. Then he eased the knife out and stood silent as he watched the man drop like a fallen tree, facedown, to the hard cobblestones.

Kate had not moved or dared even to take a breath as the deadly action unfolded. She stood in place, arms hanging loose at her sides, shaking with fear and repulsion. Marco was off to her right, still groaning and groggy, his head throbbing from the heavy hit he'd taken, his legs too weak to stand.

"Grab your friend and get in the van," the driver said, unshaken.

"What about him?" Kate managed to stammer, pointing a shaking finger at the body resting by her feet, a pool of dark blood spreading out from around his waist.

"He stays here," the driver said, turning toward the van. "And so will you and your friend unless you both get in the van now."

Kate managed a few unsteady steps toward Marco, reaching down for him, resting her fingers on the small of his neck. "We need to go," she whispered.

He looked up at her through a pair of blurry, tear-filled eyes. "What have we done?" he asked.

The driver started the van, and Kate could hear the shift in gears from neutral to first. She helped Marco to his feet and pulled open the side panel, holding him in place as she did. She eased him headfirst into the middle seat and waited as he leaned over and came to rest on his side. She then stepped into the van and slid the door closed, her eyes frozen on the man they were about to leave behind. A man murdered for three sculpted works, which to her, was for no reason at all. It was one thing to want to possess a great work. It was even acceptable to go to great lengths to acquire such works. It was, after all, what treasure hunters had done for centuries. But to kill for them or to die for them seemed to her to bring the world she was now so very much a part of up to new and much more dangerous levels. And she knew there could be no turning back once the journey down such a dark road began.

The van took off, engine churning, lights dimmed, down the dark strada, the Midnight Angels safely in the rear, rescued from the shuttered walls of a secret corridor, the first victim of their escape now lying dead on a quiet street.

CHAPTER 24

"There's been a breach," said Edwards, barely able to control his anger. He was standing in the middle of an empty street, across from the Excelsior Hotel, a light rain starting to fall about him. "I want to know how it happened."

"We were prepared for it," the man said. "There was no way we were going to leave the kids hanging on that street. We had our people in place, anticipating a move from somewhere. And when the guy popped, we had it handled."

"That's not the point," Edwards said. "We had a guy come at Kate with a damn pipe, Russell. No matter how many of our people we had on the ground, there was no way that should have happened."

"I get it, Richard," Russell said. "But look, as of last week, there were at least a dozen of the Raven's men in town, and who knows how many more have been brought in since. On top of that, this city is prime turf for art hunters, gallery thieves, curators looking for a find. There were maybe a hundred ways this might have leaked out, and not all of them could have been stopped by us."

"She could have been *killed,* Russell. To me, that's an entire universe removed from a simple security malfunction. On top of that, they didn't go and hire local, didn't bring in someone paid to simply scare her and her friend away. Which might have worked. Instead, they opted for brawn over brains and came within a flash of killing Kate."

"We have an ID on the contract," Russell said, nodding in silent agreement. "From what little we could gather on his background, he's not a player in the art world and I doubt that he had a clue what could have been in the van, or cared a whit about it even if he had. He's a thug, hired to scare and to harm."

"He may not have known what was going to be placed in that van," Edwards said, "but the one who hired him did. It doesn't surprise me that word found its way to the Raven. What does surprise me is the speed with which it happened. We need to find out who it is and what else he or she knows and has passed on, and we need to do it now."

"Do you trust the boy?" Russell asked. "Kate's friend?"

"Do you even need to ask?"

"I had him checked out early on, when he first came across Kate's radar," Russell said. "There was nothing there. This time, I'll have our guys poke a little deeper, see what we can turn up, if anything."

"He's a start," Edwards said, "but if he's a part of this, he's only a small piece. We need to get to the primary, and the sooner we do that, the better."

"I'll double the security around the area where the Angels have been hidden," Russell said. "And ramp up coverage on Kate as well."

"Hold off on that," Edwards said. "I don't want too much attention brought to the hiding spot, at least not yet. The Raven will be monitoring our moves, and he'll notice if we increase the number of our people in any one location."

"Well, as of this morning, not a peep out of the museum," Russell said. "It's as if the lift never happened."

"The museum might have been in the dark about the

Angels being in the corridor themselves," said Edwards. "Whoever hid the works did their best to keep a low profile. The Uffizi may know they're missing or they may not. Either way, they won't show their hand until they need to."

"Until I secure the breach, I'm going to put a hold on everything else we got working in the city," Russell said. "Is that okay with you?"

Edwards nodded. "As long as it doesn't take too long," he said. "We have to seal this up. Once word gets out, it might be too late to prevent a further betrayal."

"Who knows you're in the city?"

"Besides you and Rita?" Edwards asked. "No one. And if possible, I want it kept that way."

"How does she play into this?" Russell asked.

"Rita will have a role. I'm just not sure what that is yet."

"She won't be as good as her father," Russell said, "if that's what you're hoping."

"Don't be so quick to judge," Edwards said. "I'm willing to wager she might be better, in a totally different way. Not as brutal, but equally as effective."

"We'll know whether you're right on that soon enough," Russell said. "I have a feeling there's not going to be much in the way of downtime on this job."

"Are we set for tonight's meeting?" Edwards asked.

"Pretty much," Russell said. "I need to tighten one or two screws, but it's all perimeter detail, nothing crucial."

"Just to be safe, though, make sure you check out the people scheduled to come, even those we know well. No one is above suspicion. I don't want to be caught off guard twice in less than twenty-four hours."

"What about Kate?" Russell asked.

"What about her?"

"She still doesn't know you're in town, and she might

be a little rattled from what happened at the lift. Maybe she would welcome the sight of a friendly face."

"That will have to wait," Edwards said. "I'll connect with her when the time is right. For the moment, let's keep the focus on our inside problem. Who that person is and how close to us he or she is will affect Kate more than anyone. Her safety and the safety of the Midnight Angels cannot be sacrificed, whatever the cost."

"I should have some credible information in a few hours," Russell said. "We'll take some hard looks at anyone who might have reason to be unhappy with the Society and stands within the Raven's reach. This business always comes down to a question of easy money. I need to find out who in our group is most in need."

"Any chance we're dealing with more than one loose thread?" Edwards asked. "That there might be a rogue team within the Society?"

"There's always a risk of that, no matter how tight the organization," Russell said. "There is always the temptation to reach for a bigger cut. But we screen and vet our people for months before we even consider a first meeting. It might be possible for one or two bad seeds to filter in. But a whole splinter group? With all the checks and internals we have in place, I would give something like that the longest possible odds."

"It's happened before," Edwards said. "And, at the time, there was no one who was held in greater regard than the Raven."

"We have no one in the Society today who's even in the same league as the Raven," Russell said. "We learned a harsh lesson from his betrayal. No one has been allowed the access he had and the power he could wield. There was not one aspect of the business he didn't know about or have input into. That's the risk you run when you groom someone to succeed you."

"That's what happens when you groom the *wrong* someone," Edwards said.

"If there's a loose wire under our feet, rest assured, Richard, I will find out who it is," Russell said, "and I'll deal with it."

"Not right away," Edwards said. "We need to know who it is and who he is now working for, that part is abundantly clear. But we also need to keep the spy in our midst alive, at least for the run of this mission. He can be an important asset that we shouldn't be quick to dismiss."

"That will work once, maybe twice if we catch some luck," Russell said. "You can't expect it to go much further than that."

"All I need is just the once," Edwards said. "After that, our spy will have served his purpose and no longer be of any use to us or to the Raven."

"In that case, we might as well keep our hands completely clean," Russell said. "Leave it to the Raven to bring our traitor to a well-deserved death."

"You'll need to make one more phone call before we allow that to happen," Edwards said, "just to complete the picture."

Russell smiled. "Our police contacts will be notified."

"Don't go local," Edwards said. "They'll be looking to come in and simply make an arrest."

"But you want more," Russell said.

Edwards thought a moment, then nodded. "A lot more," he said.

CHAPTER 25

IT WAS A COOL SUNDAY MORNING, TWO DAYS after the Midnight Angels were lifted out of their hiding place, and the bells of Florence were clanging, the streets filled with citizens of all ages moving, willingly or not, toward the closest church and the start of high mass, the first step in what would be a leisurely day of food, drink, and family gatherings. It is a weekly ritual that helps frame the fabric of most any town, but it is especially true in Florence, a modern city that happily wraps itself in the warmth of its medieval traditions.

The past still resonates in Florence's present, no more strongly than early on a Sunday morning. The windows of the stone homes are opened wide during the spring and summer weeks or are slightly ajar in the colder months, allowing the smells of percolating sauces and grilling chickens or fresh-cut roasts crackling in warm ovens to wind their way down the ancient stone paths. Music mingles with the sounds of the street—children laughing; teenagers marching in hand-locked pairs, their voices rising as they make their way through the various squares that lead to the ornate church doors; clusters of tourists moving with the flow, some stopping to take pictures and buy gifts or a panino at the various stores and stalls catering to their desires, most just enjoying the vibrant pageantry—while old men in suits they have worn for years and elderly women in equally vintage outfits slowly lead the march toward the rows of straw chairs and wooden pews of high-ceilinged cathedrals to hear the soothing words of a religion they have embraced their entire lives.

Kate and Marco walked down a shadowed path in the beautiful gardens of the Giardino dei Semplici, the aroma of the flowers and foliage mixing sweetly with the thick scent of tomato sauce filtering down from the windows and doors of the surrounding homes. "Sunday has always been my favorite day," Marco said. "No matter how sad it makes me."

"Why does it make you sad?" Kate asked.

"Look around," he said. "What do you see? Families and friends heading off to church, walking as one, and after mass they will head back home to sit and enjoy a big meal. They will spend the day telling stories, watching football, napping, playing cards, going for long walks, maybe they'll even have an argument or a political discussion. But whatever they do, they will do it together."

"And you don't have that?"

"I did, but it was for too short a time," he said. "After my father died, it was never the same. And then when my mother remarried, it all changed, and not for the better. I'm not blaming anyone. It's just something that happened. But on days like today, I do miss it."

"I know how you feel," Kate said. "I wish I had more memories of my parents. I can go back and read the work they left behind, and Professor Edwards did his best to keep them alive for me through the stories he told, but it's not the same as having them there next to you, through good days and bad."

"How do you think they would feel about what we just did?" Marco asked. "Not so much the discovery. I would imagine they would have been thrilled about that. I mean the other part. You know, the two of us removing the Angels from their hidden place. Would they approve of that?"

Kate walked with her head down and stayed silent for several moments. The question was not one she expected, and it gave her pause. Her parents were renowned and respected art historians and probably would be quick to frown on what pretty much amounted to art theft. Still, they did believe that art deserved to be seen and not hidden away, that it belonged not to collectors who hoarded it but to the people for whom the works were originally intended.

"I don't know the answer to that, Marco," she finally said. "I suppose they would want a reasoned explanation as to why I decided to move them. And I think I would have to do a lot better than thinking it was simply the right thing to do."

"Do you believe that?" he asked. "That it was the right thing to do?"

"I wouldn't have moved them if I didn't," Kate said.

"And what happens now?"

"We wait," she said, "but not for long. Soon, there will be people here with a lot more experience than we have, and it will be up to them to determine the next move."

They stepped out of the *giardino* and turned right onto Via Gino Capponi, blending easily with the relaxed mix of locals and tourists. "Do you think we should go back to class tomorrow?" Marco asked.

"I don't see why not," Kate said. "There's no reason to bring ourselves any undo attention. Besides, as far as anyone knows, we haven't done anything that would require us *not* to go to class."

"A man was *murdered,* Kate," Marco said. "And we were there, we witnessed it and then we drove away. We may not have killed him, but if we hadn't gone through with what we did, I doubt very much that man would be dead today."

"He would have killed you and me and not given it a second's thought," she said, surprised at the edge in her voice. "And if that driver hadn't been there, that's exactly what he would have done."

"And that makes it all right?" Marco asked.

"No, not all right," Kate said, "never all right. But it does make it necessary. I may not like that it does. In fact, the very idea makes my stomach churn and my head spin, but it is part of the reality we now face. We found a work of Michelangelo's that had been only a rumor for centuries. There will be people who will pay any amount of money to get their hands on such a discovery, and many of them won't stop to wonder what they have to do in order for that to happen."

"I don't want to see another man die," Marco said. "Not for any reason, not even for Michelangelo."

"Then you should step away now," she said, her tone devoid of anger or resentment. "Before you are in so deep it will be impossible to get away."

"I think it is too late for that, Kate," he said. "The time for me to have walked away might have been *before* the Angels were stolen and most certainly *before* a man whose name I don't even know was killed in front of me."

Kate turned and faced him, her eyes focused, her right hand shaking off a nervous tremor. "Then we both need to learn to deal with it," she said. "I don't like what happened any more than you do. But all I can do, all I need to do, is make sure the Angels find their way into safe hands."

"Regardless of the cost," Marco said.

"Yes, Marco," Kate said, surprised at how outwardly confident she sounded while feeling so shaken on the inside. "Regardless of the cost."

"Then what makes us so different from those who will come looking for the Angels?" he asked. "What makes our mission, whatever that is in your mind, so much worthier from the one these others might believe in with equal passion?"

"I'm sorry you even feel the need to ask me such a question," she said.

"And I hate having to ask," Marco said, "but it's something I need to know, especially now, after what happened back on that street. How far would you go, Kate, to retrieve a lost piece of art?"

"I'm very sorry that man died," she said, "even though he wouldn't have felt the same way had he left us behind. But had that happened, he would have taken the Angels and quite possibly put them in the wrong hands, to be sold on the black market for the highest sum they could acquire."

"And what would be so horrible about that?" Marco asked.

"For one thing, a work of art doesn't belong on the black market, its whereabouts hidden from view. That would betray its very purpose."

"Which is?"

"Look, I know this may not make much sense, but it's what I believe in with my heart and soul," Kate said. "Art, especially the great works, belong to the people for whom they were created. Michelangelo's David belongs here, in Florence, not anywhere else. Especially not in some private collection or in the hands of groups determined to cash it in and walk away. It is a gift, given by the artist to the people. No amount of money should be allowed to change that."

"Does the same hold true for bloodshed?" Marco asked.

"Not to me," Kate said. "But I'm not in this alone. I have no idea where this will lead and how violent it will get. I never expected to see even one body fall. That's not an image I will ever be able to erase. I would like to be able to say that will be the one and only time it will happen, but that would be more a wish than a fact."

"And what if it comes down to just you?" he asked. "What if all that stands between you and the art is someone who wants it as much as you do, for what you believe are all the wrong reasons. What happens then, Kate? Would you yourself be able to kill someone to save a work of art?"

She stopped and looked around the crowded street, the laughter and chatter blending together, the cool breeze bringing a chill. This was a conversation she had been anticipating for a few years now, only she expected it to be a philosophical discussion with Professor Edwards, held in the safety of their home library, and not one based on real events on a packed street in Florence on a busy Sunday morning with a student she had known for less than a month. She turned to Marco, brushing aside a few strands of hair from her eyes. "I don't have an answer for you," she said in a low tone.

The two continued their morning walk in silence, Kate's right hand resting comfortably in the crook of Marco's left arm.

CHAPTER 26

ROME

ANTONIO RUMORE RESTED THE PHONE INTO its cradle and rolled back in his office chair, his leg brushing against an overnight bag. He checked the time and took a casual look around the noisy, crowded room, then back at his desktop, a disheveled blend of notes, case files, and crime-scene photos. He then glanced at the detective sitting across from him, a dark-haired, petite woman in her early thirties who had just been transferred to the squad from a Venice homicide unit.

"Anna, we get any hits out of Florence in the last three days?" he asked.

The woman shook her head. "You looking for something in particular?"

"Not sure, yet," Rumore said. "I got a heads-up call that something is working there, but I'm not sure what. I was hoping maybe something popped across one of your report sheets."

"Pretty quiet all around, actually," Anna said. "A few small-time jobs here and there and a foiled attempt at a museum in Milan. Other than that, not a blip."

"Wouldn't be like my source to call and point me in a direction just to waste my time," Rumore said. "For him to have his nose in the air, something must be going on. I'm going to take a few days in Florence to check for myself."

"Are you asking me along?" she said. "Or just thinking out loud?"

"A little bit of both," Rumore said. "How long have you been with us now? Two weeks?"

"Monday will be the start of my fourth week."

"And have you had any out-of-office assignments yet?"

"Does going out to lunch with Vincenzo and Arthuro count as an out-of-office?" Anna asked.

Rumore smiled. "Look, even if we go there and come up empty, which will probably be the case," he said, "it might be a good experience for you and a chance to get out of the office. Get to know your way up there, make a few contacts, while I snoop around and see if my source's information pans out. If you would rather not go, it's not a problem."

"You usually work alone," Anna said. "I don't want to get in your way."

"You won't," he said. "Besides, I read up on your case files. You were a very active and accurate homicide detective working in a city where it is very easy to dispose of a body. My guess is you have less than twenty-four hours before the deceased either floats out to sea or is mutilated by the grinders under the canals."

"Closer to eighteen, and that's pretty much reaching the maximum time allotted," Anna said.

"Well, both my tipster and my stomach tell me if what is going on in Florence is even close to being true, then we're going to be looking for more than a work of art," Rumore said. "We're going to be ankle-deep in bodies. If that's the case, it would be a great benefit to have someone around who can break down blood splatter as easily as marble chips."

"And what if we come up empty?"

"We'll have a few days in Florence and not be stuck

here," Rumore said. "To me, it sounds like a winning situation."

"Is your source pointing you in any particular direction?"

Rumore quickly surveyed the room, then looked back at her. "Nothing concrete, but enough to make me think a big score has found its way into the city."

"When would we leave?" she asked.

"If you agree to go, we could be on the road in less than twenty minutes," Rumore said. "I can make it thirty if you need to gather a few things together."

"They told me you're not one to waste time," she said.

"Especially when there's so little of it to waste," he said. "So, are you in or would you rather stick around here and wait until Vincenzo and Arthuro get up the nerve to ask you out to lunch again?"

"Your car or mine?" Anna asked as she pushed her chair back, then stood and walked to the edge of his desk. Rumore nodded, taking note of the tight black skirt and expensive lavender blouse topped by a jacket whose designer he couldn't quite nail. The low-heeled pumps, he knew, were Ferragamo, and the two-tier earrings hanging just above her neckline were purchased at one of the high-end jewelers on the Via Venuto. Her tan was dark and deep and her body was toned.

"What do you have?" he asked.

"I've got an Alfa Romeo, two-door convertible," she said, adding a smile. "After four years working in Venice and going to most every crime scene by boat, I got used to moving fast. This was as close as I could get to a speedboat."

"A very expensive speedboat," Rumore said, "especially for a cop."

"I'm the only cop in the family," Anna said, "the rest are all in banking and commerce, my father the most successful of the bunch. On top of that, I'm an only child. It's not hard to get special treatment under those conditions."

"As impressive as it would be, we'll take my car," he said. "I need to bring along some equipment, and the trunk space of an Alfa leaves a lot to be desired. You can make use of it once we're up there. I have a cousin who owns a motorcycle dealership in Florence, and he allows me to tool around the city, testing out the latest models."

"Fair enough," Anna said. "I'll go and get clearance for the trip and then meet you out in front."

"Don't you want to know what car I drive?" Rumore asked.

"A Benz," she said. "Four-door sedan. It's the car of choice of the Rome Art Squad, or so I've guessed from the number of them parked in the downstairs garage."

Rumore folded his arms across his chest and nodded. "Don't worry about the clearance. That's already been taken care of. I called Albertini before you got in. He fully supports the trip and you joining me on it."

"How did you know I would agree to go?"

"I didn't," he said, "which is why I asked Albertini to have orders ready in the event you passed on the offer. I didn't think they would be necessary since I didn't figure you for the type of cop who relished sitting around an office."

Rumore stood, swung his suit jacket across one shoulder and moved down a narrow aisle, heading for the elevator bank at the rear of the large squad room. "We'll grab an early dinner once we get to Florence," he said, craning his neck toward Anna. "Mama is not only a great cook, she's a great source of information. If something is brewing out on those streets, she'll know about it."

"Mama?" Anna said, following close behind. "I was told you were from Naples."

"I am," Rumore said. "The mama in Florence considers every single man in Italy her son, especially the ones with hearty appetites. The same, I would wager, is true of the young women who walk through her restaurant's front door. So, be prepared to eat and drink well, be loved to death, and, if you're very lucky and pay close attention, you'll also leave there knowing a lot more than you did when you walked in."

He stopped at the elevators and pressed the Down button, turned and waited as Anna approached.

"Are you expecting trouble?" she asked.

"I always expect trouble," he said. "It's my nature."

"You have an idea who we might be up against?"

"I won't know for sure until we get to Florence," Rumore said, "but there's been large-scale movement from two major groups in the last week or so, all moving north. And I doubt they're heading there for a taste of Mama's pasta with artichokes."

"What do you think they're after?"

"Criminals are all the same and all want the same, whether trolling the art world or selling nickel bags on street corners," Rumore said. "The only difference between the two is a diploma and various degrees of sophistication. If they end up with other people's money in their pockets, they have fulfilled their mission. And it doesn't matter to them how many have to die for that to happen. It all boils down to cashing in on the score."

"I can tell already you're going to be a fun time," Anna said.

"You have no idea," Rumore said.

He waited as the elevator door slid open, watched Anna walk in and then followed, pressing hard on the button for the main floor. "Okay if I ask you one more question?" she asked, the cable wires squeaking loud enough to cause alarm.

Rumore nodded as he breezed through the messages on his BlackBerry. "Do it quick," he said, "before the elevator cords snap."

"Is any of this personal?" she asked. "I mean, the action that may be going on in Florence?"

Rumore put away his BlackBerry and waited as the elevator door to the main floor opened. He held it in place for Anna and glanced at her as she moved past him. "It's *all* personal," he said, "no matter the city, no matter the crime. It's *all* personal."

CHAPTER 27

FLORENCE

THE RAVEN LOOKED AT THE WEARY YOUNG MAN standing against the water-stained brick wall, the hard rushing currents of the Arno only a few feet away. The man was shirtless, his jeans torn and soiled; blood oozed out of his mouth and from a gash just above his right eye.

"You have failed me, Vittorio," the Raven said. "That we both know. What I don't know is whether you did so out of incompetence or greed."

"I would not betray you, sir," Vittorio stammered. "I would never do that."

"So you failed me through negligence and stupidity," the Raven said. "Am I supposed to derive some comfort from that sorry fact?"

"I didn't fail you," Vittorio said. "I hired the best available man I could find on such short notice and I followed your express wish to have as few people involved in the plan as possible."

The Raven walked along the wet ground, thick patches of weeds and grass lining the wall and shoreline, the sounds of water rats scurrying about their nests blending in with the low rumble of the flowing river. "That man is now dead," he said, "and the police are seeking his killer, which may well lead them to you. To me. And as bad as all that sounds, it is not the worst part of our sorry tale, is it?"

Vittorio stared wide-eyed at the Raven and managed to shake his head.

"No, our little saga ends with neither of us knowing the whereabouts of the three Angels plucked out of the corridor under our very gaze by two college students," the Raven said, the anger in his voice unmistakable. "And I have myself to blame for such a sad ending since I was the one foolish enough to hire you to complete what I perceived to be a simple task."

"We knew they had a van," Vittorio said, "and had hired a driver. We were told the driver was local and not someone who wanted anything more than easy money for a late night getaway. No one figured he would step in the way he did."

"There is no 'we,' " the Raven said. "There is only you, and here is a question for you to ponder—why wasn't the driver handled first? He would have been, after all, a witness to a murder, and would have needed to be dealt with at some point, so why not make him disappear while the children were off collecting the Angels?"

Vittorio swallowed hard, aware no answer he could come up with would suffice. "I will find the Angels for you," he said, reaching out for the only lifeline he could imagine. "Allow me that one final chance. Please."

"Have you ever heard of lo squillo?" the Raven asked, ignoring the man's plea.

Vittorio's legs weakened and his hands clutched at the brick wall, his fingers scratching against the sharp edges, helping to steady a body that only wanted to surrender to fear. "Just rumors," he managed to blurt out. "Never knew anyone who ever saw one."

"They are truly fascinating creatures," the Raven said. "They are a hybrid, a mixture of water rat, eel, beaver, and God only knows what else. It took centuries for them to evolve into their present state where they live in the shallow depths of the Arno and along its shore. They are more than mere rumor. They are very real indeed, as many as five hundred of them living in the river behind us and under the dark edges of the shrubbery along the shore. You do believe me, don't you?"

"Yes," Vittorio said. "Yes, I believe you."

"I'm not so certain," the Raven said. "I sense doubt."

"I have no reason to doubt you," Vittorio said, "none at all."

"I have an idea," the Raven said, turning his attention to the flowing river at his back. "Why not go in and see for yourself? Test the waters and see if any of the squilli rise to the occasion? What do you say?"

"I'm not much of a swimmer," was all Vittorio could mutter.

"That shouldn't be a deterrent," the Raven said. "The current is so strong, even the best swimmer would be tossed about. And not being able to swim will be useful if you do happen upon a squillo, since they're very much like sharks and respond to movement rather than smell. But if they do happen to spot you, it would be best to remain as still as possible. They have very sharp front teeth and will look to wrap themselves around your lower limbs and then bite into the veins just below the back of your legs. And there they will stay until they have drained you of enough blood to satisfy their thirst."

"You can't do this," Vittorio said, no longer able to keep his composure, tears flowing freely down the sides of his face. "You can't."

"I could stand here and slice you to pieces myself, if that's your preference," the Raven said. "But you don't stand the slightest chance of survival if you choose that route. Going into the Arno, attracting little attention, letting the water take you as far as the current will allow, would seem to me to be the best available option. Other than the horrible pollutants you will swallow along the way, you might well survive the ordeal. That is, of course, unless one of the squillos manages to get a bite into you. That would, indeed, be a truly horrendous way to die. But I'll leave the final decision to you."

"I'll find the Angels for you," Vittorio begged. "I swear it."

"Oh, the Angels will be found," the Raven said. "It just won't be you who finds them."

Vittorio took quick looks to his left and right, the sun fading over the large shadow of the Duomo, and pushed himself away from the wall, standing on unsteady legs. The Raven came up behind him, moving with silent steps, and jolted him upright, gripping a hard hand around Vittorio's throat, cutting off his air passage. "I would prefer to see you go into the river alive," the Raven whispered. "But if you choose to float rather than attempt to swim, then I will do my best to accommodate you."

Vittorio nodded, a stream of saliva forming at the corners of his mouth, and struggled to get his words out. "I'll try to swim," he said.

"Wise choice," the Raven said. He released his grip and gently ushered the frightened young man toward the river's edge.

There, the Raven tossed Vittorio to the ground, watching him land on the soft dirt of the shoreline, the foamy brown water brushing over his arms and hands. "Hurry it along," he said. "The later it gets, the stronger the tide. If you hope to have any chance of survival, I would suggest you not fight the current and let it be your guide. Or perhaps you'll get lucky and a squillo will emerge and put you out of your misery."

Vittorio was sobbing loudly now as he entered the murky water. The Raven reached down, grabbed the young man's right ankle and held it in place. He pulled a switchblade out of the pocket of his dark brown jacket and snapped it open. He ran the sharp end of the knife across the lower end of Vittorio's right calf, watching a thin line of blood emerge. He then let go of the calf and allowed the young man to float off to an uncertain future.

"The squilli are more likely to show themselves if they smell blood," the Raven said as he snapped the blade back into its place.

He stood by the side of the Arno as the current swept Vittorio deeper into its center and closer to a painful encounter with a creature that only hours earlier had been nothing more than folklore. As soon as the young man was out of his line of sight, the Raven turned and walked slowly up the muddy banks of the Arno, back toward the center of the city.

CHAPTER 28

"YOU SHOULD REALLY GET THIS BICYCLE FIXED," Kate said, sitting uncomfortably on the thin handlebar just inches from the gears, careful not to brush against Marco's hands, his knees occasionally jamming against her legs and back.

"What's wrong with it?" Marco asked.

"The tires need air, for one thing," she said. "The gears could use some oil, and the chains are so rusty they look like they could snap any second. Other than that, you are good to go."

"Americans have zero appreciation for anything old," Marco said.

He enjoyed this time with Kate on his bike, and knew, despite her constant harping, that she felt the same way. She had put both his status as a student and possibly his life in serious danger with her actions, and while he remained apprehensive about their relationship and where it would ultimately lead, he did find himself attracted to her. What he dare not ask, what he feared to know, was whether she felt the same about him. He wasn't certain if he was merely a local friend she viewed as both good company and a trusted aide in her dangerous quest, or if there was a deeper meaning to her feelings.

When it came to women, Marco had often struggled with bouts of insecurity, conscious of his low standing within the clear class boundaries that remained strong but unspoken in Italian culture, and he didn't know if those borders extended across an ocean and impacted Americans in the same way. Most especially, Americans with Kate's academic and financial lineage, both of which he could not help but find daunting. Still, despite it all, he had developed strong feelings for her and knew he would be crushed to discover that those passions were not mutual. So, in typical Florentine fashion, he kept them bottled up, at least for the time being. But, deep in his heart, he realized that in a short span of weeks, he was, for the very first time, in love.

"You're flinging that accusation to a future Michelangelo scholar," Kate said. "*I* appreciate the old in art and design and sculpture and architecture. I'm just not overly fond of it when it comes to rusty old bikes, especially when we're traveling across cobblestone streets."

"It's still faster than walking," Marco said.

"Not by much," Kate said.

They were circling Piazza Santo Spirito, a quiet square crammed with the workshops of seasoned furniture restorers and dominated by Il Palazzo Guadagi on the corner abutting Via Mazzetta. Marco knew it was one of Kate's favorite spots in the city, and he glided around the piazza several times, allowing her multiple views of the sixteenth century structure, with its teardrop-shaped window etchings.

On the start of his fourth turn around the square, as he eased his bike closer to the statue gracing the center, he felt a strong pair of hands reach for the rear of his bike and bring it to a grinding halt. The short stop forced Kate to jump off the bar and tumble to the pavement, her hands and knees taking the brunt of the fall. Marco let the bike clatter to the street, then stood facing a man several years older, with thick arms hidden under a torn blue sweater and tight jeans. He had a stern face highlighted by a four-inch jagged scar that covered the center of his nose like a thin bandage.

"Where are they?" the man asked, his voice coated with a heavy British accent.

"Where are what?" Marco asked, casting a quick glance at Kate, watching as she slowly rose to her feet.

"I don't like bullshit," the man said. "I like answers."

"He doesn't know anything," Kate said, standing now on unsteady legs behind the man.

The man turned away from Marco and cast a sideways glance at her. "I figured as much," he said. "So know this. If you don't start spewing out some answers, your friend here will be the one feeling the pain. Get it? You talk or he bleeds."

Marco looked at Kate and slowly shook his head. She caught the look but kept her attention focused on the man with his back to the statue. "You plan on doing that here? In a square filled with shops and people? Which village idiot sent you?"

"Smart-ass," the man snickered, "just as I was told. I'm holding to my words and trust me on this—I will cut your friend in half as fast as you can blink. He'll have bled out before any concerned citizen will know he's hurting."

Kate took a deep breath, saw the man's right hand curled into a half fist, cupping the thin edge of a long blade. She looked at Marco and knew he would not be able to escape from a professional's swift move. And then she took a furtive glance around the square, couples walking slowly by them, lost in their own conversations; shop owners finishing up the day's assigned work, eager to please the customers milling about their goods.

"I'll take you to them," she told the man.

"How far?"

"That depends on you," she said. "We'll have to bike slowly since you will be following us on foot, so I'm guessing about ten, maybe fifteen minutes."

The man smiled. "You think you'll be able to get

away from me on that rickety old bike?" he asked. "Is that your plan? I can throw my knife even better than I can swing it. If you make that your play, your friend will die."

"We won't try to escape," Kate said.

The man stood for several quiet moments, his right hand still curled over the blade, the heartbeat of the quaint square echoing on all sides. "Get on the bike, then," he finally said. "And bring me to the Angels."

Marco lifted his bike off its side, not exactly sure what Kate's real intent was, not fully believing she would simply hand over the Midnight Angels without putting up some fight or devising an escape route. He sat on the bike, peddled over toward Kate, and waited as she jumped onto the thin bar. She squeezed in between the gears and him, his arms awkwardly placed around her as he gripped the two handles. "Are you sure about this?" he whispered.

"Let's go," Kate said to both Marco and the man, who was standing by the bike, gripping a handlebar with his free hand. "Head down Via San Martino and take the second left."

"Keep it slow, simple, and smart," the man said, his eyes flashing threat.

"Just keep up with us," Kate said. "You found us in the square. You should be able to follow a bike through the streets."

"Especially this bike," Marco said.

They moved together in an uneasy formation down Via San Martino and through the narrow side streets branching off it, past open doorways to apartment buildings and small stores selling everything from leather-bound diaries to suits, fashionable evening wear, children's books and toys. Throughout the early portion of the ride, Kate kept her gaze forward, not speaking, pointing out the turns she wanted Marco to make, the route he should follow.

They were about six minutes into the ride, the side streets getting narrower, with few cars and even fewer people. Marco knew their location but was not at all sure of their destination. As he made a right onto Via Barbadori, he could only guess Kate was leading them back toward the Ponte Vecchio, though he was unclear why. He could tell she was tense, her fingers gripping the steering shaft as if they were on a high-speed motorcycle ride through the Italian countryside. And he knew she was scared, her silence a clear indication of the concern that weighed on her mind.

"How much longer?" the man asked, his voice giving Marco a jolt, breaking the quiet that had engulfed them.

"Any minute now," Kate said. "Make a right at the corner of Via de' Bardi at the start of the Ponte Vecchio."

"Are you sure?" Marco said in as low a voice as he could.

Kate moved her right hand off the handlebar and patted his right knee. "It'll be fine," she said. "Don't worry."

Marco eased the bike into a sharp turn around the low curb that brought them onto the wider paths of Via de' Bardi, street merchants working both ends, hawking their high-end knockoffs to tourists looking for on-the-cheap buys. "Pull up next to the tall guy selling the handbags," Kate said.

"And then?" the man asked, glancing up and down the active street.

"You'll get one step closer to the Angels," Kate said.

BANYON HELD A LEATHER wallet in his hand and nodded to the tall African standing with his back to the Arno. "How much?" he asked.

The young man spread the fingers of his left hand. "Five," he said, smiling. "Good price."

"It would be," Banyon said, "if I were holding real leather, but I'm not. Is it a fair price for a knockoff?"

"Three euros, then," the African man said.

"I'm not here to bargain," Banyon said. "I'll pay the five. I just wanted to be clear on what it is you're selling and I'm buying."

The African stared at him and nodded. "Five," he said, "for what you hold."

"You just closed a deal, my friend," Banyon said.

He handed the African a five-euro coin, then slipped the thin brown wallet into the front pocket of his cream-colored safari jacket and stepped onto the curb. Leaning over the low brick wall, he surveyed the luxury apartment buildings lining the other bank of the river. He marked the angles of the sun and the shade as they blended together and crisscrossed the Arno and onto the street at his back. He listened for the rumble of passing cars and scooters and took note that traffic was on the light side, especially for the time of day. There were a number of pedestrians on both sides of the street—some locals in a rush, others the usual assortment of tourists, folded maps in hand, not sure they were headed in the right direction but not too concerned about it if they weren't. He always found Florence to be one of the most relaxing cities to visit, the people who called it home clearly in love with their town. That low-key manner seemed also to affect the tourists, causing them to dial down their excitement and simply cherish the moments spent in the company of the masters in the museums, the churches they would venture into, and the unforgettable if overpriced Tuscan fare.

Banyon was always struck by the way Florence seemed to be a city of both the very young and the very old. It was almost as if middle age was a period spent in some other place. But more likely it was because the young and the elderly were those with the time and desire to be out and about, leaving the city's engines to be run by those hidden away in banks and office complexes. Whatever the reason, he found it a most pleasurable city to visit and one of the easiest to navigate, and he greeted an assignment in Florence with fondness. He was always eager to get here and slow to make his way back.

It was also one of the best places in the world, he believed, to kill someone.

The Florence police department was well-trained, but it was a small force and tended to gravitate toward the larger squares and main thoroughfares. As far as he could tell, in all the years he had worked his trade as the dark muscle of the Vittoria Society, there were few undercover officers walking the streets. And if there were any on duty, they would be in the neighborhoods where there was a possibility of terrorist sleeper cells. Florence didn't have a high-crime track record and muggings were rare, which to Banyon meant the police stationed throughout the city were mostly concerned with street traffic and any disruptions to normal patterns. They were not as skilled as a New York plainclothes or uniform cop might be in reading a person's body language, looking for either intent or the potential for malice, which made it all the easier for a professional, especially one as experienced as he was, to blend in with a crowd.

Turning away from the Arno, he spotted Kate and Marco rounding the corner on the young man's bike, the mark keeping pace with them, his occasional glances to the left and right the only signal that he was at all apprehensive. Banyon walked back a few feet from the tall African man, who was nestled between another merchant moving sweatshirts and T-shirts and a shuttered kiosk. The African ignored him, his eyes focused on the old bicycle slowly veering his way and the smile of the young woman astride the front bar.

Banyon walked toward the kiosk and waited, looking once again at the Arno as its heavy current moved downstream, pushing its way out toward higher waters. It was, he thought, the most polluted river in the world.

And, somehow, the most charming.

KATE CAUGHT SIGHT of the African and waved in his direction. She saw him leave his post, step in front of the large table covered with an array of leather goods and spread out his arms in welcome.

"What now?" the man walking alongside them asked.

"An old friend," Kate said.

She jumped from her seat on the bike and ran the several feet that separated her from the narrow sidewalk to greet the African with a tight hug. "Oh, Francis, you have no idea how happy I am to see you again," she whispered, her arms around his neck, feeling his strong hands on her back.

"It's been much too long," Francis said.

"How are Hanna and little Francis?" Kate asked. "He must be so grown by now. It's been years since I've seen either one."

Francis gently released his hold on Kate but held onto her right hand. "There will be much time for us all to catch up," he said.

"Let's get on with our business, shall we?" the British man said, moving close to Kate and Francis, his back to Marco, who still sat on his bike, legs stretched out.

Francis positioned himself between the intruder and Kate, shielding her with his back as he turned toward Marco. "That is a very old bicycle you have," Francis said. "It must be a gift from someone who loved you very much. There would be no other reason to keep it."

"It was my father's bike," Marco said.

"I guess you didn't hear me," the British man said, stepping closer to Francis. "I have business with your lady friend and you're in the way."

"I know your business," Francis said.

The man glared at him, the knife sliding slowly down his arm and into the palm of his right hand. "Get out of my way," he said.

"As you wish," Francis said, his body still shielding Kate, one foot on the curb, the other on the edge of the sidewalk, inches from the table filled with leather goods.

The man peered over Francis's right shoulder to look at Kate. "Bring this game to an end now," he snarled.

Kate shook her head.

"Not the answer you wanted, is it?" Francis said, flashing a wide smile.

The man swung the knife blade low and fast, his wrist at an angle, the aim meant to slice Francis from left to right. With a quick flick of his hand, Francis caught the man's wrist in midswing, then leaned forward to land a powerful head butt across his face, producing a violent gush of blood. Reaching out his other arm, Francis held the man, turning him away from the leather table toward the low brick wall between the Arno and the shuttered kiosk. The British man's head drooped and his eyes were glassy. Francis looked at him and said in a soothing voice, "The Angels are close enough for you to touch."

"With cold hands," Banyon said.

He stood next to Francis now and swung open the small wooden door leading into the darkened kiosk. Francis pushed the man into the entryway and then stepped aside, casting a quick look down the street to his right, noting that their actions had garnered little attention. He then looked at Kate. He held her eyes, controlling her fear, even as the three soft muffled shots sounded from Banyon's weapon, the British man falling down, head to one side, dead inside the stone silence of a shuttered kiosk.

Banyon locked the door to the kiosk, shouldered his weapon, walked past Francis and Kate and down the center of the street.

Marco stood frozen in place on his bicycle, having witnessed the entire bloody event. His front arms, locked onto the handlebars, were trembling, and his entire upper body shook. Kate had her hands cupped around her mouth, muzzling a scream. She didn't move as Francis walked toward her, lifting a leather shoulder bag off his table. "Take the bag and your friend and get away from here," he told her, his voice calm and steady.

"Did he have to die?" she managed to say.

"There was a time when our business was more like a chess match," Francis said. "Now, it has become a death match, with casualties on both sides. Don't ever lose sight of that."

"What about the Angels?" Kate asked.

"They are safe," Francis said, "at least for now."

"Where can we go?" she asked. "They know what we look like. It won't be long before someone else will be on us."

"When you are off this street, look inside the shoulder bag," he told her, gently leading her toward Marco and the bike. "You will find an address in there. It is a safe place that will allow you both to rest and get some food."

Kate draped the bag over her head and shoulder and reached up to kiss Francis on the cheek. She jumped on Marco's bike and waited. "It will be okay," she told him, her voice urging him to start pedaling.

"It will never again be okay," Marco said.

CHAPTER 29

"I STILL DON'T UNDERSTAND WHY YOU ARE here," Giovanni Saltieri said, "asking me all these silly questions about a robbery when we have had no robbery occur."

"You've been in this job how long now?" Clare Johnson asked. "About six, maybe seven years. That right?"

Saltieri nodded, tempted to reach for a fresh cigarette from the open pack of Lords resting on his desk next to an ornate letter opener. "It will be seven years this fall," he said.

"Your job includes responsibility for the Vasari Corridor, correct?" Clare asked.

"I am responsible for the entire Uffizi," Saltieri said, "and that would include the corridor."

"Can I ask a stupid question?"

"Ha," Saltieri said. "The ones you've asked so far have been plenty stupid."

Clare sat back and crossed her legs, her black skirt revealing plenty. "Why is part of the corridor sealed?" she asked.

Saltieri paused before answering. "It is being repaired," he said. "Once that work is completed, we will determine whether or not it should be reopened."

"Besides you, who has access to the sealed-off portion?"

"I can't answer that and I won't until you tell me where this line of questioning is headed," Saltieri said.

"I've agreed to meet with you because of the favors you have done for me in the past. But now this conversation is starting to cross into areas that should be of no interest to you."

They were sitting in Saltieri's third-floor office in the Uffizi, a large room highlighted by wall-to-ceiling portraits of counts and dukes from the glory days of Florence. His desk was large and imposing, making him appear shorter than he actually was and, in ways she could not explain, adding at least ten years to his age. As befit his position of director of Uffizi security, Saltieri was impeccably dressed and stylish in manner and tone.

"Look," Clare said, "you've known me long enough to know I don't like to waste time, mine or anyone else's. So for me to come up here and start asking about the sealed-off portion of a corridor no one—and I emphasize *no one*—is allowed to visit, there must be a good reason, wouldn't you agree?"

"Yes," Saltieri said, "except I have yet to hear it."

"You will, trust me," she said. "But before we go there, I need some more information to see if I'm even close to being on the right track with this. My instincts tell me I am. But I still don't have enough to wrap my hands around, and until I do, it's all just talk to me."

"Stay within the boundaries," Saltieri said, "and I will do my best to answer your questions. But I will be more than angry if you aren't as forthcoming with me. That's as fair a deal as I can offer."

"Do you keep any art in the sealed portion of the corridor?" Clare asked.

"Not as a rule," Saltieri said. "But that's not to say that, on occasion, when the need arises, we don't place pieces there."

"Are there any kept there on a permanent basis?"

Saltieri stared at her, smiled and slowly shook his

head. "Have you ever been in the sealed portion of the corridor?"

"My understanding is that no one is allowed access," Clare said, "other than you and people employed by you."

"Well, if you *had* ever been in there, you would know it is not the place to put a work of art, *any* work, without expecting it to be ruined," Saltieri said. "And you know me well enough to know I would never allow that."

Clare uncrossed her legs and leaned forward, placing her hands on Saltieri's desk. "Let's be clear," she said. "We both know what that corridor is used for, since we've both made money off it down the years. If I were looking to hide a work of art, especially a work that was only rumored to exist, that sealed corridor would be my first stop, and you would be the first man I would see."

"Is that what this is about?" Saltieri asked. "You have a painting you need to keep out of the public eye?"

"Not exactly," she said.

"Then *what,* exactly?" he asked.

"Were *you* keeping any work out of the public eye?" she asked. "And take a minute before you answer. I don't need to tell you how severe the legal ramifications are for such offenses, especially in this country. So you can sit back and talk to me and we will work out an arrangement that, as always, will be beneficial to us both. Or I'll leave here and speed-dial the Art Squad in Rome."

Saltieri pulled a Lord cigarette from the pack, jammed it into a corner of his mouth and lit it with a butane lighter he kept by the side of his phone. He took a long, slow drag and leaned back in his chair. "The works were hidden long before I stepped into this job," he said. "All I did was simply follow the dictates left to me by the gentleman who preceded me."

"Save the Good German bit," Clare said. "What's down there?"

"Have you ever heard mention of the Midnight Angels?" Saltieri asked.

"Sure," Clare said. "That rumor has been around since my father's time, even well before. There have been lots of stories about them, but far as I can tell, not by anyone who has ever seen them. It sounded like more myth than reality."

"They were commissioned by a secret benefactor of Michelangelo's shortly after he completed work on the David, which would have made him about twenty-seven years old at the time," Saltieri said. "The benefactor, long rumored to have been a member of the Medici inner circle, wanted a work that would serve as a masterful follow-up to the piece that had rapidly given rise to Michelangelo's legend. The seven Archangels, the guardians of the very gates themselves, chiseled in perfect form, was that follow-up work."

"Which Michelangelo either never completed or didn't even bother to start," she said. "At least, that's the extent of the stories I've heard."

"Only partly true," Saltieri said. "He never managed to complete the work, or at least no one so far has been able to prove that he did. But he did indeed begin it, working on it either full- or part-time for close to two years."

"How far did he get?"

"He completed three of the Angels, as far as anyone has been able to determine," Saltieri said. "Through the years, there has been a great deal of gossip in the art world, especially among the high-end collectors, that a fourth Angel does exist, but up to now there have never been any actual sightings. And if a work can't be seen, how then can it be thought to exist?"

"But you know three of the Midnight Angels exist?" Clare asked.

"And they are exactly as they were intended to be," Saltieri said, "a true example of a genius at work."

"How long have they been kept in the corridor?"

"From what I can gather, roughly fifteen, perhaps as many as twenty years," Saltieri said. "Prior to that, they had been hidden in Rome, in the basement of a private gallery near the Vatican. Before then, I don't know where they were kept, but I can imagine they were moved quite frequently."

"Is there a reason they were never made public?" Clare asked.

"Sometimes myth is of greater value to sustaining a legend than reality," Saltieri said. "The mere thought that such a work as the Midnight Angels might exist gave an added dimension to Michelangelo's already immense legacy. In many ways, keeping them out of the public eye further fueled the impression that they were not only real, but that they were his most inspired work."

"How much do you figure them to be worth?" she asked.

"If they were to be placed at auction, I would estimate they would fetch anywhere from $100 to $150 million each," he said. "On the open market, the price could very well triple, especially now with both the Russians and an array of terrorist groups eager to invest heavily in art."

"How much of that would find its way into your pockets?" Clare asked, knowing the intent of the question would sting.

"I think you've taken up enough of my time," Saltieri said, glaring across the desk. "Now, unless you have anything of consequence to add, I suggest we end our day as it began—as friends."

"I do have one more question," Clare said.

"Then ask it," he said.

"When was the last time you personally saw the Midnight Angels?"

"I'm not at liberty to give out information of that nature," Saltieri said. "That is Uffizi business as well as *my* business, and that's where it will stay."

"Fair enough," Clare said, standing and tossing the strands of a Prada bag over her right shoulder. "I need to get going, anyway. You were just my first stop. And I'll do my best to keep a lid on what was said between us."

Saltieri stood and walked around his desk, stepping onto the thick Oriental rug that lined the center of his office, and over toward Clare. "You never did say why you were in Florence," he said, gently placing a hand on the small of her back.

"That's because you never did ask," she said.

"I'm asking now."

"I'm working on a fresh case," Clare said.

"If I can be of any assistance, you know I'll be there for you if it's at all possible," Saltieri said. "Even though I must confess to complete ignorance. I haven't heard word one on a lift of any kind from any of the high-end museums, and that is the sort of information that usually finds its way to my desk quickly."

"It's a newborn," Clare said. "Not even the police are aware of it, so far as I can tell."

"So then, you came to see me on background?" he asked. "I wish you had made mention of that from the start. I wouldn't have been as resistant as I might have appeared."

Clare reached for the handle of the thick wooden door leading out into the foyer. "I would hardly consider you background," she said. "Not on this case."

Saltieri stiffened but held onto his calm demeanor. "Which makes me what, then?" he asked.

"You're either one of the primaries," Clare said, "or one of the targets."

The color drained from his face and the thin edges of his lower lip began to twitch. "The Midnight Angels?" he asked. "If that's what you're implying, you are way off base. It just isn't possible."

"They're in the wind," Clare said. "You don't need to believe me, you can check for yourself. Now, even though I have my doubts that you know much about what went down, there are going to be quite a few people looking in your direction. I can give some cover, if you think you'll need it. But I'm not in the business of giving away any help for free."

"How long can this be kept quiet?" Saltieri asked.

"Twenty-four hours more," she said. "Forty-eight if you're lucky."

"What can I do to help?"

"Take me to where the Midnight Angels were kept," she said. "I would like a look at the crime scene before the police do."

"And can I expect coverage from you in return?" Saltieri asked.

"Anyone can give you coverage," Clare said. "I'll go a big step further, but only if you help me. And only me."

"What's your offer?"

"I'll keep you alive," Clare said.

She turned away from Saltieri and walked into the foyer, the click of her pumps echoing across the marble floor as she made her way toward the back stairwell and out of the Uffizi.

CHAPTER 30

EDWARDS SIPPED A GLASS OF PINOT GRIGIO and watched as a trio of men in fishing outfits, ski hats, and thick rubber gloves lumbered through the front doors of the otherwise elegant restaurant, pushing three large hand trucks filled with the day's fresh catch. He was sitting alone in a corner table set for three, a large basket filled with bread sticks resting alongside a flower arrangement and a burning candle. He looked out across the expansive dining area, crowded with a comfortable mix of quiet couples and groups of friends. Edwards always looked forward to dinner at Fuor d'acqua, not only because it served the freshest and best fish in the city, but because it catered mostly to locals. He also found the locale, in the middle of Via Pisana in the oldest part of the city, to be a place that gave him room to breathe, allow him his quiet space and clear his mind while he feasted.

Edwards had been in Florence for only a few hours and already was feeling the burden of this latest mission. In the four-day span since Kate and Marco moved the Midnight Angels from their long-hidden crib, two men had been killed, a dozen new recruits were flown in by the Raven's crew, and he'd put in a request to Russell by way of Rita to double the presence of the Society within the city limits. And this was on top of the small army of freelance art hunters and thieves who regularly set foot in Florence hoping to latch onto a hot property. He also knew the temperature would rise the moment the police working the cases discovered links between the two dead men—and they would completely boil over when the museum finally decided to report the theft.

He was weary, and the battle had yet to begin.

This sensation of dread mixed uneasily with the need to step back and carefully weigh each move. He usually enjoyed the challenge that came with each new discovery—forced to outfight and outwit his opponents, get to the intended target before the police and the hunters, clear the work out of the danger zone and find it a proper home, and make every decision while on the run. He had thrived under the adrenaline rush such assignments produced. But such was not the case with the Midnight Angels, and he imagined it was due to the fact that for the first time since he became head of the Vittoria Society, Kate was now at the center of the hunt.

He had always known that this moment would arrive, just never anticipated it would be for such a rare find and under such violent circumstances. He was also aware, perhaps more than any other member of the Society, that the implications of such a discovery—assuming it became public—would be both a good thing and a bad thing for himself, the organization, and Kate. It would bring media and law enforcement scrutiny, a harsh exposure of the manner in which their business was conducted. And that was something he wanted to avoid at all cost.

"I took the liberty of ordering for both of us," the Raven said, standing in front of the table, his hands at rest on the back of the chair opposite Edwards. "I didn't think you would mind."

"Not at all," Edwards said, watching as he pulled out the chair and sat down. "It's been a long time. And, if my memory is on the mark, the food we ate back then would not be found on any high-end restaurant's menu."

"We shared a brisket of beef on a hard roll," the Raven said. "We were huddled in the front seat of a Ford, parked across the way from the Museum of Natural History, shivering in the cold, waiting for Frank and Andrea to complete another of their escapades."

Edwards nodded and watched as a young waiter poured white wine into a perfectly chilled glass and set it before the Raven. "I never regret a moment of those early days spent in your company, David," he said. "It's a shame that time didn't last as long as we all thought it would."

"It lasted as long as it was meant to, I suppose," the Raven said.

"So what brings you to Florence this time?" Edwards asked, deciding to bring a quick end to the memory lane excursion.

"A rare find," the Raven said. "Or, to be more precise, the rumor of one. No doubt you've heard such talk yourself. Otherwise why leave the sanctity of the classroom? Unless, of course, you simply were craving a good meal."

"I never put much weight in rumors, David," Edwards said. "I find them to be a waste of time. I only allow facts to influence any decisions that need to be made. But once I'm convinced of the actual proof of a find, then I allow no one to stop me from bringing it in."

"Well put," the Raven said. "Spoken like a true disciple of the Westcott theory of lost and stolen art. And you've had many impressive victories down the years to illustrate your point. But with this one, I must warn you. This one will belong to me."

"It's not just the two of us this time," Edwards said. "Not just the Society against the Immortals. There is someone else in the mix now and we both need to be careful."

"Kate may be new to this," the Raven said, "but she doesn't seem slow to learn. Much quicker, I would wager, than the two dead men the local police are hoping will lead them to a few useful clues."

"I knew that, sooner or later, you and I would need to finish this . . . *thing* between us," Edwards said. "I think we both realize that with the discovery Kate has made, our moment has arrived. Only one of us can have it. But I need you to promise me that regardless of what happens between us, Kate won't be harmed."

"You were always the most dramatic of our little group," the Raven said, dismissing the plea. "With what's at stake, knowing all you know about me and what I have accomplished, why would you even entertain the thought that I would worry myself over her welfare?"

"You were in love with Kate's mother," Edwards said. "We all knew it."

"People with little to do tend to talk," the Raven said. "And we both know that no one has as much idle time as an academic."

"It went beyond talk. I think Andrea was infatuated with you, at least for a while."

"That was a very long time ago, Richard," the Raven said. "I have done my best to dissolve my memories of that period of my life. And none of it—no matter if the gossip surrounding myself and Andrea was true or false—has anything to do with the situation facing us now. So if you are mentioning it in order to dredge up some, I don't know, *nostalgia,* it's all for naught. I will do what I need to do to claim the Midnight Angels as my own."

"For a man such as yourself, who claims to be an avid student of history, you can be a complete idiot," Edwards said, his words weighed more with sadness than regret. "Especially when it comes to your own history."

"If you want to know whether Andrea and I had an affair, all you need to do is ask me," the Raven said. "At this point in our lives, there really is no reason to get cute with the facts."

"I *know* you and Andrea had an affair," Edwards said. "And as much as that troubles me, it has never changed my own feelings toward her."

"How admirable of you."

"What does concern me is Kate's well-being. Right now, you are the biggest risk to that."

"And you think whatever affections I may have had for Andrea can sway me to treat Kate differently from anyone else standing in my path?" the Raven asked. "If that's the case, then you know nothing about me."

"I know what you're capable of, David," Edwards said. "I've lost more than enough members of the Society over the years to bear witness. What I don't know is, will your need to feed that hunger, your desire to succeed regardless of the human cost, carry over to someone like Kate?"

The Raven smiled. "Why should I factor her safety into my plan?" he asked. "Tell me why, Richard. Is it because she's young and new to our business? Or is it because she was Andrea's only child?"

Edwards leaned across the table. "It's because she might also be *your* child."

The words had their effect. The Raven sat still for several moments, looking away from Edwards, his gaze off into the distance. "And you base your little theory on what evidence?" he managed to say.

"The timing of it all," Edwards said, sitting back in his chair. "Your romance with Andrea lasted, as far as anyone could figure, about six months. It was a tough time, as you know, for the Society. It was no secret that there was disagreement between Andrea and Frank as to the direction we should go. Nor was it a secret that there was a great deal of affection between the two of you."

"I was always under the impression that few, if anyone, knew of our involvement," the Raven said. "I suppose that's an error made by all secret lovers."

"It didn't escape Frank's attention," Edwards said. "There was a high level of tension between the two of them during those months."

"And how does this relate to Kate?"

"Think back, David," Edwards said. "Try to remember. Your affair with Andrea broke off for reasons known only to you and her, but what I do know is the break was abrupt and left bitter feelings on both sides. Then, a bit more than a month later, we were all told that Frank and Andrea were expecting a baby. Now, it could be nothing more than mere coincidence and that Frank is indeed Kate's father. But you have to admit, the timing does leave it open to doubt."

"Is that all the proof you have to go on?" the Raven asked. "If so, it seems to me you're being rash. It's not like you to make such an emotional assumption."

"I *don't* have proof," Edwards said. "But there have been enough clues dropped along the years to make me think I'm right."

"You have a hole card, Richard," the Raven said. "You are too smart to have entered into such a discussion without one."

"Kate is the best person I know and one of the brightest I've ever been around," Edwards said. "There is a kindness to her that never fails to remind me of Andrea. She always looks for the good."

"But . . ."

"There is an edge to her," Edwards said. "She's fearless. It is something she had even as a child. I always expected to hear a certain level of complaining whenever we would begin training for the next level in martial arts or fencing or archery. Most little girls would have preferred to be at home or with their friends. Instead, Kate embraced the challenges of the field."

"And you attribute this dedication to me?" the Raven asked.

"There's a coldness to her technique," Edwards said. "It's hard to explain. But when I watched her through all those training sessions, I saw you on those fields and in those gyms. She relished the competition and found pleasure in taking down an opponent. Frank and Andrea resorted to hard tactics when the need arose, but they were always troubled by them. I have probably gone much further than I ever thought I would in that area, but it took a number of years to get to the point where I could barely justify the violence. I don't think it will take Kate quite so long to adapt."

"I have never been disappointed listening to your various theories, Richard," the Raven said, "whether they related to art history, lost artifacts, love affairs gone wrong, and now, family lineage. But our conversation changes nothing. I won't let anyone get in the way of my claiming the Midnight Angels as my own. I will eliminate whoever blocks my path—whether that person be a former friend or even my own flesh and blood."

"I didn't tell you about Kate because I expected you to leave here eager to change your ways," Edwards said. "I thought, after all these years, it was something you needed to be aware of."

"Does Kate know of the history?" the Raven asked.

"No," Edwards said, shaking his head slowly. "She adores her parents and I didn't see the point in doing anything that might diminish that."

"Yes, having me as a father would certainly put a dent in their sainted memories," the Raven said. "But, if you prefer she not know, I won't betray you in that regard."

"I need more than that, David."

"She is next in line," the Raven said. "I will be rid of you at some point, and if I can eliminate your successor as well, that will leave a major void in the Society, one I fully intend to exploit. So, the answer is no, there will be no deals made."

Edwards sat back and stared across the large dining room, the fingers of his right hand rubbing his wineglass. "Then one of us will have to kill you," he said in a soft voice.

"I wish you both luck in the attempt," the Raven said. "Unless, of course, you agree to the one condition under which I would be willing to spare not only Kate's life, but yours as well."

"Which would be what?"

"Surrender the Midnight Angels," the Raven said. "Tell me where they've been hidden and walk away. If you care about Kate, it should be an easy decision."

"The Angels are not mine to give up," Edwards said.

"Spare me the sales pitch, Richard. I find the notion of giving lost works back to some predetermined owner nauseating."

"Which leaves us where, then?"

"Where we have always been," the Raven said, "on opposite ends, waiting for the other to make a fatal error."

"One final point, if I may," Edwards said.

"It's your bar bill," the Raven said.

"Kate doesn't know how her parents died. She was told it was an accident."

"How noble of you," the Raven said.

"That will change before I leave Florence. She'll know how they died and at whose hand. She will then finally have a reason to want you dead, David. Just like me."

"I look forward to the battle," the Raven said. "And in the event I end up killing you before you find that special moment to have your heart-to-heart with Kate, I give you my word—she will die knowing the truth."

He pushed his chair back, stood and stared at Edwards for several seconds. "And don't think for one moment there will be any hesitation on my part. She will die knowing her parents were sinners more than saints and that the man who trained her and raised her did his all to keep her in the dark about the reality of her existence. And she will believe every single word."

"What makes you so sure?" Edwards asked.

The Raven smiled and leaned across the table, both hands resting flat across the starched white tablecloth. "You tell me, Professor," he said, "what daughter, caught in such a dire situation, would not believe the words spoken by her father?"

"You deserve all that's coming to you," Edwards said.

"We all do," the Raven said.

Then he nodded, turned and walked silently and slowly out of the crowded restaurant.

CHAPTER 31

KATE AND MARCO STOOD IN THE CENTER OF the second-floor room, their bodies rigid, their faces fields of anger and confusion.

"The outside lock wasn't broken and we were the only ones with a set of keys," she said. "And the windows are too small for anyone to climb in."

"But someone *did* get in," Marco said, "and however he did it, the Angels are gone."

Kate paced the room in a tight circle, her sneakers making an occasional squeaking protest when she abruptly stopped or turned. She thought back to all the people she had talked to—those who helped arrange the lift of the Angels from the corridor and those who had designated this place, the second floor of a jewelry exchange on the edge of the famous bridge, as the ideal hiding place, shielded from public view, yet perched atop one of the busiest and most protected streets in Florence—and couldn't think of a single person who would betray her. All of them had been lifelong members of the Vittoria Society, loyal both to the organization's cause and to each other. And yet, here she stood, at a loss to explain the disappearance. "I can't believe it," she said in a low voice. "I just can't believe it. They're gone. The Midnight Angels are gone. Vanished."

"I know you trust the people who helped us," Marco said, choosing his words with care, "but could there be one of them who, for money or whatever, would be willing to put aside his or her allegiance and betray you?"

"No," Kate said. "It isn't about money or power for them. They believe in the work the group does. They wouldn't turn their backs on it now, especially not with a find this precious."

"How can you be so sure?" he asked. "You don't really know these people. And those Angels are worth a fortune."

"I'm not sure about anything anymore," she said. "Maybe I've been too trusting. But, on the other hand, I was very trusting of you and I'm not standing here accusing you of conspiring to take the Angels."

"I wouldn't take them, Kate," Marco said, lowering his eyes, knowing he had still not won back her full confidence, regardless of the dangerous path he'd ventured on in his desire to please her. "If my word isn't enough for you, then perhaps the fact I wouldn't know where to hide them or who to sell them to will make you feel better."

She looked down at the crowded street corner and shook her head. "I'm sorry," she said, her voice suddenly softer. "I didn't mean to hurt your feelings. I just can't get my head around the fact that we've lost the Angels."

Marco shrugged. "What do we do now?" he asked.

"It's back to square one," she said. "We found the Angels once, maybe we can find them again. Though I'm at a loss as to how to do that."

"How long do you think they've been gone?" he asked.

"I checked on them around eleven last night," Kate said.

Marco glanced at his watch and stepped next to her. "That's roughly a ten-hour head start," he said, "which is probably not enough time to move them safely out of the city."

Kate walked away from the window and glanced around the sparsely furnished, wood-paneled room. "They were moved with care," she said, "by someone who knew what he was doing. There isn't any marble dust or chips on the ground or against any of the walls. And it was done in darkness, late into the night when the storefronts on the bridge are shuttered and no one's around."

"That means whoever took them already had access," Marco said, "there was no need to break the alarm code or the front lock, further removing him from drawing anyone's attention."

"But he couldn't have been alone," Kate said. "That would require leaving the Angels unattended and a parked van somewhere nearby, unguarded. Even you and I knew enough not to take that much of a risk."

"Well, we seem to be able to figure out how it was done," he said. "Now if we could only just piece together who did it."

"Whoever undid the alarm and unlocked the front door did so without any fear or concerns," Kate said, "which means he or she felt they were letting in someone they knew and trusted. And whoever it was had been here before. Look around. Nothing has been jostled or put out of place. Also, there are no dust prints anywhere. You remember how dusty our sneakers got when we moved the Angels? Not just out of the sealed corridor, but up to this room? They were covered in marble dust, which is totally understandable given how old and fragile the Angels are. Yet there's not a speck to be found anywhere."

"Which means he either covered the bottoms of his shoes or left them at the door."

Kate nodded. "And was meticulous enough to have the area cleared of any signs he had even been here."

"A professional," Marco said.

"More than just a professional," she said. "He knew about the work that was in here. Its history. Its importance. And he cared enough to treat it with respect."

Marco studied her. "Are you trying to say you know who did this?"

"I'm just thinking out loud," Kate said. "There could have been a breach, someone who compromised the Society and sold us out. It could even have been a request from another member of the Society to have the Angels transferred to an even safer place than this one."

"If that were the case, wouldn't you have been told?" he asked.

"Maybe not," she said. "We're being followed, there's no secret about that. Even amateurs like us can pick out the men on our trail. Why risk the safety of the Angels by telling me they were going to be moved?"

"The people chasing us could have been just as careful as anyone from the Society," Marco said. "They would also know there would be a lot less financial worth to the Angels if they were damaged."

"If you're right," Kate said, "then the Angels are probably on their way out of Florence, lost to us forever."

"So where do we go to find the truth?" he asked.

"Back out on the streets, make ourselves as visible as possible," Kate said. "If the people on our trail are still following us, that would mean they're still on the hunt for the Angels. There would be no other reason for them to care about us otherwise."

"And if there's no one out there looking for us?" Marco asked. "What then?"

Kate turned away from the small window and slowly walked past him. "Then they're gone," she said. "They are lost to us. It will be as if they never even existed. Gone for good."

She kept her head down as she walked out of the small shop and onto the crowded stone pavement of the oldest bridge in Florence.

PART TWO

PARADISO

"No one thinks how much blood it costs."

—Dante Alighieri

CHAPTER I

JOSEPHINE MARIA COLLINS GLARED AT THE Raven, her eyes boiling with hate, ignoring the stench of his thin cigar, her arms pinned to her sides by the thick cord tied around her waist. It held her in place to a wooden pole in the center of the room.

The Raven stood across from her and smiled. "We never did hit it off, you and I," he said with a slow shake of his head. "I was never sure why that was, exactly. I suppose some people are just not meant to be simpatico."

"Or maybe I figured you for the turncoat you actually turned out to be," Josephine said. "You had the smarts to work with Frank, Andrea, and the professor. You just didn't have the spine. You're nothing more than a criminal."

"Possibly true," the Raven said. "Yet Frank and Andrea are now long dead. As for the professor, well, let's just say for the moment he and I stand on equal footing, but I expect that situation to resolve itself in short order. And then there's you and your beloved little shop. What to make of all that?"

"The years have only made you all the more insufferable," Josephine said. She didn't even glance at the two young men in dark jackets who stood off to the sides, awaiting their next order, instead focusing the full weight of her scorn on the Raven. Then, abruptly, she laughed. "The *Insufferables*. That would be a more apt name for your group than the Immortals, which isn't even original, let alone true. You and the rest of them will be forgotten the moment you die."

"I didn't come to listen to you blather, old woman," the Raven said.

"And I know you didn't come to shop or have a cup of tea," she said. "Which leaves us with only one thing. And if that's why you're here, then you've wasted not only my time but yours."

"I know you didn't take them," the Raven said. "But you know who did. What I think you might know—and what I would very much like to know—is where they are at this very moment."

"The Midnight Angels are in Florence," Josephine said with a wide smile, "where they belong."

The Raven dropped the thin cigar to the ground, stepped in closer to Josephine and slapped her twice across the face, each blow leaving behind a red stain. A tear formed at the corner of her right eye, but she didn't make a sound.

"I have nothing more to say to you," she said. "I might die today, but I will die knowing you will never possess them."

He stepped away from Josephine and glanced at the two men standing on either side of her. "I'm getting nowhere, as you can see," he told them. "Perhaps you can persuade her to approach our situation with a more open mind."

The Raven leaned against a bookcase stacked three deep with books and manuscripts, and folded his arms across his chest, indifferent to the muffled screams and muted cries less than ten feet away. He perused the assorted books, then reached up and grabbed a tattered copy of an early edition of Victor Hugo's *The Hunchback of Notre Dame,* leafing through several pages. He looked over at Josephine, now streaked in sweat and blood, the bones of her hands disfigured, her legs hanging limp, held in place by the thick cord wrapped around the wooden pole.

"This is a very valuable copy," he said to her, holding up the book. "You should take better care of your collection. It would be worth a lot more if it were in mint condition."

Josephine opened her eyes and glared at him. "I don't keep them because of what they might be worth," she said in a soft voice, blood pouring down the corners of her mouth. "I keep them because of what they mean to me and to the people who come here. I don't expect a mercenary such as you to understand such sentiments, nor do I care to explain them."

The Raven tossed the Hugo novel to the floor, walked over to Josephine and clutched her face in his right hand. "Here's something I expect you to understand," he said. "Whether you tell me about the Midnight Angels or not, I will let you live. At least long enough to stand here and watch your precious shop with all its priceless memories burn to the ground."

Josephine was caught off guard, her face now colored as much by fear as by pain. "There is a great deal of history in here," she stammered, "too much to be destroyed. Even a monster like you should understand."

"There's no profit in it for me," the Raven said with a slight shrug. "So why even bother to make the effort? Now, if I were given a reason, then perhaps I could be persuaded to let one or two trinkets go."

Josephine looked around her shop through tear-filled eyes, the memories unfolding as if they were scenes from a movie preserved in her mind, the countless nights spent in witty and warm conversation surrounded by close friends and devoted associates all coming vividly to life. The echoes of the tales spun by the many visitors were all there to be heard; the carefully orchestrated plans for the daring undertakings of the Society were also there to be rehashed and put back into play. But most of all there were the faces of the men and women who had come through that battered front door and affected her life in ways she could never imagine. She froze on the image of a younger version of herself, filled with the passion and energy of her cause, geared to take on the unseen and unknown enemy, poised to help unearth and rescue yet one more lost artistic treasure, the thrill of it all worth more than any sum of money she could ever imagine. It was a journey worth taking, and for the first time since she saw the Raven earlier in the day, Josephine Maria Collins managed to smile.

"Do what it is you came here to do," she said. "The quicker the better."

He moved his lips close to her ear, his hand holding a firm grip on her bruised and tearstained face. "There is something I want to tell you before you die," he whispered. "I will leave this city the owner of the Midnight Angels, and I will leave behind two other bodies to keep you company in the afterlife—your esteemed friend Professor Edwards and young Kate herself. I will be rid of you all, each of you knowing you have failed. Now stand here and watch, old woman, and let the last sight you see be the rising flames."

The Raven released his grip and nodded at the two men. "Burn it to the ground," he said as he made for the front door, "and we'll see which burns quicker, old paper or old flesh."

"Did she tell you anything?" the younger of the two asked.

"Not in so many words," the Raven said. "But she served her purpose and is of no further use to me."

"There's some valuable work in here," the older man said. "Seems a shame to torch it all."

The Raven turned and glared at him. "See anything you would like?" he asked.

"I wouldn't mind getting my hands on one or two of the folios she has stashed on those top shelves," he said, pointing to an antique hutch to the left of the bound woman.

The Raven walked back into the heart of the room and stood across from the older man. "Show me a work that has caught your eye," he said.

The man stepped around a small table set for three, hopped onto a stepladder and swung open the glass door to a floor-to-ceiling bookcase. He stretched for a book on a top shelf and then stepped down and walked back toward the Raven. "It's the earliest edition of any work by Vasari I've ever seen," he said, handing the Raven the book. "Out in the marketplace, with the right buyer, it could fetch as much as two hundred, maybe even three hundred thousand."

The Raven held the book in his right hand and ran the fingers of his left along the frayed leather spine. "It's damaged, and therefore worthless," he said. "As is most anything else you would find in this place. It was not her intent to collect and care for great works in order to sell them for profit. If it were, this place would be spotless, the temperature would be controlled, and no one would be allowed to go near these books."

"She was sitting on hundreds of thousands of dollars," the man said, absorbing the lesson the Raven had passed his way. "And she let it all go to waste."

The Raven shrugged, glancing over at Josephine.

She stared back hard at him, the force of her hatred evident, despite her pained expression. "You have earned your place in hell," she said.

"And when the time comes, I will take it with pleasure," the Raven said, with a slight bow of his head.

He made his way around the tables and watched as

one of the two men lit a cloth napkin and tossed it on top of a stack of books and papers. The older man held a revolver and was walking toward Josephine. "No need to waste a bullet," the Raven said, freezing the man in his step. "Let the flames do their work."

CHAPTER 2

KATE MADE THE TURN OFF PONTE ALLE GRAzie and walked with studied care down the slope that would lead her to Via dei Neri. She was alone and lost in thought, her mind filled with images of the Midnight Angels and the chaos and bloodshed inspired by her discovery. She had been in Florence for such a short period of time, yet already thought of the city as her home, and, despite the many dangers she had encountered, she knew it was where she wanted to live. It was the place she thought she could accomplish her finest work, where she would best be able to take the incomplete dreams and desires of her parents and see them come to fruition. It was also where she felt closest to them. She realized her passion for the city's most famous artist had evolved into a personal obsession, but she had always found comfort and solace in the words and works he left behind, and now, more than ever, she felt a human connection between herself and a man long dead but still very much a living presence on the streets of Florence.

Kate crossed onto the wide Via dei Neri and stopped to gaze into the window of Piccolò Slam, a clothing store that catered to men and women of her age. She took note of the man who stepped in next to her, a chocolate gelato cone in one hand and a small batch of paper napkins in the other. Through their reflection in the glass, she could tell he was looking at her.

She turned to face him. "You have chocolate on your cheek and chin," she said in Italian. "And if you don't eat quickly, you will stain your expensive jacket."

"I was a slow eater as a child," he told her, responding in English, "and a sloppy one as an adult."

"What do you want?" Kate asked.

"I would like to finish my gelato without ruining my jacket," he said. "And perhaps a minute or two of your time."

"Why should I give you any time?" she asked.

"I have a great answer for that one," he said. He reached into the front right pocket of his jacket, careful not to spill any of the gelato, pulled out a small black leather pouch and flipped it open. Kate glanced down and saw a photo ID on one side and a policeman's shield clipped to the other. He let her look at it for a moment, then snapped it back in place.

"How do I know it's real?"

"Because if I meant you any harm at all, I wouldn't need to flash a fake badge and ID in order to make that happen," he said, finishing off the last bits of his gelato. "I'm here to help, and if you are as smart as I'm told you are, you'll take it."

"What sort of help do you think I'm in need of?" she asked.

"Let's walk while we talk, shall we?" he said, pointing the way back up Via dei Neri. "I always find the conversation moves at a crisper pace when people are on the go, which is one of the many reasons I hate having to talk to anyone in an interrogation room."

"Is that why I'm not under arrest?"

"Why would I need to arrest you?" he asked. "It's not as if you found a long lost work of the Renaissance world's greatest artist and helped mastermind its theft. Now, *that* would be a reason to put cuffs on you and drag you to the nearest police station. But you didn't do that, did you?"

Kate hesitated for a moment, then started to walk back up the wide street by his side. "What do I call you?" she asked.

"Captain Rumore, if you want to keep it formal," he said. "Otherwise, you can just call me Antonio or Rumore, either one."

"Antonio, what's a member of the Rome Art Squad doing in Florence?" Kate asked.

She took note that he seemed pleased she'd called him by his given name. He had a calm and confident manner, and she felt at ease in his presence as well as safe. She was also quick to notice that he was the most handsome man she had ever seen in her life.

"Hey, now," Rumore said, "it's me who's supposed to be asking the questions, not you. Let's try to stick to some sort of proper procedure."

"Okay," Kate said. "What would you like to know?"

"Do you know how this street got its name?" Rumore asked her.

"If I were to guess, I'd say that since the word neri means black, it was named after the Florentine Black partisans. It might also have been named after the Neris, a very well-known and wealthy sixteenth-century family."

"Both excellent guesses," Rumore said.

"But both wrong," Kate said.

"Yes, very," he said. "In truth, the street is named after Francesco Nori, whose family was as close to the Medicis as one could get."

"And Francesco was the one who saved Lorenzo's life," Kate said, "during an assault in the cathedral. He took the blows meant for Lorenzo and died in his place."

"The Pazzi assault," Rumore said. "Fourteen eighty-seven. The family had a few homes on this street and, over time I would imagine, Nori became Neri and thus a street was born. I doubt he envisioned it to be the shopper's delight it has turned out to be, but then again, not much else is known about Francesco other than that he died in place of his friend."

"That's something great to be remembered for," Kate said.

"Three people have died in the last few days," Rumore said, his manner and voice still relaxed and in control, "since the rumor surfaced of an artistic find that would net the owner many millions. That sort of talk tends to bring everyone out from under his pile of wood, looking for the golden goose, or in this case, three very special Angels."

"And you think I know something about that?" she asked.

"If I only thought it, I would have stayed in Rome to work on my other cases and let the locals handle this," Rumore said. "Instead, I'm here, actually foolish enough to believe you are indeed the person of most interest."

"But you can't prove it," she said, "at least not yet. Otherwise I would have been taken into custody long before you had a chance to finish that gelato."

"How about I work with what I know, or at the very least suspect with a great deal of confidence?" Rumore said. "Let's take the first two bodies, both male, professional in the criminal sense, and each one connected to one degree or another with an organization led by a man known both in the underworld and in the art world as the Raven."

"But that's not an organization to which I belong," Kate said. "Unless you believe otherwise."

"*Per l'amore di dio,* no," Rumore said, shaking his head and brushing off the accusation with a wave of his hands. "In fact, you stand in the very opposite direction of where the Raven's group—the Immortals, in case you're curious—lies. But the third victim, now she presents an entirely different portrait. Would you like to know why?"

"I'm a sucker for a good story," Kate said.

"Her name was Josephine Maria Collins," Rumore said.

He casually glanced at Kate and got the reaction he was hoping to see. She clearly knew the woman, and just as clearly didn't know about her death. Somehow, the second part gave him a sense of relief. He came to Florence not sure exactly what he would face, knowing only that the city was electric now with the news of the Midnight Angels theft and was filled with a variety of warring camps, prime among them assorted members of the Immortals and the Vittoria Society. He had no doubt the young woman standing across from him, her reflection mirrored in the glass of a Ferragamo store, was the mastermind behind the theft. But he couldn't yet imagine her as the one whose orders left two men for dead on the city streets, and he knew there was no chance of her ordering the torturous death of Josephine and the burning of her shop.

Rumore had enough experience with the methods of the Vittoria Society to know they were a reactive organization when it came to acts of violence and never sought to initiate a killing, only responding in defense or retaliation. That left the Raven and his group, and he was just as well versed in their mode of operation, having personally chased down three members of the Immortals only six months earlier, after they made a daring, if foolish, attempt to steal a Monet from a private gallery in the center of Rome. The botched heist had cost two security guards their lives, and a visiting tourist was only recently cleared to return to work, still suffering from the effects of the multiple wounds he sustained during the ordeal. They were a nasty bunch, and the Raven was at the top of the target list of every Art Squad detective in the world. But no one wanted to bring him down more than Rumore. The Raven would be the ultimate prize, and his capture alone would bring to a close at least two dozen unsolved art thefts and black market discoveries.

But the Raven had proven to be an elusive prey, clever enough never to leave behind a trail worth following, deadly enough to kill anyone who would alert the authorities as to his whereabouts, his careful and precise planning keeping him several steps ahead of even the most dogged detectives. Still, Rumore was not deterred. He had learned a valuable lesson very early in his police career—patience was the best weapon one could employ against any criminal talent, especially one as good as the Raven.

He glanced over at Kate and knew that if she had indeed orchestrated the theft of the Midnight Angels, perhaps at the behest of the Vittoria Society or even acting on her own, then she would be very much in the Raven's scope. He could piece together enough secondary evidence to hold her for questioning in at least two of the murders, perhaps even dig up one or two witnesses who could place her at the scene, or put the squeeze on her school friend and wait for him to break under the weight of the questions and the threat of a long prison term. Or he could let her float free, maintain his distance and wait for the pieces of the Midnight Angels puzzle to fall into place, hold his hand until the Raven surfaced. Then perhaps he could make the move he had longed to accomplish for years. Rumore found it ironic that the key to the capture of the deadliest and most elusive art criminal in the world potentially rested in the hands of a beautiful young student in Florence who specialized in studying the works of the master himself, Michelangelo.

Based on what he had read and recently observed, Kate acted much older than her actual age, a trait he found very appealing. It was not a unique occurrence for him to meet young women who were both attractive and intelligent. But a woman who added wisdom to that mix as well as a taste for adventure was a combination he knew would be difficult for him to resist.

"How did she die?" Kate asked after several moments of stunned silence.

"There never is a good way to die," Rumore said, "but hers was one of the worst. She burned to death, tied to a wood beam inside her shop."

"Do you know who did it?" she asked, tears rising but her voice now containing an angry edge.

"I have a pretty good idea," Rumore said. "But an idea alone doesn't hold up in a court of law, so what good is it, really?"

"Did you know her?"

He nodded. "I met her a few years back on one of my first Art Squad cases," he said. "She proved to be of valuable assistance, and over time she became a friend. She meant a lot to me—though, I guess, not as much as she meant to you."

"I didn't see her as often as I would have liked," Kate said. "But whenever I walked into her shop, she made it seem like we had been together forever. I loved her. She was more than a friend, she was part of my family."

"If I'm correct in assuming who killed Josephine, then I also know he won't stop with just one friend," Rumore said. "He'll kill anyone close to you to get what he wants. He won't stop until he is stopped."

"But if I turn to you for help, maybe all that will go away," Kate said. "Is that what you would like me to believe?"

"You'd be a fool to believe it at this moment," Rumore said. "You don't know me, haven't had a chance to have me checked out, aren't even sure if I'm an honest detective or on someone's payroll. You'll put that all in motion before we meet again, but in the meantime I want to assure you I will do my very best to keep an eye on you and try to keep you safe."

"Why?"

"For very selfish reasons, I will admit," Rumore said. "I don't think you had anything to do with the murders of those two men we never did get around to discussing, but I have a hunch you could point me toward those who did. And then there's the matter of the Midnight Angels. Now you won't admit to me that you had any prior knowledge of their existence or that you had anything to do with their theft. But, you see, you don't have to. All I need to do is look around and see all these criminals, art hunters, black market operators, various members of the Immortals and the Vittoria Society, all coming together in one city with one purpose and with only one name on their lips—yours. Now, why do you suppose that is?"

"They could all be wrong," Kate said. "They could all be wasting their time hunting for something they only *think* exists. Rumors of the Midnight Angels have been around for centuries, and as long as those rumors exist, there are people—some with good intentions, most not—who descend on a city like Florence looking to bring reality to what they have heard. What makes you think this particular hunt is any different?"

"No one had ever found them before," Rumore said. "The Lord himself knows that some of the very best in two fields—academic and criminal—made many an attempt at their discovery, only to leave the city encased in dust and disappointment. Some stayed as long as three years, haunting the halls and basements of every museum and gallery, reading and rereading Michelangelo's words, hoping to find that magical, hidden clue, staring at his work until their eyes appeared ready to melt, looking for that sign, that hint of where an incomplete masterpiece might rest. No one succeeded, until you arrived."

"I don't have them, Captain," Kate said. "I give you my word."

"I know," Rumore said with a nod and a deep breath. "They've been taken again. It's all pretty amazing, no? The Midnight Angels lay hidden for centuries with no one even coming close to unearthing them, and now, in a matter of hours, they are found and taken twice by two different individuals."

"I didn't expect you to believe me," Kate said, surprised at his quick response. "I didn't realize detectives were that trusting in nature."

"I can't speak for all of them," Rumore said, "but I'm usually not."

"Then how do you know I'm not lying?" she asked.

"You're still alive," he said. "If the Raven thought you had the Angels, he would have gone after you, instead of trying to pull information out of Josephine."

"She died because of me, then," Kate said.

"She died because of the work she chose to do," Rumore said. "It was no secret she was a member of the Society and believed in their cause with deep passion and conviction. Her devotion to that cause probably led to the murder."

"And where do you stand on that cause?" Kate asked.

"I'm a detective in the Rome Art Squad," Rumore said. "That is my higher purpose. My work is very simple—I arrest art thieves, no matter how honorable their intentions might be. So, for now and for as long as you remain a suspect in my eyes, you and I walk on opposite sides of the street."

Rumore nodded to her, like a gentleman taking leave of a woman he was courting, then turned and walked back up the old street whose history he knew so well.

CHAPTER 3

EDWARDS HELD MARCO UP AGAINST A DARK stone wall, in the middle of a dank alley just off the Viale Duca degli Abruzzi. The late night darkness was inching toward early morning gray, the sun still at least an hour from rising, and the streets were silent and empty.

"What is it you want from me?" Marco asked, his upper body trembling, his face and neck streaked with lines of cold sweat.

"The truth," Edwards said. "And neither one of us is leaving here until I hear it."

"I *have* told you the truth," Marco said. "I'm not who you think I am. I have nothing to do with this group you keep talking about. I'm just a student, same as Kate. You must believe that, sir."

"I *would* believe that had you not been seen talking to a member of the Immortals just yesterday in a café in Piazza Santo Spirito," Edwards said, his anger checked, the force with which he held Marco enough to cause welts on the young man's arms. "What were the two of you talking about?"

"He was a tourist," Marco said, "or claimed to be. I was having a coffee and he asked me how much of a hike it would be to get to Piazza Michelangelo. I gave him my opinion and he moved on. The entire conversation lasted no more than thirty seconds, and the person you had spying on me should have told you."

Edwards released his grip, turned and stood with his back against the wall, alongside Marco. "I need to know about your relationship with Kate," he said. "Is it serious between the two of you?"

"Kate is my friend," Marco said, "and I like her very much. I would do anything for her and would protect her in any way I could."

"That's quite a bit of devotion to someone you've known for such a short period of time," Edwards said, "especially someone who has put you at potential risk for a long prison term and possibly even placed your life in danger."

"Doesn't friendship always come with a price?" Marco said.

Edwards looked at the young man and smiled. "Does she know?" he asked.

"Know what, sir?"

"That you care for her," Edwards said, his tone toward Marco softening. "Beyond friendship, I mean."

Marco looked at Edwards and shook his head. "I know who you are and I know how much Kate means to you," he said. "And yes, I do care for her very much, which is all the more reason why you should believe me when I tell you I would never do anything that would bring her harm."

"You might not mean to do anything hurtful," Edwards said, "but you are up against forces that will exploit you. She has confided a great deal in you, and you have borne witness to the Angels themselves. You were part of the theft and were with her when she hid them. That's a lot of information for someone fresh to our game to possess."

"I'm part of this now," Marco said. "It was not something I sought, believe me. But I'm too deeply involved to walk away from it now, assuming that's what you're suggesting I do."

"I came here to gauge whether you could be trusted as we move forward," Edwards said. "Now, while I think the answer to that question is yes, I'm not sure you're up to what the mission might require. And that does give me pause."

"What mission?"

"How far would you go to protect Kate?" Edwards asked. "And to protect the Midnight Angels?"

"I would do anything in my power to protect her," Marco said with certainty.

"Would that include the taking of a life? Think about it."

"It's not something I ever thought I'd have to decide," Marco said.

"Few do," Edwards said, "but here it is for you now, and if you remain determined to continue on this journey with Kate, it is a question to which I need an honest answer."

"And if I can't give you the answer you want, what happens to me then?" Marco asked.

"You go back to the life you had prior to meeting Kate," Edwards said. "There would be no need for you to see any of us ever again. We'll be of no threat to you, unless you decide to do something stupid with the information you currently possess."

"Even so, how do I know that either one of those groups won't still decide to come after me?" Marco asked.

"At the moment, you're not on any police department's radar, and even if you did catch the eye of an enterprising detective, he would have little in the way of proof to question you, let alone hold you in custody," Edwards said with a degree of assurance. "As to the Immortals, Kate will remain their main target. If they wish to retrieve the Angels, they won't waste time chasing after you. It is Kate they will need to confront."

"I've never held a gun," Marco said, his voice lower, knowing what he wanted to do, yet fearful of the consequences of such a decision.

"Not everyone is able to kill," Edwards said quietly.

"How much danger is Kate in?" Marco asked.

"More than you could imagine."

"Then what kind of a friend would I be if I left her now?" Marco said.

"Not much of one," Edwards said. "But at least you would be cut clear from a situation not of your doing, free to go about your studies, a career, a life."

"I'm afraid it's not going to be that simple to be rid of me," Marco said, determined. "I'll stay by her side and do whatever I can to keep her safe."

Edwards listened and nodded, staring down at the dark, mangled stones by his feet, his hands thrust deep inside the pockets of his khakis. "One more question, then," he said. "This one more out of curiosity than anything else."

Marco wiped the sweat from his brow with the right sleeve of his blue shirt and looked over at Edwards. "I doubt it can be any more difficult to answer than all the others," he said.

"Do you ever plan to tell Kate how you feel about her?" Edwards asked. "Or will you simply wait until she has it figured out on her own?"

"No, sir, I will not tell her," Marco replied with a slight smile. "I'm afraid the limits of my bravery only extend so far."

Edwards grinned. "We are all cowards when it comes to women," he said.

"Do I tell Kate that we've met?" Marco asked.

"Not just yet," Edwards said. "So far I've managed to keep my presence unnoticed, and I would like that to continue for at least another day, maybe two. It makes it easier to accomplish what I need to get done."

"And I assume you're aware the Angels are missing once again," Marco said, curious as to what reaction, if any, the statement would illicit from the professor.

"It's a small city and an even smaller profession," Edwards said. "Word travels very quickly in our circle. But I have faith in both you and Kate. You uncovered them once. You'll do it again."

Marco walked to the other side of the narrow alleyway and reached for his bicycle. He sat on the seat and curved his feet around the pedals. He glanced up at the morning sky, the sun slowly making its way above the rooftops to bring with it a warm day. "Is there anything else, sir?" he asked.

Edwards shook his head. "A new bike wouldn't be such a bad idea," he said. "Has anyone mentioned that to you before?"

Marco lifted the kickstand and started to peddle down the rocky street. "Only everyone I meet, sir," he said, before disappearing down the alley and around a bend.

A thick wooden door behind Edwards swung open and Russell Cody stepped out, handing the professor a fresh cup of coffee. "What's the verdict?" he asked.

"He cares for her," Edwards said. "And the affection is real. He's not savvy enough to fake it."

"Can he handle himself?"

"No, but it won't be due to any lack of courage," Edwards said. "He shouldn't get in our way, if that's what you mean."

"But what if he does?" Russell asked. "What if he manages to do something that puts either Kate or someone else from our crew deeper into danger?"

Edwards sipped his coffee. "Then get him out of the way," he said. "Fast."

CHAPTER 4

CLARE JOHNSON SAT AT A CIRCULAR TABLE near the bar in a small room off the lobby of the Hotel Excelsior and sipped a green apple martini. She smiled when she saw Antonio Rumore enter from a side door, catch her eye, and walk toward her table. He nodded at the bartender as he approached, rested his hands on the back of the chair across from her and returned the smile.

"Now I *know* there was a theft," he said, "because you're in town."

"I ordered you a double Fernet on the rocks," Clare said. "And they serve lunch and snacks in case you came in hungry."

Rumore sat and waited as a waiter in a white jacket and black bow tie rested a thick glass filled halfway with the harsh-tasting digestive he had been drinking since he was a small boy sitting across the table from his father. He lifted the glass, raised a half toast to Clare, and took a long swallow of the cold Fernet, a drink invented by monks during the Renaissance and said to be favored by both Michelangelo and da Vinci, making the potion one of the few pleasures in life enjoyed by both men. "Are you here on a case?" he asked.

"You go first," Clare said. "Things must be very quiet in Rome for you to take the time to come up north, and sniff out a rumored robbery—and that tells me you have a bit more information about what went on than I do."

"Who are you working for this time, Clare?" Rumore

asked. "And don't hand me your insurance card. Who's your partner in this?"

"Frankly, I'd like it to be you," she said. "I can't do what I want to do on my own, but with your help, I might be able to get there."

"And what is it you want to do?"

"Bring down the Raven," Clare said. "Not his organization. That's spread out too thick and too wide for any one job to accomplish. I'm talking about him personally. In handcuffs or on a slab, it makes no difference to me."

"You've done business with him in the recent past and both of you walked away with quite a tidy profit from each pairing," Rumore said. "That job in Lisbon three years back alone brought in fifty million euros apiece, and that comes on top of your insurance retrieval commission. Now, I don't mean to sound cynical, but why would you want to turn your back on such a lucrative situation?"

"It's personal," she said. "Would it be okay with you if we left it at that?"

"No, Clare, it wouldn't," Rumore said. "If I have to trust you, I need to believe you. And right now, I don't."

Clare finished her drink and sat back. She was wearing a sleek black pantsuit with a small string of pearls wrapped around her thin neck. Her eyes sparkled under the twinkling lights of the barroom and she stared down at her hands, folded in front of her as if she were a schoolgirl. "I was engaged to be married about eight years ago," she said. "He worked for an art house out of London. Handsome, sweet, crazy mad over me."

"*That* I believe," Rumore said.

Clare smiled. "My father would have liked him, even though he might have wondered how one man could go through life being so honest."

"And your father would have despised the Raven," Rumore said. "Your father was the best of the cat burglars, but he treated the profession and the works he stole with respect, and he understood the boundaries. He would not have been happy to see you do business with a man without limits."

"I had my reasons," she said, "and believe me, if Pops were still alive and I had made him aware of the entire story, he would have happily embraced my plan. Then again, if Pops had been alive, then maybe Glen would be, too."

"In what way was he connected to the Raven?"

"Not in any way," Clare said. "He was aware of him, of course, as is anyone who works in the high-end galleries, and he knew to be wary, but that's the extent of their relationship."

"Did he know about you and your connections to him?" Rumore asked.

Clare slowly shook her head. "I was involved with the Raven a long time ago," she said. "Sometimes it seems so far in the past I can barely remember it, but it's there and it has come to haunt me to this very day. I fit all the clichés—young, naive, swept up by his looks, his charm—and by the time I realized what kind of man he truly was, well, the bed had already been made. But as honest as I had been with Glen, it was one part of my life I felt too ashamed to share. I thought he would end up hating me for it."

"But then the Raven decided to hit Glen's gallery," Rumore said, trying to piece the scenario together and make it a bit easier on Clare, "and you tried to talk him out of it."

"And you can imagine how far that got me," she said. "Instead, he came up with an alternative plan, one that would guarantee both my involvement and Glen's safety, and I went along with it."

"What went wrong?"

"Nothing," Clare said. "The Raven's plan went exactly as he plotted it out, from the break-in to the sale of the stolen pieces. It was executed to the letter—there weren't any prints left behind and not a single clue that could be traced back to anyone involved in the heist, myself included."

"But the Raven likes to have a cover on *all* his tracks," Rumore said. "It helps to limit his risk involvement. He wouldn't see you as a threat, since you were a participant in his scheme."

"And Glen wasn't," Clare said, her eyes misty, her hands resting flat on the surface of the table. "The Raven waited a few weeks before making his move. I was back in the States, working with the Art Squad in Boston, and Glen was busy prepping a new exhibit, both of us working long hours, as usual, putting a big dent on our cellphone minutes."

"How?"

"He was on his way home the day before the official opening," Clare said. "It was so late that it was closer to daylight than night. He was just about half a block from his apartment, walking on an empty street, when a car jumped the curb and ran him down."

"Did you get all this from the police report?" Rumore asked.

Clare shook her head and wiped at her eyes. "I didn't have to see any police report," she said. "The Raven called my cell and gave me all the details I needed. He wanted to give me enough of a warning so I wouldn't miss Glen's funeral."

Rumore caught the waiter's eye and signaled for two more drinks. They both sat in silence as they waited for the liquor to arrive along with two long glasses of flat mineral water and a small bowl of assorted nuts. "Yet with all that, you continued to do business with the Raven," he said, "to this very day. Now unless he's holding something over your head I'm not aware of, that wouldn't appear to me to be the reaction of a grieved lover."

"You're not one for a warm bedside manner," Clare said, taken aback by his harsh tone.

"I'm a detective," Rumore said, "not a doctor. I didn't come here to offer comfort. I'm here to find out what you wanted and why."

"I knew I was going to get him for what he did to Glen," she said, her voice now stripped of all emotion, cold and matter-of-fact. "I knew it the minute I heard his voice over the phone. But I also knew he would expect it and be primed for any suspicious move I might make. So, instead I brushed Glen off as just another in a line of lovers long forgotten, and continued to work my deals with the Raven whenever the opportunity presented itself. I needed to let the time pass, the memory fade, the trust build. I needed to let the perfect moment arrive."

"And that moment is now?" Rumore asked.

"Yes," Clare said. "I can't think of a better time or a more convenient place. The setup is perfect and all the players are lined up in their proper order. All I was missing was a cop, and then, lo and behold, you showed up, the final piece to my elaborate little puzzle."

"I admire your determination, even though I'm still not totally sold as to your true motive," Rumore said. "Then again, you must forgive me my suspicious nature, but it comes with being born a southern Italian. So tell me, what makes you think this is the perfect time to bring the Raven's run to an end?"

"I've agreed to help him retrieve and remove the Midnight Angels," Clare said. "He may not completely trust me—he's no better than you in that department—but he feels he needs me because my international contacts offer him the cleanest way to move the Angels once they're out in the marketplace and guarantee him his biggest return."

"That's assuming the two of you will be the ones who end up in possession of the Angels," Rumore said.

"I don't want him to end up with the Angels," Clare said. "And he won't, especially if I have you working on one end and the Vittoria Society fighting him on the other. Toss in a handful of those freelance art hunters roaming through the city, and the odds in his favor dwindle considerably."

"His group is not one that can be dismissed lightly," Rumore said. "They may not leave behind any prints or clues, but they're never shy about blood."

"I don't dismiss them," she said, "though I am counting on the Society to contribute their share to the body count, and at the very least keep the Immortals on their guard. Meanwhile, the Raven will be busy tracking the girl and her young friend. If he is indeed going to end up in possession of the Angels, then she will be the one who leads him to them."

"What do you know about her?" Rumore asked.

"Not much more than what you've most likely already dug up," Clare said. "I just wouldn't be as quick as some to place her name in the inexperienced and naive category. Just because she hasn't been in this type of situation before doesn't preclude her from being very adept at handling it."

Rumore finished off his drink and sat back, giving the ornate room a quick glance. He noticed a young couple off to the side, clasping hands, sharing a quiet moment, and a middle-aged man, portly, balding, and alone, contentedly working his way through what was no doubt an expensive bottle of Montepulciano, a red glow to his cheeks and a smile on his face. Rumore always thought of Florence as the perfect city in which to be a tourist. Due to its size and the attitude of its residents, it lacked the frenzied pace of cities like New York or Paris, allowing a visitor a relaxed chance to devour all that the town had to offer—from its vast trove of Renaissance works to the finest in current fashion to the best in Tuscan cuisine. It was also a small city, and therefore easy to manage by foot, a fact he always relished after spending far too many days and nights caught in the congestion and madness of Rome. He watched as a tall, long-haired young man in a suit well past its prime sat behind a large piano near the entrance to the room and began to play the first few bars of an old Frank Sinatra song long loved by Italians, "Strangers in the Night."

Rumore turned back to Clare, her face and eyes sparkling under the glow of the low-wattage lights and the burning candle at their table, and smiled. "So, tell me," he said. "Where do I fit into this great plan of yours?"

Clare was quick to return the smile. "Well, Detective," she said, "I'm awfully glad you asked."

CHAPTER 5

EDWARDS RESTED HIS ARMS ACROSS THE STONE archway of the small bridge and looked down at the angry brown tide of the Arno heading toward the sea. Dusk had descended on Florence, the city streets already lathered in a light, early evening mist. Kate stood next to him, her back to the river, one foot resting over the other, hands buried inside the side pockets of a tan jacket. It had been two days since his meeting with Marco.

"You could have told me you were here," she said. "You didn't have to make me guess."

"This was the safest way," Edwards said, "for you and me."

"Why did you have to move them?" she asked, turning her head to gaze at his profile.

"I needed to make sure the Raven couldn't get to them," he said. "The spot you chose was good, but too many people knew about it. I had to find a more secure location."

"Where are they?" she asked.

Edwards looked across at her and turned away from the Arno. "Riddle me this," he said.

"Oh, not that," she said, burying her face in her cupped hands. "I wasn't any good at it as a child and I don't think I've become any better."

"I'll start you off with a solid clue," Edwards said, "and then leave you time to figure it out. Sound fair?"

"Make it a really good clue," Kate said, lowering her hands. "Not one of your usual, cryptic ones."

"I will," he said, "you have my word. But before we get to that, we need to have a serious talk, one we should have had years ago. I kept putting it off for a number of reasons, all of them having to do with me. I would delay it even further if I could, but since I'm not certain how our little adventure here will conclude, I think it's best you hear what needs to be said from me."

"Are you all right, Richard?" Kate asked, resting a hand on his arm. "You're not sick, are you?"

"No," he said, "it has very little to do with me. We need to talk about your parents."

Kate stiffened. "What about them?" she asked.

Edwards took a deep breath and gazed down at the rough current of the Arno, its dark waters agitating against the shoreline, grudgingly moving forward, bringing waste and debris along with it. "Most of what I told you about them was the truth," he began. "They were two very special people, masters in their field, generous of heart and spirit, madly in love with each other and with you. They were a passionate pair, and what they set out to accomplish changed the art world for the better and ensured their legacy. There will never be another couple quite like them, and for all of that you should be very proud."

"What haven't you told me?" Kate asked.

"They didn't die in any accident," Edwards said. "They were murdered, killed by a man they once trusted and counted as one of their own."

Kate took two steps back, the lights of the city beyond the bridge now a whirling blur, the sounds of the passing scooters and cars echoing like drumbeats in her ears. The fingers of her right hand dug into the hard rock of the bridge wall, clutching onto the ancient stone as if it were a soft pillow. "Why did you lie to me?" she managed to say.

"It was a decision made by your parents and passed on to me," Edwards said. "They were always aware of the risks their work forced them to encounter, the ultimate price they might have to pay. You were so young, they thought losing them would be hard enough without having to know how it was their fault. It was a good lie, Kate, the kind told only by those with the deepest feelings of love in their hearts."

"Is he still alive?" she asked. "The man who killed my parents?"

"Very much so," Edwards said. "But maybe not for long."

"Do you know him?"

"Yes. At least, I thought I did," Edwards said. "There was a period of time when I considered him a friend. He was a scholar for whom your parents had the highest of hopes, but he allowed a hunger for riches and the damage caused by a love affair turned sour to force him to abandon the dream Andrea and Frank envisioned. Instead, he devised a more lethal and lucrative approach to securing the world's missing art treasures. Over time, his goals became the very opposite of ours."

"And what exactly are our goals?" Kate asked.

Edwards shrugged. "We find lost treasures and return them to their owners, whether they be a family or a museum or even a city. That part I think you've already figured out. But the lengths we go to in order to achieve our goal gets a bit more complicated."

"I've started to pick up on that, too," Kate said. "Three people have died. Josephine was one of them. She was tortured and her shop was burned to the ground. Is that part of the lengths we go in order to achieve our higher purpose?"

"Look, I don't expect you to embrace all of this at

once," Edwards said, "and I wish you had a lot more time to take it in and sort it out. But this is the time the issue put itself on the table, and this is the moment when we need you the most."

"You mean the Vittoria Society?" she asked. "I'm starting to get the idea it's more than a group of academics and scholars seeking a common purpose."

"It's that and much more," Edwards said. "It is the very group founded by your parents and now run by me and maybe, someday, you. That is why you were raised as you were, with that very purpose in mind."

"And what if it's not something I wish to do?" she asked. "What happens then? Do I no longer serve a purpose?"

"That is your call to make," Edwards said. "But before you move toward making any decisions, there is something you should read."

He pulled a thick leather-bound book from under his left arm and handed it to her. "What's in it?" she asked, taking it from him and cradling the book against her chest.

"The truth about your parents," Edwards said. "It's a journal they both kept for you to one day read. You know them now only through their work. This takes you beyond that point and gives you as honest a glimpse of them as you'll get. They held nothing back, and while some parts may make for painful reading, I think by the end you'll come away loving them as much as you do now."

"So you've read it?" she asked.

"Yes," he said, "several times, in fact. Nothing underhanded, mind you, it was at their request. They felt the man raising their daughter should be allowed entry into their private world as well. I was to pass it on to you when I felt the moment was right, and I can't think of a better time than right now."

"Did you find anything in the book that *surprised* you?" Kate asked.

"Yes," Edwards said. "I'm certain you will, too. But regardless of what you read, come away knowing this—your parents led full lives and loved each other deeply. You'll find, however, if you haven't already done so, that life often gets complicated, forcing us to venture down roads we never envisioned entering. That's as true for your parents as it is for you and me. Please bear that in mind as you read their journal."

"What are you trying to tell me, Richard?" Kate asked.

"That it's time for you to think of your parents as people, as flawed as anyone else," he said. "It is what they would have wanted. What they deserve."

Edwards leaned over, wrapped his arms around Kate and kissed her gently on the cheek. "Read with an open mind and a forgiving heart," he whispered.

He released his hold and began a slow walk toward the south end of the Ponte Santa Trinita, a stiff evening breeze blowing against his face.

KATE SAT ON the stone ledge of the bridge, her back to the Arno, opened the journal and began to read the words her parents left behind. Each passage was written with a clear purpose and a level of sincerity not seen in any of the academic works of theirs she had read and reread countless times. These were the words of a concerned mother fretting over leaving behind her infant daughter to venture off in search of a missing work of art, or the worries of a father too weary to continue a quest he had begun to grow skeptical about but still determined to see it through. She learned, as she moved through page after page, how the two met and fell in love, despite the reluctance of both to settle down to what they initially presumed would be a stuffy existence on a university campus, battling for tenure and having to endure a series of endless and fruitless arguments at a string of cocktail parties over the value of one painting over another.

As dusk turned to night, she discovered that it was her mother who initially conceived of the idea for the Vittoria Society, but that her father was the one who streamlined its goals and duties, expanding it from a small group of like-minded academics to an all-out force complemented by art hunters, forgers, mercenaries, hired guns, private collectors, insurance investigators, and auction house insiders, all working under the guise of a similar goal: to locate and preserve lost or stolen artistic treasures, not merely for profit—though there was enough of that to help fill Society coffers around the world—but for the sheer joy of the art itself.

Kate wanted time to stop and leave her just like this, alone on the *ponte*, bathed in the glare of an overhead streetlight, getting to know her parents in ways she had never dreamed. She read about their adventures, which took them out of their offices and away from home to explore places far removed from the sealed world of academia—the wild hunts for the missing piece; the daring escapes and the bodies that were left in their wake, both of friend and foe. It was as thrilling a read as anything she could find in the novels by Alexandre Dumas or Victor Hugo, her parents leaping off the page as modern-day swashbucklers, living life to its fullest.

She read of the private moments Andrea and Frank shared with her as a child: her mother doting over her choice of clothes and hairstyles; her father always on the lookout for some small adventure the two could share, whether a horseback ride through the backwoods of their Maryland summer cottage or a sled ride down the slopes of a sun-drenched New England afternoon.

The most insightful moments in the journal came during the quiet times—often late in the evening, dinner and dishes done, Kate sitting on a thick upholstered couch between her mother and father, laughing along with the two of them as they regaled her with tales of their travels abroad and the wide and eccentric variety of people they encountered.

Kate paused from her reading, resting the book facedown next to her leg, and looked out across the city of Florence. She had just read that it was her parents' favorite city and the site of many of their exploits, one more breathtaking than the next. She knew now what they had in mind for her, and what Professor Edwards's mission had been—to prepare her in every way to be part of the Vittoria Society, regardless of the dangers she might confront, the obstacles she would encounter, or the fierce opposition she would potentially face. Her parents had lived and died for the sake of the Society, and to fail to preserve it and expand its mission would be failing them in the most crucial way. As she sat on that bridge in the middle of a Florentine night, she felt, perhaps for the first time in her life, the full pressure of her destiny. It was an overwhelming realization, and one that left her on the verge of tears.

She picked up the journal and continued reading, now turning the pages with some trepidation, mindful of the professor's words of warning, and when she finally did come across what he had only dared hint at, it hit her with such force that she lurched forward, nearly dropping the book, clutching onto the light pole for support. She closed her eyes and took several long and deep breaths, choking back the bile building at the base of her throat.

The words were written in her mother's hand, each sentence clear and concise, offering no excuses, parsing no blame, simply stating the facts as they had occurred. Andrea and Frank had been on the hunt for a stolen

Cezanne, and brought along both Professor Edwards and a young scholar they were mentoring to aid in their quest. The trail of clues forced them to separate. Frank and Richard went off to Lyons to search for the supposed thieves, while Andrea and David—described as handsome, filled with boundless energy, and with a superior intellect—trekked back to London to follow the path of the money that was scheduled to change hands. On their third night in England, hiding in a remote cottage in the countryside, waiting out a freezing rain soaking the winding roads of the small town, they built a fire from straw and loose twigs and discarded furniture, and huddled close to it in order to keep warm.

Andrea confessed in the pages of the journal to a silent crush on the remote young man she and her husband had taken under their wings, and before the first light of morning rose above the cottage she succumbed to her secret desires. It was the beginning of a two-year affair, a period in which Andrea felt disjointed and confused, torn between the genuine love she held for Frank and the physical attraction that existed between her and David. From his end, Andrea felt David was not as conflicted, wanting to lay claim to both her and the Society, then still in its infancy, as his own. Andrea knew it could not go on much longer; her relationship with Frank was beginning to fray at the edges and she sensed that while her husband was aware of the situation, he was not yet prepared to confront her. She also saw how it pitted Professor Edwards and David against one another, turning once close friends into bitter and potentially lethal adversaries.

As Kate read the painful words her mother had so carefully put down on paper, she caught a glimpse of a woman she had never envisioned—torn apart by two men, waging a disturbing tug of war between love and infatuation, fearing the final results of whatever resolution would eventually emerge. Andrea wrote with clarity and sincerity, but could not escape the shackles of the emotional dilemma she was forced to confront. It would take the exposure of David's unquenchable thirst for power and the ease with which he could betray those closest to him to make Andrea finally aware of the folly of her affair and the risk she had run in chasing away the one man who truly loved her, free of any conditions or assurances.

Kate tore through the pages now, the hours of the night slipping past her, the city silent and far removed from the private world she was immersed in, a world that until this day had been kept at a distance. She felt a sense of relief as she read the section where her mother confronted David and dismissed his request that she leave Frank and turn the Society over to the ambitious and ruthless young man. "If you could only have one," Andrea had said to David, "me or the Society, which would you choose?"

David had not hesitated in responding, and hearing his calculating and chilling words, Andrea realized the full extent of her mistake. "There is no need for me to choose," he said to her, "for I can't conceive of one without the other."

"But if there were only one?" she asked again, fearing she already knew the answer, "what then?"

"I would choose the one that will be remembered long after both of us are gone," David said. "We can each find someone to comfort us and carry us through, but the potential rewards the Society can bring, the power it can accumulate and the riches that will follow? It is too precious to ignore."

"The Society is not yours for the taking," Andrea had told him. "It never will be."

Kate brushed the tears from her face as she read about her mother's reconciliation with her father and how easily he forgave her, despite the obvious pain the affair had caused him. She bore the brunt of her guilt for the rest of her life, never managing fully to come to grips with the reasons why she had embarked on the affair, especially when she was forced to confront the fact that she had never fallen out of love with Frank or in love with David. "I have been in the arms of two men in my life," Andrea wrote. "One was a man I should have never been with, and the other is a man I should never have been apart from. That I betrayed one for the other is what I will always find unforgivable."

Then, as she continued to read, and believing the worst was over, Kate was hit with a passage that shook her to the core, her hands trembling and the words barely legible as she fought to hold the journal steady. It was a section three paragraphs long and written in a straightforward manner, the words uncluttered by any show of emotion. It dealt with Andrea's pregnancy, which she had kept to herself for the first three months. She did so not out of any concern about losing the baby or any uncertainty as to whether she would even have the child. She kept it quiet for as long as possible because she was not sure who the father was—David or Frank. "Then," she wrote, "I made a clear and simple decision. Frank was my husband and the man I truly loved, and therefore was the father of my child. There would be no need to conduct any tests or discuss the matter any further. The baby I carry belongs to the two of us."

Kate closed the journal and stepped down from the side of the bridge. She held the book close to her chest and walked toward the dark and silent streets. She needed to do what her mother had done before her—separate her emotions from the facts confronting her at the moment—even though she remained uncertain whether she had the inner strength and clear sense of purpose to accomplish such a feat. As she walked, she realized there were three huge truths she needed to come to terms with.

The first was that her parents had died at the hands of the man she had come to know as the Raven. Those, she could seek to avenge.

The second was that he was the very same man who was the lover her mother knew as David. That, she would need to digest and eventually forgive.

The third was that the Raven could very well be her father. And that fact was the one that frightened her to the point of surrender.

She turned a corner and was now in Piazza Santa Maria Novella. She found an empty bench, sat and stared out at the empty square and realized that whatever else she would confront in the days ahead, from this moment forward her life would not be the same.

Now, after so many years and so many unanswered questions, she finally knew her parents for who they really were, and she felt a closer attachment to them than ever before. She also was now fully aware of the goals of the Society and her place in helping to achieve them. She had a better understanding of the power and scope of the organization that was built by her parents and nourished by Professor Edwards, and she realized how crucial it was for her to carry out those responsibilities.

Kate gazed at a cluster of pigeons seeking out crumbs and pecking at tiny specks of food. Behind her, she could feel the warmth of a rising sun, the start of a new day.

CHAPTER 6

THE FIAT 124 CRUISED THROUGH THE NARROW side street, made a sharp right, rear tires squealing, and took dead aim at Kate and Marco. The two were out for a run, Kate needing to burn away some of the tension she felt from reading her parents' journal, Marco tagging along more out of concern than desire. It was early morning and they were running along the rim of the Boboli Gardens. Kate turned as soon as she heard the rumble of the engine and the sharp shifting of the gears. She slapped at Marco's arm to get his attention away from the sounds of Zuccero blasting through his iPod and pointed toward the entrance to the Pitti Palace. "Let's get in there quick," she said. "He's coming pretty fast."

Marco turned and saw the Fiat, now less than five hundred feet away, and picked up his pace. "A driver and second man in the seat next to him," he said. "Maybe they're just trying to scare us."

"How's that working for them so far?" Kate asked as she took a sharp curve and ran through the Palace gates and the entrance to the Gardens.

"This way," Marco said, pointing at a path to their right, shaded on all sides by thick shrubbery. "We can run in between the trees. Not even a car as small as what they have can manage those turns."

Kate skidded to a stop. The Fiat 124 had ground to a halt just off the entrance to the Palace, and the two men were out now and chasing after them on foot. "Looks like they thought of that, too," she said. "We need to outrun them and get to the other side of the park."

"Do you think they have guns?" he asked.

"I would say that there's a very good chance," Kate said, "and an even better chance that they plan on using them on us."

"Then yes," Marco said, picking up his pace and rushing toward the shrubs, "I am more than up to the run."

Kate and Marco sprinted, the two men giving chase, close enough to be a threat but not within range of getting off a clear shot. The few pedestrians in the Gardens were spread out, casually going about their chosen tasks of quick runs, brisk walks, or casual strolls through one of the most serene stretches of land in the city, unaware of the potential danger in their midst. It was still too early for the daily army of tourists to walk the lush Garden paths, making the sounds of harsh breathing, pounding steps against dirt and pavement, intermingled with birds chattering in the tree coverage, the only noise.

As they rounded a sharp turn down a stretch of dirt road surrounded by tall pines, Kate stepped on a large rock and turned her ankle, sending her on a hard face-first sprawl to the ground. Marco stopped and rushed to her side, looking up to see the two men charging hard to make up the distance between them.

"Help me to my feet," Kate said. "And then start running and don't stop until you reach the other end of the Gardens."

"I won't leave you behind," Marco said, lifting her off the ground.

"They don't need to catch us both," she told him.

"Why not wait and find out what they want?"

Kate turned to see Captain Antonio Rumore step out

from the tree cover, wearing a Roma sweatshirt and sweatpants, the ring around his neck coated with sweat.

"What are you doing here?" she asked, both surprised and relieved to see him.

"Same as you," Rumore said, smiling at her and giving a quick look to Marco. "Out for a run on a beautiful morning."

Kate caught the look and turned to Marco. "This is Antonio Rumore," she told him, "a detective from Rome who seems to be following me."

"And I don't seem to be alone in that," Rumore said, reaching out a hand for Marco, who shook it.

The two pursuers were no longer running, but now walked casually toward the three of them. The detective waited until they were close enough to hear him without having to shout and smiled. "You can really improve your time if you run in more appropriate clothing," he said, pointing at their jackets, slacks, and loafers.

They were both young and sturdy, and Rumore could tell from the bulges beneath their jackets and at the base of their right feet that they each had at least two weapons, possibly more if they were brazen enough to have guns tucked in the backs of their waistbands. He took two steps to his left, shielding both Kate and Marco as best he could from the sight line of the men, and let his hands dangle at his sides, taking a relaxed pose free of any hint of menace.

"It looks to me like you came here to run," one of the men said to Rumore, "and it would be smart for you to keep to that."

"You left your car illegally parked near the Palace entrance," Rumore said. "That's very much against the law so I was forced to call it in. A truck should be there any minute now to pick it up."

The second man, stockier, with thinning hair and a pale tint to his skin, moved his right hand closer to the inside of his tan jacket, while he stared hard at Rumore, seconds away from a draw and a shot.

"I don't have a gun on me," Rumore said. "So if you make your move, remember you'll be taking down an unarmed man. An unarmed *policeman*."

"My favorite kind of target," the second man said.

"I also don't have a cellphone," Rumore said.

"So?"

"Doesn't it make you a little bit curious as to how I called in your car to the police?" Rumore asked.

Marco, standing behind Rumore, saw them first—four heavily armed officers, in flak jackets and carrying automatic weapons, two partially hidden by thick shrubbery and two edged behind a row of trees, all weapons trained down on the two men.

The second man froze in place while the first stepped closer to Rumore, fully aware of the police officers circling in. "No one wants a shootout," he said in a low, controlled voice. "Other than leaving the car where it shouldn't have been left, we haven't done anything that calls for police involvement."

"You're carrying concealed," Rumore said, "and the last time I checked the rule book, that had a big red mark next to it. And you were also chasing these two kids through the Garden, which would lead a suspicious man like me to conclude that there was some level of malicious intent."

"What do you want from us?" the first man, the more brazen of the duo, asked.

"You need to tell me what I don't know," Rumore said. "I'll help you by filling you in on what I do know. You work for the Raven, but since you were given a simple catch and grab, I figure you haven't been working for him very long."

"We were brought in about a week ago," the first man said.

"Where were you supposed to bring the girl once you had her?" Rumore asked.

The two men looked at each other and then lowered their heads, unsure which of the two punishments they faced—the wrath of the Raven or the weight of the law—would be more severe.

"A private home," the second of the two said after several more seconds of silence. "Up by Piazza Michelangelo."

"What about the boy?" Rumore asked.

"Him, too," the man said. "He was insurance in case the girl didn't talk."

"Otherwise he was collateral," the other man said. "Either way, not an essential piece."

"How heavily is the house guarded?" Rumore asked.

"Not sure," the first man said. "I was only given an address and a time to deliver."

Rumore turned and faced Kate and Marco. "It has a bit of risk to it, I'll be the first to admit," he said to them. "But it does have a number of advantages."

"What does?" Marco asked, not bothering to mask either his confusion or his fear.

Kate was the one who answered. "We go with them, Marco," she said in a calm voice. "We let them follow through on the plan."

"*What?*" Marco said, startled. "Why would we do something so stupid?"

"Well, you would not exactly be alone," Rumore said.

"And what will you be able to do?" Marco asked.

Rumore stepped up closer to Kate and Marco and lowered his voice. "To be honest, this isn't your decision," he said to Marco. "You heard what the man had to say about you—collateral. The Raven sees you or he doesn't, it won't matter. It's Kate he wants, and it's Kate's call as to whether or not she goes into the house."

"If she decides to go, then so will I," Marco said. "I won't leave her alone with those cavemen."

"That would make two of you I would need to get out of there safely," Rumore said. "And that will make it twice as difficult to succeed, increasing the chance you both won't come out alive."

"He's as much a part of this as I am," Kate said.

"That sounds like you've already made up your mind," Rumore said. "I'll have as many people as I'll need covering the outside of the house as soon as we determine its location. I'll take care of the inside and get to you before any harm can be done."

"How do we know that for certain?" Marco asked.

"You study art," Rumore said to him, his eyes still on Kate, "working your way toward a master's degree. I imagine, then, that you must be very good at what you have chosen to do. Are you?"

"Yes," Marco said with confidence, "I am very good at it."

"So am I," Rumore said.

He held his look on Kate for several seconds, then gazed over toward the officers waiting by the shrubbery and signaled for them to approach. He looked at the two men standing and waiting, both still unsure whether they had made the safer bet by placing themselves in the center of whatever ploy the police devised.

"You were clear as to what might happen if we let you take us in," the second man said, "but you didn't say what kind of a deal our cooperation gets us."

"That's right," Rumore said, "I didn't."

"Is there a reason?" he asked.

"Here's all you and your friend need to know," Rumore said. "Neither one of you is in leg irons on your way to jail. No one is putting a call in to the Raven and telling him you dropped the ball on a straightforward assignment. You're both going to where you were supposed to be going—a safe house—and delivering the target you were asked to deliver. What that does is keep you alive and out of prison. That's the best I can offer."

"And if you land the Raven?" the first man asked.

"Then we'll have something to talk about," Rumore said.

The two men nodded, and Rumore gestured for two armed officers to step forward. "Get them their car back, unload their weapons, and then let them have their guns. Have them give you the exact location of the safe house and the time they were supposed to bring the girl there. Then have three units standing by, ready to move. Get as much detail as you can and then double-check it with as many trusted sources you can find. Also, run their names through the database. Let's see how they've earned their keep these past few years."

The officers grabbed the two henchmen and walked down the sloping hill and away from the tree coverage. Marco stood next to Rumore and watched as the group veered left and disappeared behind a statue. Kate was leaning against a tall pine tree, her arms folded across her chest, head down, alone with her thoughts.

"I know you won't believe this, but you don't have to worry about me once we're in the house," Marco said.

"You're right," Rumore said. "I don't."

"I might surprise you," Marco said.

Rumore stared at him for a few moments. "What are you looking to get out of this?" he finally asked. "I mean, you don't seem to be in it for the adventure. You have no connection to the Society. Yet, here you are, ready to put your life on the line for a girl you barely know."

The question caught Marco off guard, even though after his conversation with Professor Edwards, he felt better prepared to answer it. "I like her," he said. "Do I need more of a reason than that?"

"If you were going out on a date, no," Rumore said. "But you're going to be risking your life, and for that you might want to go with something stronger."

"It's reason enough," Marco said.

"We'll soon find out," Rumore said, leading him over toward Kate.

"How much time before we need to go to the safe house?" Marco asked.

"Two days, minimum," Rumore said. "We'll try and get as much information as we can before we move. In the meantime, you and Kate will be free to go about your business."

"Is there anything you need me to do once we're in the house?" Marco asked, standing now next to Kate.

Rumore nodded. "Don't get her killed," he said.

CHAPTER 7

RUSSELL CODY WAS ROWING THE SCULL DOWN the center of the Arno, moving against the heavy tide, his upper body and legs straining with every pull on the thin wooden oars. It was the dawn of what promised to be another in a string of warm and pleasant days. Cody was only fifteen minutes into his journey and already the top half of his white Chicago Blackhawks T-shirt was drenched and his face and neck were coated with a thick sheen of sweat and he couldn't have been any happier. He was as devoted to his ninety-minute daily workouts as he was to Professor Edwards and the Vittoria Society, an organization on whose behalf he had orchestrated many a murder—all of them, he truly believed, justified.

Russell plunged the oars deeper into the dark, choppy waters, the homes and buildings on both sides of the river silent and imposing, the city streets still free of tourists and congestion. As he rowed, he ran through the hurdles that currently faced the group as they closed in on adding the most valuable discovery in decades to their arsenal. He knew that if they could secure the Midnight Angels, it would forever seal the reputation of the Society, the goals of its founders finally achieved. The plan he and Edwards had begun to put in place was indeed a strong one, with one troubling unknown—this would be their first venture with Kate in the mix, and no one knew how she would respond to the dangers and the pressure. She had the proper pedigree, of that he was fairly certain, and she also had all the academic credentials required, but she had never been in a tussle of any magnitude, let alone one that pitted her against the Raven and his ruthless arsenal of mercenaries.

Russell had been through dozens of battles with Edwards by his side and never once questioned either his courage or his dedication to the cause. With this fight, however, he was worried about the professor's close attachment to Kate and the dangers that could flare up and devour such a relationship. In all his time as one of the Society's key security planners, he never had to concern himself with family considerations, even in the years Frank and Andrea ran the group. He had grown not to think of them as husband and wife but rather as two determined professionals. Russell did not know if Edwards and Kate, working together for the very first time, could bring that level of discipline to the job. And he knew where there was doubt, there was always increased risk.

On top of those inherent problems, there was the skill level of the opposition to consider. Russell knew the Raven and the Immortals were more than prepared to turn the quest for the Midnight Angels into their last great stand, their best shot to do irreparable damage to the Society and step into the spotlight of the art retrieval world. The word had spread rapidly throughout the art underground that the Society was in a weakened state—their two main enforcers, Russell and Banyon, talk had it, had left their best days behind them; the professor, while skilled and able, was never a fair match when pitted against the Raven; Andrew MacNamera, the most feared operative in the Society, had been reduced to a wisp, his battle with cancer consuming the bulk of his remaining days; and their heir apparent was a novice yet to be tested in the field.

Yet, despite it all, Russell felt confident and in control.

The odds were heavily tilted toward the Society, especially in terms of manpower and money. Also, over these many years, they had built a more sustainable structure of street and boardroom connections on both sides of the art world, able to reach into galleries, private museums, art collectors, black market dealers, and police departments for valuable aid and information. And nowhere else were they better situated than in Florence, the city where the Society maintained its deepest network and greatest clout. Its members considered the city their home turf and believed that if they could not best the Raven on streets that so thoroughly favored them, then their entire quest would be doomed.

And Russell Cody did not expect to leave Florence with empty hands.

He had never failed on a mission entrusted to him by the Society in the past, and he was not prepared to make the retrieval of the Midnight Angels—his most important task to date—the first failure. In past years he had battled for precious prizes against a number of high-echelon members of the Immortals, but a matchup with the Raven had always been elusive. Now, with so much at stake, Russell felt this would be the truest test of his skills.

He pulled the oars from the water and held them aloft, content for the moment to allow the swirling tides to dictate his path. He slid one of the oars into the scull, reached down for a white hand towel and wiped a row of thick beads of sweat from his face and forehead. He took in a deep breath, his only regret in the world being that he had neglected to bring along a bottle of water. It was a peaceful and serene morning, the early sun slow to rise, the thick mist surrounding the banks and the lower end of the city just beginning to evaporate, giving the surroundings a nineteenth-century feel. He peered out beyond the row of bridges and buildings and rooftops, and from where he sat Florence looked no different to him on this beauty of a morning than it might have several centuries earlier, when true masters walked across its cobblestone streets. He took in the truly magnificent scenery and smiled at the magical city spread out before him.

He lost the smile the second he caught the glare of the rifle scope.

It was coming at him on the flat end of an approaching bridge, and Russell knew he had little time to react. He dropped the hand towel and gripped the oar, sliding it back into the water and trying to maneuver his scull in a pattern that would help make him a less stationary target. He had committed the unpardonable sin of the professional—left himself vulnerable and without any viable escape options. He could toss himself into the river, but knew he would never be able to survive its strong and whirling currents or the dangers that lay beneath the churning waters. He could also drop down, lie flat and stretch out in the base of the thin boat and make himself harder to hit, except then he would be at the full mercy of the river. He also didn't know if he was up against a lone gunman or a slew of them hidden at various points along the upper banks. Given the early hour, he had little hope that either a passing car or pedestrian would take notice of any gunman, shrouded as the shooter would be by both mist and secure location. Rowing upstream, as far away from the bridge as possible, was also not an option since the current would be much too strong for him to push against and only cause his boat to slow to a crawl, making him a sitting duck.

In the end, Russell Cody knew he was not the kind of man who ran from an adversary. He had been schooled in the hard ways of the cold professional, and the first and last rule of that education was to attack your opponent head-on. He estimated he was at least half a mile away from the shooter, and given the time of day, weather conditions, and the stillness he presented as a target, it would be a difficult but not impossible shot to take. He glanced down at the small duffel bag resting against his right leg, the black grip of the semiautomatic handgun clearly visible and within quick reach. If the shooter was patient and waited until he was closer in range, then maybe he stood a chance of getting a kill shot off. It was a gamble, but one he was more than willing to take. "Well," he said to himself, "time to find out if I have any kind of luck left."

Russell pulled at the oars with all the strength he had, cutting through the waves with a hard stroke, moving the scull downriver as fast as it would go as the second bridge drew closer. He released one of the oars, allowing it to float on its own in midair as he bent down, grabbed his weapon and rested it under his right leg. He caught the oar and gave it yet one more violent tug against the harsh, dark brown water.

He was now within fifty feet of the shooter.

The slap of a choppy cross-current wave saved him from the first shot. The high caliber bullet nicked the left side of the boat, sending thick chips of polished wood into the morning breeze. He bore down hard on the oars one final time and then leaned back in the scull, the gun held firm in his right hand, his eyes on the approaching bridge. He waited a number of seconds, his breath coming out in an easy rhythm, his heart racing as much from the workout as from fear.

Then, as a line of shadows descended across the shoreline, Russell caught a glimpse of the shooter, crouched down, resting on one knee, the other leg steadied against a stone embankment. The gunman had reset his rifle, and Russell knew he was now within easy range. With one swift move worthy of a man twenty years younger, Russell let go of the oars and tilted the boat sideways with the weight of his body and a pull of his left hand against the punctured rail. He got off two quick rounds before the scull tilted over into the river, Russell floating above the polluted waves, shielded by the shell of the boat. He waited until he was sure the scull had safely passed the bridge, then released his grip and swam with mouth and eyes closed against a current eager to pull him deeper into its hold.

He swam with tired arms and weakened legs, the hard rowing having exhausted him. He cut through the water, aiming for the closest shoreline, swimming just below the surface in an attempt to make his movements smoother and to lessen any attention he might be getting from any number of gunmen waiting for him aboveground. He wasn't sure if he had scored a hit on the shooter, but knew that his bullets caught the man off guard. If the shooter was a lone wolf sent to take him down, utilizing the element of surprise, then he might be in the clear once he made it to shore. But if there were more than one shooter and they were spread out across both sides of the river, then he was in for a long morning. Or, really, a short one.

Russell made it to the shoreline, hands and knees scraping against the harsh brown sand. He rolled over into a pile of wild shrubs, still moist with dew. There, he rested for several long minutes, catching his breath, the foul smell of the grass and wild roots strong enough to burn his nostrils. He saw a cluster of river rats scurry away, headed back to their nesting hole, annoyed by the unexpected disturbance.

Russell remained as still as possible, ignoring the horrible odor, wondering what terrible disease he risked getting simply by laying down in the slime and muck of the Arno. He was buried too deep in the shrubs to be warmed by the morning sun but was hidden from the view of any casual observers walking along the streets above.

For the moment this foul stretch of earth seemed to be the safest place in the city.

He closed his eyes when he heard the approaching footsteps, and knew then that his efforts had all been in vain. He rose slowly to his feet, wiped the thick, wet sand from the back of his pants and glanced over at the Raven.

"I didn't think you cared much for the water," he said. "You being so adverse to the sun, I mean."

"Don't let appearances deceive you," the Raven said, staring down at a lone rat making its way through the brush. "It's just that I prefer my beaches to be rodent free."

"A tan's a tan," Russell said.

"It all depends, I suppose, on the circles you travel in," the Raven said.

"I never figured my run would end this way," Russell said, quick to take a firm measure of the situation and assess the Raven's intent. "People in our line of work always expect to go out in much more dramatic fashion."

"It doesn't have to be the end," the Raven said. "In fact, it could be a fresh start. That is, of course, something only you can decide."

"You mean come work for you?"

"Would it be so horrible?" the Raven asked. "The work would be the same, the pay doubled. And good men like you are hard to find."

Russell glanced up at the sun and then across the waters of the Arno, a smirk spreading across his face. "I don't think so," he said in a low voice.

"I admire your loyalty," the Raven said. "I never get enough of that from members of my group."

"Can't say I'm surprised to hear that," Russell said. "Your hiring practices leave something to be desired."

The Raven shrugged grandly. "I don't suppose you would have any idea where I might locate the Midnight Angels?"

"Not only do I not know where they are," Russell said. "I don't even know what they are."

The Raven smiled and pulled a handgun from his waistband. "That's too bad," he said.

He raised the gun, equipped with a silencer, and fired three shots, all at close range and all finding a critical mark. Russell crumpled slowly to the edge of the shore, his hands clutching his chest as he dropped face-first onto the sand. The brown water lapped the side of his head, small, foamy waves mixed with the flow of blood oozing out of his body.

The Raven stood above him, took a quick look at the streets in the vicinity, and observed no prying eyes. He fired one final round into the back of Russell's head, placed the gun back in its safe spot, and walked along the shore toward the Ponte Vecchio.

CHAPTER 8

KATE QUIETLY RIFLED THROUGH HER PURSE looking for loose change with which to buy coins for the washing machine and dryer. Marco had already handed her the three euros he had in the front flap of his shirt. It was nearing 5:00 P.M. on a rainy Sunday afternoon and they were the only people in the Laundromat off a side street, not far from Piazza Santa Croce. She had lugged two duffel bags filled with two weeks' worth of wash, while Marco's dirty clothes were bundled and tucked under his right arm.

"I don't get it," she said. "You practically change your shirt every hour and I've never seen you wear the same jeans longer than two days in a row, and yet I'm the one with all the dirty clothes."

"There are a few positives to having a mother living close by," Marco said. "Not many, but enough to occasionally make a visit worthwhile."

"You don't see her very much," Kate said, stuffing a coin into the slot. "And you talk about her even less. I know the two of you aren't close, but don't you think she misses you, even a little?"

"I love her very much," Marco said, not looking at Kate, searching out the closest laundry machine to use. "I don't want you to get the impression I don't. But she has her own life and her own family, and I'm not a part of that anymore."

"You're part of her family, too, Marco," Kate said.

"Maybe not in the same way as when your father was alive, but you're her son, and no mother ever breaks free of that bond."

"I can only imagine how difficult it was for you to lose your parents at the age you did," he said. "I was devastated when my father died, and even though many years have passed, I'm still not over it. But in a way we're very lucky, you and I, having something like that happen to us."

"Lucky how?" she asked.

"To this day, my father remains very much alive to me," he said. "In many ways, more so than my mother. And I feel the same is true with you, with both your parents. You have kept them alive all these years, through their work and through your memories. They are there for you anytime you need them, no matter where you are or how late in the day it is, and that will always be true. No one can ever take them from you, just as no one can take my father from me."

Kate stuffed her clothes into two small washing machines, separating by color as well as by need. "That's all true, Marco," she said, "but you know you can't turn to a memory when you have a problem. And I don't mean just when it comes to situations like we find ourselves in now, but in simple day-to-day moments—what dress should you buy for that party or what should I say and not say at that next job interview. Just to have them here to talk to, like I'm talking to you, going over the most mundane parts of an uneventful day."

"*Do* you have any uneventful days?" Marco asked, hoping to get a smile in return.

Kate didn't disappoint him. "Yes," she said, "believe it or not."

"Then there's hope for us, still," he said.

The tall man in the thin leather jacket walked into the Laundromat and let the door slam behind him. There was no attendant in the room, just small sets of security cameras mounted in the corners of the ceiling. Two overhead fans spread warm air and dust, and music blared from a static-filled, in-house stereo system. Marco had his back to the man and looked toward the rear of the Laundromat, his eyes moving past a row of coin-operated machines that offered a variety of soaps, detergents, and bleaches until he closed in on the door partially hidden by a corner wall, a small latch lock in place. He turned his head, hoping to catch Kate's attention, but saw that her gaze was already focused on the man, now standing less than five feet from them both.

The man's thick-soled boots made streak noises against the tile floor as he walked past the coin machines, the rumble of the dryers and the whirling of the washing machines drowning out all other sounds.

"I don't suppose either of you have any spare change?" he asked.

"We used it all to run our machines," Kate said. "But there's a store a few meters away that will give you all the change you need."

"So long as you buy something," Marco said. "It's the owner's only rule. He hates to do anything for free."

"Most people do," the man said.

Kate looked at the crumpled white shirt in the man's right hand. "That's not quite a full load you have there," she said.

"I'm a limo driver," he said. "I always carry an extra shirt in the car, cleaned and starched, part of the job requirement. But I've been on the move for the last two days, driving the same client around. I haven't had a chance to get back home and clean up. We were supposed to have headed back to Milan hours ago, but she's insisting on having drinks and dinner with some friends. At this rate, by the time I get home it will be close to sunup, and I don't want to sit behind the wheel of my car for all that time smelling like a dog left out in the rain."

"I was about to start running my load," Marco said. "There's plenty of room. You can toss your shirt in with my clothes if you don't mind mixing it with my dirty batch. It would be a lot cheaper than running a machine just for one shirt."

"No," the man said. "I don't mind."

Kate and Marco stood silently side by side, casting an occasional glance at each other, as the man tossed the bundled white shirt in with Marco's load.

The man had a wiry but muscular build, and Kate caught a glimpse of a long angular scar along the right side of his neck. "At the very least," he said to them, "I owe you both a coffee."

"Don't worry about it," Kate said, "but thank you. We both have some reading to do and work we need to catch up on, and an empty Laundromat seems the ideal place to accomplish those goals."

"Are you both students?" the man asked.

"*Everyone* under the age of thirty in Florence is either a student, or a tourist," Marco said.

"What about you?" Kate asked. "Do you live in Milan?"

"I live where the work takes me," the man said, his dark eyes examining her. "The spring and summer months, I prefer to stay up North, and as long as there are tourists willing to pay top dollar to be driven around Italy, then that's a habit I won't need to break."

"So you've been doing this work for a while, then?" Kate asked. "Being a driver, I mean."

"Five years this January," the man said. His body was relaxed, at ease in the company of the two students in the dust-filled Laundromat. He had maneuvered himself casually between them, his back to Marco, his full attention on the young woman with all the questions.

"Don't you keep an extra set of clothes in the trunk?" Kate asked. "In case you get caught in the rain, or if you need to change a flat and your jacket gets torn?"

"You sound more like a policeman than a student," the man said. "Is there a problem?"

"Not so far," Kate said.

"There shouldn't be any," the man said.

"How often do you get down to Florence?" Marco asked. His tone was lighter, more conversational.

"When it's busy, maybe three, sometimes as often as five times a week," the man said. "It's a fast ride up and down, especially if you avoid weekend traffic. And the client can take in the sights and be back in his hotel room before it's too deep into the night."

"When you're in town with clients, you take them to the usual spots?" Kate asked. "The Duomo, the David, the Palace—those places, right? I mean, nothing out of the ordinary, side trips into smaller neighborhoods or out-of-the-way restaurants where only the locals eat?"

"No," the man said, shaking his head. "Clients want to see the places they've heard or read about. They want to see what they don't have back home."

"What about you?" she asked. "Are you interested in seeing any of those places for yourself?"

"Me?" The man pointed to his chest. "I don't even care about the sights they *do* want to see."

Kate moved away from the coin machine. "Then how did you know this Laundromat would be here?" she asked. "Only local cars and cabs with Florence plates are on this street. It caters to students and foreigners staying at hostels. The closest you could have parked would have been about a half mile up from the church. That puts you about seven city blocks from here and a long way from your client, who may decide to cut short her meal and be eager to get back to Milan, which would be hard to do if she can't locate her driver."

The man nodded, impressed. "That's not a problem," he said. "My client is familiar with the city. In fact, she was the one who told me about this place. She also told me I would find you both here."

"I don't know many people with their own personal drivers," Kate said, suddenly feeling cornered in the large room, her mouth dry.

"This one you do," the man said. "Not by name, I don't think. I wasn't even told her name."

"Why did she send you here?" Kate asked.

"Nothing too complicated," the man said. "She wants to talk to you both. There's no rush. We can even finish the laundry. When you're ready, we'll take a little walk and meet up at the car."

"And from there?" Kate asked.

"From there, I'm afraid we're all in the same boat," the man said. "Our final destination will be determined by the client."

"And what if we decide not to go?" Marco asked.

The man looked briefly at him and then turned back to Kate. "I don't think we'll need to explore those options," he said in a tone as matter-of-fact as if he were discussing the day's weather.

"We'll go with you," Kate said, "as soon as the clothes are out of the dryer."

"Good idea," the man said.

FORTY-FIVE MINUTES LATER, Kate and Marco were walking with the man down a narrow street, heading for Piazza Santa Croce. The day had turned dark and overcast, with the rumble of rain clouds looming in the distance. Marco carried one of Kate's duffel bags, slung over his right shoulder, his head down, feeling physically fatigued. The heavy toll of the past few days had finally kicked in, and he was now convinced that what had once seemed an innocent adventure was destined to end in the most violent way. He had been advised, by both the professor and the detective from Rome, simply to walk away, told that he'd taken the journey as far down the road as he could handle and that the safe bet would be to return to the student life he had so eagerly sought. Instead, he allowed bravado and his concern for Kate to cloud his usually sound judgment. As a boy and now as a young man he had always been acutely in touch with both his abilities and limitations. He was also aware of how quickly and how anonymously death could strike, without any hesitation or warning. He had seen it firsthand with the death of his father. And now, here on the streets of the very city where he was born, he had the distinct feeling that he was within striking distance of his own demise.

Kate had her own concerns, walking alongside the man in the leather jacket, a duffel bag cradled in her arms. There were elements of the man's story that troubled her. The prime question revolved around his client. What if it wasn't a woman she might have heard about? What if the man worked for the Raven instead? As matters stood, the Raven was expecting her and Marco to be delivered to him at the safe house, so why bother going to the trouble of tracking them down at a Laundromat? Why risk something going wrong out in the open, in full view of witnesses, when he could have her in a place where he would be in full control? And if she could rule out the Raven, then who was this woman and what role did she play in all this?

They turned a corner and entered a wider street, this one filled with pedestrians, many weighed down with packages containing clothing and wine. "Is this your first time driving this client?" she asked the man, keeping her tone casual.

"No," the man said. "When she's in Florence, I'm her regular driver."

"What does she do?" Kate asked.

Marco slowed his step and gave a quick look her way, wondering what she was hoping to gain with her questions.

"Does it matter?" the man asked. "She wants to see you, and I'm the one picked to take you to her."

Kate stopped and rested her duffel bag next to her leg. "It does matter," she said, "if not to you, then certainly to me and Marco. We need to know who it is you're taking us to see. And until we find out, neither one of us is taking another step."

"That would be a mistake," the man said, unable to hide the fact that this flustered him.

"Take a look around," Kate said. "There are far too many people on this street for you to do anything that would cause attention. There's a police car parked one street away, just past the gelato store. I'm sure they would respond if they heard me scream, which would leave you in a bit of a bind."

"What is it you want?" the man asked.

"Who are you taking us to see?" Kate asked. "No more games. I want the truth and I want to hear it now, or I'll stand here, the rest of the night if I must."

"He is taking you to see me," Clare Johnson said, standing in front of Kate, a light, cream-colored raincoat flung across her shoulders.

"Who are you?" Kate asked.

"Someone you need to talk to," Clare said, "your friend there, as well. And the sooner that happens, the better for all parties concerned."

"Talk to you about what?" Kate asked.

"I can be a big help to both of you," Clare said. "Help you to navigate your way through your current problem. I mean, let's be honest, shall we? If the two of you don't get some help fast—and I mean the *right* kind of help—then the reward for all the trouble you went to will end up in someone else's hands."

"What do you mean by the right kind of help?" Kate asked.

Clare turned and started to walk down the street. A dark sedan, engine running, was parked close to the corner, the man in the leather jacket within several feet of the driver's side door. She stopped and glanced at Kate over her shoulder. "That is something you'll have to discover for yourself."

CHAPTER 9

EDWARDS STRADDLED THE DUCATI 999, THE ENgine coughing out a thin line of white smoke from its silver exhaust pipe. One foot resting on the wet pavement, the other balanced against the curb just outside Harry's Bar, he glanced in the right side mirror. There, he saw the two men sitting in a black Mercedes sedan, their faces shielded by thick clouds of misty white cigarette smoke.

He carefully slid his black helmet over his head, careful not to dislodge an earpiece and wire attachment. "You still with me?" he said into a small microphone latched to the inside of the helmet.

"I can't leave you now," Banyon said in response. "You still owe me for that job in Tokyo, three years ago."

Edwards smiled at the memory. "Forget it, my friend," he said. "That's one check I'll never live to cut. You weren't supposed to be there, remember?"

"And if I hadn't been, then you wouldn't be here," Banyon said.

"They're three cars behind me," Edwards said, "two in the front, possibly one laying low in the back."

"You want them tailed or nailed?" Banyon asked.

"I've played enough games," Edwards said. "He went hard after Russell, and it's time we did the same to his crew."

"Let's take them out for a ride, then," Banyon said. "Head for the autostrada going south toward Rome. I'll be close enough on their tail to stop them if they get too close to you."

"There's a rest stop about ten, maybe fifteen kilometers up," Edwards said. "I'll swing into that and stop for a coffee and the men's room. If he follows me in, I'll deal with him there."

"In that case, I'll do my best to keep one of them alive for you," Banyon said.

"If it's only to be one, then I would suggest it be the driver," Edwards said. "But who am I to tell a man such as you his business?"

"Keep an eye out for a second car," Banyon warned, "either on the streets or up on the big road. It would make sense for them to have a lead car in place. If they don't, then it's a simple tail and report."

"It might still be that, even with two cars," Edwards said. "The Raven can't afford to go all-in on Kate telling him where the Angels are. I'm his safety net. He has to figure if she tells anyone else, it will be me."

"Or he might have guessed that you already have the Angels," Banyon said, "which would make you his primary."

"There's really only one way to ever know anything for sure," Edwards said, kicking the Ducati into gear and venturing into the light traffic.

He checked his mirrors and saw the Mercedes pull out of its spot and ease into the lane, a small plumbing truck the only vehicle separating them. He passed Banyon's black Ferrari and watched as Banyon made a fast U-turn, neatly dodging an oncoming metro bus to fall in line behind the trail car.

"Glad to see you still have all your reflexes," Edwards said, "even at your advanced age."

"Just wait till you see me drive and shoot," Banyon said. "That's when I'm at my very best."

"I hope so," Edwards said.

He stopped at a red light, released the handlebars of the Ducati, and checked to make sure his two handguns were still snug in place, easy to get to when the moment called. He tilted the bike slightly to the right, gripped the bars and brought his right hand down on the throttle as soon as the light turned green. He veered right, then swung a sharp left and was on the highway within seconds, the black sedan in pursuit.

He stayed in the right lane and shifted gears, going fast enough to keep ahead of the Mercedes, but not so fast as to suggest he knew he was being followed. Edwards now moved at too quick a pace to notice Banyon's car, but he was confident his friend would be there when needed. The traffic was light, the hour relatively early, and the weather still a few weeks away from the hint of fall. He moved the Ducati into the center lane and then made a quick tilt back to the right, smiling as he saw the Mercedes do the same, confirming for certain he was indeed their mark.

The rest stop was less than three miles away when a second car—this one a dark blue Audi SUV with tinted windows and chrome risers—inched up alongside the bike. He saw the rear passenger side window roll down and glimpsed the tip of a high-powered gun leaning against the door panel. Edwards quickly downshifted and let the Ducati slow as he moved back into the center lane, right behind the Audi. He saw frantic movement in the backseat as what appeared to be two gunmen rearranged their positions and shifted their weapons back in his direction.

Edwards took his right hand off the bar and reached for his handgun, pulled it and aimed at the back window of the Audi. He fired off three rounds, smashing glass and sending the car veering and screeching to the left and the right. He then kicked into higher gear and moved to the left lane, closing in on the driver's side, gun in his right hand. He exchanged a look with the driver, a young, portly man in his midtwenties with the thin collar of a blue blazer hugging his neck and a Roma soccer team hat pulled low on his head, shielding his eyes. A light, misty rain had started to fall, making the smooth roads slick and harder to navigate.

Three shots rang out from the rear of the driver's side, one of them nicking two of the spokes on the back wheel of the Ducati, momentarily causing the bike to veer, forcing Edwards to steady his grip and ease his hand off the throttle. He gave his mirrors a quick glance and saw the black Mercedes in the right lane, three car lengths in back of the action. There was no sign of Banyon in any of the lanes and there was less than a mile to go until the first rest stop.

The windows of the Audi were now lowered on all sides, guns at the ready, waiting for Edwards to venture closer into range. He slowed the Ducati down further and pulled out his second gun, cradling them as he steadied the bike down the center lane of the highway. The Audi slowed as well, the gunmen leaning farther out their windows, taking dead aim at him. The Mercedes held steady, a safe distance removed from what promised to be an all-out firefight.

The black Ferrari seemed to appear out of nowhere, zooming in on the right-hand side of the Audi, cruising just a few yards ahead of it, Banyon behind the wheel, a .357 Magnum held firmly in his right hand, pointed at the front of the car packed with shooters. Banyon took dead aim at the engine block of the car and fired off five rounds into the right side of the hood. From the rear,

Edwards let loose with a volley of bullets, all targeting the gas tank and the rear tires. He then switched gears, swung the bike around the back of the SUV, coming within inches of the chrome bumper—smoking tires, shouts, and misguided gunfire all erupting from the swerving vehicle.

Edwards leaned his bike hard right, his helmet mere inches from the pavement, and zoomed past the SUV to swing into the rest area. He downshifted and eased into a parking slot facing the road. Releasing the clutch, he brought down the kickstand with the heel of his boot and shut off the engine. Lifting the helmet off his head, he cradled it across his chest and watched as the SUV bounced off the highway, careened against several trees, then flipped over into a ball of thick smoke and shooting flames. He waited as the black Ferrari followed the SUV off the road, idling to a stop a safe distance away, and saw Banyon get out of his car and walk toward the smoldering Audi, knowing he was not heading over to help but rather to finish off the kill.

That left the Mercedes.

Edwards knew it would be parked somewhere in the rest area, its occupants waiting for him inside, either in one of the minimarts or possibly in the men's room, betting that the odds inside closed confines favored them more than a shootout in an open-air lot. He rested his helmet on the seat of his Ducati and, still facing the road, put a fresh clip in each gun. He then took a deep breath, patted down his hair and jacket, and walked toward the minimart, in the mood for a double espresso and a hot panino.

He checked his watch, then took a quick look around the half-mile-long parking area, filled at this hour with minivans, motorcycles, hired sedans, and buses. He always liked the rest areas on European roads, especially those in northern Italy. The food was always fresh, tasty, and inexpensive—mostly sandwiches, freshly baked pastries, and small pies. He found it a refreshing and welcome break from the long string of gas stations and fast-food outlets that dotted the highway landscape when he traveled cross-country back in the States.

Edwards smiled at the dark-haired, middle-aged woman working the minimart counter just off the rest stop entrance, ordered Genoa salami and fresh mozzarella on a small toasted roll, and handed her his receipt. That was another European habit he found pleasure in: deciding what you wanted, paying for it, and then ordering it. He felt it made a line move faster by eliminating last minute indecision.

He scanned the small place, made up of six tall, circular tables, no stools, and a corner area filled with napkins and sugar packets next to a register where a pudgy young man stared up at a TV monitor above his head. Just off to Edwards's right was the sliding door entrance to the market itself, where he spotted a half-dozen shoppers loading up on fresh milk, water, and snacks suitable for a lengthy road trip. To his left and down a wide corridor, past a string of coin-operated soda and juice machines, were the washrooms, the women's on one side and the men's just around a sharp corner.

The woman handed Edwards his toasted roll, nestled in a plastic napkin, and slid a small cup of coffee next to it. "Were you out there when that loud explosion went off?" she asked.

He shook his head. "Sounded to me like maybe a flat and the driver lost control of the car," he said. "That's why I stick with motorcycles."

"I pray no one was hurt," the woman said.

Edwards nodded in agreement, took his toasted bread and coffee and turned toward the sugar counter. He was stirring in three packets into what he knew would be an excessively strong cup of espresso when he spotted the two men walking in. They were both young and fit, moving with closed fists and hard looks, heading his way and not too concerned whether he was aware of their presence. The taller of the two—his thick dark hair heavily gelled and his face flushed—stepped in next to Edwards and rested an elbow on the sugar counter.

"We need to talk," he said. "The men's room would be the best place, but out here is just as good. And understand, if there's any trouble, we're on orders to shoot to kill. And if someone who came in here for a bathroom break gets in the way, so be it."

Edwards sipped his coffee and took a thick bite out of his toasted sandwich. "Get yourself something," he said, chewing his food slowly, "your friend, too. Whatever is going to happen here between us—talk or worse—it would be best if it took place with our stomachs full."

"You were lucky out on the highway," the tall man said. "The guys sitting in that SUV weren't very good."

"But that's not the case with you and your silent friend," Edwards said. "That's why the Raven put you two in the lead car."

"You're the smart one in this group," the man said. "So, if this goes the way it should, then maybe all three of us stand a good chance of leaving here alive."

Edwards finished his sandwich and espresso and wiped at the corners of his mouth with the edges of a paper napkin. "Let's take a walk," he said, turning away from the two men and heading toward the bathrooms just beyond the snack machines.

He pushed open the men's room door and stepped into a small puddle, water from the rim of a cast iron pipe directly over his head slowly dripping down. He walked to the middle of three sinks, cupped his hands under the faucet and waited for the water to flow. He didn't look up when the two men followed him in, watching as an old man in a tattered brown traveling coat eased past them and made his way out.

"Is this the part where you rough me up?" Edwards asked.

"It doesn't have to go there," the tall man said. "You know what we want to know. Just tell us and we'll let you get back on your bike and be on your way."

"You called me the smart one only a few minutes ago," Edwards said. "So, how smart would I be if I believed that you plan to let me out of this bathroom alive?"

"Do you know where they are?" the man asked.

Edwards nodded. "Yes, I do," he said.

"Then we can make a fair offer," the man said. "You tell us where the Angels are and we leave the girl alone. If you pass on it, there are men in the city ready to grab her. Once he has her, you know he'll do whatever he needs to do to get her to talk."

"You make it sound so simple," Edwards said.

"It can be," the man said, "if you let it."

Edwards turned away from the sink and stood facing the two men. "And if I choose not to take the simple approach?" he asked. "Decide to let the girl fend for herself? What does your plan call for then?"

"You know the Raven better than anyone, is my guess," the tall man said. "It's not the path I'd suggest but it's your call to make."

"I suppose there are worse places to die than in a men's room at a pit stop just outside Florence," Edwards said. "Though, I must admit, I had always envisioned a more romantic finale."

The tall man eased the left flap of his thin jacket aside and raised his right hand toward the handgun jammed against his hip. The second man walked with his head down and hands folded behind his back, bracing himself against the sink behind Edwards.

"I imagine you placed a sign outside," Edwards said, "which explains why we've been here alone for such a long period."

"What good is a men's room when the toilets are overflowing?" the tall man said, smiling.

"You let no one in," Edwards said with a nod. "That was a smart move. But you did make one mistake."

"Educate us, Professor," the tall man said.

"You didn't check to see who was already in," Banyon said, emerging from a tight corner of the large room. He had a gun in each hand, both with silencers attached and aimed at the back of the tall man.

"I haven't pulled my weapon," the tall man said, his eyes on Edwards, his words directed to Banyon.

"Then that was your second mistake," Edwards said, coldness now lacing his voice.

He whirled toward the man behind him and deftly and with one furious motion plunged a knife deep into his stomach, not releasing his hard grip until his victim dropped to his knees, his right hand grasping the edge of the white sink, his eyes open wide, his mouth unable to form words. Behind him, Edwards heard the three soft pings of the silencer and low groan of a dying man. He pulled out his knife and turned just as the thin man fell facedown onto the marble floor.

Edwards stared up at Banyon, the smoldering guns still clutched in his hands as two thick trails of blood began to pool around his feet, and shook his head. "You ever wonder at what point the goals of the Society begin to mingle comfortably with those of the Immortals?" he asked.

"There *are* differences," Banyon said.

"Well, then, perhaps you can remind me what they are," Edwards said. "It would be nice for me to hear them spoken out loud."

"It will be my pleasure," Banyon said, "soon as we dispose of the bodies."

CHAPTER
10

THE HOUSE WAS BIG, STONE, WHITE, AND SE-cluded. it was a renovated thirteenth-century structure framed by manicured lawns and thick shrubs and trees that kept it all but hidden from the winding streets below. It was a half mile from Piazza Michelangelo, and the entire expanse of the city could be seen from the bay windows that dominated the large first-floor sitting room and second-story master bedroom. The ceilings were thirteen feet high, and a series of portraits of dukes, duchesses, and earls lined the walls, while thick Oriental rugs rested on marble floors.

Kate stood in the center of a large reading room on the second floor, Marco to her left. The door to the room was locked from the outside and the drapes were drawn, two large floor lamps bringing them their only light. A small fire smoldered in the stone fireplace just to Kate's right. Outside, she could hear light rain pelting the windowpanes.

"If he's as smart as everyone says he is," Marco said in a hushed voice, "he will know this is a trap."

"Maybe," Kate said. "But let's not give him any extra help. Let him figure it out on his own. Don't let him see it in your eyes or hear it in your voice."

"I'm scared," Marco said, "and he will hear and see that."

"You are *supposed* to be scared," she said. "He'll expect you to be."

"And you?"

"I'm twice as scared as I've ever been in my life," she said.

"What are you going to tell him?" Marco asked. "I mean, when he asks you about the Angels."

"I'll have no choice but to tell him the truth," Kate said. "I don't know where they are and I'm not at all certain who has them."

"He won't believe that," Marco said. "If he thought anyone other than you knew where the Angels were, those people would be standing here instead of the two of us. He'll just assume we're lying, and that will make him angry, and as has been mentioned often enough, I'll be the first to feel his anger."

"Rumore won't allow that to happen," Kate said with a degree of reassurance, "either to you or to me."

"You can think of him as your protector, if you wish," Marco said, an edge to his words. "But somehow, I can't imagine my safety being his primary concern."

Kate smiled and pressed her right hand against his face. "That's because you're jealous," she said.

"I have no cause to be jealous," he said, caught off guard, both by Kate's touch and her correct reading of his feelings. "Even though you must admit you are somewhat taken by him."

"I only just met him, Marco," she said. "But I was pretty impressed by how he handled those two men in the Gardens. He took what should have been a confrontational situation and turned it to his advantage without breaking a sweat. And he made the plan he came up with sound as if he had worked on it for weeks, instead of just inventing it on the spot."

"He's a detective," Marco said. "That's what he's paid to do. And the plan isn't all that wonderful, trust me. He's out there, safe and surrounded by dozens of other police officers, while we're in here forced to confront a danger we should be avoiding at all costs."

"It's all very flattering," Kate said.

"What is?"

"Your jealousy of Rumore," she said.

The door behind them swung open and the Raven walked in, escorted by the two men from the Gardens. "I'm glad to see you could make our little meeting," he said. "It's always a pleasure to see you."

"I don't think we were left much choice in the matter," Kate said.

She looked directly at him, seeing him not only as an adversary, but also as the man who might be her father. The very notion that she would have to view him as both flushed her face red with anger and trepidation. She wondered if he ever had such thoughts himself, or if he had learned long ago simply to keep his focus on the matter facing him at that moment. Or maybe he didn't even know the full story, had no idea of the history the two shared.

"There is always a choice," the Raven said, "regardless of the circumstances. It always boils down to a question of need. You made the decision to come here because you felt it was in your best interest to do what you could to protect the life of your young friend. Now, that's an admirable trait in most professions, but a damaging one in ours."

"That would mean something if I thought we *were* in the same profession," Kate said. "But I'm not a thief."

"You are so much your mother's daughter," the Raven said, his eyes betraying the slightest hint of emotion. "I'm happy to see all the years spent under the tutelage of the professor didn't completely dull your spirit. You've managed to keep it alive."

"I understand my mother meant a great deal to you,"

Kate said. She took several steps closer to him, only a few feet separating them. "Is there any truth to that?"

"There is as much truth to those words as to any you might say," he answered.

"Then you can stop all of this now," Kate said. "You can show me how much my mother and now her memory means to you by letting me go, along with Marco."

"I see you also inherited your mother's romantic side as well," the Raven said, a smile spreading across his face, his hands gently gripping the back of a chair. "There is only one problem with that idea."

"What?"

"I care for the Midnight Angels more than I ever cared for your mother," he said.

"Then you didn't know her as well as I thought."

"Perhaps," the Raven said. "Or maybe I knew her better than anyone else. Your mother lived for the work, and if she were as close to the Angels as I am, then she would allow nothing to stand in her way."

Kate nodded. "I have no idea where the Angels are."

The Raven lost the smile and the relaxed manner, the muscles of his face tensing, his hands clutching the back of the chair with a harder grip. He stared at Kate and then gave a quick glance in Marco's direction. "By this time," he said, "you have some idea of the kind of man I am. You have heard or maybe even witnessed what I am capable of. If indeed you neither possess them nor know where they are, then you cease being of any use to me. Have I been clear enough?"

"Yes," Marco said. "But she's telling you the truth. She has no idea where the Angels are."

"How is that possible, since you were the dynamic team that found them, then retrieved and then hid them?" the Raven asked.

"We'll admit to that," Kate said. "But just like we took them out of their hidden home, someone else found them and took them from what we obviously thought was a secure location."

"Why am I to believe that?" the Raven asked.

"I don't care whether you do or not," Kate said. "It's the truth."

"Well, I'll need you to prove that for me," the Raven said. "And believe me when I tell you that those moments will not be pleasant ones."

"Don't forget to start with me," Marco said, shaking his head in defeat. "It's okay. I've been forewarned."

"You're also naive," the Raven said. "Your death will not matter one bit to the young lady to whom you so clearly have sworn your devotion. Our methods may differ, but make no mistake. She and I share the same goals."

"I don't have the Angels and I don't know where they are," Kate said.

She did her best to maintain her composure, but couldn't hide her fear. Her legs felt lifeless and she could feel a tremble in her right hand and was certain the Raven had noticed it as well. The nape of her neck was damp, and the excessive heat in the room made it difficult for her to take a full breath. She had spent large chunks of her life preparing to fulfill this role, but as she stood there, her body just a few ticks away from twitching, she realized that no amount of training could ever prepare her for the reality of such a moment.

"Then we have reached an impasse," the Raven said. "And the only method I know to remedy such a problem is a very painful one."

The door behind him opened and three men walked in, one of them holding a thick roll of leather.

The Raven didn't turn to face them. "Strip the boy of his shirt and spread him out on the table," he said, his eyes moving from Kate to Marco. "Tie his hands and bind his feet. If nothing else, I'm a complete fool for religious symbolism."

Kate shouted, the panic finally taking full command of her body. "I don't know where they are," she said. "You have to believe me!"

Two of the men grabbed Marco and ripped open his blue shirt, the white circular buttons scattering to the floor, then dragged him toward a table in the corner of the room. Marco put up minimal struggle, realizing how little effect it would have on the two much stronger men. He caught Kate's eye and saw the cold look of fear on her face, as if the blunt force of the truth had finally hit. She now knew what he had known all along—they were students who had placed themselves in the middle of a struggle between forces stronger and deadlier than any they could possibly imagine. She might have thought she was ready for such a move, and perhaps with more time and training she would have been, but the moment arrived too soon and with not enough warning for her to anticipate all the dangers that would rain down upon them.

"I don't know what my mother saw in you," she said, her voice low, her eyes focused on the Raven, consciously avoiding Marco as he was laid out with arms spread across the long table in the corner. "It is difficult to imagine she would risk losing the only man she loved for someone so pathetic."

"Then you clearly know as little about your mother as I initially imagined," the Raven said. "And you know even less about me."

"I know what I see," Kate said. "A man consumed by greed who reverts to murder and torture in order to acquire works of art only so that he can sell them. That is not a man my mother could ever love. That much I *do* know about her."

"And you think her goals were so different?" he

asked. "Or your own? You're much too intelligent to believe that. Simply look at the life you've led—beautiful home, the best schools, travel whenever and wherever you chose to go. How do you suppose all that was paid for? And then there's the Vittoria Society, praised far and wide as the most altruistic benefactors. Yet, here they are, the richest organization of their kind in the world, and there you stand, ready to step up to the throne when the professor's day is done. Once you piece all those threads together, dare to tell me the difference between your mother and me."

Kate stood silent for several moments, the heat in the room becoming even more oppressive despite the bottom of the curtains furling in the evening breeze of the gardens below. "My mother would not have stood for this," she finally said. "She might have given her all to acquire the works, but there were certain lines she would never have crossed."

"And I might have done the same," the Raven said, "had she chosen to remain by my side."

"You chose the work over her," Kate said. "You made that very clear."

"She *was* the work," the Raven said, his voice betraying him with a small break. "That was what I could never convey to her. There was no separation between the two. Not in my eyes. I loved them both dearly. To this day I do. And now that I've cleansed my soul, I'm afraid it's time to get to the matter before us. You know what it is I desire. All you need to do is tell me."

Kate looked across the room at Marco, the two men holding him down, his legs hanging over the edges of the table, his upper body trembling, his eyes closed. "I wish I could," she said. "I wish I could."

The Raven took a deep breath and walked with his head down toward his employees. "Break two of his fingers," he ordered, "and let her hear him scream."

"Wait," Kate pleaded from across the room, not sure what to say next, wondering just what signal Rumore was out there waiting to hear before moving in.

The Raven held up his right hand and, along with the two men, turned to face her.

"I can tell you where I hid them once we got them out of the corridor," she said. "From there, maybe you and your men can figure a way to pick up the trail and locate them."

"I'm afraid that's not good enough," the Raven said. "I'm an art hunter, not a detective."

He glanced at one of the men and nodded. Within seconds Marco's sharp scream echoed through the room and nearly brought Kate to her knees, tears forming at the corners of her eyes, her hands clasped across her mouth.

"I'm so sorry, Marco," she whispered.

"Shall we continue?" the Raven asked.

Kate turned toward him, lowering her hands from her face, and then, fueled with anger and hate, she rushed him, her shoulders at chest level, sending them both to the ground. Rolling off of him, she got up and ran toward the double doors leading to a small patio. She grabbed a thick, porcelain vase as she moved, avoided the reach of one of the Raven's men, and swung the doors open, tossing the vase out the second-floor window and standing there as she heard it smash onto the rock garden pavement below. Then she peered out into the semidarkness, hoping to see some movement, hear the police presence as they pressed into action, but got nothing in return other than a warm breeze brushing her face. She froze when she felt the Raven wrap his arms around her waist.

"Now what did your little action accomplish?" he whispered, "other than ruining what I can only assume was a rather valuable vase?"

"You may as well kill me now," Kate said, anger overcoming any fear. "I will never help you. Never. So do what it is you do best. Otherwise, know that I will make you taste defeat."

"Finally, you sound like your mother," the Raven said. "Perhaps there is hope for you after all."

"Let Marco go," she said. "This is between the Society and the Immortals, and he has no place in either group. Leave the fight where it belongs—between the two of us."

"And if I agree, will I then hear from you what I need to know?" the Raven asked.

"You have my word," Kate said.

The Raven released his grip on her and turned to step back into the room, leaving Kate standing alone on the patio. He looked over at the two men hovering uncertainly above Marco. "Let the boy go," he said. "He is no longer of use to me."

"That's funny," Rumore said, "I was about to say the very same thing. Just goes to show it might be true—criminal minds do think alike."

He was standing in the open doorway, three heavily armed officers forming a tight circle behind him, the hallway beyond filled with cops with automatic weapons at the ready.

The Raven recovered quickly from his sudden shock. Assuming there were as many if not more officers outside, he assessed the situation and formulated the quickest escape path he could envision in the scant seconds available to him. He had been in the hunt for a long time, and learned years earlier that while the true professional needed to be prepared for the unexpected, it was only the very skilled who had the capacity to improvise a successful plan. "And here I always thought Florence to be the safest city in Italy," he said to Rumore. "I will make it a habit from this moment on to always lock my door."

"It's a good rule no matter what city you happen to be in," Rumore said. He walked into the room and looked at Marco, now straddling the table, his damaged hand cradled in the palm of his good one. He made eye contact with Kate, still standing on the patio, then turned back to the Raven. "It would be another good idea if you had your men lay down whatever weapons they might have hidden under those clothes. With all these cops around, there's sure to be one or two looking to take someone down, and your boys do seem to fit the profile."

"It seems you have the upper hand," the Raven said. "That does not often occur with me."

"That request about the guns?" Rumore said. "That goes for you as well."

The Raven held out his arms and kept his hands open, fingers spread.

"Okay, then," Rumore said, taking several steps deeper into the room, "let's try and take this nice and easy, shall we?"

"I await your orders," the Raven said.

Rumore turned to one of the uniformed officers standing to his left. "Take the kid first," he said. "Get him to a doctor and have that hand taken care of."

The uniformed man nodded, hurried across the room and gently took Marco by his elbow. "Don't worry about your shirt," he told the boy. "We have blankets for you downstairs."

As Marco walked slowly past Rumore, he glanced up at the detective. "I'm sorry if I let you down," he said.

"You're a lot tougher than you think," Rumore assured him, with a pat on his shoulder. "You bought us time."

"What about him?" Marco asked, tilting his head toward the Raven.

"Yes, please, what about me?" the Raven said. "Do you think you have enough to hold me longer than it will take my lawyer to drive up from his office in Rome?"

Rumore moved around the room, hands at his sides, the uniforms buzzing behind him, placed in position for a takedown. He was impressed by the calm exhibited by the Raven, at least on the surface. He had learned that one of the marks of a professional criminal was to act as if he or she had the upper hand, no matter how dire the situation. The Raven's henchmen lacked that skill, and stood with their shoulders sagged, waiting for the handcuffs to be slapped on. Marco was just happy to have survived an ordeal that could have easily ended up doing much more damage than it did. As for Kate, she had yet to move from her place on the patio. He was not sure if it was fear keeping her there or the fact that she thought it best to stay out of the way and let him and his officers do what they came to do.

But it was the Raven who concerned Rumore.

He was nothing at all as he had imagined him, despite all that he'd read of the man's many rumored thefts and more heinous crimes. The Raven was athletic in build and moved with a dancer's grace, each gesture measured, each action and reaction made to solicit a response he already seemed to anticipate. But more than anything, it was his calm demeanor that troubled Rumore. It seemed as if he knew what was going to happen next, long before anyone else had come even close to anticipating it.

"Maybe you should tell your lawyer to take his time coming to Florence," Rumore said, eager to regain the momentum crucial in any confrontation. "The kidnapping charges alone will allow us to hold you for as long as necessary. Then, we tack on felony assault, maybe even stretch it to attempted murder and the threat to do bodily harm with intent, and the magistrate will have more than enough to seal the paperwork and hold you without bond."

"In that case, you leave me with very little choice," the Raven said.

"I don't think I'm leaving you with *any* choice," Rumore said.

"Trust me when I tell you, Detective," the Raven said, flashing a cold smile, "there is *always* a choice, no matter the circumstances."

"What's yours?" Rumore asked.

The Raven stared at the detective for a quiet moment and then turned toward the patio and bolted. Rumore surprised, chased after him, watched him wrap an arm around Kate and whirl her so he stood behind her, his left arm around her waist. The revolver clutched in the Raven's other hand was pointed at the young woman's temple.

Rumore tried to maintain professional composure, doing his best to ignore the fact that he had allowed himself to be duped, falling into a conversational trap the man had so expertly weaved, instead of going by the police textbook and making the arrests as soon as he entered the room. He had committed one of the cardinal sins of police work—never lose control of a situation. Now, the rules would be dictated by the criminal and not the cop, and he was helpless to do anything more than listen.

"What do you want?" he asked.

"It would seem obvious, no?" the Raven said. "I take the girl and depart your company. You can take solace in the fact that I'll willingly leave behind my men to do with as you please. They are of no use to me."

"There are at the very least twenty-five officers surrounding the house," Rumore said, "and about another half dozen or so working the first two floors. And not one of them reports to me. I'm not from this city and I have limited jurisdiction, if that."

"Not my problem," the Raven said. "I either leave here with Kate or you can come and cradle her dying body. I would prefer the first solution, which seems so much cleaner. How about you?"

Rumore glared at the Raven and then turned to one of the uniformed officers. "Find your captain," he said to him. "Explain the situation and ask him to have his men pull back from the house."

"*All* his men," the Raven said. "I wouldn't want any stray scopes pointed in my direction."

Rumore looked at Kate, silent and shivering in the Raven's grip. "You okay?" he asked.

She nodded.

"I'm sorry I screwed up," Rumore said. "But I want you to know three things. I will find you. I will get you home safe. Do you believe me?"

"Yes," Kate said.

"Oh, out of curiosity," the Raven said, nearly glowing with his victory, "what's the third?"

"That you won't leave Florence alive," Rumore said.

CHAPTER II

EDWARDS STOOD BESIDE CLARE JOHNSON AND stared up at the magnificent structure of the Duomo. It was just past nine in the morning the day after the Raven had made his daring escape.

"It truly is a marvel," he said. "A simple and elegant design, built not to last for decades, but for eternity. I'm always left amazed at the level of craftsmanship and never tire of looking at it, finding something new and unique each time I do."

"Not everyone was so charmed," Clare said. "Michelangelo hated it. He claimed it was nothing more than an inflated shelter for pigeons."

"If it wasn't touched by his hand, he considered *any* work insignificant," Edwards said. "The burden of genius, I suppose."

"While we're on the subject of genius," Clare said, "you seem to have been caught a bit flat-footed by our mutual friend. He has Kate now, which means he's close to having the Angels. He had her targeted from the start, regardless of who actually possessed them. Which begs the question, what are you going to do about it?"

"What I always planned to do," Edwards said. "The Raven wasn't the only one who came into this with the goal of leaving town with the Angels."

"Then the deal we have still holds?" Clare asked.

Edwards looked away from the Duomo and turned toward her. "How you manage to keep them all straight in your head is a wonder to me," he said. "After all, is there anyone involved in this that you *don't* have a deal with?"

She smiled and wiped stray strands of hair from her face. "I haven't totally locked in with the cops yet," she said, "but give me a bit more time. Look, Richard, we each work our own way, using our own methods. I want those Angels as much as you, Kate, the Raven, or anyone else."

"Well, you're honest in that regard," Edwards said.

"The only secrets of our trade involve finding where the art is hidden," she said. "The rest of it—alliances, friendships, real or faked, who sits on whose side of the table—that all gets found out in less time than it takes to make the connections. I've never made any bones about how I go about my business. The best deal offered me is the one I'll take."

"Could you arrange a meeting between me and the Raven?" Edwards asked.

"I could," Clare said, "but I won't unless I know the reasons why, and not just those on the surface. You need to tell me as much as you can about what you have planned. You might be surprised—I could be of some help."

"What is it you want?" Edwards asked. "I mean, besides the Angels? That's the short-term goal. I'm asking about the long-range plans."

"What makes you think I've made any?" she asked.

"I heard a story about your dad a few years back," Edwards said. "He was planning a job, a fairly big one in a city he was unfamiliar with and with an alarm system that had yet to be broken."

"Those aspects would have appealed to him," Clare said with a smile.

They were now walking on the perimeter of the Duomo, past the stands hawking Florentine souvenirs and the tourists with their digital cameras pointed in all directions.

"It was a private museum, just outside Denver," Edwards said. "The owner was an avid collector of modern art and a quiet buyer of stolen Renaissance works. Over the years, he had managed to latch onto about a dozen masterworks, some known, one or two only rumored to exist."

"Which one was my dad going after?" Clare asked.

"All of them," Edwards said. "Here he was, in a strange city, working against an alarm system that any sane person would tell him couldn't be cracked, and he was going to clean this guy out of every black market painting he had in his collection. He knew it might end up being the toughest job he ever went out on, so he took time in the planning, worked and reworked every angle, read books about the city, articles about the man, studied the designs of the house, took mail order courses on advanced alarm system technology. He worked that job for three years before he made his move. In other words, he was thinking long-term."

"Just like you think I am," Clare said.

"You can't hide from your bloodline," Edwards said.

"So, tell me, did my dad get the job done?" she asked.

"You ever hear a story where he didn't?" Edwards asked. "He cracked the code, got the paintings, and ended up with enough of a cut from his score that I doubt he ever once worried about the cost of the education he bought you."

The two walked in silence for several minutes, taking in the sounds and sights of the crowded street—the restaurants and cafés preparing for busy lunchtime traffic; the front men for stores selling everything from leather goods to perfumes to pottery, advertising their wares in the middle of the passing crowds; the smiles and looks of wonder mixed with confusion on the faces of children new to the city, clutching their parents' hands, staring up at buildings that had been put together by hand and designed by men working free of the weight of modern technology.

"I do have a long-term goal," Clare said. "But it doesn't affect you, at least not directly. I won't share it with you just yet, but someday soon I will. For now, just know we're not working on opposite ends of the field. It just might sometimes appear that way."

"Can I count on your help against the Raven?" Edwards asked. "I know you've done business with him in the past, and there has also been talk about a romantic connection that ended on something of a sour note. None of that matters to me unless it affects this current operation."

"Will he hurt Kate?" Clare asked. "Is she in danger from him?"

"I wouldn't be enjoying our little walk if I thought there was the slightest chance of that," Edwards said. "The Raven has a number of reasons not to harm Kate, prime among them that she's his key to getting his hands on the Midnight Angels. He'll do his best to put a scare into her, but for the moment at least she's safe."

"He might be holding her, but he's not the only one who wants to get at Kate," Clare said. "Just take a walk down any street in the city and you'll find someone connected to the art world. On my way over to meet you, I caught a glimpse of the Frenchman who is now fully employed by the Russian mob to bring them as much lost and stolen art as he can find. And as you're aware, to the Russians, cost is no object—though they would much prefer that payment be shelled out in blood as opposed to cash. This business has changed so much in such a short period of time. It was always brutal, but now it's like working in a war zone."

"I heard the Frenchman had found his way here," Edwards said. "But as good as he is, he'll be nothing but fodder to the Raven. That goes for the dozen or so other hunters walking the side streets. The Raven won't ever deal with them, and he certainly won't allow them to harm Kate."

"What makes you so certain?" Clare asked.

"I know my opponents," Edwards said.

"Do you have an idea of where the Raven might be keeping her?" she asked.

"As a matter of fact, I do," he said.

"I'd be a much more receptive partner if you made a better effort at sharing your information with me," Clare said. "It would go a long way toward strengthening the bonds of trust that exist between us."

"We don't actually have a bond of trust," Edwards said, smiling. "More like a bond of convenience."

"Well, sometimes that works even better," she said, returning the smile.

"You risk putting yourself into a very dangerous corner," he said, "with all these moves you're attempting. All it will take is for one of them to backfire and there will be no hesitation on anyone's part to put you down."

"You don't know what I'm planning," she said. "You only think you do. And I'm more than capable of handling myself, regardless of the situation."

"I'm not saying you're not good at it," Edwards said. "I am saying that you run the risk of floating too many balloons. One of them is bound to pop."

"I didn't realize you cared about my well-being," Clare said.

"I don't, not really," he said. "But I have come to respect you and appreciate the help you've given the Society in the past. But there comes a time, Clare, when you have to stop pitting one side against the other and wager that you'll come out ahead regardless of who ends up the winner. And that time is now."

"Look, I've done business with you in the past, as well as with the Raven," she said. "And sometimes I'll cut a deal with the cops or with the galleries. I really never went out of my way to make that a secret. It's all part of my job—whatever it takes to get the works back into the right hands and at the right price. But I won't do anything that hurts the girl. On that, I give you my word."

"No offense," Edwards said, "but I'll need more than your word before I can believe you."

Clare nodded, stopped walking and leaned against the driver's side of a parked car. "What do you need?" she asked.

"In order to get Kate back and away from the Raven," he said, "I'll need to let him know where the Angels are hidden. At least that's one of the options I'm considering. Now, he won't just hand her over, since he won't be sure whether I'm telling the truth. But he will let her stay with someone he's in bed with, so to speak, while he goes off in search of the works."

"And you want me to double-cross the Raven," Clare said, "so you can safely send him off on a wild-goose chase. Yes?"

"On the button," Edwards said.

"Now with you being so eager to set up the Raven," she said, "how can I be sure you're not just as eager to set me up?"

"I'm taking a chance on you," Edwards said, "and you'll be taking one with me. By the end of the play, we'll both know if either of us was less than truthful. That's my only offer. But I need to know if you're in before I walk away from here."

Clare moved away from the car, gazing over at a cluster of boys running and kicking a soccer ball in between the small packs of moving tourists. "You can count on me to do my part, Professor."

CHAPTER 12

The Raven walked down the center aisle of the quiet church and made a left at the altar. He caught a glimpse of a young nun sitting in a second pew, her hands folded, head bowed in prayer, as he made his way toward a rear stairwell, the walls and ceiling shrouded in shadows from dimmed lights and votive candles. He found his way to the basement, cold stone floor and thick concrete walls keeping out both any warmth and potential intruders. A series of hanging lightbulbs lit the way to a massive wooden door marked with a sign that had the word DANGER stenciled across the front in four different languages. He turned the old, rusty knob and walked in.

Kate was sitting on a rickety wooden chair, her hands bound, her feet tied to the legs of a large table that dominated the room, a coal-burning stove at her back offering the only warmth. The Raven nodded to the two men standing guard. "I can only imagine my guest must be as hungry as I am," he said. "Go out and bring us back two decent meals. And make sure you're not followed. I prefer to eat my lunch free of unwanted company."

The men walked past the Raven and out of the room.

"I gave you some time to yourself," he said to Kate, "with the hope it would allow you to give some serious thought to the situation you currently are in."

"You know, for a man allegedly as smart as you are,"

she said, "you can be pretty dense. But despite that, you're concerned. I can see it on your face."

The Raven smiled at her. "In what way?" he asked.

"You're starting to have doubts," she said to him. "You hide it pretty well, acting as if you are always in complete control, but you're not really sure what your next move should be."

"And you have come to this conclusion based on what?" the Raven said.

"Based on the fact that you are starting to doubt whether or not I actually do have the Angels or know where they are," Kate said. "I mean if I did, I more than likely would have told you by now. I probably would have told you back at the house, right after you hurt Marco. But, even if I had remained strong back there, I would have certainly cracked down here, in some dingy basement, freezing cold, tied, and bound. Still, I haven't said a word. I'm either the bravest woman you've ever met or I've been telling you the truth all along."

"Your friend, the young man," the Raven said, "is it possible he talked more than he claims? Stumbling on such a rare find is not something someone as naive and inexperienced as he seems to be could keep to himself. More than likely, he would brag about his discovery."

Kate shrugged, her arms and legs aching from the stiff position she had been placed in and were numb from the tight bonds. "Not one person he might have talked to would have known how to move the Angels, or where to move them. If Marco told anyone where they were initially hidden, the Angels would now be in the custody of the Rome Art Squad."

"Which then leaves, as always, the professor," the Raven said.

"I never told him where they were hidden," Kate said, surprised at the accusation but seeing the logic.

"You wouldn't have to," the Raven said. "Richard

knows you better than anyone. He understands how your mind operates. And he has enough men in Florence to help him in such a quest, perhaps even a tracker who could report back to him exactly where you shielded the statues from view."

"He wouldn't do that and not tell me," Kate said, her tone defiant.

"In that case, you don't know your beloved professor as well as you might think you do," the Raven said.

Kate was about to respond but was silenced by two loud, hard knocks on the door.

The Raven swung the door open and was surprised to see the same nun he had spotted earlier in the entryway of the church. He glanced down at her feet and saw two large plastic bags filled with packages and containers resting against her legs. "Are you lost, Sister?" he asked.

"No," the nun said, "I think I'm in the right place. You wanted some food brought down, is that correct?"

"That is true," the Raven said, taking several cautious steps back. "But you were not who I sent to get it."

"Your friends are upstairs," the nun said. "In the first confessional booth, the one just across from the high altar."

"That doesn't sound like my friends at all," he said.

The nun glanced over at Kate and then glared at the Raven. "We all seek out the Lord when death is at hand."

He reached for the gun he kept jammed in a side holster, but was too slow. The nun moved with a professional's skill and speed. With three quick gestures she entered the room, closed the door behind her with a rear kick of her right boot, and had a semiautomatic jammed against the Raven's chest. "I've already killed two today," she said. "A third would not be a problem."

Despite the gun against his ribs, the Raven managed a slight smile. "What order do you belong to?" he asked.

"I'm Sister Rita of the Sisters of No Mercy," the nun said.

She reached into a side pocket of her vestments, pulled out a switchblade, and pushed the Raven with the hard edge of the gun closer to Kate, until she was within reach of the young woman. "Lift your hands up to me," she ordered Kate, her eyes square on the Raven.

Kate pulled her hands up and watched as Rita snapped open the switchblade and began to slice at the twine that bound her.

The Raven stayed motionless, seemingly more amused than threatened by the situation. "You're pretty good with that," he noted after Rita had cut Kate's bonds. "I must applaud the professor on his recruiting methods. I would never have thought to solicit recruits from a convent."

"Some nuns are married to Christ," Rita said. "Others are married to their work. You just have to know where to look."

Rita watched as Kate undid the ropes around her feet and then stood. "He has men stationed outside the church," she said to Kate, nodding toward the Raven. "We'll have to make as fast a getaway as possible. Can you drive a car?"

Kate nodded.

"How well do you know the side streets?" Rita asked.

"I've walked most of them, never driven them, though," Kate said.

"That's going to change today," Rita said. "I'm going to need you to maneuver the car while I try to keep his men from getting close to us."

"Do you have a destination?" Kate asked.

"Yes."

"Then you should drive," she said.

"You won't get far," the Raven said. "Not all my men are easy to kill."

"Perhaps not," Rita said, her gun still pointed at him. "But you most certainly are."

Kate pulled the Raven away from the nun and threw him down on the chair. "I'll tie him up," she said. "That should keep him out of commission long enough."

"A couple of bullets will keep him out of commission for good," Rita said.

"He'll get his due," Kate said as she bound the Raven's hands and feet to the back of the chair, "just not here and not now."

"Your actions won't win any points with me down the road," the Raven said, his voice lower. "You'd be better off getting rid of me, as the good sister proposes."

"I don't expect anything from you," Kate said. "But I'm not a killer like you."

"Then there is still much for you to learn," the Raven said.

Kate checked the knots on his hands and feet, then straightened, took one final look at him, and followed the nun out of the basement, slamming the door behind her.

CHAPTER 13

DUSK HAD SETTLED ACROSS THE LARGE CEMETERY on the outskirts of the city, less than a fifteen-minute drive from the center. The grounds were pristine, and a dozen rows of thick marble walls standing twelve feet high lined each side of the stone walkway. There were about a hundred headstone markers on each side of every wall, highlighting the names, birth dates, and dates of death of the bodies resting within the walls. As a rule, Italy does not allocate thousands of acres of precious land to its dead, preferring instead to inter them in family mausoleums or walls, which more often than not are marked by votive candles and flowers, changed weekly by the regular visitors who come by to pay their respects, either out of habit or desire.

Edwards stood between two large walls, gazing up at unfamiliar names long deceased, framed photos the only reminder that they once walked the same soil. Andrew MacNamera stood to his left, one hand in a pocket, the other cupping a lit unfiltered cigarette.

"I'm sorry I had to call you into this," Edwards said, "given your condition. It was something I sought to avoid."

"Dying is not a condition, Richard," MacNamera said, "it's a fact. Besides, I've never been one to sit idle by the sidelines."

"You'll have all the action you crave in a matter of hours," Edwards said. "The Raven has called in as many of his group as he could spare, even pulled some off operations he had working in other parts of the world. He is making his stand on the fight for the Angels."

"He has also put out heavy offers to a number of freelancers who were floating through the city or close enough to get here," MacNamera said. "But he could call in the 101st Airborne and it wouldn't matter to the outcome."

"How do you figure that?" Edwards asked.

"This will come down to three people—you, Kate, and the Raven. The rest of us are merely collateral."

"Do you think he has figured out by now that Kate no longer has the Angels?" Edwards asked.

"I would imagine he suspected that for some time," MacNamera said. "My guess is he only put her in jeopardy to get your attention and force you to turn your focus toward protecting her instead of the Angels. Meanwhile, his people have been turning the city upside down looking for where they might be hidden. Given all that, I have to admit, I'm surprised he has yet to find them."

Edwards gazed over at his old friend and smiled. "You want to stay alive in this business, always think as your adversary thinks," he said. "I was told that many years ago by a man much brighter than me, remember?"

MacNamera returned the smile, followed by a harsh cough, and nodded. "And I see you've heeded the lesson," he said. "At least well enough to have the Raven and his bunch running in circles."

"You want to hide something," Edwards said, "the best way to do that is put it in a place where everyone can see it. If you're up for a short walk, I can give you an example to illustrate my point."

"Lead the way," MacNamera said, dabbing the corners of his mouth with an embroidered handkerchief.

They walked in silence down the stone path leading to the mausoleums stretched out around the sloping hills. The cemetery was serene at this hour, a light mist covering the tips of the grass and small trees that dotted the landscape.

"If you're going to die," MacNamera said, "you could do a helluva lot worse than end up in such a beautiful place."

"I never took you for the sentimental type," Edwards said.

"What can I say? You start leaning in that direction," MacNamera said, "when you start getting close to the finish line."

They stopped in front of an ornate white stone mausoleum, a black, locked iron gate with ANGELA AND FRANCO BUONARROTI chiseled above the entryway, below a design of two young angels on bended knee. Edwards reached inside his jacket and pulled out a small string of keys. Standing on the top step of the mausoleum, he took a quick look around and caught a glimpse of MacNamera's approving smile.

"Any relation to Michelangelo?" MacNamera asked him.

"I didn't take the trouble to find out," Edwards said, jamming a thin key into the lock. "It was a fairly common name for quite a few centuries, so the chances are there wasn't any connection. But, like it or not, they're in his company now."

He swung the gate open and stepped in, followed closely by MacNamera, who closed it as soon as he entered the frigid room. There were headstones carved into all four walls, each with the names of deceased members of this particular branch of the Buonarroti family dating back to the eighteenth century.

In the center of the room, one large white cement coffin was the final resting place of the family patriarch.

"Give me a hand here," Edwards said. "We need to tilt the coffin on its side."

"Then you should have brought a crane and a construction crew," MacNamera said.

"You're a lot stronger than you think," Edwards said, grabbing one end of the coffin. "Now just grab the other end and push it up."

The two men lifted the coffin and placed it on its side, resting it on the stone ground.

"It's pure Sheetrock with a hard layered coat," Edwards said. "Even if, on the odd chance the Raven did send any of his men in here to take a look, they would see nothing more than a family at eternal rest."

A thick white shroud covered the opening. Edwards got down on both knees and gripped one end with a hand, gazing up at MacNamera with a look of sheer joy. "All men should witness at least one rare work of beauty before they leave this earth," he said. "Set their eyes on a gift few others have seen. I'm sure you would agree."

"With all my heart," MacNamera said.

"Then here is yours, my friend," Edwards said, casting the white shroud aside. "Be witness to the Midnight Angels."

The two men stared down into the squared-off center of the opening. There, deep inside the well, positioned gently next to each other, were the three uncovered Angels, the rarest works of Michelangelo ever found.

"I always thought the David was the most perfect work I would ever see," MacNamera finally said. "But these far surpass that."

"If the information we have about them is true, he was not yet thirty when he began work on the project," Edwards said. "That would have made him nearly four years older than when he finished the David. He would have been that much more experienced, that much more a polished sculptor."

"There's more to it than that," MacNamera said. "These were sculpted with a passion and a fervor missing in the others. Work of genius though it may be, the David was chiseled on defective marble and under the dual duress of time and money. These, however, were worked on with care, patience, and love. I've never seen anything like them."

"No one has," Edwards said, "and it's quite likely no one ever will."

"I can see why the Raven is so desperate to get his hands on them. These would fetch a hefty price if they were ever put on the private market."

"If you believe the talk among the art hunters," Edwards said. "Not a penny less than 400 million euros."

"To quite a few of those hunters, roughly 430 million in cash is worth dying for," MacNamera said.

"Four hundred million euros *each*," Edwards said.

"Do you plan on leaving them here?" MacNamera asked.

"For now," Edwards said, "at least while the battle with the Raven still rages."

"And then?"

"Then it will be up to Kate," Edwards said. "The decision is hers. If she follows the dictates of the Society—and there is little reason to believe she won't—she will need to determine who the Angels rightfully belong to, where it was that Michelangelo wanted them to reside."

"She'll make the right decision," MacNamera said.

"We can't fail her, Andrew. And we can't fail the Society. We need to rid her path of the Raven once and for all."

Andrew MacNamera wiped at his neck and brow, his eyes still on the Midnight Angels. "Let's get at it, then," he said. "I'm not getting any younger."

Edwards glanced at MacNamera and watched him make a vain attempt to stifle a blood-soaked cough. "Are you sure you're up to this?" he asked.

The older man smirked. "As of today, Richard, if my doctors are to be believed, I have less than two months to live. That makes me the most lethal weapon you possess. Now, I suggest we let the Angels rest in peace and go out to ensure their enemies will do the same."

CHAPTER 14

THE SMART CAR ROARED PAST THE ANCIENT walls, bounding across the cobblestone streets, dodging pedestrians and stands, small engine running at peak power, Rita, still dressed as a nun, was behind the wheel, shifting gears as adeptly as a Formula One driver. Kate sat on bended knees in the small passenger seat, a gun in each hand, gazing through the small rear window at the two men on Vespas in fast pursuit.

"That must have been one very special convent you went to," Kate said to Rita, "teaching you how to shoot *and* hot-wire a car."

"We didn't spend *all* of our time in prayer," Rita said, hugging the corner and making a sharp right around a leather goods store.

Kate crossed her arms over the back of the front seat, the guns still in her hands. "You would think they would have taken a shot at us by now," she said.

Rita turned left and caught a glimpse of a Fiat racing down from an adjoining side street. Farther up the tight street, she saw the brake lights on a parked taxi flash. "They're looking to box us in," she said. "We have another car in the mix just behind us and a cab up ahead that will act as the lead car. The Vespas will probably swing over and follow us on parallel streets, coming in and out as necessary."

They ran a stop sign and nearly collided with two bikers, Rita veering the car close enough to a café to send two tables hurtling. "I can't get a clear shot," Kate said, "and I don't want to risk hitting a bystander."

"That will stop us," Rita said, "but it won't stop them, if they decide to fire. For now, though, it looks like they'd like to take us down alive, or at least you, anyway."

A yellow taxi came roaring down a narrow street and slammed into the driver's side of the Smart car, sending it smashing against the stone entrance of a law office. Though dazed from the collision, Rita managed to downshift and slam her foot on the pedal, smoke coming off the rear tires as she kept the car rolling forward. "There is one negative to using this small a car in a speed chase," she said, "and you just witnessed it. It can't take a hit."

Kate jumped into the small opening that passed for a backseat and slammed out the rear window with the butt ends of her guns, the hood of the taxi only inches from the fragile bumper of the Smart car. She could see the driver and the man sitting next to him, his right hand hanging out the passenger-side window, a cocked revolver gripped tight between his fingers.

"They're going to try to get us from both ends," Rita said. "Three streets ahead, there's another yellow taxi coming toward us, and he's moving at collision speed."

"Can you turn down a side street?" Kate asked without looking away from the taxi now bumping against the rear of their car.

"I don't have much control of the wheel," Rita said. "I might make it, but not fast enough to clear us from the two cabs."

Kate made eye contact with the man on the passenger side of the taxi, then lifted her gun and fired two shots into the center of the windshield, hoping the driver would swerve the vehicle and reduce its speed. She achieved neither result and took a deep breath, bracing her back against the passenger seat of the Smart car, her feet against the rear board. She raised her guns, poised to take out the driver.

A black unmarked sedan came out of a side street then and slammed into the Smart car, shoving it into a narrow driveway, the front end of the small car crushed, two of its tires blown, the air smelling of burnt rubber.

The driver of the taxi in pursuit quickly shifted gears, but to no avail, as he ran smack into the side of the black unmarked sedan. The second pursuing cab, which Rita had spotted earlier, came at the cars from the opposite end of the street, screeching to a halt inches from the unmarked black sedan. Smoke filled the air and approaching sirens wailed from all directions as people leaned out of tiny windows, wooden shutters pushed aside, to get a better glimpse of the action.

Antonio Rumore stepped out of the unmarked sedan and fired into the smoldering taxi. He took out the driver as several bullets aimed his way missed their mark. He pulled a second gun from a shoulder holster and, spreading his arms out, fired at the damaged cabs on either side. After emptying his clips and letting them drop to the ground, he whirled in a 180-degree circle, reloaded his weapons and resumed firing. Shots dented the sides of the unmarked sedan and blew out a tire, but Rumore stood his ground. He emptied his second and final clips, then lowered his arms, bowed his head and waited for the silence to take hold.

Within seconds he was surrounded by heavily armed police officers fresh on the scene. He looked up, scanned the street, then turned to a uniformed cop holding a semiautomatic weapon. "What's the damage?" he asked.

"Four dead," the cop said, "two in each of the taxis. And you're wounded. From here it looks like a flesh wound that just pierced the shoulder, but you might feel better having a doctor tell you that. A second ambulance will be here in about a minute, maybe less."

"What about the women in the Smart car?" Rumore asked.

"The nun is pretty banged up, has a head wound that's going to need stitches, and maybe a broken leg," the officer said. "The girl in the backseat just seemed shook up, but they're taking her in for observation to be sure."

Rumore holstered his guns and walked toward the ambulance now parked halfway up the street, back doors open, siren lights twirling. The nun was already in the back, ministered to by two young EMS technicians. Kate was on a gurney, a sheet covering her up to her chest. She smiled when she saw him.

"You're bleeding and I'm not," she said. "So why am I the one on the gurney?"

"Italians love to pamper their women," Rumore said.

"I always thought that meant music and food," she said. "I didn't know about the shootouts."

"It was a risky move, and it could have turned out to be a very bad one," he said. He was standing at her side now, his right hand gently brushing the hair away from her eyes. "It was my only choice to keep you alive, and I just could not let anything happen to you."

Kate gazed up at him and smiled. "Is it because you still think I know where the Angels are?"

Rumore shook his head. "I would have done it even if you had never found the Angels," he said. "And I would do it again, just to see that smile."

"You might have been killed," she said, her voice cracking from strain.

"I did my best to avoid that," he said. "But would you have missed me?"

Kate nodded, reached up and held his hand close to her face. "They told me the woman who saved me is going to be fine, but she'll be in the hospital for a few days."

"I guess it helps to have God on your side," Rumore said.

"How's Marco doing?" Kate asked.

"He's in a police car on his way to the hospital," Rumore said. "He'll probably get there before you do. He was positioned a few miles from here, on the other side of the Arno and heard it all on the police radio. But they're ready to take you now, *mia cara*. I'll come and see you soon."

"They'll only keep me there for a few hours," Kate said, "and then send me home."

"Not to worry," Rumore said, smiling. "I'll find you."

"And can you not crash into me when you do?" she said.

"I'll do my best," he said.

Rumore nodded at the two ambulance attendants standing nearby, watched as her gurney was lifted into the rear, and gave her a final wave as the doors closed. Then he turned to a uniformed officer standing off to his left.

"I think I'm going to need another car," he told him, the remains of his unmarked sedan still smoldering in the warm air behind them, the body and tires punctured with bullet holes.

CHAPTER 15

THE FAMED PIAZZA SANTA MARIA NOVELLA WAS nearly barren. It was closing in on three in the morning, and most of the residents of the square were hours away from greeting a new day. The massive train station that stood behind the church in the center of the piazza was also still, an occasional train chugging into a rail stall, either from a distant city or in need of repair or fuel. There was a chill in the air and a thin layer of fog shrouded the piazza that through the centuries had been a home to scholars, painters, and poets, among them Henry Wadsworth Longfellow, Henry James, and James Fenimore Cooper. The Italian storyteller Boccaccio set the opening of his most famous work, *Decameron,* in the church, while the frescoes of both Filippino Lippi and Ghirlandaio graced its interior walls.

The piazza was the gateway to Florence, a resting stop for nobleman and peasant, tourist and resident, an irregularly shaped square dominated by two stone obelisks that rested on the backs of savage-looking bronze turtles. It was in the piazza that the Medici dukes first introduced chariot races to the city in the sixteenth century, and it was there, along the stone walkway, that couples met, lovers parted, friends got reacquainted, and families reunited. And it would be here that two lifelong enemies would arrive in order to bring their blood feud to its violent conclusion.

The Raven was the first to step out of the shadows of

the imposing church, walking slowly, hands by his sides, heading toward the center of the square. "Do you know that of all the famous and infamous people who have stayed in this square, it was only William Dean Howells who truly grasped its beauty," he said. "The rest of them, even those who called Florence their home, never saw it for what it was."

"That's because you have to seek out the beauty," Edwards said, sitting on a folding chair he had found resting against a wall of a shuttered café. "It doesn't overwhelm, like Santa Croce. You need to take time to absorb what's here, and not many are willing to do that."

"That's part of what made you and me stand apart, Richard," the Raven said. "We were always willing to seek out the beauty, regardless of time and cost, knowing that if we did indeed find it, we would be rewarded."

"But we did choose separate paths to get there," Edwards said, "and we always had different motives."

"The end result was the same, however," the Raven said. "We both became wealthy and powerful men, in debt to no one other than ourselves. And, yet, here we stand, in the middle of one of the grandest piazzas in all of Florence, one of us destined to die at the hand of the other."

"And of course it's impossible to run from one's destiny," Edwards said.

"We can, Richard," the Raven said, "you and I. All we need to do is unite and we can be as we once thought we would be—partners in the pursuit of lost treasures."

Edwards stood and walked closer toward the Raven. "The possibility of such a thing has long since passed," he said. "I would not be able to bend to your rules any more than you could bend to mine."

"Is it merely that?" the Raven asked. "Or is there

more to your dismissal of me than the fact that I sell my discoveries for the highest sum? Is there something else?"

"You tell me, David," Edwards said. "You always were the one with the answers."

"I think it all has to do with Andrea," the Raven said. "I think it is the simple fact that she chose to rush into my arms, not yours, which has burned inside your soul all this time. I'm not the only art hunter with whom you have competed over the years, but I am the only one you seek to destroy."

"I loved Andrea, more than I've allowed even myself to admit," Edwards said. "But I wasn't blind to what she had with Frank. I never would have done anything that had the potential to hurt them. And, even if I were so inclined, such feelings ended as soon as Kate was born."

"So you chose to relinquish the woman you loved for the man you believed she loved," the Raven said. "I always thought you were a romantic, but I never realized the extent of your foolishness. And as for your beloved Kate—well, she could just as easily have been your child as she was Frank's or possibly mine."

"Yet despite the very real possibility that Kate could be your daughter," said Edwards, his tone suddenly hardened, "you would kill her to get your hands on the Midnight Angels."

"I'm as sentimental as the next guy, Professor," the Raven said. "But I would kill *anyone* to get to the Midnight Angels."

"Then look no further, old friend," Edwards said. "I'm the one you want. I have them, and if you want them, it is me you need to kill."

The first bullet landed against pavement, and the second chipped a side of a stone wall. Both shots came from up high but from different directions. Edwards moved swiftly and took cover in a narrow alleyway between the church and a small apartment building. He pulled a gun from his waistband and scanned the piazza, looking for the Raven, now hidden behind a clump of trees on the side nearest the train station.

"I hope you don't mind," the Raven shouted across the square, "but I brought along some friends."

Three more shots rang out, one shattering glass, the other two lodging into the side of the apartment building. Edwards leaned against the soot-stained bricks and took a deep breath.

"A final act between two old friends," the Raven said. "It doesn't get more dramatic than that."

Edwards moved from the wall, scanned the rooftops and aimed his gun in the Raven's direction. He fired off two quick rounds, then ran out of the alley and to his left, hugging the sides of the buildings as he sprinted toward the corner, the ping of bullets landing against stone, both at his feet and above his head. He turned the corner and raced out of the piazza, running full tilt through the dark and empty streets of Florence, the Raven and his men in pursuit, covering both ground and rooftops.

Edwards cut through side streets, moving fast, running low and steady as he made his way toward the Ponte Vecchio, the silence of the night broken only by the sounds of his footsteps across cobblestones and the drone of an occasional passing scooter. Few cities slept as soundly as did Florence.

Edwards was not fooled at all by the quiet that seemed to engulf him. He knew he was being followed, and wanted to bring the fight to higher ground and more open terrain. He needed to lure the Raven to the fight, knowing well his history of steering clear of head-on confrontations, allowing his minions to handle the dirty deeds he often required. As he raced through the streets, the stones slippery and moist with dew, he recalled many other races through cities across the globe, times when he was either the hunter or prey, all in the name of the Vittoria Society.

He had done his best to keep Andrea and Frank Westcott's dream a reality. He did his best to maintain the integrity of the Society, but he was also enough of a realist to know that its goals could often only be achieved through the cost of a life.

He had few regrets—not for making the sacrifices required to prepare Kate to replace him at the helm, and not for any of the actions that allowed the Society to achieve its exalted status in the art world. After this day it might all change, and he knew that if his run was indeed coming to an end, he could not have envisioned a more fitting conclusion than to leave the Society one of the rarest finds ever uncovered in the art world—Michelangelo's Midnight Angels.

Edwards came to a full stop and looked around the quiet streets.

The sky overhead was crammed with stars, and the roar of the Arno could he heard in the distance. The Angels were in a secure location, and on the rooftops above him and across the alleyways that surrounded him members of the Society were taking their positions, preparing to do battle with the Raven and his Immortals, each soldier awaiting his signal. In a matter of moments the peace of the night would be broken and the city of Florence would turn into one large battleground, where blood would flow and bodies would fall, all in the name of art.

Edwards reached into the side pocket of his jacket, pulled out a flare gun and aimed it toward the starlit sky.

He fired off one round, watching the flare zoom straight up, waited for the quick pop and the flash and then tossed the gun into a trash can on the corner. He ran up a narrow street, opened the door to a small private home, and disappeared inside.

CHAPTER 16

RUMORE REACHED INTO A SMALL WICKER BASket, grabbed the half loaf of fresh Italian bread and ripped off a thick slice. He rested it against the small plate by his left elbow and nodded.

"It's not the Angels I'm after at the moment," he said. "It's the Raven I want. If I capture him, he might lead me to them or he might lead me to dozens of other stolen works. My job is to retrieve lost and stolen art, and the best way I know to do that is to arrest the best art thieves in the world. Right now, he's the one I want."

He was sitting in the rear garden of Trattoria Pandemonio, a restaurant as popular with the locals as it was with tourists, thanks to a first-rate menu and wine list, a stress-free ambience, and Mama, a petite and engaging dark-haired, dark-eyed woman who treated every customer like a long-lost relative. Her warmth and energy filled the restaurant and made it a home to all who frequented it. It was a favorite place of Kate and Marco's, and to their surprise, they soon discovered it was also a favorite of Rumore's.

"How do we know we can trust you?" Marco asked. He was sitting next to Kate and across from Rumore, his right hand in a small cast covering his broken fingers.

Rumore dipped the slice of Italian bread in an olive paste spread across the small plate and shrugged. "If I took the time to count, my guess is the two of you, either together or separately, have broken at least half a dozen laws just in the time I've known you," he said, looking from one to the other. "If I wanted to, I could easily have you locked away for as long as I'm in town, and for even longer than that. But you're not behind bars. You're sitting here, across from me, waiting for Mama to bring you a plate of pasta with artichokes and tomatoes. Does that answer your question?"

"You know how the Society functions?" Kate asked. "I would imagine this isn't the first time you've crossed the same paths the group has, looking to land the same lost or missing work."

Rumore shook his head and took a bite of the bread. "No," he said. "I've worked with them before and found them to be a big help in securing the work. It doesn't mean I approve of the methods they employ. But we do share similar goals—to return the art to whomever it was intended."

"Then there's no problem," Kate said, smiling. "You collect the Raven and we take the Angels. You get what you want and we get what we need."

"I don't have that kind of authority," Rumore said. "I can't simply allow this work to slip from my grasp. This isn't some marble bust of a Roman emperor no one remembers. This is Michelangelo, and to find a work of his, dating back to his own time, will be a discovery that will get the full attention of practically anyone with the slightest connection to the art world. This is not an ordinary find, Kate. This may well be the biggest find ever. It will need to be protected, and not even the Society with all of its resources is up to that task."

"But you think the Rome Art Squad would be?" Marco asked, not meaning his question to come off as sarcastic as it did.

"You think they hand us a museum pass and send us on our way?" Rumore said, doing little to hide both his anger and his impatience. "There isn't anyone in the world better at this job than we are, and right now I'm exactly what the two of you need and who you need to trust."

"Then we work together," Kate said. "I move ahead with my plan and you move on with yours, but we'll function as a team. You're right about one thing—we might be able to take the Raven's group on our own. The Society has more members and can be just as lethal when confronted. But there are a lot of hunters in the city not affiliated with either organization. Some of them might just back away if they heard the Rome Art Squad was also on the scene."

Mama came up to the table, holding three warm platters filled with pasta smothered in a thick artichoke and tomato sauce. She placed a dish in front of each of them and smiled. "You all look so serious," she said. "You eat now and don't worry. The problems will all still be there when you're finished."

They ate in silence for several moments, relishing the food. Rumore broke off another piece of bread and signaled the waiter for three more glasses of wine. "If I agree to what you propose," he said, "it means I'll be letting both of you out of my sight for any number of hours. A lot can happen in that time, most of it bad. Don't forget, the Raven's chasing you, you're the key to everything he wants, and I just won't let anything happen to you."

Kate gave Rumore a warm smile and a nod. "I'm ready for this, Detective," she said.

"Why do you care so much?" Marco asked Rumore, not even making an attempt to hide his jealousy.

"It's my job," he said, his voice cop hard. "I don't have to like you, which, by the way, I'm starting not to. But I usually prefer it to be the bad guys who get taken down, not some kid in over his head."

"Is that what you think?" Marco asked. "You don't think I can be of help?"

"You're a good kid and you care for Kate," Rumore said. "But these are professionals waiting out there, willing to do whatever needs to be done to get what they came to Florence to get. As little as three weeks ago your biggest concern was the condition of your crappy bike."

"I'm not leaving her side," Marco said. "No matter how much you want me to."

"You want to ask her out on a date, be my guest," Rumore said. "Once this is over, I'm back in Rome and you'll be back in class with plenty of time to decide which movie you want to take her to see. All of that can happen, but only if you get out of this now. If not, I can't guarantee you'll live long enough to see the inside of another classroom."

Kate reached for Marco's good hand and held it. "I don't want that to happen," she said. "The detective is right. He's where he belongs, this is what he does. And I belong here as well. This is my life. You're the only one here who didn't ask for any of this."

Marco stared at Rumore and reached for his wineglass. "You're right," he said after a brief pause. "I didn't ask to be put in the middle of this. But I went with Kate because I am her friend. And it is for that same reason I will stay in the middle of this, no matter how it might turn out for me."

Rumore finished his wine, wiped his pasta plate clean with a sliver of bread, and then brushed aside a handful of crumbs from his side of the table. "It's your call," he said to Marco, "and I don't have to like it or agree with it. But I will tell you this—if I even think your involvement is putting Kate, me, or any other cop out there at risk, then I will pull you out of the scene faster than you can tell time. You'll be invisible in a matter of seconds."

Marco stiffened and moved his hand away from Kate. "I might surprise you, Detective," he said.

"You might at that," Rumore said.

Mama was heading back toward the table, minus the smile, a concerned look spread across her thin, handsome face. Rumore pushed back his chair and met her halfway down the narrow aisle. "What is it?" he asked.

"It has begun," she said, glancing over his shoulder at Kate and Marco.

Rumore wrapped his arms around Mama and gave her a warm hug. He then turned, walked back to his table and stood over Kate and Marco. "I think," he said, "the wise move would be to skip dessert."

CHAPTER 17

EDWARDS MADE THE LEAP FROM ONE RED brick rooftop to another, a gun in each hand, firing at the two men in pursuit behind him. He landed with a soft thud, rolled across the hard tar and came up on both knees, waiting for the men to get closer. Two bullets came at him from behind, off an adjacent rooftop, the shooter crouched behind a small, soot-stained chimney. He bent down and searched for cover, firing in both directions as he moved toward a rusty tin door swaying in the breeze. He checked his ammo clip and then took a quick look down at the bridge four stories below. There, he spotted a group of gunmen going at each other from both sides of the street.

Edwards reached the door and heard the approaching footsteps. He whirled, fired, and then ducked down into the stairwell, hearing the grunt and hard fall of a wounded man. He turned the corner of the stairwell, gazed down the rail opening and saw three men approach from the steps below. He knew others from above would soon follow and that he could ill afford to allow himself to be cornered. There were four apartment doors on the floor, and he tried turning the knobs on two of them, to no avail, before hearing a third, in the far corner closest to the next flight of stairs, slowly creak open. An elderly woman, in a nightgown and robe, peered out and nodded for him to come forward.

He rushed to her door and watched as she swung it open, offering him entry.

"Are you sure?" he asked her. "The men following me will shoot anyone who gets in their way."

"All the more reason for you to come in," the old woman said, waiting until he was in her foyer before she quietly closed the door behind him.

Edwards glanced around the small apartment and ran to the kitchen window, which overlooked the street below. He saw three men down on the pavement, pools of blood forming around them under the misty overhead lights, and two others badly wounded, resting against the rear doors of parked cars. He turned to look at the old woman. "Is there a place in here for you to hide?"

"What are you going to do?" she asked.

"It's too high to jump and I'm too tired to run," he said, "so that means I'll have to let them in."

"Let me do that," the old woman said. "They won't be expecting me and that will give you a better chance."

"I told you I didn't want you to get hurt," he said.

"In that case, let me have one of your guns," the old woman said, reaching out her right hand. "Don't worry. It won't be the first time I shot a gun. My husband was a municipal policeman and would often take me with him on hunting trips. My aim might be a bit off, but I have surprise on my side."

Edwards stared at the old woman and then leaned over and kissed her gently on the cheek. He handed her one of his guns and walked toward the front door. "There's a round in the chamber," he said over his shoulder. "Fire off your rounds fast and then move even faster to that closet next to the sofa. Get in there and stay down and don't come out until you know it's safe."

"And what about you?" she asked.

"Signora," Edwards said, with a hint of weariness, "I'm afraid my night has just begun. But if I make it through, I promise to come back one day and show you my gratitude."

"I'll hold onto the gun until you do," the old woman said.

Edwards stepped to the far side of the door. The old woman buried her hand and gun in the right sleeve of an ill-fitting bathrobe and opened the door. There were four men in the hallway—two on the landing and two positioned near her apartment. "It's the middle of the night," she said, giving an angry touch to her words. "What are you doing in here?"

"Never mind that," the one closest to her said. "Are you in there alone?"

"Look at me," the old woman said, "and guess the answer."

"Did you see anyone else come down the hallway?" he asked. "Maybe somebody who woke you from a sound sleep?"

"That would have been you," the old woman said.

"She's lying," a second man—the one standing on the top step of the far landing—said. "You can see it in her face."

The man closest to the old woman moved several steps nearer to her, the gun in his left hand held down and loose. "Is my friend correct?" he asked her. "Are you hiding something from us?"

The old lady looked up at the man and turned away, stepping back into her apartment. Edwards jumped from behind the door, legs spread wide in the open doorway, and began to fire, spraying his bullets from one end of the hall to the other, sending the men scurrying for what cover they could find. He dumped an empty clip to the ground and slammed in a fresh one. Bending down, he grabbed the wounded man's discarded gun, then lifted him to his feet, turned him face out to the hallway and started to move forward, firing his weapons as he did.

He reached the stairwell and headed down, turned and carefully maneuvered from step to step, one eye on the targets around him. The wounded man was weighing him down, and had taken several slugs to the chest and legs in the mad assault to get at Edwards. He was on his last breaths and his upper body was starting to spasm. Edwards released him, fired three bullets up the landing and then ran down the stairwell, taking the steps two at a time.

He made it back out to the street, his hair matted to the sides of his head and his left shoulder bleeding from a flesh wound. He rested against a stone wall for a few moments, taking deep breaths and relishing the calm and coolness of the street. He sprinted to the corner and turned right, staying close to the shelter of the walls as he moved down a deserted street lined with shuttered shops. He could hear the rush of the Arno on the other side of the low buildings and knew he was getting close to where he needed to be. He had less than an hour before the sun would begin to rise, costing him the cover of darkness. It was then that he spotted the dark blue car, a BMW, parked tail first between a private home and a shuttered trattoria. The side windows were blackened and the lights off, but he could make out the rumble of an idling engine.

Edwards didn't need to check his ammo clip to know he was running low. He also knew that if the car had come for him, there was nothing he could do to avoid it. His shoulder wound was now gushing blood and his right leg ached from a blow it had suffered in the hallway battle. He felt this left him with only one option.

He decided to take it.

Lowering his head, Edwards took several steps deeper into the street, the BMW parked one hundred meters away and to his right. He picked up his pace as he drew closer, then turned toward the car, running at an angle and firing bullets into the driver's window as he did. By the time he reached the front end of the idling car, he was out of breath and out of bullets. He stepped into the alley, swung open the driver's door, and saw only shattered glass and torn leather. The motor was on but the interior was empty. He looked around to his left and right and saw or heard no one. He had no weapon and was leaking blood. His heart was pounding so hard he could feel his chest move, and for a brief moment Richard Edwards was as close to panic as he had ever been in his life.

"Thank the Lord I decided to head out for a smoke." The low, raspy voice came from deeper in the alley.

Edwards smiled, took a breath, and turned to see MacNamera walking with slow and steady steps toward him, a thin line of smoke covering his head and face.

"I will never ask you to give up cigarettes again," he said.

MacNamera peered into the car and noted all the bullet holes and glass fragments littering the front seat. "You drive," he said, "since you're already bleeding. And I'll fill you in on what you should know on the way over."

"You wouldn't have any extra ammo clips?" Edwards asked, brushing some of the glass off the seat and onto the pavement. "I wasted them all blasting out the window of your new car."

MacNamera slowly made his way to the passenger side and slid the door open. "It's actually your car," he said. "Or I should say the Society's? I picked it up from a garage about ten kilometers outside the center. As to weapons and ammo, I wouldn't concern myself. I packed the trunk with all manner of useful items."

Edwards sat behind the wheel, slipped on the seat beat, and eased the BMW out of the alleyway. "You're a gift from heaven, my friend," he said. "I would be lost without you."

"Gift from hell would be more fitting for our task," MacNamera said. "But either way, I appreciate it."

"We're down as many as seven, maybe eight men," Edwards said, "and that's just what I could make out from the rooftops. There could be all sorts of hell breaking loose throughout the city."

"That there certainly is," MacNamera said. "It seems as if you're not the only one who has decided to make this your final stand. The Raven seems equally insistent."

"Are any of the outsiders getting into the mix?" Edwards asked, easily navigating the deserted streets.

"Not yet," MacNamera said. "More than likely they're waiting it out, watching to see who emerges less bloodied, and with the Angels in their possession."

Edwards brought the car to a slow stop, shifted the gears into neutral and looked over at MacNamera. "He's better at this end of it than I am," he said, "always has been, and now here I am playing right into his hands."

MacNamera gazed out the side window for several moments and then turned back to Edwards. "The Raven has had more experience," he said, "but experience doesn't always win. And playing into his hands does have its advantages."

"Such as?"

"He wouldn't be expecting that to be your move," MacNamera said, "which might mean he'll think it a ruse and hold back, waiting for your real plan to emerge. By then it could be too late for him to rebound."

"He'll be there already," Edwards said, "expecting us."

"Well, expecting *you,*" MacNamera said. "He's been

told that I'm out of commission. I have made it my business to be put off the Raven's radar."

"I have never gone into a job filled with such doubts," Edwards said. "I worry about the choices I've made, the approach I'm taking. I'm not sure why, but these last few days have left me feeling adrift."

"It means you're getting better at what you do," MacNamera said. "Face it, Richard, when you were first handed the reins of the Society, you were a much younger man and with that splendid age comes a carefree spirit and a sense of invulnerability."

"I'm not *that* old to have those feelings suddenly vanish," Edwards said.

"You're old enough," MacNamera said. "And much more aware of the consequences of your actions. You've been in enough violent scraps to get a sense of your mortality. Plus, there's the matter of Kate."

"What about her?"

"She's ready to step into your place," MacNamera said. "That means no matter how this particular escapade turns out, the Society will be in capable hands. And that worries you. The fears you have, Richard, are for Kate. You've been through too many a battle to cower at the thought of the next one now. But this is her first taste of the action, her first glimpse of spilled blood, and you don't know for certain if she can handle it."

"What do you think?" Edwards asked.

"I think Kate is as much your daughter as she is Frank's and Andrea's," MacNamera said. "And knowing that, I am free of worry. You should be as well."

"I have never worried about her skill," Edwards said.

"So what concerns you, then?"

"The letting go," Edwards said. "I'll be losing both Kate and the Society in one fell swoop. Up to now, those have been my anchors, nurturing both, taking pride in watching them grow and develop, and now neither of the two will need me. My mission will be complete. I'll be irrelevant."

"Would you prefer to trade places with me?" MacNamera asked with a harsh laugh.

Edwards turned and looked over at his friend of many decades. "No," he said. "But I do hate the thought of losing you. In our line of work, it's not often we find friends."

MacNamera turned away from Edwards. "In that case," he finally said, "the Raven may have bitten off a bigger bite than even he can swallow—two desperate men and a young woman out to claim her destiny. That's a powerful force to push back against."

"That's what I'm counting on," Edwards said.

He released the brake, shifted gears, and eased the car back out onto the streets.

CHAPTER 18

THEIR BACKS TO A CLOSED STALL ON THE PONTE Vecchio, Kate and Marco gazed up at the windows of the Vasari Corridor, the dim light of early dawn about to break.

"I hope Rumore's informant was correct," Marco said. "On the surface, it doesn't make sense. Why would the Raven choose this place to do battle?"

"In a way, it makes perfect sense," Kate said. "There are multiple escape routes here—the Pitti Palace on one end, Palazzo Vecchio on the other, the church of San Felicita in the middle. Besides, the corridor itself is lined with nothing but windows. No matter what occurs inside, the Raven knows he will have to make his way *outside,* and this affords him the best routes."

"But what about all the security?" Marco said. "He might be able to get away from us, but how does he escape the guards?"

Kate looked at him and smiled. "We did it, and we had no idea what we were doing," she said. "Besides, there won't be as much security as you would normally expect to find. Rumore is having the place cleared, except for a handful of selected officers."

"Why would he go and do something that foolish?" Marco said.

"He didn't share his reasons with me," Kate said, "but I'm sure one of them had to do with the issue of trust. The Raven has countless people on his payroll, so it would make sense that any number of them might be security guards."

"A bit ironic, isn't it, that our adventure might end where it began?" Marco said. "Had we not found the Angels, this would be just another wonderful morning in Florence, and the only people walking those halls would be tourists, guides, and guards—and not a single one of them would be at risk."

"This day has been coming for decades," Kate said, "back to when I was a little girl. If it wasn't the Angels, it would have been some other unexpected discovery that set the events in motion. No matter what, though, it was going to happen."

"Do you think it's worth it, in the end?" Marco asked. "You could lose quite a bit here today if it turns against us, people you care about and who have been a close part of your life for years. All for sculptures whose existence Michelangelo himself never even bothered to acknowledge."

Kate turned away from him and gazed down the street leading away from the Ponte Vecchio, the morning chill not yet burned off by the arriving sun, the nearby Arno making itself heard.

"It was worth it for my parents," she said in a barely audible voice, "and it is worth it for Professor Edwards and for every member of the Society. The same holds true for the Raven and his group. And yes, it is worth it for me. It is who I am. It is who I'm choosing to be. I think that's what Rumore was, in his own direct fashion, trying to tell you back at the restaurant. You are the only one here today who hasn't chosen this."

"I'm here because of my concern for you," Marco said. "I value the discovery that we made together, but forgive me, despite its artistic merit and financial value, I don't see the point in having to kill someone in order to secure the works. Does it truly matter to the outside world if the Angels belong to the Society or the Immortals or to some private individual who paid a king's ransom for them? Who possesses them should be of no importance. I think even Michelangelo himself would agree with that. I doubt very much he would have encouraged murder, even if it were in the name of art, especially his own."

"It matters to me," Kate said, her words lit, her feelings bruised by his remarks. "It has never been about possessing any of the works the Society has discovered. In fact, the opposite is what has always held true and will continue to be the one rule that guides us. It is not just about keeping the works alive but also allowing those works to be kept by the very people or place for which they were intended."

"I didn't mean to anger you," Marco said. "I guess it's more my nerves talking than me. It's changed me, meeting you and setting out on this path, pretty much following your tracks. For the better, I think. I always seemed to live in fear, not wanting to draw attention to myself, preferring to leave things as I found them, often the last to get involved in any sort of activity that had the slightest chance to have a light shine its way. And I still lack the courage it takes to tackle such challenges, certainly to the degree you do or to the level of Rumore. I guess what I'm trying to tell you is I'm afraid. Not just for myself, but for both of us."

Kate leaned closer to Marco. "I'm afraid, too," she said quietly. "That's why I'm so glad you're with me. I know you will be there to protect me. Remember, it's always the brave ones who show the most fear."

"Then I'm the bravest man in the world," Marco whispered back.

She moved her head away from his neck, gazed into his eyes, then reached up and kissed him.

CHAPTER 19

EDWARDS WALKED DOWN THE STEPS OF THE first portion of the empty Vasari Corridor, his footsteps silenced by thick carpeting, small drops of blood dripping down his fingers from his shoulder wound. His path was bordered by large portraits of dukes and duchesses now centuries deceased, relatives of the rich Medici bloodline or benefactors of the arts. There were 1,200 such portraits in all, covering the more than one-mile-long corridor, each kept dust free and away from the potential damage of direct sunlight. Every fifteen feet or so a small circular window overlooked the streets below, each one designed by Michelangelo himself on assignment from the Medici family. He was told to make the windows so it would be easier to look out than to look in. In place of a railing, a thick rope ran through a series of iron handles, serving as a guide down the massive corridor, broken up every quarter mile by a locked prison gate, opened four times a day by a guard. A security camera rigged in the top left-hand corner of each room backed up the human surveillance.

The ceilings were high and solid, the width of the hall about a dozen feet, the walls made of stone. The corridor began at the Palazzo Pitti, passed over the church of San Felicita, then crossed the entire length of the Ponte Vecchio, which, at the time it was built in 1565, had been a marketplace that sold fresh slaughtered pigs. At its farthest point north the corridor spread out to the right across a threshold that ran along the Uffizi, where a small bridge allowed access to the Palazzo Vecchio. There was one large window overlooking the Arno. Then there was the quirky detail toward the end of the corridor: One of the walls was not as thick as the others. This wall, flat and smooth, bordered the bedroom of a Renaissance family not eager to move their home to accommodate Giorgio Vasari's vision. So Vasari, not one to waste time, built around their home.

On the surface, the Vasari Corridor was one of the safest and most secure locations in Florence.

"It's magnificent, is it not?" the Raven asked. He was standing several feet away from Edwards in the middle of the stairwell, arms folded across his chest. "The artwork leaves a bit to be desired, I admit, but the structure itself is stunning."

"The paintings are originals," Edwards said, turning to gaze up at one of them—an austere-looking woman with dark hair pulled rigidly away from her face, and eyes the shape of almonds. "They would still net you a nice profit on the black market."

"It would take a dozen such corridors lined with thousands of ghastly faces to fetch the price I seek," the Raven said.

"Then I suggest you go in search of them, because the Midnight Angels will never belong to you."

"Not even if I agree to spare your life?" the Raven asked. "Or hers?"

Edwards shook his head and moved closer to the Raven. "It ends here and now," he said.

"And I will have the pleasure to witness it," MacNamera said. He was standing a half-dozen steps above them, the ever-present cigarette hanging from his lower lip.

The Raven lowered his head. A small smile creased his face, his eyes on Edwards. "And here I trusted you would be all alone," he said. "How very foolish of me, wouldn't you say?"

"How 'alone' was our friend David?" Edwards asked MacNamera.

"Two of his men were in the lower portion of the corridor," MacNamera said, "and a third was hidden in the passageway over by the Uffizi. They are no longer Immortals."

"You always thought yourself better at this game," Edwards said to the Raven, "and, in many respects, you were right. But with such an accomplishment there comes a price, and yours is to never be trusted."

The Raven held his smile as he glared at Edwards. "Your instincts are on the mark, which is probably why Frank and Andrea chose you over me. That was their error. True, you did make the group large, rich, powerful. But I would have made it all that and more. I would have made sure the Society was feared. Were I in your place and had my hands on such a rare discovery, no one would have dared threaten to take it from me."

"The thing about words, David," Edwards said, "is they never guarantee a result. You are no closer to the Angels now than you were before their discovery. You've gained nothing and have lost much—the streets of Florence are littered with the bodies of your men."

The Raven leaned closer to Edwards and widened his smile. "None of those poor souls mean anything to me," he whispered. "I am not a general who cares about his troops. But I believe you are."

He spun away from Edwards, crouched down on one knee, pulled a gun from a side holster and aimed it at MacNamera. He fired off three rounds, finding his mark with two of them. The force of the bullets caused MacNamera's arms to flail out, and he landed faceup with a muted thud on the carpeted steps, the unlit cigarette now resting across his still and bloodstained chest.

Edwards grabbed the Raven from behind, the weapon tumbling to the ground, and the two men slid together down a number of steps. Edwards struggled to get a grip on the Raven, hampered by his shoulder wound and the damage to his leg. The Raven rained hard punches on his shoulder and chest, further weakening his hold. A knee to the groin and a sharp hook to the stomach allowed the Raven to maneuver away from Edwards and get up to a kneeling position. As he reached for the discarded gun, Edwards caught him from behind and wrapped his good arm around his neck, bracing a knee against the center of his back, the Raven gasping for air, the gun still out of reach.

An elbow thrown by the Raven then landed square in Edwards's stomach and forced him to loosen his grip. It allowed the Raven to push Edwards up against a wall, the professor's wounded shoulder taking the full brunt of the hit, causing him to gag for air.

On his knees, his wounded arm dangling by his side, Edwards's face was a mask of welts and emerging bruises, his vision clouded by the blood splattered across his nose and eyes. The Raven stood up, grabbed the thick white rope that served as a railing, and wrapped it in a U-shape around the professor's neck. He stood above him now, working at full strength, pushing down on Edwards with his right knee wedged into the small of his back, lifting the rope upward, straining to drain him of air.

The Raven used the wall to enforce his back and stretched the rope with the full force of his upper body, Edwards futilely tugging at the rope, eyes closed, desperately trying to get back on his feet. "Where is your beloved Society now?" the Raven shrieked. "Where are they when their leader is most in need?"

Edwards reached up and scratched at the Raven's face, the desperate movement of his fingers digging deep into flesh and causing thin rivers of blood to flow down the other man's right cheek.

"And where is your successor?" the Raven continued, ignoring the pain, tugging the rope even harder, eager to draw out a last painful breath from the mouth of his longest living enemy. "Where is the young woman you gave up so much to raise? Why is she not here to see this? Smart enough to uncover a master work, but not clever enough to deduce where we would meet?"

The Raven could feel the life before him slipping away, and gave the rope one final, vicious tug before releasing it. He leaned against the blood-smeared wall, watching the professor crumble to the floor, his head resting on one step, his body curled on another. "Perhaps she simply didn't care enough," he whispered. "Perhaps indeed she is mine after all."

The Raven looked down at the body of Professor Richard Dylan Edwards, head of the Vittoria Society, for a few quiet moments. Then he stepped around him and slowly made his way down the steps of the Vasari Corridor.

CHAPTER 20

"STAY DOWN AND KEEP AWAY FROM THE DOOR," Rumore shouted to Kate and Marco, sliding two semi-automatics toward them across the cold floor. "And use these if anyone not wearing a badge or a uniform walks in here. Understood?"

"Where are you going?" Kate asked.

"I need to clear the air with some friends outside," Rumore said, standing by the mausoleum doorway and checking the clip load on the two guns he held. He turned to look over at Kate and Marco, both taking cover under the side of a large coffin in the center of the room, plaster and marble debris flying all around them. "And remember, only come out if it's me telling you to. Otherwise, stay in here and do your best not to get killed."

"I'm still not clear why we're here instead of the Vasari Corridor," Marco said. "I mean shouldn't we be more concerned with capturing the Raven?"

"I *wanted* to be here," Kate said, "with the Angels."

They huddled in the old English cemetery, in the Buonarroti chapel, their faces only inches from the resting place of the Midnight Angels, not knowing that in the center of the city, inside the halls of the Vasari Corridor, Professor Edwards lay dead. Marco stretched out his hand and grabbed the gun left for him by Rumore, his small cast not a hindrance. Kate already held her weapon in her hands. "I still don't know how the detective knew the Angels would be in here," he said to her, "and we couldn't figure it out."

"I told you, I was never any good with Richard's clues," Kate said. "I also don't have an entire unit of cops and a dozen local informants out there looking for the answer. Rumore does."

"As it turned out, those informants don't only work for the police," Marco said. "They must have also spread the word to the Raven's gang."

Kate ducked under a heavy fuselage of bullets against stone and then lifted herself to her knees and peered at the door. "We have to help him," she said. "There have to be at least six gunmen out there, maybe more. He can't take them all on his own."

"He told us not to move from here, remember?" Marco said.

"I heard him, Marco," Kate said. "But he needs help, and right now we're the only ones who can give it to him."

Above them a series of bullets shattered glass, nicked against the thick wood door, and chipped the base of the tombs on the walls. Marco was down on hands and knees, the smoke in the room causing his eyes to water. "There's only one way out," he managed to say, "and they are bound to see us coming out the door. We'll be easy targets."

Kate ran from her side of the large coffin over toward a window close to the door, her sneakers hitting shattered glass. She crouched under the window and raised her head just enough to peer outside. "Not if they're ducking our bullets," she said. "They won't be expecting return fire. If I were them, I would guess the cop is the only one with a weapon. If I start firing to cover you on your way out and then you get to a safe spot and cover me, they won't know how many guns they're up against. That might give Rumore enough time to pick off a few."

"All I understood of that is that I'm going out the door first," Marco said.

"Just run low and shoot straight," she said. "They're not expecting it and that might buy you the time you need to reach tree cover."

Marco crawled over toward the door, the floor littered with dust, marble, and broken glass. He reached the wall, got to his knees and grabbed the handle. "Tell me when to go," he said, "because if we wait for me to make the move, we'll be here all night."

Kate rested her gun against the windowsill and looked over at Marco. "Now!" she said and opened fire.

Marco swung the door open and headed into the darkness, bullets coming his way, firing back two of his own, crisscrossing toward a row of pine trees to his left. When he got close enough, he took a full dive into a clump of leaves and wet grass and then rolled down a slight slope and lay there, the gun held in both hands, his heart beating hard against his chest. He turned on his stomach, made his way to a small boulder resting among the row of trees, and used that for cover. He tried to stand but his legs and upper body were shaking and he had trouble catching his breath. He closed his eyes and made a vain attempt to compose himself, knowing he had only a matter of seconds to do so before Kate came running out the mausoleum door.

"Fire two rounds into the tree cover." It was Rumore's voice, coming at him to his left, his body sheltered by darkness and foliage. "But wait until she comes out. I'll move in closer and clear a path for her. Together it should be enough to get her to a safe spot."

Marco opened his eyes, leaned his head out, and waited for Kate to emerge. As soon as he saw her race out, he cupped his hands around the gun and fired two bullets into the darkness. He then turned and saw Rumore walking straight out into the line of fire, his arms stretched out, a gun in each hand, firing off a volley of rounds, standing in the open ground, his body as much a shield for Kate as his weapons.

Kate ran off toward the right of the mausoleum, stopped to fire a round and then dove behind a row of bushes. She came up on her knees and fired off a second round, a loud grunt in the distance proof that the bullet had found its mark.

She zipped off bullets from the right, Marco let off the occasional shot from the left, Rumore working the middle, shooting rounds in every direction, pausing only to drop used clips and jam in fresh ones. The shooters moved among the shadows and the treeline, using the safety of the cemetery walls to reload and regroup. There were at least eight in motion, with only one of them down from a wound.

Rumore circled around one wall and held his position, his back resting against cold granite. He heard two men speaking in hushed tones to his right, tilted his head and saw them on the other side, both crouched down, guns pointed out toward the mausoleum. He jumped out between the walls, making just enough noise to be heard. The two men turned in his direction, caught the weight of his bullets and fell, one on top of the other. Rumore ran toward the men, grabbed their weapons, pulled ammo clips from their waistbands and then raced back into the fiery darkness.

He now stood in the center of the cemetery, firing in every direction except where he knew Marco and Kate were laying in wait, looking to force the gunmen into the open. Two came at him from his left, firing as they ran. Rumore caught one with a bullet to the chest. The other nicked the detective's leg, sending him down to one knee and forcing a gun loose from his hand. Rumore and the gunman exchanged heavy fire, now only a few feet apart, bullets ripping at their feet and above their heads before the kill shot found its mark and the gunman landed face-first onto the hard pavement, inches from the detective's side.

Rumore never heard the shooter coming at him from behind. He had his head down, reloading one weapon and reaching for a second, his back a leather-jacket-clad bull's-eye. The gunman lowered his weapon, crouched into a shooting position and prepared to fire.

The sound of two shots caused Rumore to turn and face the shooter. He caught the stunned and pained look on the man's face seconds before he fell to the ground. To the left of the shooter he saw Marco, hot gun held in both hands.

Rumore stood and ran over to Marco. "You okay?" he asked.

"Yes," Marco said. "Are you?"

"I wouldn't have been, if you hadn't shown up," Rumore said.

"What about your leg?" Marco asked, eyeing the blood coming out of the gaping wound just above Rumore's right knee.

"I know how to limp," he said. "There's at least four more out there we need to find."

"I didn't mean to kill him," Marco said, nudging his gun toward the fallen shooter.

"I know," Rumore said. "But he meant to kill you."

KATE WAITED FOR the shooter to walk past. She was lying flat, the grass cold and wet on her back, her gun raised. She lifted her legs to brace herself and knocked aside several loose rocks. The noise caught the shooter's attention and he whirled and fired down in her direction. Kate rolled away from the bullets, came up standing to his left and fired two bullets, both finding their mark. Down to her last shot, she moved toward the fallen man to retrieve his weapon.

The force of a man's grip yanked her off the ground.

He had one hand around her throat and a sharp knife in his free hand was lifted toward the sky. "I got you now," he whispered, his rough skin brushing against her face, harsh breath causing her to flinch.

She jammed the heels of her sneakers into the soft ground and then slammed two heavy elbow blows into the pit of the man's stomach. The force of the blows, combined with their unexpected arrival, sent the knife to the ground and the man down to his knees, clutching his stomach, gasping for air. Kate whirled and hit him across the face with two fast close-fisted blows, then grabbed the knife. The man looked up just as she crossed in front of him, the knife clutched in her right hand, the blade pointed at him, her hands as steady as her grip.

"I'll take it from here," Rumore said.

Kate didn't look up when she heard the familiar voice, and she held her position. A bevy of police cars and ambulances, sirens wailing, were closing in on them, wheels shrieking just near the cemetery entrance.

"They're all down, Kate," Rumore said. "Except for one or two, who ran off when they heard the calvary rushing in."

"What about Marco?" she asked, the adrenaline beginning to slow.

"He's okay," Rumore said. "He's got my back, just in case I'm wrong about the other gunmen."

She looked away from the man and glanced at Rumore, now standing next to her, his leg bleeding, a gun in his right hand pointed at the shooter. "Marco has *your* back?" she asked.

"Yes," Rumore said with a nod. "Perfect man for the job, it turns out."

CHAPTER 21

KATE CRADLED PROFESSOR EDWARDS IN HER arms, her face resting against the top of his head, Rumore and Marco standing by her side. The Vasari Corridor was now a twenty-first century crime scene—yellow tape placed around the areas of the shooting; CSU technicians taking swabs of blood from the walls and the floor, bagging bullet fragments and dusting for prints and evidence.

Kate gently rocked back and forth, let the tears flow down her cheeks as she fought back the urge to vomit. "I'm so sorry, Richard," she whispered. "I should have been here for you. I did what I thought you would have wanted me to do—protect the Angels."

Rumore leaned down next to her, one hand resting gently on her back. "They will need to keep his body in the morgue for a few days," he said. "After that, you will be allowed to fly him home."

Kate listened and nodded. "He'll be buried next to my parents," she said. "They would want him there with them. He was as much a son to them as I was a daughter, and as close to a father as I'll ever know."

"I'm sorry, Kate," Rumore said. "My men had the entrances covered, but they must have entered through the passageway by the Pitti or perhaps some other entrance that we're not even aware exists. Each one—MacNamera, the professor, the Raven—knew the secret ins and outs of this corridor. It made it difficult to keep track of them. Still, we should have prevented what happened."

"Do you know where the Raven is?" Kate asked.

"We have an idea," he said. "That gentleman you took down in the cemetery has helped confirm our suspicions."

"Will you tell me?" she asked.

"This is no longer just your business, Kate," Rumore said. "This is a police matter. It should have been all along. I allowed it to go too far, but now I won't risk another death, especially yours."

She turned to look up at him. "I'll find him on my own if you don't tell me," she said. "This has been my fight all along and I'm the one who needs to finish it. The Raven is waiting for me, no one else."

"The professor and his friend were two of the best the Society had," Rumore said. "And the Raven took them down alone. He's a professional and you're not. I can take it from here and I will bring him down, that I promise you."

Kate rested the professor's head slowly and carefully on the top step, then stood and faced Rumore. "The Raven murdered my mother and father," she said, barely able to get the words out. "And now he's killed the man who raised me and loved me as if I were his own child. He needs to be put down, and I'm the one who needs to do it. If I can't make you understand that now, at this moment, then you never will."

Rumore stared at her, then glanced down at the body of Professor Edwards and nodded. "I'll give you ten minutes," he said. "If you can't finish it by then, it will fall to me."

"Where is he?" she asked.

A new voice echoed through the corridor. "The Salone dei Cinquecento," Clare Johnson said, walking toward them, "in the Palazzo Vecchio." She now stood three steps down from Rumore, Marco, and Kate, her eyes fixed on the body of Professor Edwards. "The police have the building cordoned off," she said, "but he uses a network of underground passageways to get around."

"What are you doing here?" Rumore asked.

"Officially," she said, "I'm here to assess any damage done to the portraits and to the corridor itself. My company handles the insurance. Unofficially, I came to see if I could help. Richard was a good friend to me and an even better one to my father."

"How do you know where the Raven is?" Kate asked.

"Because I'm supposed to meet him there in fifteen minutes," she said.

"Why?" Rumore asked.

"The fact that you may have him surrounded, Detective, is of little importance to the Raven," Clare said. "He came to Florence to get the Midnight Angels, and he won't leave until that goal is met, and he thinks I can be of help."

"Is he right?" Rumore asked.

"I could be of help to him, if I wanted to be," Clare said. "But then I would be on my way to see the Raven and not here talking to you."

Kate walked down the steps separating her from Clare and stood inches away from the taller woman. "Is he alone?" she asked.

"As far as I know," she said. "He knows I hate to talk business in front of people I don't trust."

"I don't believe her," Marco said, looking from Kate to Rumore. "She could be working for the Raven."

"She probably is," Kate said, her eyes still on Clare. "But I do think she's telling the truth."

Rumore reached for Kate's arm and turned her toward him. "If you're going to take him," he said, "you need to hit first."

Kate nodded. "Where did MacNamera park his car?" she asked.

"Two streets down," Rumore said. "Why?"

"There's something in his trunk I want," Kate said.

"What?"

"A gift from the professor," Kate said. "I think it's time for me to share it with the Raven."

CHAPTER 22

IT IS THE MOST SPECTACULAR ROOM OF ITS kind in the world.

The Salone dei Cinquecento was built in 1495 to accommodate the members of the Greater Council of Florence, then numbering five hundred. The vast artworks that line the floor, ceiling, and walls of the room were designed to celebrate the great military victories of Florence and include Michelangelo's famed Genius of Victory and frescoes by both Leonardo da Vinci and Giorgio Vasari. The walls, which run as high as the average height of a town house, display a composition of battle scenes, portraits, and paintings representing the four elements of earth, water, air, and fire, while the thirty-nine panels of the ceiling present highlights of the life of Cosimo I, his achievements made all the greater by the money he paid to the artists to have his memory so honored.

The Raven paced about the great hall, head down and buried in thought. Despite an overwhelming advantage in both manpower and weaponry, his Immortals had yet to secure the Midnight Angels, having been either outfoxed or outgunned by the smaller number of more determined members of the Society. He did see a silver lining in the bloodshed, however. Word of the death of their leader would soon filter through the streets and perhaps give some of them pause.

The Raven had been caught off guard by the arrival of

the cop from Rome, and his presence indeed posed a dilemma. Normally, he would have no qualms about dispatching a member of any force, but he was well aware that the murder of a captain from Italy's most respected squad would bring with it an avalanche of police, and he could ill afford that cascade.

The key, he knew, was still Kate. She had proven to be as resourceful as he imagined, but much more difficult to subdue. He wondered whether the death of her beloved professor would weaken her resolve or merely strengthen it, and while he was prepared to kill her if he must, the thought did not please him, and he found that very fact a troubling one. He took it as a sign of weakness, and that was something he had never allowed in himself.

The Raven walked quietly down the center of the vast hall, gazing from one battle scene to the next, taking solace from the fact that he would have thrived in such times. He believed he would have ranked among the best of the Renaissance men, walking among kindred spirits who valued duplicity and treachery as much as fine works of art.

He heard the whizzing sound of the arrow before he felt the sharp pain of its point piercing through his right thigh. The shock of the blow caused him to fall to one knee. A second arrow came at him like a wooden missile and embedded itself in his left shoulder. He gasped aloud at the pain and looked around the vast room for the culprit, surprised to see Kate walking toward him, her figure lit by the light at her back from a large second-level window. He glanced at his wounds, blood oozing slowly out of both, then looked back across the room at Kate.

"I heard mention that you were proficient with a bow and arrow," he said.

She rested her bow against the side of Michelangelo's

winged Genius of Victory and ventured closer. "You fought Professor Edwards when he was at a disadvantage," she said, "with wounds to his leg and shoulder. I thought it only fair you share the same handicap when you fight me."

"You are proving yourself to be a worthy adversary," the Raven said, grimacing as he slowly made it back on his feet. He moved several inches closer to her. "And I might add, much more dangerous than I first imagined."

"You rise to the level of your opposition," Kate said. "Or so I've been told."

"It need not end this way," he said, his eyes now focused on Kate's every movement. "You have it within your grasp to move the Society in any direction you choose, and a merger is one possibility that should not be quickly dismissed."

"My parents are dead because of you," she said, "and now so is my guardian. They were the only family I had, and they're gone, all because of your greed, your jealousy, and your hatred. If I ever merged the Society with your organization, it would be a betrayal of their memory."

The Raven was close enough to reach out for her, standing on unsteady feet, a small puddle of blood forming around his boots. "I take it, then, that your answer is no."

"I would rather die," Kate said. "In fact, I will do all that I can to destroy what you have spent decades building."

"A lofty goal," he said, "but a bloody one as well. What do you suppose your parents would make of it?"

"They're not here, remember?" Kate said. "I am."

He leaned his head closer to her. "But for how long?" he whispered.

The thin blade of the knife came out of his right hand and slashed Kate across her left arm and chest, cutting through her white blouse and slicing its way through several layers of skin. She was as surprised by the cut as she was hurt by it, and instinctively raised her right hand to ward off further blows. The Raven grabbed the back of her hair and tossed her violently to the ground, hovering over her, his feet straddling her prone body. Kate tried to roll over and get to her feet, but to no avail as the Raven bent down, swinging his knife with skillful abandon against her back and legs, the floor around them soon coated with a slippery gloss of blood.

Kicking hard at him, Kate landed a blow against the embedded arrow, forcing him to grunt loudly and back away for a moment. It was enough time to allow her to reach for a small caliber gun in her waistband. Holding it with her right hand, blood streaking down her fingers, she fired off a shot, barely missing him. A hard kick against her wrist sent the weapon hurtling across the gleaming floor.

The Raven reached down and whirled her around, staring at her with a cold, hard look. He bent to his knees, resting them on top of her shoulders, and smiled when she grimaced from the pain. He held the knife point down against her chest. "Before you die," he said, "would you like to know if I am indeed your father?"

"Spare me one final lie," she said.

The first bullet struck the Raven just above his chest and forced the knife from his hand. The second found center mass and sent him sprawling faceup to the floor. Kate froze for several seconds, then turned her head when she heard the approaching footsteps. She closed her eyes in relief when she saw Rumore approach, the warm gun still in his hand.

"I told you ten minutes," he said. "And not a second more."

Kate crawled over toward the body of the Raven until

her face was inches from his. She saw a smile crease his trembling lips.

"The Angels," he rasped, "are they all I imagined them to be?"

"More," she said.

The Raven held the smile and nodded. "You do your father proud," he said.

Then he closed his eyes and his body shuddered one final time.

CAPTAIN RUMORE HELD KATE in his arms and carried her across the vast floor of the Salone dei Cinquecento. She rested her head against his warm neck, her arms resting comfortably around his shoulders. "I'm getting blood all over your shirt," she said.

Rumore smiled at her. "I promise never to wash it," he said. "It will give me something to remember you by."

She lifted her head and waited as Rumore turned his face toward hers. "I could easily get used to having you around, Detective," she said, staring into his eyes.

"I can make that happen," he said.

Kate nodded, then lowered her head, again resting it against the side of his neck, and closed her eyes.

Holding her to his chest, Rumore walked across the grand hall, his footsteps echoing through the vast room. He turned to glance at the Raven, whose body was at rest, surrounded by portraits of great battles of the past, warmed by the sharp rays of sunlight shining down from the large windows.

He then looked down at Kate, her face streaked with blood, strands of hair shielding her eyes, her wounded body resting softly against his. Her battle was finally over, her sculptures saved.

To Rumore, she seemed so at peace.

An angel brought to earth.

EPILOGUE

KATE WALKED WITH HER HEAD BOWED ACROSS the Piazza Santa Croce.

She was glad to be back in Florence and a return to a normal life. It had been three weeks since the Angels were secured. In that time, she had allowed her wounds to heal and had flown back to America to attend to the burial of her beloved Professor Edwards.

He was laid to rest next to her parents, his funeral attended by dozens of academics and friends and various members of the Society. She saw to it that fresh flowers would be placed weekly in front of each headstone. Above Edwards's name, she had inserted a photo taken many years ago, when she was a child, the four of them standing together, Kate held aloft by her mother, surrounded by her father and Richard. They were then as they were meant to be—a family.

And it was how they would always be remembered.

Kate walked past the imposing statue of Dante, guarding the entrance of Santa Croce, and smiled when she saw Rumore and Marco standing on the top steps. Racing up, she jumped into their arms and gave each a long and grateful embrace.

"I missed you both so much," she said, trying her best not to shed tears.

"Florence wasn't the same without you," Rumore said.

"And neither was eating at Mama's," Marco said.

"But that will change soon enough. She's expecting us there for lunch and has promised to prepare a feast in your honor."

"Sounds like heaven to me," Kate said. "But before we go, do you mind hanging out for just a few more minutes? I need some alone time with the big guy."

Rumore shook his head. "The third man in your life," he said.

"He's much too old for you," Marco said. "And he only lives for his work."

"But he is rich," Rumore said. "That could make up for all his other deficiencies."

Kate patted their cheeks and smiled. "You can talk about me while I visit his tomb," she said.

Kate went up the final steps, swung open the door to the church and disappeared inside.

MARCO STARED DOWN at Rumore's Ducati motorcycle parked in the piazza alongside his rusty bike. "I guess she'll want to ride with you," he said.

"I wouldn't be so sure," Rumore said. "She likes things simple and old. And your bike tops the list in both categories."

"It was my father's bike," Marco said. "It's all I have left to remember him by."

"I know," Rumore said. "Kate told me."

"Listen," Marco said. "I can step away from this, if you prefer. Let's face it, if she had to make a choice, she would choose you."

Rumore looked at him, smiled and patted him gently across his back. "Good luck to us both," he said. "*In bocca al lupo.*"

"What happens next?" Marco asked. "I mean, after today."

"I go back to Rome and my squad," Rumore said. "There are always more bad men out there like the

Raven than good men like you. They'll keep me busy for as long as I want. And I guess you and Kate head back to class. At least until her next adventure comes along."

"You think there will be another?" Marco asked.

"I would count on it," Rumore said.

"Did she tell you?" he asked.

"Tell me what?"

"What she did with the Midnight Angels?"

"I didn't ask," Rumore said. "As far as I know, they still haven't been found."

"I didn't ask her, either," Marco said. "But I'm sure if they did exist, she left them safe and sound, exactly where they belonged."

"I would bet my life on it," Rumore said. "And yours."

KATE STOOD BEFORE the large marble tomb of Michelangelo and smiled up at his sculpted face. Behind her, groups of tourists were packed three deep, gazing at the tombs that lined both sides of the church. Michelangelo was at rest directly across from Galileo and next to his old friend Dante Alighieri, three giants dominating a church filled with the remains of the Renaissance greats.

"I hope you're pleased with what I did," she whispered. "Even if you're not, you don't have much choice. You're stuck with just me now. Mom and Dad are gone and so is Richard. I'm all you've got left, and you're all that's left of my family. I won't know what to do if you ever leave my side. But somehow I don't think you will. Somehow I think you'll always be there, and I'll always love you for it."

CLARE JOHNSON GLANCED out the window of an apartment overlooking Piazza Santa Croce, her face shielded from the sun by a thin white curtain. She leaned farther out when she saw Kate depart the church and walk toward Marco and the detective. A man in a dark shirt and slacks stepped in next to her and gazed down into the square.

"They don't seem so imposing," he said.

"That's because you don't know any better," Clare said. "But it was that not-so-imposing trio that took down the Raven and prevented him from taking possession of the Midnight Angels."

"Some good came out of it," the man said, turning his back on the square. "The Immortals belong to you now, and we are the better for it."

"Can the flattery," Clare said, "it doesn't fly with me."

"Do you wish them followed?"

Clare shook her head. "No," she said. "Leave them alone. We have plenty of time to catch up."

"What about the Angels?"

"They're safe," Clare said. "I'm certain the girl saw to that. And while we can't get to them, no one else can, either."

"So what's next?" he asked.

"How about we take a cue from our friends in the square," Clare said, "and go out and enjoy what's left of the day."

"Do you wish to walk or ride?" the man asked.

"What did your old boss the Raven prefer?" Clare asked.

"He always walked when he had the chance," the man said.

Clare nodded and turned away from the window. "In that case," she said, "bring the car around. My walking days are at an end."

KATE, MARCO, AND RUMORE stood in front of the Ducati 999 and the beat-up bicycle. "I see we have two chariots awaiting us," Kate said. "Which shall we take?"

"I think today we should all be allowed to ride in style," Rumore said. He caught the sad look crossing Marco's face and turned to the young man. "It would be an honor for me if you allowed me a ride on your father's bike," he said. "In return, you and Kate can take my Ducati and drive it over to Mama's place."

"I've never driven a Ducati before," Marco said, stammering. "What if I do something wrong and cause some damage?"

Rumore straddled Marco's bike, reached into the front pocket of his jeans, pulled out a set of keys and tossed them his way. Marco caught them in midflight. "If that happens," he said, "then I might have to shoot you."

Kate and Marco watched Rumore pedal through the piazza and down a side street, heading toward the restaurant. Marco got on the Ducati, put the key in, and started the powerful engine. He grabbed a black helmet off one of the handlebars and handed it to Kate, waited as she put it on and then reached for a second one from the other bar and squeezed it over his head. Kate got on behind him and rested her arms across his waist. He kicked up the stand and slowly shifted gears. The Ducati lurched forward and gently made its way through the piazza.

"Way to go, Marco," Kate said.

"Do you really think Rumore would shoot me if I damaged his bike?" Marco asked her, navigating his way down a side street.

"Yes," Kate said.

"That's some friend to have," Marco said, turning to give her a quick smile.

"Yes he is," Kate said, resting her head on Marco's back. "And so are you."

* * *

IN THE DARKNESS of the church, five feet below the tomb of Michelangelo, the Midnight Angels stood, one next to the other.

Their arms were stretched out, palms up, wings open and ready for flight. Their faces gleamed and their eyes looked up at the tomb of their creator.

They were where they belonged.

At rest with Michelangelo.

In peace.

At home.

ACKNOWLEDGMENTS

I OWE SO MANY FOR THE INSPIRATION AND guidance they willingly gave in helping me complete this book. Since my heart is always somewhere in Italy, I will begin by thanking Massimo and Nico of the Excelsior Hotel in Florence, who worked their magic and got us into the Vasari Corridor at a time when no one was allowed. They are simply the best at what they do.

And to the dozens of others who are lucky enough to call Florence, my favorite city, home: from Mama to the owners and staff of Buca Mario and Sostanza to the jeweler who collects American license plates to the young woman at the herbal pharmacy who allowed me access into the shuttered basement of a place where both Michelangelo and da Vinci came for their herbs—I owe my deepest thanks.

The best way to keep Michelangelo alive is to do what comes naturally in Florence—walk. His presence is everywhere, in every angle of every church, museum, street corner. All you need do is look. And nowhere is his presence stronger than in the church at Santa Croce, where his body rests and where I spent endless hours in his company. There is no finer guide in all of Florence.

To my man Keith Bellows, editor-in-chief of the *National Geographic Traveler,* who has been kind enough to allow me to write about Italy for his terrific magazine going on ten years now; and to Jayne Wise, his gifted senior editor who makes the words better and each endeavor a challenge not a chore. Thank you both.

My editor, Mark Tavani, was a godsend. He helped guide me down a fresh path, always ready to take an idea and make it better, patient, talented, determined to get it right. The result is a book we both can be proud of. He is also, hands down, the best line editor I have ever had the honor to work with. Plus, he speaks and writes a little Italian, which means I can't put anything past him in either language.

To the rest of the team at Ballantine: from the great Gina Centrello who has always been in my corner, to the very classy Libby McGuire and my pal of many decades, Kim Hovey—thank you for all you have done. To Brian and to the many copy editors, art directors, sales and marketing men and women who worked so hard over so many years on what is now eight books, always making them read and look better, I am in your debt.

To Suzanne Gluck, the best and smartest book agent on the planet, and her A-team at WME—way to go, Idaho! Add to this mix Rob Carlson without whom no deal is possible and without whose friendship I would be at a loss; Lou Pitt who never stops working and never stops caring; Tom Collier who does it all with style and class; and to the immortal one himself—Jake Bloom, the champ still holding the crown after all these years.

To my many friends who listen and allow me to vent through every book with every pain, real or imagined, I thank you. Most especially in this round: Dr. L., the GM, Ed F.; Big Hank; Peter L&O; Leah; Liz "I took the wine" Wagner; Fred and Pat; Frank, PJ, and the gang at AGS; Andy K.; Coates B.; Big Steve; Christopher and Constantino; Dr. C.; and the great crew at East Side Animal and South Fork Animal Hospitals—for taking care of my posse.

To Susan—thank you for putting up with me for way

too long a time and for planting the seeds of an idea that grew into this book. You have always been my MVP and I can't imagine my world without you in it.

To Nick—you have heart, charm, and passion—and are never shy about letting me know if an idea of mine should be flushed.

To Kate—you are simply the best. Your achievements alone leave me in awe. With both of you, I am honored to be your dad.

And to Gus and Willow—the two greatest dogs in the world and yes, Casper, you, too (the world's oldest cat): You three will forever be the coolest ones in any room you walk into or any backyard you happen to stumble upon. You have more than earned your treats.

AUTHOR'S NOTE

THIS BOOK IS A WORK OF FICTION.

But, according to a number of noted Michelangelo scholars, as much as thirty percent of the master's work remains undiscovered to this day.

The Midnight Angels may well be one of those works, out there somewhere, waiting to be found.